I'll Be Killing You

I'll Be Killing You

Beverley Armstrong-Rodman

iUniverse, Inc.
New York Bloomington

I'll Be Killing You

Copyright © 2008 by Beverley Armstrong-Rodman

All rights reserved. No part of this book may be used or reproduced by any means, graphic, electronic, or mechanical, including photocopying, recording, taping or by any information storage retrieval system without the written permission of the publisher except in the case of brief quotations embodied in critical articles and reviews.

This is a work of fiction. All of the characters, names, incidents, organizations, and dialogue in this novel are either the products of the author's imagination or are used fictitiously.

iUniverse books may be ordered through booksellers or by contacting:

iUniverse
1663 Liberty Drive
Bloomington, IN 47403
www.iuniverse.com
1-800-Authors (1-800-288-4677)

Because of the dynamic nature of the Internet, any Web addresses or links contained in this book may have changed since publication and may no longer be valid. The views expressed in this work are solely those of the author and do not necessarily reflect the views of the publisher, and the publisher hereby disclaims any responsibility for them.

ISBN: 978-0-595-52966-7 (pbk)
ISBN: 978-1-4401-1294-2 (cloth)
ISBN: 978-0-595-63019-6 (ebk)

Printed in the United States of America

iUniverse Rev. date 11/26/08

Also By Beverley Armstrong-Rodman

Murder is a Family Matter

Baa Baa Black Death

Cast of Characters

Cassandra Meredith – an unwilling witness to murder
Victoria Craig – the loyal friend who lives for adventure
Stephanie Chapman – the beautiful artist who has no time for men
Kitty Winfield – Steffie's partner in Aunt Aggie's Attic
Jack Willinger – the detective who has a special reason to catch the killer
Bud Lang – the partner who keeps Jack out of trouble
Dave Meredith – the husband with the big secret
Harold Johnston, aka John Duncan – the "I'll Be Killing You" killer
Joseph Warner – the motel owner with a newly found conscience
Muffin and Sugar Plum – Cassie's clever cats
Miss Rosie and Petie – Kitty's adorable felines

Acknowledgements

My wonderful husband Ward, who keeps me laughing

My son Greg, and daughter Heather, who helped with technical "stuff"

My sister Jean Archer, who is ageless in her faith and enthusiasm

My buddies Judith Kennedy and Carson Martin, who once again helped with the legwork

My friend Faye Amadio, the computer wiz, who always manages to transform my sketchy ideas into great covers.

The helpful detectives from the Panama City Beach Police, and from the Niagara Regional Police

Chapter One

First came the desperate, high-pitched scream. It cut through the thick, warm air, like a scalpel slicing through flesh. Then came the dull, moist sound, which could only be called a "splat"!

This calm Florida night was made for lovers, definitely not for horrible noises such as "splat." The stars sparkled like tiny fireflies, and there wasn't even the hint of a breeze. It was well after midnight, probably closer to 2 o'clock, and not many people were stirring at the elegant Edgewater Beach Resort. All good vacationers were in bed, dreaming sweet dreams of the fun-filled days to come. It was preternaturally quiet, as if the warm Florida night was holding its breath – waiting, just waiting.

"Splat"! What kind of sound was that? It reminded Cassie of a watermelon falling from a high balcony onto the tiles below. It had that hollow, moist thud to it. Unfortunately, it was not a watermelon falling from a high balcony. Cass knew exactly what it was, and the knowledge made her heart do the old elevator drop right down to her painted toes.

It was a woman, a very unlucky woman, who had made that calamitous noise, and Cassandra Meredith had seen and heard it all. The incident, (a kind word for a tragic event), was destined to change her life alarmingly, although she had no way of knowing that, at the time. She knew that if she ever heard that sound again, she would connect it to an innocent woman, well, presumably innocent, flying through the air to her ignominious death.

Up to this point in time, it had been a wonderful evening. The four friends had gone to dinner at an Italian restaurant just up the road.

They had returned to Cassie's condo in Tower III, and had packed for their much anticipated cruise. They were leaving very early the next morning, to catch a flight to Fort Lauderdale, and then board their ship in Port Everglades.

Uncharacteristically, Kitty Winfield and Steffie Chapman, the third and fourth members of this "girls night out" party, had chosen to finish their packing, and get to bed at a decent hour. They were both party animals, but the past week of fun in the sun had been hectic, and they wanted to be rested, and full of energy, when they boarded that gorgeous cruise ship.

Cassie and her closest friend Victoria Craig, on the other hand, had decided to make one more trip to the hot tub, and have one more glass of wine, before finishing the mundane chore of packing. It turned out to be an unfortunate decision.

Luxuriating in the warmth of the tub, Cassie was quite willing to wait, while Vickie fetched the wine. They weren't even supposed to be in the hot tub after midnight, but they were being quiet, and since Cassie was a condo owner in this glamorous resort, she had no qualms about breaking that rule. As long as they weren't disturbing anyone, what difference did it make? As things turned out, it made a huge difference, but who could have known?

Cassie's leg was aching a bit, as it did occasionally when she had done too much walking. That's why the hot tub had seemed to be a good idea.

"Classy Cassie," as her friends called her, had been a dancer in her earlier days. She had even owned a dance studio at one time. An unfortunate skiing accident in Switzerland, however, had ended her dancing career, and eventually she had sold the studio. On occasion, the leg which had been broken, ached alarmingly.

Now in her late forties, her life had taken an entirely different turn. Much to her amazement, she had inherited a huge amount of money – around twenty-six million dollars, and she was still trying to get used to the idea. Because she still had guilt feelings about the money, she was finding that it helped assuage the guilt, and made her happy, to share with her three closest friends. The cruise was her treat, and the four of them had been planning for it all the previous winter.

While waiting for Vickie to return with their wine, Cassie had been gazing up at the condo towers, enjoying the solitude, but wondering why her scalp was tingling.

When Cassandra Meredith's scalp began to tingle, (which, fortunately for all concerned, it didn't do too often), it was always a warning that something bad was about to happen. Her tingling scalp never failed her.

For the past few minutes it had been tingling like crazy, and she was feeling uneasy. She wished that Vickie would hurry back with the wine. Suddenly she didn't like being alone down here on the deck, which surrounded the huge lagoon pool. The beach, with its white sugary sands, looked ghostly, and unfriendly at night, and she realized that she might have been foolish to stay down here alone, while Vickie went for replenishments.

Edgewater was a gated resort, and was totally safe, or, as safe as any gated community can be, but Cassie's imagination had abruptly kicked in. It had been her experience that there was always room for unexpected and unpleasant things to happen, and she had a gut wrenching feeling that something unpleasant was coming her way.

The previous summer, back in Niagara Falls, she had suffered a frightening encounter with a serial killer, who called himself "The Black Sheep." Prior to that, she and Vickie had become seriously entangled in a string of murders, to the point that they themselves were slated to be the next victims. They agreed that they had had enough of mysteries and murders to last them a very long time.

Now, however, on this beautiful night, Cassie could picture all sorts of evil coming towards her from that ghostly beach. During the day, it was alive with adults and children, sunning themselves, laughing, and splashing in those gorgeous turquoise waters of the Gulf of Mexico. At night, however, all alone on the pool deck, she could conjure up a dozen different scenarios, none of them good.

She had turned herself around in the tub, so that she was facing out towards the water, and towards Tower III. She didn't want anyone sneaking up on her from the beach. Although she tried to tell herself that she was getting all bent out of shape over nothing, she didn't believe a word of it. Something was wrong.

Suddenly she had heard voices, and had looked around hopefully for the source. It would be reassuring to know that she wasn't alone. It took a moment before she looked up at Tower III, and saw that a man and woman had come out onto the balcony on the tenth or eleventh floor. There was no light on that balcony, but the living room behind it was lit up, so that the figures appeared in silhouette.

They seemed to be struggling, but it looked to be an unfair match. The woman appeared to be small and slight, while the man seemed to be tall and hefty. Cassie had stared in disbelief and horror, as he suddenly gave the woman a vicious blow to the side of her head, picked her up as if she was a rag doll, and threw her off the balcony.

Chapter Two

Cass let out a sound which resembled a squawk. It certainly wasn't a scream. Some subconscious inner safety button had switched on, telling her that it was neither smart nor prudent to scream. In the still of the night, however, her frightened squawk was loud enough to attract the man's attention. He stared at her, as she scrambled out of the hot tub.

She couldn't see his face, just his size, but she knew he was looking right at her. She could feel his hostile eyes upon her. It was fairly light on the deck by the most easterly hot tub, and she wondered in a panicked sort of way, whether he could make out her features. It seemed very important that she remain anonymous to the man staring down at her.

In her haste to get out of the hot tub, and because she was looking up over her shoulder, she banged her shin very hard on the cement edge. The sharp pain brought hot tears to her eyes, as she limped to the chair, swept up her towel, and headed for the body. She would have preferred to rush up to her condo and hide, but had to see whether there was any chance that the woman was still alive.

"This isn't happening. This is NOT happening," she muttered to herself. It was like a little mantra which she was repeating over and over. If she said it often enough, maybe what she had just seen would go away. Maybe it really had not happened. Ya, right. And maybe a purple cow was going to dance a jig right here on the deck!

She and Vickie nearly collided, as Vickie rushed towards her, a look of disbelief on her face.

"Did you see?" cried Cassie, clutching her friend's arm. Vickie was still grasping the two plastic wine glasses in her hands, although most of the wine had splashed out of them.

"Yes," gasped Vickie, her brown eyes looking big and dazed. "I saw her in mid-flight. There was nothing to break her fall. I think she landed right in front of the Bimini Bar." Then her irrepressible, off the wall sense of humour kicked in, and she couldn't resist adding, "She must have been awfully anxious for a drink."

"Vickie," groaned her friend, trying not to grin at the silly remark. "She didn't fall. She was pitched like a bag of garbage." Cass looked up again at the condo balcony, which was now empty. Where had the killer gone? Was he on his way down here to kill her too, because she had seen him?

"Come on, we have to get out of here. He knows I saw him, and he might be coming after us."

"What? Who saw you, what are you talking about?"

"The guy who threw her over," said Cassie, in a patient tone. "Let's check on her. I'm sure she's dead, no one could have survived that plunge, but we'd better make sure. Then we'll head for the elevator, and try to get out of here before he shows up. We really don't need to be involved in any more murders."

"That's for darn sure," agreed Vickie, realizing that this wasn't simply a tragic accident. It was apparently something much more sinister, and they definitely didn't want to be entangled in any way, especially not as witnesses.

They reluctantly looked at the body, but it was a horrible sight. There was no doubt that she was dead. There was a lot of blood, and her head looked strangely misshapen. They both stood staring, momentarily frozen to the spot.

Finally Cass grabbed Vickie's arm, and said "Come on, there's nothing we can do for her now. Let's run for it. I hope she was only semi-conscious when he pitched her over. Maybe she didn't really know what was happening, although she did scream. Then she just fell so quietly. It was pitiful. I saw him give her a vicious blow to the side of her head before he threw her. Didn't you see him at all?"

The sight of the woman had been sickening, and Cassie was chattering on non-stop, as if to keep herself from thinking of all that blood and gore.

"No. All I saw was this body hurtling down, and landing with an awful wet sort of noise. I just assumed that she had fallen. Listen, kiddo, you know I love your penchant for melodrama, but this is serious. Are you really sure that you saw someone actually throw her over?"

"Vickie, I'm telling you, a great big guy hit her on the side of the head, then picked her up, and without any hesitation, he just lifted her right over the railing and heaved her. We'll have to call 911 as soon as we get upstairs. Come on, he's likely on his way down at this very moment. We can't let him see us. He won't be happy about any witnesses to his dirty deed."

"Well shit," groaned Vickie. "It sounds as if you've just landed us both in a pile of doo-doo up to our armpits. Can't you ever stay out of trouble?"

Like all people with over-active imaginations, Cassie tended to hyperbole. Her stories were always entertaining, because they were usually slightly, or in some cases, grandly, exaggerated. In this case, however, Vickie realized that they could be in immediate danger. If Cass was scared, then so was she.

As they ran to the condo, a small man and a tall woman came flying around the corner. They had either seen her fall, or had seen her land. "Is she dead?" asked the man, as he swept past them, and peered at the body. The tall thin woman gasped, and made a retching sound. Cassie hoped that she would have enough sense to barf in the bushes, and not all over the crime scene.

"Yes," said Vickie and Cassie in unison. "She's very dead," added Vickie.

"Did you see what happened?" asked Cassie hopefully. She didn't want to be the only witness.

"No. We're in the condo on the first floor, right over the Bimini, and my wife was looking out the window. She saw her land."

"Too bad," muttered Cassie.

"We'll contact 911," called Vickie over her shoulder, as she dragged Cassie into the elevator.

Just as they entered elevator number one, the doors to elevator number two opened, and a tall, heavyset man emerged. He stared at them malevolently, and took a step towards them, as the doors to their elevator closed in his face.

They saw his big hands trying to hold the doors open, but he was a moment too late. The elevator doors closed firmly, and it lurched its way upward.

"Oh shit. That was the guy. I'm sure of it. He's the one who threw her over the balcony," said Cassie. "He got a good look at both of us. Shit, Vickie, I was so hopeful that this would be a quiet holiday, with no mysteries and no monsters."

"Okay," said Vickie, who also had a wild imagination, and who was usually the hot-headed one of the pair. She didn't have reddish-auburn hair for nothing! "Let's get ourselves into the condo and think this through. We could be in serious trouble here, but maybe that wasn't the guy at all."

The elevator was never exactly fast, but at the moment they felt as if they were on a slow boat to China.

Suddenly Cassie pushed the button for the 7th floor.

"Good idea, kiddo. You're trying to fool him into thinking we're getting off there, aren't you?"

"Yah. It might put him off our trail for a while anyway, at least until we can figure out what to do."

"Do you know what floor he was on when he pitched the gal?" asked Vickie.

"I don't think it was the top one, so it must be the one right above us." Cassie was squinting her eyes in concentration.

Eventually the elevator reached their floor.

Vickie handed the two plastic glasses to Cassie, as she fumbled for her key.

They knew that the little ploy of pushing the button for the 7th floor wouldn't fool the killer for long, so they both heaved sighs of relief, as they entered the condo, and double-locked the door.

"Do you think we should turn out the lights?" Vickie asked, being careful to stand away from the picture window.

"No, he might be looking up here to see which condo we're in. If he sees these lights go off now, he'll be pretty sure it's the right one."

"Yes, but most of the condos should be in darkness, because it's 2:30 in the morning. Ours will stand out like a beacon, with all these lights on," reasoned Vickie.

"Oh shoot, I don't know what to do. What I do know is that we're in a lot of trouble. That guy just murdered a woman, and you and I may be the only two witnesses. Dammit, why does this always happen to us? We seem to attract danger like flowers attract bees. I knew something was wrong, because my scalp was tingling, but I never expected anything like this."

"Well, Miss Cassandra, you do get us into some interesting predicaments. If only our flight was a little earlier, we could get out of here right now. Getting the heck out of Dodge sounds like a good idea."

They stared at each other as the seriousness of the situation hit them like a grave-digger's shovel.

The night, which had started out so happily, had just deteriorated into a scene from Nightmare on Elm Street.

Chapter Three

The logical thing to do, of course, was to call the police immediately. Cassie was just about to dial 911, when Vickie grabbed her arm.

"Wait a minute, let's just think about this."

"What are you talking about? We have to call the police," frowned Cassie.

"Maybe not," said Vickie, raising her eyebrows. "Somebody else in one of these condos must have heard her scream. Maybe several people did. Also, there could have been quite a few people who actually saw her fall. They'll have called the police for sure by now. If we call and say that we actually saw the guy doing the dirty deed, what do you think will happen?" She immediately answered her own rhetorical question. "We're going to get tied up in the investigation, and we're going to miss our flight in the morning. That means we'll miss our cruise. Are you prepared for that?"

"Oh Vic, that seems to be a skewed way of looking at things, but I do see what you mean. Still, someone was murdered tonight, and we can identify the killer. That should take precedence over the cruise, don't you think? Besides, wouldn't it be considered obstruction of justice if we don't tell?"

"Woa. Hold up there, pal. Can we actually identify the killer? I'm not sure about that. I didn't see him on the balcony. All I saw was that poor woman doing a swan dive."

"Well, we saw him get off the elevator. I'm positive that was the guy. He was tall and brawny, just like the man up on the balcony. You can't deny he tried to force our elevator doors open. Why else would he do that, unless he wanted to talk to us, or scare us, or maybe strangle us. We have to give the police a description. It's just the right thing to do. You know it as well as I do."

Vickie knew that technically Cassie was right. In a complex this big, however, with three towers on this part of the beach, it made sense that someone else would have seen the murder. It was late, but surely everyone couldn't have been in bed. Maybe someone taking a moonlit stroll on the beach had looked up and seen the actual murder. Maybe someone in the next condo had heard the argument before the woman plunged to her death. There could have been several people in the towers, looking out at the precise time that the struggle had occurred.

People got up to go to the bathroom in the middle of the night. It made sense to believe that someone else had seen or heard something. She and Cassie couldn't possibly be the only two in the entire complex who were in the unfortunate position of being eyewitnesses. At least this was what she was telling herself, as she tried to reason with Cassie.

As they stood there in the safety of their condo, they whispered back and forth, discussing the pros and cons of calling the police. Before they could reach a decision, however, they heard a commotion down on the deck. They hurried out to the dark balcony, and craned their necks to see what was going on. They couldn't see too much, but there were police there, and paramedics. Heaving sighs of relief, they realized that they didn't have to call 911. The decision had been made by someone else. The police really arrived quickly too. That was excellent. Now they needn't get involved. Whew! What a relief!

Suddenly Cassie gasped, and turned to Vickie in dismay. "My bracelet, Vic. My gold bracelet – I've left it down by the hot tub. I took it off before we got in the water, and I put it on the chair with my towel and cover-up. After I saw that poor woman plunge to her death, I scrambled out of the water, grabbed my things off the chair, and forgot all about the bracelet. I guess I was in shock. I must have knocked it off the chair when I scooped up my towel."

Vickie looked at her in disbelief. The heavy gold bracelet was a cherished possession of Cassie's. Her husband Dave had given it to her, and it had her name engraved on it. If the killer happened to find it anywhere around the hot tub, he would know the name of the witness.

That was making things way too easy for him. They had to get that bracelet before the killer found it.

Not even stopping to put on dry clothes, and not even stopping to think that they might run right into the killer, they took the elevator back downstairs. No elevator had ever seemed slower than that one. It had been travelling like a snail on the way up, but now it was moving like an old woman with arthritic hips.

They tried to look nonchalant as they mingled with the small crowd, which was gathering around the body. They didn't see anyone who looked remotely like the man who had come out of the elevator, and who had stared at them with such animosity. They didn't know whether that was good or bad. If he had been there in the small crowd, they could have pointed him out to the police, and he would have been arrested on the spot. Still, they felt safer not seeing him anywhere.

They sauntered over to the hot tub, trying to be as inconspicuous as possible. There was no one around it, and they were able to have a quick look. Unfortunately the bracelet was nowhere to be seen. The chair on which Cassie had deposited her towel, her cover-up, and the infamous bracelet, was empty.

Cassie couldn't believe such bad luck. She had lost that beautiful gold bracelet which had been a peace offering from Dave. He had given it to her after an argument they had last year, before one of his seemingly unending trips abroad. It was bad enough that she had lost it so carelessly. Worse still was the fact that if it was the killer who found it, he now would be able to track Cassie at his leisure.

Was she making too much of it? Would he really have reason to follow her back to Niagara Falls and try to silence her? Would she be looking over her shoulder the rest of her life? Would the rest of her life be a very short time?

Surely the killer would realize that she hadn't been able to see his face clearly way up there on the balcony, and in the dark. Yes, but he would also know that she had a good look at him when he stepped out of the elevator. She groaned at the remembrance of his hostile face, and his big brawny physique. He was the stereotypical killer of every movie she had ever seen. She knew he would need to get rid of her.

Chapter Four

Neither friend said a word as they headed back upstairs. They simply stared glumly at each other, wondering how or why fate had once again selected them to be put in the middle of a dangerous situation. They both understood all too well that if the killer had found the bracelet near the hot tub, it would be very easy for him to find out to whom it belonged. Cassie owned her three bedroom wrap-around at Edgewater, so, undoubtedly, he could get her address from the office. This was a very bad turn of events.

Both women were silent, as they sat in the darkened living room, trying to think their way out of this dilemma.

"What an absolute bummer," exclaimed Vickie, pulling on the hair at the back of her neck. This was a habit she had when she was nervous, or trying to think.

"Wouldn't you just know that you would be the one to be sitting down in that hot tub, when that hulk decided to pitch his little friend, wife, lover, whatever, over the balcony. I'll bet it's the first bad thing that's ever happened here at Edgewater, and good old Cassandra had to get herself right in the middle of it." She shook her head in disbelief, as she gave Cassie a friendly poke on the arm.

"You're just darn lucky that you're the one who came back up here for the wine," retorted Cassie. "Otherwise, you would have been the poor sucker sitting down there all alone, hearing that 'splat'. Honestly, Vic, that was the most awful sound. I wish now that I hadn't looked at the body. Blah, that poor woman."

"I know. I can't believe how much blood there was. There was other stuff too that might have been brain matter. Ugh. Even if she had managed to survive the fall, which was impossible, she would have been a total veg. It looked as if her head just burst like a ripe melon. I don't want to think about it, or I won't be able to eat for a week."

"Well, thanks for that graphic picture. I'll never be able to look at another melon."

"I wonder who she was. You know, she could be someone we've met this week, someone with whom we've chatted. We could have met her walking the beach, or sitting in the hot tub, or having a drink in Oceans. What a horrible way to die. I just hope she died of fright before she hit the tiles." Vickie was up now, pouring them more wine. She figured it was always good to calm the nerves and put things in perspective.

"I wonder why he killed her," mused Cassie. "Were they lovers, or business partners, or is he just a psycho who gets off on killing women?"

"Damn, I wish he hadn't seen us at the elevators, if indeed he was the one," said Vickie.

"I'm sure he was. He was the same build, anyway, and he certainly looked at us in a very unfriendly way. Besides, he didn't say anything like "Did you just hear a scream?" which is what an innocent person would have said. Damn damn, double damn. If only I hadn't worn that bracelet down to the hot tub. I guess it really doesn't matter though. If that was the killer in the elevator, he got a good look at us, and he would likely be able to find out who we are anyway, even without the bracelet."

"Look, the guy will be picked up by the police probably within hours. Someone will know who he is, and he won't be any danger to us. He's likely in custody already. After all, they'll know who's staying in that condo, and once they have his description, how hard will it be to find him?"

As soon as she had spoken, she realized the meaning of her words, "once they have his description." Here she was trying to talk Cassie out of calling the police, while it was likely true that she might be the only person able to tie that big hulk to the crime. She might be the only person who could give a genuinely good description.

She heaved a sigh. She really didn't want Cassie getting them involved in another murder. They'd had enough of mysteries to last them a couple of lifetimes, but right was right. There was a moral obligation there to stand up and be counted.

"Okay Miss Dudley Do-Right. Let's not think any more about it just now. We've still got some packing to do, and a great cruise ahead of us. Surely we can figure out something. Maybe you can mail in your description," she laughed. "It's just that we've planned this for so long, and darn it, we're not going to let it spoil things for us, or for Kitty and Steffie. This is going to be the cruise of a lifetime."

Cassie grinned at her friend affectionately. "Right on, Pollyanna. Let's finish the packing before we make a decision. Maybe we'll figure something out while we pack. We likely won't be able to sleep, so we might as well stay up and enjoy ourselves."

"Good idea. We'll sleep on the plane. Let's just take another peek down there and see what's happening," suggested Vickie.

Cassie grinned again. Good old Vickie. She just couldn't resist any excitement or danger. It was in her blood. How many times over the years had she dragged Cassie into some dangerous situation, just through her curiosity and love of action and intrigue. Then she always somehow managed to blame Cassie for getting them involved. What a gal! This time, however, it was Cassie who could be leading her friend into a mess of intrigue and peril, through no fault of her own.

She just hoped that the killer would be arrested quickly, and there would be enough evidence against him, that they would never have to testify. Cass knew, however, that there was a wide road between hope and reality.

They opened the sliding door very quietly, and looked down on the surreal scene below. The police, medical examiner and paramedics were milling around. The police photographer was taking pictures from all angles, being careful not to step in the dark puddles and rivulets of congealing blood.

Two policemen were talking with some of the people who were huddled in little groups in front of the Bimini Bar. Just a few short hours before, that bar had been so active and noisy, so full of music and laughter. Now it was dark and silent. Outside of it, people were shrugging their shoulders, shaking their heads, pointing up toward the higher levels. It was as if everyone wanted to be involved somehow in the excitement and drama of the moment.

"You know, I think your original idea was the right one. We have to call 911 and tell them what you saw. Let's do it anonymously. You call, tell them about the man who threw her over, describe him, then hang up. That way your conscience will be clear, the police will have a description of the killer, and we can go off on the ship without any self-recriminations. What do you think?"

"I think that's a possibility," said Cass slowly. "You realize, of course, that we'll have to find a phone off the Edgewater property. They could trace any 911 call right to here, so there wouldn't be any point in trying to be anonymous. We can't use cell phones either. I just wish that Jack was here. I'd feel a lot better if I could talk to him," she muttered.

Jack was a detective on the Niagara Regional Police force. He had played an important part in the murders three summers ago, and the Black Sheep killings last summer. More importantly, however, Jack was the love of Cassie's life, at least there were times when she told herself that he was. Other times her good sense prevailed. Unfortunately, he had been married to someone else, as was Cassie, and they had to pine after each other, and think about what "might have been" from a distance.

Cass knew that Jack's wife Darla had died several months ago, when she fell down a flight of stairs. Apparently Jack had come home and found her dead. The rumour was that she had been drinking. Somehow, the fact that Jack was now free, complicated matters. Cass, of course, was not free, but she couldn't stop herself from thinking about the possibility of leaving Dave, and running off with Jack. It was a type of teenage pipe dream. Even thinking such thoughts made her angry with herself. Dave was a great husband, and she loved him, at least she used to love him. Now she wasn't quite as sure.

They had endured plenty of ups and downs in their marriage, but she would never leave him. Marriage was forever, and she had made her choice a long time ago. Still, it was difficult not to dream the impossible dream. There were moments, like this one, when Cassie really wanted the comfort and safety of Jack's arms.

How quickly things could change in a person's life, she mused, as they headed down to the car, to make a short trip to a public phone.

Chapter Five

There was no possibility of sleep for either woman the rest of the night, so, after finishing their packing, they quietly went back out onto the dark balcony. They couldn't help but be drawn to the activity below.

Paramedics, the medical examiner, and police, still milled around. They were examining the body, (which Vickie, in her usual pragmatic manner, proclaimed was really just a pile of mush).

They were also taking a few more pictures, and talking with the people who had gathered. The rubber-neckers all seemed reluctant to leave, in case they missed any more excitement. This was much more than they had expected. After all, Edgewater Beach Resort was a delightful place meant for fun and laughter. It was not a place for murder and mayhem. It occurred to Vickie that it looked a bit like a movie set, except that the main character would never do another film.

Cass and Vickie felt somewhat better now that they had called the police, and given what little information they had. Their consciences were almost clear, and they could concentrate on having a great time on the cruise.

Unfortunately, seeing that woman take the plunge, had spread a gloomy pall over both of them. In the presence of such unexpected death, it was difficult to focus on frivolous things such as a Caribbean cruise, with all expenses paid for three of them, thanks to Cassie's generosity. They, however, were determined to make the best of a temporarily bad situation.

For various reasons, they all really needed this cruise, and had looked forward to it for several months. The previous summer had been disturbing, and in some ways shocking for all of them. Not only had a friend and colleague been strangled by the serial killer, who called himself the Black Sheep, but Kitty had been attacked and nearly killed by the same man.

Fortunately for her, all three of her friends had arrived just in time to fight him off. He had been killed in the ensuing melee, and they had suffered through the trauma of not only escaping death, but also of causing death, all in the space of a few horrendously frightening minutes.

After that excitement, Cassie had spent most of the winter remodelling her spacious and beautiful new home, which overlooked the mysterious green Niagara River. Among other changes, she and Dave had added a large room which would be Cassie's library, and an even larger sunroom. It had wonderfully padded window seats, on which her beloved cats Muffy and Sugar Plum, could sit and watch the fascinating things which went on outside. The house was very large, and provided a safe and interesting environment for the two spoiled but charming little felines.

Running Cassandra's Cattery took up most of her time. It had been her first project after receiving her inheritance. It was a haven for homeless cats, and it was her pride and joy. She had patterned it after Hemingway's estate in Key West, where the descendants of his first polydactyl cats roamed within high garden walls. With the hours spent at the cattery, and the time spent planning, remodelling, and moving to the new home, Cassie was ready for a vacation.

Her husband Dave was in their new home now, overseeing final touches to the painting and remodelling. He was moderately content to stay there while Cassie went off with her friends on this much anticipated cruise. He was now getting antsy, though, and would be leaving for Europe shortly after she returned.

Dave enjoyed travelling in Europe, tracking down new musical talent for his agency. Unfortunately, Cassie was beginning to doubt his motives. With all the money they had now, there was no need for Dave to continue his work, but he loved it, and the freedom which it afforded him. He had half-heartedly promised Cassie that this would be his last trip without her, but she wasn't convinced.

She sometimes teased him that she suspected he had another wife stashed away in Europe, because he spent so much time there. Yes, she was only teasing, but occasionally the unwanted thought pierced her heart like a sharp icicle.

Anyway, she really felt that at this moment in time, she needed to get away, think about her marriage, think about Jack, relax, and recharge her batteries. Getting involved in another murder case was the very last thing she wanted or needed. Perhaps that was why she almost allowed herself to be persuaded to catch that early morning flight, instead of staying and helping the police any way she could.

The anonymous call to the police had made her feel ridiculous, and cowardly. Her innate sense of honesty and integrity kicked in, and by the time Kitty and Steffie wakened, she had set things in motion.

She was gradually learning that with the money she had inherited, she could make things happen. A few phone calls, some work on the computer, and everything was arranged. She would stay and talk to the police. She had a small jet on standby, and as soon as the police were through with her, she would catch up with the ship at its first port of call.

She had wanted Vickie to go on with the other two, but Vickie was adamant that she would stay with Cassie. They would just make this part of the adventure, and they would both enjoy the rest of the cruise much more for having done the right thing. At least that was what they thought. They had forgotten that fate often steps in at unexpected times.

When Kitty and Steffie wakened, they were shocked at the news of the murder, and disappointed that they had missed all the excitement. They were also sorry to be leaving Vickie and Cassie behind, but were persuaded that their two friends would only lose a day of the cruise. There was nothing they could do about it anyway. It was a done deal.

The four women were extremely close friends. Cassie and Vickie had been chums since elementary school, and were closer than sisters. As children, they had loved mysteries, and ran around picturing themselves as Nancy Drew. Now, however, they weren't quite so interested in getting involved with murder and mayhem.

Three years previously, they had been the intended victims of a crazed member of Cassie's family, and had endured and escaped kidnapping, fire, and even killer bees. These days they were quite content to relax and read murder mysteries, rather than being involved in them. Unfortunately, however, like it or not, it seemed that they were being dragged into trouble once again.

Steffie and Kitty were co-owners of a very popular boutique in Niagara Falls, called 'Aunt Aggie's Attic'. Although very different in temperament, they got along beautifully.

Steffie was an artist, and had an artist's temperament. She was divorced from an abusive husband, and had recently lost her younger brother to a brain tumour.

Kitty was always getting herself enmeshed in one romance after another, and at the moment was very involved with a popular mystery writer. She had come very close to being killed by the Black Sheep strangler, and she was now enjoying every day as a bonus. Life seemed sweet, and the four women were looking forward to the Caribbean cruise, with great anticipation.

The flight out of the small Panama City airport was uneventful. Arriving in Fort Lauderdale, they barely had time to look around, before they were loaded onto the shuttle bus, which took them to Port Everglades, where their cruise ship was waiting.

Steffie and Kitty were a very attractive pair, and several of the men boarding the shuttle bus, looked at them with undisguised interest.

Kitty hated her unruly curly blond hair, but everyone else thought it suited her. She also had big blue eyes like Cassie. There was a delicate, rather ethereal quality to her looks, which seemed to make her very attractive to the opposite sex. Men always wanted to cuddle her, and protect her. Kitty's problem was that she fell in love too easily, and was always extricating herself from complicated relationships.

Steffie was definitely an eye catcher. She was the tallest of the four friends, and had raven black hair. Kitty wasn't the only one who thought she looked like a Tahitian princess, with her blue-black wavy hair and high cheekbones. Today she was wearing lavender – her favourite colour. Her calf-length skirt was a filmy material, with the uneven, flouncy bottom so popular at the moment, topped with a lacy lavender sweater.

Actually, as they stood talking and waiting to board the shuttlebus, they looked like two models, and attracted many glances from other women, as well as most of the men.

Kitty was enmeshed in a torrid, but long-distance romance with her latest love, Mitch Donaldson, a popular writer of mystery novels. Because Kitty lived in Niagara Falls, and Mitch in Toronto, it was proving to be a long-distance affair. It seemed that Mitch was always on the road, promoting one of his books, or holed up in his loft, writing the next one. Kitty was crazy about him, and was sure now that this was the real thing. Time would tell, but she, her family, her friends, and even her two cats, thought that Mitch was a great catch.

Steffie was free as a bird, having escaped from a somewhat abusive marriage. She had foolishly forgiven her handsome husband the first time he hit her, but the second time was the last. She had waited till he was out of the house, had cut up all his clothes in a theatrical act of revenge, and had flown to Toronto to start a new life.

She and Kitty met at a computer class, and became instant friends. When Kitty inherited her grandmother's home in Niagara Falls, the two women picked up stakes, moved to Niagara, and opened a boutique. Much to their surprise and delight, it had become popular with the tourists who flocked to Niagara Falls, as well as the locals, and was now a real gold mine.

At this point Steffie wasn't dating anyone seriously. She was enjoying her freedom too much, and was wary of getting herself into another sticky situation. Kitty, however, always the romantic, was silently hoping that her friend would find a partner on this magical cruise.

Chapter Six

The cruise terminal in Port Everglades was a huge building in which they had to line up, verify their tickets, show their identification, and try to contain their excitement. It was a bit chaotic, as two thousand passengers all tried to push and shove their way into the proper lines at the same time. Fortunately, every single person seemed to be in a good mood. The noise level was high, the terminal was hot, but laughter was plentiful.

As Kitty and Steffie patiently waited their turn, they chatted excitedly. It was fun looking around at the people who would be their shipmates for the next ten days. They came in every shape and size, and it was interesting to see the variety of fashions. They ranged from dressy pantsuits to sloppy T-shirts and jeans, from elegant skirts to short shorts, from shape hugging tube tops to baggy shirts.

The ages seemed to run from early twenties to late seventies. Steffie even noticed, to her chagrin, that there were a few families with screaming, whining, rambunctious kids. Steffie did not like children. She found them noisy, undisciplined, and totally obnoxious.

She did, however, love old folks. She volunteered one afternoon a week at the Niagara General Hospital, and worked unfailingly and lovingly with the geriatric patients. She called them her "crinkly-wrinklies," which always made them laugh. She seemed to have boundless patience and empathy with the trials, tribulations and fears suffered by the elderly, and they, in turn, loved her energy, enthusiasm, and humour.

She wished she had her sketch book handy right now, as she noticed a white-haired lady who appeared to be all alone. She had a cool elegance, which made her stand out in this motley crowd. She had fine patrician features, and must have been a real beauty in her youth. Steffie also noticed that the woman was wearing some very expensive looking rings on both hands. The errant thought crossed her mind that this elderly lady was foolish to be flaunting those diamonds so casually. What an invitation to be robbed, she thought, shaking her head.

The next few hours passed quickly, as they found their luxurious cabin, unpacked a few necessities, toured the ship, and headed for a bar.

They were anticipating adventures on this cruise, and would be disappointed if nothing extraordinary happened. Both Kitty and Steffie were as full of devilment and love of new challenges as were Vickie and Cassie. All four had laughingly talked about finding some new mystery to solve, while basking in the sun on deck, or trudging through the straw markets in the islands. They were mostly kidding, but half hopeful that something exciting and out of the ordinary might happen. They certainly weren't thinking about one of them witnessing a murder, and possibly being stalked by the killer! They had something less dangerous and more fun in mind.

They stood on the top deck, drinks in hand, as the great ship gradually made its way out to sea. They waved at the receding shoreline, although there was no one there to see them off. How different it used to be, thought Kitty, remembering old movies she had seen.

It certainly wasn't as romantic as the old days, when the excited passengers would throw miles of confetti ribbon down onto the loved ones they were leaving behind, as the huge ship set out to cross the ocean. In those movies there was always someone waving sadly from the shore, to a loved one on the ship, and the audience knew without a doubt that something either wonderful or tragic was going to happen to that passenger.

Today most of the crowd seemed a bit blasé. Many of them had done cruises before, so they knew exactly what to expect. They laughed and waved to no one in particular, raising their glasses in a toast to those being left on shore, but there wasn't quite the same feeling of expectation there had been in the movies. Kitty loved those old movies, and couldn't resist her favourite game. "Okay, Stef, tell me at least four stars who played in the Titanic movie from 1953," she asked, with a grin.

"Oh, great," groaned Steffie. "We're setting out on a big ship into the middle of the Caribbean Sea, and you want to remind me of the Titanic. You've got a wicked streak, Kitty," she laughed, shaking her head.

"Actually, that's a pretty easy one," she said, after a moment's thought. "I think Barbara Stanwyck was in it, and Clifton Webb," she said slowly. "But now, who else?" she muttered, pursing her lips and frowning. She had changed into her red bellbottoms, and white sailor blouse. Her lustrous black hair was pinned up on her head, with tendrils falling softly around her lovely face. No wonder all the men were giving her the eye.

Kitty guessed that Steffie would be fighting them off with a stick. What male could resist a gal who looked like Steffie, and who was smart, funny and artistic as well. Her ex husband must have been a total idiot to mistreat her the way he had.

"Just tell me when you're ready to give up," Kitty grinned, taking another sip of her champagne.

"Hope you don't mind if I help you ladies out a bit here," interrupted a good-looking fellow with a mischievous grin. "I couldn't help but overhear your game, and it sounds like fun. I'd like to play too, since I know at least two more characters from that movie." He seemed to have eyes only for Steffie, as he spoke.

"Well, of course you can join us," laughed Kitty, with a sidelong glance at Steffie, who was looking quizzically at the handsome stranger. "My pal here seems stumped on what I thought was a pretty easy one."

"First of all, let me introduce myself. I'm Brad Butler, and I'm a veterinarian from Toronto. I'm taking my younger sister on this cruise as a graduation present. She's just graduated, and is now a full-fledged veterinarian too. She's going to be working with me, and I couldn't be more proud of her. She's just gone back to her cabin for a minute, but she'll be up here soon, and you can meet her. Her name is Jillian, and before she gets here, let me tell you that Robert Wagner and Thelma Ritter were in that movie."

"Hey, you're good," said Kitty with approval. "Now that you mention those names, I think I remember Richard Basehart being in it too. You're welcome to play with us anytime," she laughed at the slight double entendre.

They stood in a little group by the railing, as the shore gradually disappeared. Actually, they were now too busy talking to take much notice.

This was what it was like on cruise ships. Friendships were made in the blink of an eye, and sometimes broken or forgotten just as quickly. Time would tell about this one. He was a real hunk though, no doubt about that, and he couldn't take his eyes off Steffie.

Well, he'll be disappointed, thought Kitty, who was very protective of her friend. Steffie simply wasn't interested in any new relationship at the moment. She was enjoying her freedom too much. At least that was what Kitty thought, but the way Stef was smiling and chatting with him, she wondered. She was always on the lookout for a good man for Steffie, and maybe Dr. Brad Butler would be the one. He certainly seemed interested.

With the sun shining brightly against the bluest of blue skies, and a gentle breeze tugging at their hair, and with the joyful sounds of people laughing, and glasses clinking, they felt as if they were sailing into paradise. The only disappointment was that Cassie and Vickie weren't here with them, to share these first exciting hours on board.

When the shoreline was becoming distant, they all retired to an upper bar, where the barstools were designed to look like mermaids standing on their tails. The décor on the ship was gorgeous, and this particular bar was delightful.

Brad Butler was turning out to be as charming and funny as he had first appeared, and his petite and pretty sister Jillian, was just as appealing.

A couple of hours after the great ship set sail, they had to go to a lifeboat drill. That was fun, but a bit sobering. Learning how to put on those orange life jackets, and memorizing the location of their particular lifeboat station, put a lot of ugly pictures into their heads. It highlighted the fact that they really were out in the ocean now, and there was nothing but miles and miles of endless water all around them. The lifeboats seemed very small when they visualized them bobbing along on all that water. The thought of being cast adrift in one of those boats was not very palatable.

By the time the friends went back to their room, did a bit more unpacking, and changed their clothes again, it was time for dinner.

"I wonder who we'll have at our table?" mused Kitty.

"Well, at least with the 8 o'clock seating, we shouldn't have any families with squalling kids," said Steffie.

"Steff, you're going to get yourself the reputation of a grumpy old curmudgeon. You shouldn't let people know how much you dislike the little darlings," laughed Kitty.

"You're right," agreed Steffie with a grin. "I promise I'll behave, but, if we walk in there and see any little brats at our table, feel free to just throw me overboard, and put me out of my misery."

They were interested to see that they had been placed at a table for eight, but so far no one else was there. Just as they sat down, however, the elegant woman Steffie had noticed earlier, arrived. She introduced herself as Martha Carrington from New York. Next to arrive was a white-haired gentleman who walked with a cane. His name was Jonathan Smithers, and he was from Kentucky.

To their delight, the last two people at the table were Brad Butler and his sister Jillian. They all laughed when he told them how he had done some fast talking to get himself and Jillian placed at their table. He hoped they didn't mind. They all agreed that it had been a great idea, and by the end of the dinner they were very comfortable with each other.

When they had signed up for dinner, they had explained that their two friends would be arriving tomorrow, and that they all had to be seated together. They were happy to see that for tonight two places had been set for Cassie and Vickie "just in case." The dining room steward, who had heard their story, and taken their table reservations, had been most obliging. It seemed that everything was going smoothly.

After dinner, the two friends, plus Brad and Jillian, went to see the show in the main theatre. It was excellent, with lots of singing and dancing, backed up by a very good band. Mrs. Carrington said she needed her beauty sleep, and Mr. Smithers was heading for the casino.

After the show, the friends headed to the casino as well, and it was late before they finally got to bed. They had two staterooms side by side on the Sky Deck, each with two double beds, a sitting room, and a balcony. The sitting room was tastefully furnished with comfy chairs, a small bar area, a large television, and even a small safe in which to keep their passports, jewellery and money.

Since this entire cruise was Cassie's treat, they had known they would be travelling first class, but had not realized what beautiful rooms they would have. Cassie and Vickie would be in one, and Kitty and Steffie in the other. They could hardly wait for their friends to arrive. Already there was so much to tell them.

"That Brad is one charming rascal, isn't he?" asked Kitty innocently, as they turned out the lights and snuggled down.

"He certainly is," laughed Steffie. "Now don't you go getting any big ideas about matching me up with him," she chided. "He's interesting and witty, and I hope to see a lot of him on this trip, but that's all. You know very well that I'm not in the market for a relationship, so just cool your jets, Little Miss Matchmaker."

She was laughing when she said this though, and Kitty grinned into the darkness, as she thought how good Steffie and Brad looked together. She had never seen Steffie this enthused about a man, and it made her very lonesome for Mitch. She wondered what he was doing right now, and whether he was thinking of her.

They were easily lulled to sleep by the distant throbbing of the engines, and the occasional creaking, as the great ship made her way so powerfully through the gently rolling waters.

It had been a wonderful day, and they could hardly wait to see what surprises tomorrow would bring.

Chapter Seven

While Kitty and Steffie were having a fun-filled day on board ship, back in Panama City Beach, Vickie and Cassie were wishing they had never become embroiled in the entire mess.

First they had gone back down to the hot tub, and had searched again for Cassie's engraved bracelet. No luck. They checked the office to see whether it might have been turned in, but again, no luck. It had to have been the murderer who had taken it. What possible use would a bracelet be to anyone else, when it had Cassie's name on it?

Vickie asked one of the new clerks at the reception desk, whether anyone had been inquiring about Cassie. The young chap behind the desk, whose name tag said 'Darryl,' shook his head. "Nobody asked me about any Cassie," he said in an uninterested way. Clearly he had other things on his mind, or other places in which he would rather find himself. He obviously hadn't grasped the fact that he was now working at the elite Edgewater Beach Resort, and was therefore expected to behave in a certain well mannered and well informed way towards the guests.

"Oh, I got a phone call early this morning," offered a pretty young girl with a mane of tangled brown hair. "Some guy just asked if he could speak to Cassie. He didn't have a last name, so I told him I couldn't help him. Then Maria, who heard me talking to him, said he must mean Mrs. Meredith. Her name is Cassie or Cassandra, and she owns a condo here. So I told him that info, and then he just hung up on me." She sounded very aggrieved at the caller's lack of manners.

Cassie and Vickie looked at each other with concern.

"Shit on a stick," muttered Vickie. Then, putting on her most charming smile, she lowered her voice and said, "Please don't give out any information at all about Mrs. Meredith. There's a dangerous man looking for her, and you don't want to be responsible for getting her killed, now do you?"

Vickie was morphing into her 'I'll kill you myself' voice. Both the young man, and the tangled-hair girl, whose name was Tami, looked startled, then nervous.

"I'm not kidding," added Vickie, pressing her advantage. "This is a very serious matter. If anyone else calls asking for Cassie or Cassandra, or Mrs. Meredith, try to get his or her name and phone number. Tell them you'll get the info for them and call them back. That would be a great help to the police, and you'll be heroes. Just don't give out any more info about Mrs. Meredith."

She was scowling at them now, as only Vickie could do, and they both seemed totally intimidated.

"Gee, what's goin' on?" asked Darryl, with renewed interest in the conversation. "Last night someone got killed, and now someone's after Mrs. Meredith. Wow! Cool! This is the place to be! It's better than the movies," he added with an amazed look. "We sure won't say anything, but, hey, do you think anyone might want to interview us? You know, like for the TV or somethin?"

He looked so hopeful that Vickie hated to burst his balloon. "Well, you never know. Just keep alert, and tell anyone else who works on the desk or the phones, to give out absolutely NO information about Mrs. Meredith. Got it?"

Darryl and Tami stood slack-jawed. It seemed obvious that they were still in training for the front desk job. This was more excitement than they could handle. It would take time to sink in. Meantime, Vickie stomped out, Cassie trailing silently behind her, trying to subdue her desire to laugh. Vickie was funny when she got going.

The trip to the police station was an adventure of sorts. They had taken Front Beach Road to drive to the station, which was located at the west end of the beach, near the library. The scenery along the beach was gorgeous, but the station was a small, uninspiring building. The receptionist had quickly led them to an interview room, where they waited till two detectives arrived.

They were immediately chastised for not coming forth the previous evening. The two detectives seemed tired and cranky. Maybe they had been up all night. Anyway, this set a rather bad tone for the interview, and they were annoyed that they had missed their flight and first day of the cruise, just to be scolded like children. Surprisingly, no one else had seen the killer, at least no one had come forward, so the small amount of information which they had, was apparently important.

They described the man from the elevator as best they could. They both agreed that he had small, black eyes placed close together on his wide face. They didn't know whether he had any distinguishing marks, but they emphasized his size, and the fact that he had a moustache. They remembered that he was wearing light gray pants and a smart pinstriped shirt. He was also wearing a watch, which might have been a Rolex or a good knock-off.

Upon prompting, Vickie remembered that he had very thick, long brown hair, which he combed straight back. He was likely a professional man, but his size, hair, and mean facial expression, made one think of a biker or red-neck ruffian.

Cassie laid on the charm, and explained about losing the gold bracelet with her name engraved on it. She also told them that she and Vickie had missed their flight to Fort Lauderdale, in order to come forth with this information. That seemed to alleviate the tense situation, and the police eventually agreed that they could leave for the cruise, but should touch base with them again upon their return.

Cassie asked them not to let their names get into the local paper as witnesses, as they both felt somewhat threatened. Finally, it was a relief to leave the station, and know that they had done all they could. They were now free to fly to the ship to join their friends, and put all this unfortunate experience behind them.

The flight in the small jet was a breeze, and they were exhilarated when they finally boarded the ship. They attracted a bit of attention as they boarded, but that didn't bother them. Cassie, was tall and slim, with reddish blond hair and big blue eyes. In her aqua and white outfit she looked cool and elegant. Vickie was wearing yellow and white, which suited her auburn hair and brown eyes.

They were interested to see that just about every passenger was wearing shorts. Most of the women had cute little visors, or big straw hats to protect them from the sun. Most of the men were wearing baseball caps, but some also had the straw hats. Obviously they had been to a straw market in port.

Soon a steward showed them to their fancy cabin.

"This is so great, Cass. I can't believe we're finally here," enthused Vickie, twirling around in the spacious stateroom.

"I'm so glad we got these nice cabins. Hope Steff and Kitty have one just as fancy."

They were unpacking a few of their belongings, when Kitty and Steffie showed up. It was a grand reunion, with everyone talking at once. One would suspect that they had been separated for months, rather than just one day.

"Stop, stop," laughed Cassie, standing up and waving her arms. "We sound like those four women on The View. We're all talking at once, and I can't hear anything. Why don't you take us on a tour of the ship, and we'll catch up on all the details over a drink in some neat little outside bar. We've already lost a day and a half, and I don't want to waste another minute. Come on, 'carpe diem' as they say. Let's go."

That night at dinner, Cassie and Vickie met their other tablemates. They immediately liked Brad Butler and his sister Jillian. It was obvious to see that Brad was smitten with Steffie, and she, in turn, wasn't as standoffish as she usually was with men. He was very attractive, with broad shoulders, a wide, easy grin, straight white teeth, and rather unruly thick black hair. His sister Jill was quiet at first, but soon entertained them all with tales from veterinary college, and from the ranch north of Toronto, where she and Brad had been raised. She and her brother, in turn, were very interested in hearing all about Cassandra's Cattery.

Mr. Smithers from Kentucky, set Vickie's teeth on edge. His head bobbed when he talked. It reminded her of a balloon on a string, gently bobbing and waving in a slight breeze. He seemed to talk constantly, which was also annoying. She sighed inwardly as she put on a pleasant smile, and tried to look interested in his boring tales of Kentucky. There was what Vickie thought of as an "eau de pomposity" about him, and she decided that she would not let herself get stuck sitting next to him for the rest of the cruise. She would insist that the others take turns with her.

Martha Carrington arrived a little bit late. Cassie and Vickie looked at each other and raised their eyebrows, when they saw all her jewellery. Kitty and Stef hadn't warned them. She was wearing five large rings, as well as a heavy diamond bracelet, earrings and a diamond pendant.

"I thought we were told not to bring good jewellery on this cruise," muttered Vickie, sotto voce. "Not that I have any, of course, except for my beautiful sapphire ring."

"Maybe all her stuff is just paste," answered Cassie, without looking up from her plate of surf and turf.

This being the second night out, it was the Captain's night, and everyone was dressed in formal attire. Before dinner, they had the opportunity to meet the Captain, and have a photo taken with him. He wasn't the tall, glamorous type they had pictured, but he was average looking, and had sparkling eyes which were attractive. It was obvious that he fancied himself a hit with the ladies, and he did a lot of flirting with Steffie.

After dinner, they danced in the Grand Ballroom. There were enough single men on board, plus husbands with wandering eyes, that all four of the friends were danced off their feet.

It had been a marvelous night, and they were so tired that they virtually fell into their beds, promising to meet early the next morning for breakfast on deck, rather than in the formal dining room. It was fun to have all these choices.

As Cassie and Vickie lay in companionable silence in the soothing darkness, they fervently hoped that the man who had thrown the woman off the balcony, was now safely in custody. That kind of trouble they didn't need. They were glad, however, that they had taken the time to talk with the police, even though it meant that they had missed the beginning of this trip.

"We did the right thing," laughed Cassie, plumping her pillows, and snuggling down. "At least we missed all the crowds in the cruise terminal yesterday."

"True, but I'm sorry to miss one single moment of this adventure. I love cruising," stated Vickie happily, staring out the window at the stars, which seemed unusually bright and nearby.

The ship swayed slightly, occasionally lurching unexpectedly. Lying in the darkness, they could hear the occasional far away sound of laughter down a long corridor, or the tinkle of a tray of drinks being delivered by a conscientious, and ubiquitous cabin steward.

This super cruise ship was very quiet. It was only now and then that they became aware of the constant pounding of the engines. They sounded like an angry animal trying to get free. They were beating out a steady rhythm like a giant heartbeat, as the four friends from Niagara Falls gradually drifted into sleep.

Chapter Eight

There was so much fun to be had, and so few days in which to have it.

Waking up on the ship, and knowing that there was an entire day of fun and food ahead of them, was terrific. This morning, the ship was rocking a bit more enthusiastically than it had the day before, but the sun was streaming in the picture windows. Jumping out of bed, and venturing onto the balcony, Vickie saw that the ocean was much more riled up than it had been when they arrived.

"Hope it doesn't get any rougher than this," she grimaced, as she was thrown against the railing. "Yikes, I'm not going out there again for a while. That ocean does not look friendly, and it sure as hell looks deep. Come on Cass, up and at it."

Cass had slept soundly, but was now raring to go. She also ventured onto the balcony, but one look at the roiling, angry water, sent her back to the safety of the bedroom. "Shoot, we won't be able to make any port today. It's going to be a sea day for sure," she muttered as she headed for the shower.

By the time they had met with Kitty and Steffie, and had finished breakfast, the ship was rolling angrily. Even this huge ship, with its wonderful stabilizers, could not do too much to calm the rocking, as it blundered bravely on. Looking out the windows, they could see that the waves were high, and were creating huge crater-like troughs in the seemingly endless water. To make things worse, the sun had now disappeared behind some metallic looking clouds.

"We've really hit a pocket of bad weather," murmured Steffie to Brad, as they sat drinking coffee in the Crow's Nest lounge after breakfast. "Wonder how long it will last." She was also wondering whether she would be able to capture the majesty and the grimness of the waves, if she tried to paint them.

"I'm no sailor," admitted Brad, chomping on a cookie, "but I'll bet we'll be through it in a couple of hours." He had no idea at all, but it seemed like a cheerful thing to say. He was just very content to be sitting here with Steffie. She was the best looking woman on the entire ship, but much more important, she was the most interesting.

They sat in companionable silence, drinking their coffee, and looking out the picture windows at the roller coaster waves, which surrounded the ship.

The rocking and rolling got worse as the morning went on. Gradually, the public lounges and decks became relatively empty, as passengers staggered back to lie, wretched and retching, in the privacy of their cabins. The souls who did manage to stay on their feet, were the hardy ones, the ones with the cast-iron stomachs, and sturdy resolve to make the most of every day.

The dining rooms and food stations were half empty by the time lunch rolled around. Fortunately for the fearless four, they all had good appetites and strong stomachs. Actually, they couldn't take their eyes off the wicked waves, which were slapping and beating the ship in a mad frenzy.

"Are we paying extra for this show?" kidded Vickie, as they all sat by the picture windows, waiting for the cruise director to start the Catch-Phrase game.

"I don't think you could pay enough for a sight like this," said Kitty. "I wish Mitch could be here with us. He'd work it into his latest book."

As the hours passed, passengers tottered around, looking as if they wanted to be anywhere but on this bloody ship, with its constant and relentless rocking and pitching. It was as if the ship was dancing to some mad music, which only it could hear. It had taken on a life of its own, and it was now beginning to seem malevolent and fiendish.

Barf bags had appeared like magic in corridors and on stairways. Dramamine and ear patches were available at the purser's desk. The ship doctor, in his everyday regulation navy blues, took a short break from sick bay, possibly looking for more victims of mal de mer. Actually, he looked as if he might be a little sick himself. The lifeboats were swinging from their davits as if eager to be cut loose.

Steffie had read somewhere that being on board ship in a bad storm was rather like riding a camel. The ship pitched and rocked unexpectedly, seemingly with no pattern to its gyrations. At the moment this was one camel she would like to dismount!

They managed to keep themselves busy in the lounges, playing Trivial Pursuit, Catch-Phrase and bridge, all organized by the harried, but still bubbly cruise director. His forced enthusiasm was getting on people's nerves.

Somehow, it seemed much noisier onboard during the storm. The distant growling and groaning of the engines was louder. It sounded as if the engines were fighting as hard as they could to keep the ocean at bay. If you dared to open a door out onto a deck, the wind roared, and the angry waves kept up their interminable slapping with intensity and malice, against the sides of the ship. The sounds were very reminiscent of horror movies.

Inside, the noise was less threatening, but constant. There was always the clattering of dishes on one deck or another. The laughter and chattering of the passengers seemed to verge on hysteria. Music blasted from ubiquitous speakers. It was a mad symphony of sounds, a cacaphony of noises which assaulted the soul.

Eventually, however, by late afternoon, they had reached calm waters. The sun came out, the ship stopped its manic dance, and the ocean seemed to be saying "I had a little temper tantrum, but I'm fine now." Kitty wondered aloud whether this was why sailors loved the sea. It was so capricious, and so like quick-silver in its changing moods.

Brad was happy to have been correct in his predictions that they would soon outrun the storm, and he treated them to drinks in the Mermaid Bar, which had become their favourite.

The following day was a day in paradise, at least it started out that way. The water was so calm that the wake looked like a shimmering highway cut right through the ocean behind them. They were going in to Key West, where at least one more passenger was to join the ship.

Steffie and Kitty had never been to Key West, so they set out on their own to see as much of the area as possible. Cassie and Vickie had been there more recently, when they were planning Cassandra's

Cattery. They had flown down for a week, and had spent their days at Hemingway's old home. This was where the descendants of Hemingway's polydactyl cats lived and flourished.

They had spoken at length with the staff, to get ideas for the cattery, which Cassie had built with some of her inheritance. Many hours had been spent on the estate property, happily observing the cats, how they were treated, how much freedom they had, and how they interacted with each other. They had taken many pictures, and had patterned the Canadian haven after this famous one.

Today they went to the estate first, spent a couple of hours there, took more pictures, talked to more staff, then left to have lunch, visit some of Hemingway's favourite haunts, and do a little shopping.

Eventually they parted company. Cassie wanted to return a sweater which she had bought hastily in the first store they visited. Vickie wanted to find an old neighbour of hers from Vancouver, who now lived in Key West, and ran a little art shop. They promised to meet at Sloppy Joe's bar to catch the shuttle back to the ship.

Cassie got there first, and ordered a margarita, while waiting for her friend. Vickie had not arrived by the time the shuttle bus was ready to leave, and Cass was in a quandary. It was possible that Vickie had returned early to the ship. She could be scatter-brained at times, and she might have confused their meeting plans. That was unlikely though. Good old Vic was pretty reliable. Something must have happened, and Cass could feel her scalp starting to tingle.

The ship was due to leave at 5 o'clock sharp, and it was now 4:15. Cass paced up and down outside the bar, looking hopefully for any signs of her friend. Finally she decided that she had to get back to the ship, and tell them that Vickie was missing, or in some kind of trouble. She had missed the last shuttle bus, so grabbed a cab, and raced back.

After checking to be sure that Vickie had not returned, she went right to the front desk to tell them her predicament. They paged Vickie, but to no avail. Apparently she was not on the ship. The staff then contacted someone higher up. Cassie hoped it was the captain. To her dismay, the word came back that they couldn't hold the ship back for the sake of one errant passenger. Vickie could fly out to catch up with them at their next port.

This was not acceptable to Cassie. Vickie would never miss the ship on purpose. Something bad had happened. Having a lot of money had made Cassandra much more sure of herself, and much more willing and able to "take charge" in certain situations. Within minutes she was speaking directly with the captain and first mate. Laying on the charm, she argued, discussed, cajoled and pleaded. Vickie had to be found. There would be dire consequences if they sailed without her. Eventually the captain allowed himself to be persuaded. The ship would wait for one hour.

The captain, now convinced that something unfortunate might have happened to one of his passengers, and always aware of possible lawsuits, sent the port agent and two crew back with Cassie, to help her search. They would check with the hospital, the police, and the little art store to which Vickie had been heading when last seen.

Chapter Nine

While Cassie was frantically trying to find her long time friend in this lovely, but unfamiliar area, pictures of Vickie kept flitting through her mind.

She remembered the night they had broken into Jordan's house, looking for evidence against him. He had caught them, and Vickie had pretended to hurt her ankle, just to get them out of there in a hurry. Vickie had bought herself a beautiful sapphire ring after that adventure. It was a good story, and they both loved to tell the tale.

Cass thought of the time Vickie had comforted her, when she heard that Prudence was dead, and they both suspected that it was murder.

She pictured the night they brashly went out to the old house, hoping to catch a killer, but were caught themselves in a dreadful fire.

She recalled how brave Vickie had been the night she was almost raped by Willie the Weasel.

Whatever had happened to her this time, Cassie was determined to find her, and to find her unhurt, and unscathed by whatever misfortune had befallen her.

Meanwhile, the object of all this concern, gradually sat up and stared around in bewilderment. She had been lying on the ground, half under a bush. As she looked around groggily, it seemed that she was lying at the entrance of an alley, on a narrow little street she didn't recognize. There was no one in sight.

As she looked at her watch, her heart started racing. She was dismayed to see that it was after five o'clock. She must have been unconscious for close to an hour. That was not good. Did she have a head trauma? She sure as hell had a mother of a headache. Why hadn't anyone seen her lying there?

By now the ship would have sailed without her. The thought sent her into a slight panic. This was serious. She could see blood on the ground where she had been lying. Was that from her head, or was she hurt somewhere else as well? What should she do? Hell, what could she do?

"Okay, Victoria, old girl. Calm down," she muttered, forcing herself to move. She felt quite woozy, however, as she tried to stand, so she gingerly sat herself back down beside the bush.

"There's no way Cassie would have left without me," she assured herself. She found it easier to think when she spoke out loud. "The ship may have sailed, but Cassie is definitely here looking for me. She'll have half the ship crew out too. Key West is a small area," (she hoped she was correct about this,) "so they will have fanned out, starting with where she last saw me. Well, that's great, but where the hell am I in relation to where I was? How will they know which way to go? No one is going to check out this crummy little street," she wailed, as she tried to stand up again. "I have to get back to a main area where there will be people."

Bending down to pick up her purse made her stagger. Whew! She really was dizzy. Fortunately her passport was zippered securely in the pocket of her cargo pants, and her wallet and cards were still in her purse. Why hadn't her attacker taken these things? Was it not just a simple mugging? Why would he have knocked her out that way? What was the point of it? Didn't muggers usually just pull a gun on you, take your money and run?

Why had he chosen her? Was it because she was all alone on this miserable little street, or had he been following her for some other reason?

The thinking was making her dizzy again, but gradually it was all coming back to her. She had asked someone for directions to her friend's shop. Somehow she had become lost, and found herself in an abandoned, dirty area of town, where most of the stores were closed.

As she had begun to understand that she was seriously lost, she tried retracing her steps. She had realized that there was no one around, yet suddenly she could hear footsteps behind her. Turning to ask directions to get herself out of this maze, she had found herself looking at a large hulk of a man, who somehow seemed familiar. She had felt instinctively that he meant her harm, and she had begun to run.

He had caught up with her, and apparently hit her on the side of the head with something hard. That was all she remembered. He must have thought he had killed her, but why would a complete stranger want to hurt her? Why did he seem familiar?

Her poor head felt as if it was filled with cotton balls and big pins. She couldn't think clearly, and every little effort sent sharp pains hurtling around in her head like tiny porcupines gone mad. She had to get out of here and find help right away. She could have a serious concussion, and pass out again at any moment. She had suffered a concussion once before. It was three years ago, the summer she and Cassie were locked in the burning house, after being knocked unconscious. It hadn't been fun then, and it sure as hell wasn't fun now.

Along with her pounding head, and the blood on her shoulder and arm, she was breathing in short little hurtful puffs, as if she had been running. Never mind. She would worry about that later.

With a determination born of fright and anger, she half ran, half staggered, until she made it to the corner. Where was everyone? It was as if every living person had been sucked right out of Key West. As she rounded the corner, however, she gave a little gasp of thankfulness. Ahead she could see people and cars. Everything looked normal again.

"Trust me to get myself into an abandoned part of town," she mumbled, as she stumbled along. She really was quite light headed and sick, but her determination overrode her physical feelings.

She was about to go into the first little shop on the street, to ask for help, when she heard her name called. Looking up, she saw Cassie running towards her, and behind her came a policeman. Her friend had never looked so good. Vickie took a deep breath, as she and Cassie hugged without saying a word. Then they both started talking and laughing at once.

Cassie was so relieved to have found her friend, that she couldn't stop touching her and squeezing her hand. Vickie was so relieved to have been found, that she couldn't stop the tears which were welling up in her eyes. Crying was something she never did, well, almost never. In this case, however, it had been a scary experience, and the feeling of abandonment had been sickening. Who cared if she shed a few tears of relief. Cass would never tell.

With the help of the police officer, they got it all straightened out. Vickie gave her statement, they found the port agent and the crew members, and they made it back safely. By then it was well after six, but they knew that the ship wouldn't sail without its personnel. It was only as they headed right to sick bay to have Vickie checked out, that she gasped and stopped.

"Oh, God, Cass. I think I know who attacked me. I knew he looked familiar, but I didn't think I knew him. Now I do. It was the guy who threw the woman off the balcony. He's shaved his head and lost the moustache, but I would recognize those little black eyes anywhere. I know that's who it was. He had a Rolex on one arm too, just like the guy in the elevator. He's followed us here to the ship. I'll bet he's the extra passenger they were picking up in Key West."

Chapter Ten

Vickie did indeed have a concussion, although it was not nearly as bad as they had feared. She put up no fuss at all when the nurse tucked her into bed in the little ship hospital, and said that she would be there for one night at least. All she wanted to do was sleep, but they tried to keep her awake as much as possible. If she did doze off, Cassie, who was sitting beside her in the little sick bay, was authorized to waken her gently, and get her talking again.

It was a very long night for both of them. It reminded Cassie of the night at the old farmhouse. Vickie had been hit on the head, and ended up in the hospital with a slight concussion. That time too, Cassie had stayed by her side, keeping her awake, and wondering whether their nightmare was finally over.

Unfortunately, this time, she suspected that their troubles were just beginning.

Towards morning, Vickie appeared much brighter. She had Cassie crank up her bed, so that she was sitting, rather than lying.

"Look at you," laughed Cassie, shaking her head. "You look pretty darn good for someone who was left for dead. Of course, you've got a lump on the side of your head, and I don't know how you got that black eye. And, with that cannula stuck up your nose, you're quite the sight, Mrs. Craig."

Cassie, of course, was referring to the ubiquitous oxygen tubes stuck in Vickie's nostrils.

"I don't want to see myself for a while. All those lovely new clothes I bought, and I look like a damn monster," groaned Vickie.

"It must have been rather exciting, finding yourself abandoned under a gooseberry bush, or whatever it was. How the heck did you get so lost? I can't let you out of my sight for a minute. You know, you and I are just an old pair of inveterate trouble-seekers, and, hopefully we'll never change."

"Do you mean hopefully we'll never smarten up?" grinned Vickie. "I got lost because I asked someone for directions to Carol's shop, and I must have misunderstood what they said. I thought it seemed farther than it should have been, but I stupidly kept going, until I realized that I was in a shady part of town." She shook her head at her own stupidity, but then moaned and touched the bandage. "Ouch, that brute must have hit me with a fifty pound weight. You'd better be nice to me. I suspect that you're lucky you still have me around. He really meant business when he hit me. Fortunately I must have a pretty hard head."

They both laughed, and Cassie gave her a gentle hug. "I've always known that," she kidded.

There was only one other patient in the tiny hospital area. He was an old man who was having chest pains. Cassie sincerely hoped that it was a false alarm. If it was a real heart attack, he wouldn't get too much care on the ship.

At dinner the previous night, the doctor had looked great in his crisp white dress uniform with all the gold braid. Of course, most men did look great in a snazzy uniform. Today he was in his every day navy blues. He still looked good, but talking to him, Cassie found that he didn't instill too much confidence.

For a doctor this young to be working on a cruise ship, Cass suspected that he likely had been victim of a malpractice suit, and had taken off to lick his wounds and enjoy a gentler, less stressful life. He was kind though, and attentive, so she had no serious complaints regarding the care Vickie was receiving.

Steffie and Kitty dropped around to visit with her for a while. They each offered to take shifts sitting with the patient, but Cassie wouldn't relinquish her seat beside the bed. Somehow she felt responsible for Vickie's plight. If she had gone with her to find her friend Carol's art shop, instead of going off to return the sweater, none of this would have happened.

As she sat in the quiet little room, trying not to give in to the soporific effects of the gently rolling ship, she wondered about Vickie's attacker. Could he really be the same man who threw the woman off the balcony? It seemed quite impossible. Still, he certainly could have found out her name and her destination from Edgewater, and she had heard that one or two passengers were supposed to be picked up in Key West. If he had followed them here, it could only be to kill them. Why, then, had he left Vickie alive and lying on the pavement?

The more Cassie thought about this, the more she began to believe that it all fit nicely. When he hit Vickie, she likely went down like a stone. He would think that she was dead, especially if he had been in a hurry. And, of course, he would have been in a hurry to catch the ship before it sailed.

It was likely just a piece of good luck that he had spotted Vickie and recognized her, good luck for him, but bad luck for Vickie. He knew that the ship was coming in to port in Key West, and that they would likely be getting off to roam around. He would have been watching the tourist areas, and could have spotted them easily. The fact that they split up made it easier for him. He had likely opted to follow Vickie, because she headed away from the busy tourist area. It all fit.

Cass wondered where he was now? Had he boarded the ship? If so, it should be easy to track him down. She had to talk to the captain again right away. He had been so helpful after she had turned on the charm. She knew that if this guy had indeed boarded the ship, it would only be to kill her. The thought stunned her. This cruise certainly wasn't turning out the way she had expected.

Early that morning Cassie had a good meeting with the captain. He seemed to be a nice enough man. He was average height, with graying hair, and a weathered face. Well, what could you expect from a man who had spent the better part of his life at sea, she mused. She noticed again that his eyes sparkled when he talked, which made him quite attractive. He seemed a bit on the flirtatious side, but that didn't bother Cassie. She figured that he likely struck up a lot of shipboard romances during these cruises.

He appeared skeptical when she started the entire tale of the murder, and the engraved bracelet, and Vickie's mugger. He let her talk first, then asked a lot of questions. Cassie was able to answer them coherently, and that seemed to assuage his doubts.

"Well, it should be pretty simple to find him. Actually, we picked up three people in Key West. We'll check the passenger list, see who is assigned to those cabins, and arrange for you to have a look at them. We have a musician who is joining the ship to play in the band. He's replacing our trumpet player who had to fly home because of a family crisis. I would guaranty that he's not your man. I'm not sure about the other two though. They were both last minute additions. Anyway, we'll get it all straightened out, don't you worry."

Cassie went back to sick bay to check on Vickie, and was surprised to discover that they had let her go back to her cabin.

Vickie had a good sized lump on the side of her head, but other than that, she seemed fine. "I'm so tired, though, Cass. All I want to do now is have a good sleep. Thanks to you, I was awake almost all night long. Why don't you go to dinner with Steffie and Kitty, while I snooze, and I'll go to the casino with you later."

"Okay, that sounds good. Just be sure to keep the cabin door locked. Until they catch this guy, we really aren't safe. The captain is supposed to contact me as soon as they track him down, and then we'll see what happens."

"Don't worry, pal. I won't open the door to anyone until you come back. Be careful, though. It would be better if you didn't come down this long corridor by yourself. Get Kitty or Steffie to come back with you after dinner, and we'll go to the casino together. I'll be up and dressed and ready for fun by then."

Chapter Eleven

All during dinner, Cassie kept glancing around the large, elegant room, hoping to catch sight of the captain or the murderer. She couldn't understand why the captain hadn't contacted her by now. How difficult would it be to track down one large man on one ship? Cass wanted to see for herself whether he looked like the man in the elevator back at Edgewater, and she wanted Vickie to see him, and tell them whether he was her attacker.

Kitty and Steffie were having an after dinner drink with Brad and Jillian, so Cass excused herself to head back to the cabin. Cassie hadn't been on the huge ship long enough to become familiar with it, and somehow she took a wrong turn. Opening a door, she found herself on an outside deck.

It was a glorious night, with a myriad of stars in the black sky, so she allowed herself to be sidetracked for a moment. She walked over to the railing, and gazed up at the stars, wondering whether they could see them back in Niagara Falls. It seemed so far away.

She was lonely for her husband Dave, and would have liked to have him here beside her. Maybe they would have been able to regain the old magic if he was here with her. She pictured him at home in their new house, supervising all the finishing touches, and anxious for her to see how beautiful it was. He would be taking good care of Muffy and Sugar Plum. They, in turn, would be annoyed and intrigued with the workmen who came early every morning, making ugly noises, and disturbing their regular routine.

It was a beautiful house, with lots of great hiding places for her two beloved cats. How spoiled they were, and how she loved them. She missed them, and also all her little furry friends at Cassandra's Cattery. She had worked so hard to get it going, had spent a huge amount of money, and was very proud of how successful it was.

Farther down along the deck, she could see a young couple standing with their arms entwined, totally unaware of anyone but themselves. Actually, there was something in the way, so that the only way she could see them was to lean out a bit over the railing.

The moon looked huge, and it had created a silvery, sequined ribbon across the black velvet sea. It was very romantic, and she scolded herself for letting her thoughts turn to Jack. How could she love two such different men at the same time? It was a serious flaw in her character, and she despaired of ever achieving a truly happy ending.

Because she was lost in the beauty of the night, the vastness of the ocean, and the feelings of homesickness, she didn't hear the man, as he emerged from the shadows, and grabbed her from behind. He actually lifted her off her feet, and she realized that he was trying to throw her over the railing.

Terror throbbed through every part of her body. The ocean, which moments before she had been admiring as a black velvet sea, was now a black, yawning pit of evil, waiting to envelop her.

She could see herself being sucked into the ship's powerful engines. They would mangle her till she was unrecognizable. She pictured sharks swimming along beside the ship, just waiting for some delectable morsel to appear. A shark could bite her into two pieces. Possibly it would toy with her, biting off one limb at a time.

These terrifying thoughts and pictures flashed through her mind in an instant, as she tried to tear the man's arms from around her waist.

Her heart felt as if it was exploding, as she screamed and fought with all her strength. This was a life and death struggle, and, unable to loosen his iron grip, she grabbed frantically at the railing, but her hands weren't strong enough to hold on. As they gradually slipped, she turned herself just enough in his strong arms, that she was able to jab a finger into his eye, all the time screaming and screeching like a banshee.

He yelped in pain and surprise, and loosened his grip slightly. That gave Cassie the chance to attack him again, this time with her nails, which she raked down his cheek. Now he let go totally, putting his hand to his face, and looking in disbelief at the blood on his fingers.

Suddenly she was aware of pounding feet and someone yelling. "Stop that. Leave her alone!"

In the one part of her mind that wasn't frozen with shock, she realized that help had come in time. She shoved him, and staggered away from the railing, as the young couple reached her.

"Are you okay?" they cried simultaneously. "Did he hurt you?"

"Thank you, thank you. You've just saved my life," she stammered. "He was trying to throw me over the railing."

A deep voice behind her said, "No, it wasn't like that. I saw that she was going to jump, and I just grabbed her. Thank God I came along when I did. That's a terrible way to commit suicide."

Cassie was momentarily stunned at this amazing statement. Taking a good look at him, she realized that he must be the same man who had attacked Vickie. He was big and hefty, and his eyes seemed rather close together. Actually, he was a fairly decent looking man, except that he now had an overbite, which was not attractive. It must be a false bridge, which he can put in and out to change his appearance, Cass thought.

At the moment, he had relatively long wavy hair, which, she thought was likely a wig. Hadn't Vickie said that her attacker had cut his long hair? Tomorrow was costume night, and there were lots of costumes and wigs available to the passengers. He had likely been incognito all day, perhaps even walking amongst them, as they searched for a baldheaded man.

The young people were looking at Cassie in confusion. Had she really been trying to jump? She saw the looks of doubt they were giving her, and tried to explain.

"I certainly wasn't trying to kill myself. I just came out here by mistake. I took the wrong door. This ship is very confusing. Anyway, I saw you two kissing, and it made me lonely for my husband and home. This guy crept up on me, grabbed me from behind, and lifted me right off my feet. If you hadn't been so close, he would have pitched me over."

She turned to give the attacker an accusing look, but he was nowhere to be seen. Stunned, she did a complete circle. Where was he? How could he have disappeared so quickly? He must have slipped through the door back into the ship, while she and her rescuers had been talking. He had disappeared as mysteriously as he had come.

"Honestly, I wasn't trying to commit suicide," she reiterated. "He wasn't trying to save me, he was trying to kill me, and he would have succeeded without you two. I can never thank you enough."

"But why would he want to kill you? Who is he?" asked the young man doubtfully.

"Let's go inside. I have to report this to a steward or the captain. It's a long story, and I don't even understand it myself, but he's already killed one woman and tried to kill another. Looks like I was supposed to be the third victim."

Cassie was shaken at the thought of plunging into that black, bottomless water. How had this guy eluded everyone all day long? Where had he been hiding? How had he known that she would come out on the deck?

He must have followed her from the dining room, and grabbed the perfect opportunity when she went out that door by mistake. How careless she had been. She knew he might be on board. Why had she left the others in order to go back to Vickie's room by herself? Why had she been so cavalier in her attitude toward this killer?

The three of them went into a lounge, and waited while a steward was sent to fetch the captain. The young man got a drink for her, and she gulped it down with shaking hands, as she tried to explain herself. She could sense, however, that the two lovers were both unconvinced. The more she talked, the more disbelieving they became. It was the old "methinks thou dost protest too much" syndrome.

"Look, you heard me screaming. Why would I be yelling for help if I was trying to kill myself?"

"You could have been screaming because he was trying to stop you," suggested the young woman reasonably.

Cassie just shook her head in frustration. Hopefully the captain would believe her, and they would finally catch this monster.

It was half an hour before the captain appeared, looking a bit disheveled. Cassie wondered whether he had been having a little rendezvous with a passenger. He hadn't appeared at dinner, and he did seem to have an affinity for the ladies. Anyway, he sat and listened quietly, while she told what had happened. She assured him that she had definitely not been trying to commit suicide, and was grateful that he didn't seem to question her story.

He admitted that they had searched the ship from top to bottom, and had found no trace of the passenger who had come aboard in Key West. The musician and the other passenger, who had boarded at the same time, had been questioned and released. The musician was a skinny boy in his twenties, and the other passenger was a short man in his sixties. Neither fit the picture painted by Cassie and Vickie. The third passenger had not shown up in the cabin reserved for him, and had managed to elude the searchers all day.

Cass was becoming incensed. How hard was it to find one person when there were so many looking for him? Well, on a ship like this, it would be pretty difficult, she admitted to herself. There must be so very many great hiding places. Anyone familiar with ships would know just how to elude searchers. The likelihood that he had disguised himself made it even easier for him to escape detection. This guy must be pretty clever, and extremely determined to get at Cassie and Vickie, and get rid of them. Suddenly this lovely cruise ship seemed to be an unexpectedly dangerous place.

Chapter Twelve

The friends congregated in Cass and Vickie's suite, and rehashed the unbelievable events. They had difficulty accepting that the killer/mugger would have followed them to the ship. He must be desperate to get rid of Cassie and Vickie. The thought pierced Vickie's brain like an acupuncture needle. If he was here on the ship, that meant that the police in Panama City Beach hadn't been able to track him, and likely had no idea who he was, or where he was. That was not good.

Cass was disappointed and frustrated that the captain was very reluctant to broadcast to the entire ship that they were looking for a murderer. In her mind, he should have warned everyone that the man was extremely dangerous. With some 2000 passengers looking for one large man, it would have been pretty easy to find him. He could change his appearance, but he couldn't change his size.

The captain, however, didn't want to frighten the passengers, or ruin their holiday. It would also give the cruise line bad publicity to broadcast that they had a killer on board. He insisted that they would find the felon in their own quiet, methodical way, and he would be turned over to the police as soon as they reached Port Everglades, or one of the other ports.

"I don't think his quiet, methodical way is doing much good," said Steffie, in disgust. "I'm going to tell everyone I meet, so that they'll all be looking for him."

"That's a good idea," said Kitty. "I also think that the four of us should stay together for the rest of the trip. He can't hurt all four of us at once, so Cass and Vickie will be much safer. That means if one of us wants to go back to the cabin for something, all four of us will go. Agreed?"

"Agreed," nodded Vickie, reluctantly. "I don't relish the thought of meeting up with him in one of these long corridors. Of course, I don't relish the thought of meeting up with him at all," she laughed ruefully. "Once was enough. This is turning into quite the adventure, Cass. How is it that we can't seem to go anywhere or do anything without getting ourselves into trouble? I just hope you didn't pay extra for all this excitement."

"Hey, we're usually minding our own business, and trouble just comes looking for us. You remember what we were like when we were kids. We were always looking for mysteries to solve. Maybe the fates are just paying us back for our impudence and imprudence."

"Well, whatever it is, I don't like it any more. I used to think it would be fun chasing a killer, but when the shoe's on the other foot, it's a different picture. I just want us all to get home safely. Surely he won't follow us to Niagara Falls."

There was dead silence after that remark. Each of the friends was thinking her own thoughts, and digesting the awful possibility that the murderer might indeed follow them to Niagara Falls. It was a debilitating and demoralizing thought.

The next day was spent in uneasy pursuit of holiday fun. They played Catch-Phrase in the "Crow's Nest" lounge on the upper deck, and drank margaritas while sitting around the pool. Before dinner, they took a brisk walk on the Promenade Deck, and spent time choosing costumes for the big masquerade party.

The ten day cruise would be over much too soon, and Steffie was beginning to feel reluctant at saying goodbye to Brad. She had spent a lot of time with him on board, and felt relaxed and happy when they were together.

It was the first serious but short relationship she had experienced since the break-up of her marriage. She wasn't about to jump into anything though. She loved the freedom she had in her new life, and wasn't eager to get involved. Brad was a lot of fun, and she liked his sister Jillian as well, but she wasn't sure that she wanted it to go any further.

All throughout the cruise, two photographers had wandered around, taking pictures of the passengers. No matter what they were doing, eating, drinking at the bar, lounging on deck, swimming, dancing, playing bingo, their pictures were being taken. The pictures were then developed, and hung up in the long corridors, and the anteroom of the photo shop. Passengers could search for pictures of themselves, and then had the option to buy any they liked.

It occurred to Kitty, that the photographer might have unwittingly snapped some shots of the man who was stalking Cassie and Vickie. The women thought that was a great idea, and the four of them set out to check the pictures. It was a daunting task, as there were hundreds of them in no particular order other than the date.

Vickie was the first to find one. It must have been taken just shortly after he had boarded the ship, as he was still going "au naturel" with his bald head. He obviously hadn't had time to get himself any wigs or other props from the very well equipped costume room.

They all studied the picture, so that they would have a better chance of recognizing him, even if he was in disguise. Kitty spotted another one of him with a blond wig and a phony scar on the right cheek. At first they weren't sure that it was he, but the little black eyes told the tale, along with the Rolex on his wrist. They bought copies of the pictures, and showed them to everyone with whom they came in contact. Sooner or later someone had to spot him. They all hoped that it would be sooner.

The entire ship was now buzzing with the fact that there was a manhunt in progress. Rumours abounded. Some thought he was a lunatic escaped from a psychiatric hospital. Others heard that he had opened fire in a Macdonalds in Fort Lauderdale, killing nine people. How that one got started no one knew. Cassie heard that he was looking for his wife on board, because she had run away with his neighbour.

Because of all the stories circulating, there was a certain excitement in the air, an edgy attitude. You could almost smell the adrenaline pumping. People were looking at each other more seriously, and every large man on the ship had become suspect.

The four friends had a lot of fun choosing their costumes for the masquerade. They were amazed at the variety and quantity from which to choose. This was definitely an upscale cruise line. They finally decided to go as Elvis, and three bimbos in his entourage. Steffie made a very good looking Elvis, with a black wig and sideburns. The other three were hilarious, with great beehive hairdos, thick blue eyeshadow, and dresses from the sixties.

Strangely, they all felt more secure once they were in costume. It was as if they really believed that the murderer wouldn't recognize them. Brad and his sister went as Hansel and Gretel, making it more fun by reversing genders and having Brad go as Gretel. He was squeezed so tightly into the costume, that he could barely move, but that made it all the more hilarious.

There were plenty of prizes, and lots of dancing. At one point, a heavyset man dressed as Zorro asked Cassie to dance. She had the horrible feeling that he could be the one who tried to throw her overboard. There was no way she was going to take a chance and dance with him. He might dance her right out onto the deck, and try again. With all the music and laughter, no one would hear her scream. She quickly told him that she was feeling faint, and had to sit this one out with her friends. He muttered something as he walked away, but he didn't bother her again. Actually, they didn't even see him again.

There was another man who appeared to be the right build and height. He was dressed as Henry VIII, and was also wearing a mask. He didn't approach any of the women, but he did always seem to be close by. Was he watching them? Was he just waiting his chance to grab either Vickie or Cassie and do something evil? Of course, maybe he just found them attractive, and was trying to get up his courage to ask one of them to dance.

Vickie had been having headaches ever since the mugging, and she could feel a dandy coming on now. She didn't want to spoil the fun for the rest of her gang, so she mumbled that she was just going to the washroom, which was right off the ballroom. Instead, she headed down to her cabin to get herself a Tylenol. She needed to stop the headache before it got any worse, and she didn't want Cassie to know about it. Cass could be such a mother hen at times, and would likely try to haul her back to the hospital.

One thing which Vickie did not like about the ship, was the fact that all the corridors were so long and so silent. You never seemed to meet any of your fellow passengers. You never even saw the stewards, who were so good at coming in and straightening up the room as soon as they exited it.

Tonight she kept imagining that someone was following her, and she chided herself for being paranoid. She also admitted that maybe coming back alone had not been a good idea. As she quickened her steps towards her suite, key in hand, she just had to turn and take a quick glance over her shoulder. A cold wind of fear blew right over her. Coming down the corridor towards her was Zorro. He was running.

Vickie had no choice. There was nowhere to go, except forward towards her room. Heart pounding, and legs shaking in the stiletto heels, she raced ahead. She could feel her beehive wig starting to come off, but had no time to adjust it. She hoped desperately that someone would open a cabin door just as she passed it, so that she could bolt inside and be safe. No such luck. She was entirely on her own, as if she and Zorro were the last two people on earth, or at least on this luxury liner.

In her fear, she was almost past her cabin before she could stop. Her hands were shaking badly as she tried to open the door. After seconds, which seemed like hours, the door opened and she stumbled in, slamming it in the face of Zorro, who was now right behind her. She stood numbly staring at the doorknob, which was being twisted savagely. As long as he didn't have a key, there was no way he could get in, at least that's what she told herself. Those ship doors were very heavy and airtight, possibly to keep water out if the corridors ever flooded.

Her mind seemed stuck in neutral. She just couldn't think what to do. Then, as she picked up the phone and called for help, she heard voices outside.

"Sir, may I help you," said a voice with a Filipino accent. "Have you lost your key?"

There was no reply, but Vickie heard the sound of a slap, or a fist hitting a head, then a soft grunt, and the sound of something falling. Next she heard footsteps pounding down the corridor, away from her door.

She waited a moment, but heard nothing. Somehow the silence was scarier than noise would have been. When she heard a small groan, she cautiously opened the door a crack, ready to slam it again if Zorro was still there. All she saw was the little steward, who had been looking after their cabin so dutifully all week. He was on the floor, holding his head, and trying to sit up.

Vickie peered up and down the corridor, saw no one, then got him into her cabin. By the time help arrived, so had Cassie, Steffie and Kitty. They had realized that she was taking too long in the washroom, and when they checked, and couldn't find her, they had come looking for her.

It was chaotic in their room, as they all tried to get the events sorted out. The women were all cross with Vickie for having broken their pact to stick together. Vickie was shocked that Zorro had almost caught her, and angry that she hadn't had the chance to "kick his ass."

Once they realized that she was fine, they began to laugh at her appearance. Her beehive wig was perched at a rakish angle, clinging to her head like a furry monkey on its mother's back. Soon they were all laughing in a semi hysterical fashion, as they realized that once again the killer had been foiled in his attempt to hurt one of them.

In spite of having to be on constant alert for the deadly stalker, they all agreed that the masquerade party had been the most fun of the entire cruise. Vickie thought that she hadn't been that scared for a long time, but she would never admit that to anyone.

The best part of the memory was seeing herself flying down that long corridor. She hadn't run that fast since she was a kid. She'd been wearing high heels too! Good for you, kiddo, she told herself. You've still got what it takes.

That night, however, she tossed and turned, pounding her pillow, and straightening the comforter again and again. The darn guy was like a phantom, a will-o-the-wisp. He must know every nook and cranny of the ship, the way he came and went as he pleased. Still, if he was there to kill them, it meant that he was desperate, and desperate men made mistakes.

We'll get him, she promised herself. We'll lock him up and throw away the key. This thought was somehow comforting, and she finally drifted off to sleep.

Chapter Thirteen

Cozumel was their next port of call, and they were there for several hours. It was hot and sticky, but they enjoyed the little shops and the friendly people. Being careful to stay together wherever they went, they found a funky little cantina where they had lunch, accompanied by a few margaritas.

Their enjoyment was marred only slightly by thoughts of the stalker. The entire idea of being stalked didn't seem real, somehow, in this gorgeous, carefree environment. Everytime, however, that they allowed themselves to think of how he had pitched the woman off the balcony at Edgewater, had mugged Vickie, had chased her down that long corridor, and had even tried to throw Cassie overboard, they realized how serious the situation was.

Back on board, they showered and changed for dinner. Cassie expected to hear good news from the captain about the capture of the murderer. She was disgusted to hear that he was still at large. How could one man be so seemingly invisible?

All the talk at the table that night was about the stalker. Martha Carrington, the lady with all the diamonds, was worrying that he might try to steal her jewels. They all noticed that she had toned down her appearance considerably, wearing only two rings, and one necklace. She must have put the rest of her collection in the ship's safe, or at least in the small safe in her cabin.

Later that evening, they enjoyed themselves in the casino. Kitty hit a hundred dollar jackpot. Vickie was up about seventy dollars, and was smart enough to quit while still ahead. The other two lost their money within the first fifteen minutes, but they still enjoyed wandering around just 'people watching'.

After the noise and excitement of the casino, they headed to the Mermaid Bar for a quiet drink before bed. Everyone in the bar seemed to be frowning and whispering. Cassie finally asked the bartender what was going on.

"Well, apparently that guy they've been tracking, managed to get off the ship in Cozumel," he said, putting down the towel with which he had been wiping the bar.

"What?" choked Cassie in disbelief. "How the heck could they possibly know that?"

The bartender looked around, then leaned toward Cassie. "We're not supposed to talk about it, but looks like he knocked out a fellow who was built pretty much like he was, you know, big and brawny. Anyway, he stole the guy's passenger card. He would never have got through customs back in Port Everglades, but it's pretty easy to get off the ship in a scheduled port like Cozumel. As you know, they just check your passenger card, and as long as you look something like the picture, they don't even notice."

Cassie was too stunned to reply. Her heart had sunk like a stone. The guy was loose. He was free to go wherever he wanted. He had given them all the slip. Would he still come after her, or would he just stay in Mexico? How could she ever feel safe again? This was really bad news.

"Where's the man he knocked out?" she finally asked.

"Oh, he's in sick bay. They only found him a little while ago. A couple of his friends went to see why he hadn't come to dinner. When he didn't answer the phone or open his cabin door, they got a steward to go in and check on him. They found him unconscious and bleeding on the floor. The killer must have been on the lookout for someone who was basically his same height and size. Then he waited to get the fellow alone, knocked him out and stole his passenger card. It's pretty darn smart when you think about it. I'll tell you though. The guys who were checking the passengers disembarking in Cozumel are in deep doodoo. I'll bet they'll lose their jobs. What a couple of schmucks."

Cassie's stomach was in a knot, as she walked back to the table to tell her friends. "Can you believe it? Those jackasses let him get away.

He just thumbed his nose and sashayed right off the ship. Who knows where the hell he is now. He's probably safe somewhere in Mexico. He's likely sitting at a little café, wearing a sombrero and a serape, and drinking José Cuervos.

He doesn't even have to worry about extradition, because Mexico won't let him go, if he's being brought back to face a capital charge. They don't believe in capital punishment, and they don't believe in life in prison. Shit, shit, shit. He's sitting somewhere right now laughing at us." Cass was so angry that she was spitting out her words like a hissing cobra.

"Well, Cass," said Steffie, "at least if he stays in Mexico, he won't be coming to Niagara Falls to chase you and Vickie. That's good news, isn't it?"

Cassie hadn't thought about that positive part of the equation. Yes, it definitely was good in one way. The bad thing, however, was that it meant that he was going to get away with throwing that poor girl off the balcony, and with his harassment of them. He had been darn busy since that night at Edgewater. Surely his luck would run out soon, and he would be caught.

Cassie didn't know whether she hoped he would stay in Mexico forever, and leave her alone, or whether she wanted him to come back to the states, so that they could put him in prison. What a choice! She didn't want to be part of this imbroglio. In no way had she bargained for all this trouble when she planned this cruise. If only she could talk to Jack.

So much had happened to Cassandra Meredith in the past three years that she was a much tougher and more resilient person now. Still, she had a very gentle and tender side, and right now she wanted to be home with her husband Dave. Much to her shame, however, even more than wanting to be with Dave, she wanted to be with Jack.

The worst and most difficult decision she had been forced to make recently, was to stop mooning over Detective Jack Willinger, and to put him out of her life. Unfortunately, that was not easy to do. Jack's beautiful wife Darla had died a few months ago. Cass hadn't been in contact with Jack since then, but she had written him a long note, and sent flowers.

She knew that Jack would be so vulnerable right now, and she couldn't take advantage of that. She often dreamed of what life would be like with him, but knew it was not to be. She had made her marriage bed, so to speak, and now she would lie in it.

The unfortunate point was that she loved Dave, or at least she was relatively happy with him, and intended to spend the rest of her life with him. Jack was always there, though, just on the periphery of her mind, tempting and teasing. She could picture him right now, lounging against the door, one foot crossed casually over the other, grinning that special grin. She wanted to be with him, just to be able to tell him about all this mess, and get his help. Jack was a "take charge" sort of guy, and he would know what to do. This captain and his crew seemed to be dolts, and she wasn't likely to get much help from them.

The friends had another round of drinks, as they chatted with the people at the next table. They were incredulous and disgusted at the inept way in which the situation had been handled. There should have been extra staff checking people off the ship. According to a man who seemed to know a lot about the situation, one of the crew checking people off was a Filipino who didn't understand English very well, and who had poor eyesight. It was likely that a man in a gorilla suit could have made it past him with no trouble.

The big question was: were Cass and Vickie safe now, or had the real terror just begun?

The final days of the cruise went smoothly. Knowing that the killer had escaped, and was no longer on board, gave the women a great sense of freedom and safety. They dedicated themselves to having as much fun as possible in the time remaining. They went to bed late and got up early.

They did water aerobics, lazed on deck, sipping margaritas, entered a hula hoop contest in which Cassie won a prize, and pigged out on all the glorious food. Each night they listened to the fabulous guitarist in the Palm Lounge. Cassie bought copies of all the pictures which the persistent and ubiquitous ship photographer had taken of them, and Steffie managed a little time alone with Brad. They packed everything into those final days, and that went a long way toward making up for the bad things which had happened.

Somehow the great Caribbean seemed to know that their vacation was coming to an end, and it was on its best behaviour. It was so calm that they figured they could have waterskied behind the big ship. The sunshine sparkling and reflecting off the water was almost blinding. This truly was paradise.

The last day was bittersweet. They were all anxious to get home, but sad to leave this magical experience. Friendships had been made, and, although most would soon be forgotten, a few would be lasting.

There was a frenzied need to do everything today, for which there hadn't been time yesterday. All the signs of departure were there, the hustle and bustle, and the hastily packed suitcases, bulging with souvenirs and treasures. The stewards were falling all over themselves to be helpful, visions of generous tips in their heads.

Dinner that final night was an extravaganza. After the shrimp cocktails, the filets, and the lobster tails had been consumed, the lights were dimmed. To the accompaniment of a fanfare from the dining room orchestra, in came a parade of servers, carrying gleaming silver trays of flaming baked alaskas, held high above their heads. Each server was also carrying a flickering candle. It was an impressive and strangely moving sight. The delighted passengers gave them a standing ovation.

Soon they would be back to reality. Life would go on, and a different group of happy, eager vacationers would take their places. They considered themselves very fortunate, because they were going back to Edgewater for a few more days, before flying home. By then Kitty knew that she would be glad to be home. She missed Mitch very much, and she was so lonesome for little Miss Rosie and Sir Petie. She could imagine how they would wind themselves round and round her ankles, and want to cuddle with her as soon as she sat down. Yes, it had been a wonderful cruise, but she agreed with Dorothy, there was no place like home.

Steffie was looking forward to getting back to the routine of the boutique. She would likely see Brad again, but wasn't counting on anything too serious developing. Being single was too much fun.

Vickie and Cassie were going to feel much safer when they got back to the big house on the river. They would have Jack and Bud to protect them, just in case.

The burning question at the back of each woman's mind was the whereabouts of the murderous stalker. Was he hiding safely in some other country, or would he risk following them to Niagara Falls? Only time would tell what the fates were planning.

Chapter Fourteen

Their first night back at Edgewater was uneventful. They were tired, but full of great memories of a fun-filled cruise, which, in retrospect, had gone by far too quickly.

Sitting on their balcony, they rehashed some of the funny and exciting times they had shared. The passenger talent show had been a riot. There were serious people who sang or played a musical instrument. Actually, Kitty had played some jazz on the piano, and had won a prize.

There were also people who did bizarre tricks. One young fellow made strange noises with his armpits. Another guy drew a face on his stomach, put a bag over his head, and whistled, making his belly-button go in and out, as if it was doing the whistling. Weird! One woman had done stand-up comedy, and had them all laughing. Of course there were the ubiquitous jugglers, and one young boy had played the harmonica like an old pro. He had been the hit of the evening.

They all had a good laugh, remembering the steward, who had insisted on putting Steffie's nightie on her bed each night, and shaping it like the body of a voluptuous woman. He likely would have been fired if she had reported him, but after three nights, she simply hid her nightgown in her suitcase and locked it. Kitty declared that she was very offended that he hadn't done the same for her.

Steffie had found the time to do several sketches, and planned to sell them in their boutique when they got home.

No one had stolen any of Mrs. Carrington's jewels, although it must have been very tempting. She had been a charming and interesting person, once you got past all the jewellery.

All their games of Trivial Pursuit and Catch-Phrase had been challenging and fun. They had won several games, and had earned the reputation of being smart as well as attractive.

It had been fun to meet Brad and Jillian – particularly for Steffie. She admitted that she really liked Brad, and hoped to see him again, but wasn't looking for anything too serious. After being in a disappointing marriage, her freedom was very precious to her.

The Masquerade Ball had been one of the highlights of the trip, even though it had almost ended disastrously when Zorro chased Vickie to her cabin. They looked at all the pictures which Cassie had bought for them, and collapsed in hysterics at how hilarious they had looked in their costumes as Elvis and his three bimbo groupies.

No one wanted to mention how close Cassie had come to being pitched overboard, or how close Vickie had come to being left dead on that lonely street in Key West. Those events did not seem to match up with all the fun and hoopla.

After rehashing their cruise day by day, it was inevitable that they would get around to the night before they had left EBR. That was the night when the unfortunate woman had been thrown off the balcony from this very tower. They couldn't help looking at the spot in front of the Bimini Bar where her broken body had landed. Again they speculated as to what she might have done to deserve such a fate.

"Come on guys, we've got to get to bed. Tomorrow Vickie and I have to go back to the police station, to tell them everything that's been going on. I wonder if they have any clue that the murderer followed us onto the ship."

"Hope they don't try to blame you two for not giving them his description the night it happened," said Kitty.

"Well, they weren't happy with us," replied Vickie, sipping her wine. "We made up for it, though, by going to the station the next day, telling what we knew, and voluntarily missing the ship's departure. We should get some brownie points for that."

"We'll be fine," said Cassie, "but I'm too tired to think about it tonight. Let's get up and have breakfast over at Ocean's, then Vickie and I will go to the station, while you two do whatever you please. We'll all go for lunch someplace nice, maybe Uncle Ernie's or Bayou

Joe's, and then we can decide whether we're going to go parasailing or seadooing. It's supposed to be hot and calm tomorrow."

"I vote for seadooing," said Steffie.

"Me too," said Kitty loyally, "since Steff and I went parasailing the last time we were down here." They both remembered that it had been just before they got word of the murder of their friend and associate, Cleo Chandler.

"Hey, Cassie and I have done the parasailing too, and it's really wonderful. We want to do it again, and we should do the seadooing too. We'll see if we can get someone to take some videos," enthused Vickie.

The return trip to the police station was unsettling. The police had not been aware of all the incidents involving the killer. The cruise ship management obviously had been in no hurry to give out this information. The detectives looked angry and deflated, on hearing that he had disappeared from the ship in Cozumel, and was now likely hidden deep in Mexico, never to be seen again.

They had not been idle, however. What they did know was that Harold Johnston was the husband of Gloria Johnston, the deceased. He happened to fit the description given by Vickie and Cassie, and he was the sole heir to his wife's considerable fortune. If he stayed hidden in Mexico, he would never be able to access that fortune. Of course, if he came back to the states, he would have to face a trial, and if found guilty, he would never be able to get his hands on the money.

The really interesting part was that Harold Johnston was just one of the aliases used by a man named John Duncan. Three years ago his wealthy wife had mysteriously drowned in her bathtub. Five years ago Bill Gordon, (who fit the exact description of Harold Johnston and John Duncan), had a wife who mysteriously fell off a cliff on a camping trip. She had also been very wealthy. In each case, they had been married less than a year.

It appeared that Bill Gordon, aka John Duncan, aka Harold Johnston, was making a career of rich wives and mysterious accidents. The Gordon woman had died in Nevada. John Duncan's wife drowned in her home in Texas. Harold Johnston's unfortunate wife took a header off a balcony in Florida.

Vickie and Cassie could only imagine how much police work had gone into putting all this information together. They were appalled at what a really bad guy this fellow was. Apparently in the first two cases, there had been no witnesses. It was his misfortune that Vickie and Cassie had decided to relax in the hot tub at Edgewater the night he helped his third wife to fly.

"Detective Davidson," asked Vickie, "do you think he'll try to come back to the states, and if so, do you think that he would still feel he has to track us down and kill us?"

The two detectives were not about to hypothesize with members of the public. Their answers were all a bit vague.

"I do think that you need to be very careful," Detective Davidson finally said. "He may feel that if you hadn't seen him, and if you hadn't given us his description, he could have pretended that it was an unfortunate accident. The fact that you actually saw him throw her over, and the fact that you actually came face to face with him in the elevator, must have been devastating for him. It ruined all his perfect plans. We would have had no possible way of proving that he threw her over. My guess is that he has a hat full of hate for you two. He may want to kill you just to exact vengeance. I'd be damn careful until he's safely in custody."

"But that could be years," cried Cassie. "We can't spend the rest of our lives looking over our shoulders. Killing us at this point won't do him a bit of good. You've already got his description, you can likely place him at the scene, and you know a lot about his background. Seems to me you could build a pretty good case against him without us."

"Oh no. That's not the way it works. Once we get him, if he comes back that is, you'll both have to be witnesses at his trial. So far you are the only two who actually saw him. No one else has come forward. It's sad but true. You're both on the hook. He's a smart guy, so he'll know the score. As I said, you'll have to keep on the alert till he's in custody."

Cassie and Vickie just stared at each other. This was not the news they wanted to hear.

"Well, we're heading home to Canada in three more days. Will you let us know if and when you arrest him?" asked Vickie.

Cassie knew that tone. Vickie was gearing up for a bit of a fight.

"Don't worry, we'll be in touch," said ugly puss, the other detective, who had been very quiet throughout the interview. Vickie and Cassie weren't sure what his name was, because he hadn't bothered to introduce himself, but they knew they didn't like him. The way he said "we'll be in touch" sounded like a threat.

He was short and stocky, and had a head which seemed too big for his body. His brown hair, what was left of it, was greasy. The remaining faithful few strands were carefully combed over the bald spots. His suit was rumpled, as if he had slept in it. He had a bulbous nose, which made him look like a heavy drinker, and his personal hygiene didn't seem up to par. He looked at the two women as if they were a pair of twits just trying to cause trouble. Cassie had an uneasy feeling about him. She didn't like him, and she could feel that he didn't like her.

"I don't understand your attitude, detective. You act as if we've done something wrong. Where would you be if we hadn't bothered to come forward with our information?" Vickie was definitely getting belligerent.

"Well, now, little lady, I'm sorry that you feel that way. You can take my attitude any way you like. If you had come right to us the night it happened, instead of stalling around, we might have caught him before he got away. Just think about that while you're feeling hurt about my attitude," he snarled.

What now, they wondered, as they left the station. The meeting had not done anything to assuage their fears. In fact, they had gone from thinking that they were home free, to realizing that they might be looking over their shoulders for years. It was not a happy thought.

"Well, at least Detective Davidson seems reasonable, doesn't he?" remarked Vickie, as they got into their car.

"Yes, he seems okay. He's got lovely curly hair, and when he smiles his whole face lights up. It makes him look mischievous. Did you notice all the laugh lines he has around his eyes? Obviously working with creeps and punks and perverts every day hasn't jaded him."

"Not yet anyway," added Vickie. "Did you get the other detective's name?"

"No, I'm not sure that he even mentioned it."

"Well, he's one ugly dude. As a matter of fact, he's about a mile past ugly. He's sure no Mel Gibson."

Cassie laughed in agreement. "There's something about him I really didn't like. I just hope he's wrong about this Harold Johnston, aka John Duncan, aka Bill Gordon. They must have been able to trace fingerprints I guess, and tie them all to the same guy. He's been a very busy and very bad boy. It sickens me to think of him following us all the way back to Niagara Falls. Oh, I just had a weird thought."

"What?"

"Well, he likes to marry wealthy women and then kill them. What if he finds out about my money? He might decide to try to woo me, and then kill me." She was kidding, of course, but it did seem like a possible, if unlikely scenario.

"I don't think that will happen," laughed Vickie, "but if it does, don't ask me to be your bridesmaid. Of course, there's the little matter of the husband you already have. Anyway, to get back to your other thought, I don't think he'll follow us back to Niagara Falls." She said this with more conviction than she really felt. "We just have to tell ourselves that this is all over, and get on with our lives. We have some fun things to do here in Panama City Beach before we head home, and we aren't going to waste time on some killer/stalker who is likely so deep in Mexico that he'll never find his way out."

From your lips to God's ears, thought Cassie, as they headed back to the condo.

Chapter Fifteen

The following day was beautiful. The temperature was in the low 80's, and the skies were that cloudless, cerulean blue which is so common in Florida.

It seemed that everyone was out, taking advantage of the great weather. Although it was early, the skies were already busy. They saw two small airplanes flying advertising banners. One was for an insurance company, and one was for a local bar, which promised five cent wings and ten cent beer.

There were two helicopters, likely from Tyndall Air Force Base. They seemed to be doing maneuvers of some kind. Three multi-coloured parasails glided along ever so smoothly, looking like party balloons so high in the sky.

The turquoise-blue water sparkled invitingly. A yellow banana boat filled with happy vacationers, made its way carefully through several seadoos and power boats. There were even four or five sailboats skimming the surface.

The beach itself was dotted with dark blue sun umbrellas and wooden loungers. There was a holiday feeling in the air, and the four friends suspected that it continued this way right from March until late September. People came from all over the world to enjoy these beautiful sugar sands, and they weren't disappointed. There was something for everyone here in Panama City Beach, and most of it was going on right at Edgewater.

"Girls, turn around and gaze upon this sight for sore eyes!" exclaimed Steffie, with a big grin on her face.

Turning to have a look, they all began to laugh. A tall young man, likely in his twenties, was strolling along the beach. On his head was a leopard-skin sunhat. On his butt was nothing but a thong, also leopard-skin. It was the skimpiest suit they had ever seen on a man. As he passed them, they got a good look at his buns, which were totally exposed.

They all hooted, and he tipped his hat as he strutted past.

"Now I've seen everything," laughed Kitty. "Steff, maybe we should start selling them in the boutique."

"Oh sure. Can't you just see our old Rumplestiltskin friend in one of those?"

They all laughed at the picture this idea painted.

After breakfast at Oceans, the on site restaurant and bar, all four walked down the beach to sign up for the seadooing and parasailing. There was a big line-up for the parasailing, so they decided that they would rent two double seadoos, and go out together. That sounded like fun.

Fortunately the waves were small and friendly. The foursome set out, laughing and shouting to each other, as they careened wildly across the turquoise water. Steffie and Vickie were driving, and Kitty and Cassie were quite content to hold on behind. It was an exhilarating experience, as they bounced across the waves, going further and further from shore.

They stayed relatively close together, so that they could shout to each other. Vickie turned out to be by far the most daring driver, flying full tilt across the water, and fearlessly turning full circles tight enough to make Cassie squeal. For the full half hour, any thoughts of the balcony killer were expunged from their minds.

Their allotted time was up far too soon, and, sitting on the deck at Oceans, catching their breath, they thought they might do it all again the next day.

That night they went to the Salt Water Café for dinner. The food was excellent, and the piano player was very entertaining. After dinner, they sat at the bar, which surrounded the piano. They requested their favourite songs, and sang along lustily with the pianist.

Kitty, having had more wine than usual, got a bit nostalgic when the pianist played "I'll Be Seeing You." She began thinking of Mitch, and wondering what he was doing. She fervently hoped that he was not seeing Sheridan, his former girlfriend. Although he had broken off his long-time relationship with her after meeting Kitty, she knew that Sheridan still called him often, trying to rekindle the connection. She trusted Mitch, but also knew that he was a deeply thoughtful and sensitive man, who felt sympathy for his old love. It was something which would hopefully work itself out in time. Meanwhile, Kitty stared disconsolately into her wine, as her pals sang exuberantly.

It was only after they returned to their condo, and were having Spanish coffees out on the balcony, that Cassie and Vickie came up with what seemed to be a great idea. They wanted to drive down along the coast to see the quaint little fishing village of Apalachicola. Steffie was torn between going with them, or driving out to Eden state park, where she hoped to do some sketching. Kitty also wanted to see the old Eden Mansion, so it was finally decided that they would split up, two going east and two going west. They would have to rent a second car, but that was no problem.

Cassie found a good map, which would take them directly to Apalachicola along the coast road. They would leave very early, as it was probably close to a two hour drive. They could have lunch in the fishing village, do some sightseeing, and explore the little boutiques. That would leave them time to get back for a bite of dinner with Steffie and Kitty, and another visit to the hot tub. Hopefully this time there would be no balcony incidents.

The next morning was the kind of day for which Florida is famous. It was in the mid 70's, promising to go higher by afternoon. There was not a cloud to be seen in the azure sky. Just a hint of a breeze made the palms sway ever so slightly. On a day like this, all seemed right with the world.

The foursome enjoyed a good breakfast, before going their separate ways.

"Be sure to take lots of pictures of Eden," suggested Cassie, as she and Vickie got into their rental car.

"We will," promised Kitty, "and you two try to stay out of trouble, and get back here safely."

They all laughed as they waved goodbye.

"This was a great idea," said Vickie contentedly, as they crossed the Hathaway Bridge. "The sunshine is reflecting so brilliantly off that water that I can barely see the boats out there," she laughed. "I'm sorry that we aren't going to have time to go parasailing this trip, but I'd rather be doing this. Apalachicola, here we come."

Both women looked their best, as they drove along, chatting amiably. Vickie was wearing navy linen bell bottoms, with a lemon yellow top, and navy jacket. Cassie had chosen to wear a long dusty rose linen skirt, with a matching rose and white summer sweater. They were both wearing sandals. Cassie's were two inches higher than Vickie's, not too comfy for walking, but very stylish. By the end of the day, they would come to regret their choice of clothes and shoes. At this point, however, the day ahead looked to be full of nothing but fun and adventure. Unfortunately, it would be the wrong kind of adventure.

"Part of me wishes we could stay down here longer, but part of me is ready to get home. It's so exciting to be settling into our new house on the river. I'm really glad that you're going to stay a couple of weeks with me before you head back to Vancouver."

"Yes, I can hardly wait to see this new mansion of yours," laughed Vickie. "You've come a long way, baby."

"You've got that right," agreed Cassie. "You and I have been through a heck of a lot the past three years, and our lives have really changed for the better." She sighed then, and shook her head. "I just pray that John Duncan, or Harold Johnston, or whatever he's calling himself at the moment, has forgotten all about us by now."

"Well that's not likely. I just hope he's happily hiding in Mexico with no thoughts of ever coming back. I don't think the police are going to find him."

"Man, I hope you're right about him hiding in Mexico, yet I hate the thought of him getting away with what he's done. I just don't want him back stalking us."

They were silent then, as they drove along. Each woman was thinking her own thoughts, and wondering what would happen with the person they had come to think of as "Monster Man." It didn't seem real that he might actually be planning to kill them. It was so much easier to tell themselves that he was safely hidden in Mexico, and had forgotten all about them.

Coincidentally, the first stop along their route, was a little spot called Mexico Beach. Next came Port St. Joe, and, finally, Apalachicola. Both Mexico Beach and Port St. Joe seemed more modern and appealing than the fishing village of Apalachicola. There were a lot of new condos and town houses being built, and they noticed a few interesting little restaurants right on the water. If only there had been more time, they would have stopped to explore.

"You know, I never realized how many different types of palm trees there are," said Vickie, as she scrutinized the passing scenery.

"Oh sure, there are all kinds of palms," said Cassie absently. She was thinking of something else entirely. She was thinking of Jack, and how they used to love going on long drives, and looking for quaint little places where they could stop and have a treat, and maybe buy a souvenir.

"How many do you think we could name?" persisted Vickie.

Cassie sighed. "I really don't care, but let's try. There are coconut palms, royal palms, and date palms. That's a start. Now you add to it."

Vickie looked crestfallen. "You named all the ones I know, smarty. The only other one I can think of is the pineapple palm. Oh, yes, and isn't there one called the sable palm or something like that?"

"Could be. I don't really care," Cassie laughed. "What is this, a science lesson?"

"No, but it's interesting. Tell me if you think of any more."

They were silent for a while, then Vickie spoke up. "Oh, I know some more. First of all, it's a sago palm, not a sable. Then there are several kinds of fan palms. I think there's a Mexican fan palm and a Chinese fan palm. What about you, have you got any more?"

"Yes, as a matter of fact I do. I think there's a giant fishtail palm and a bird of paradise palm."

"Oh, those are good, but I've never heard of them. You likely just made them up, cheater. Did we say the king palm and the queen palm? I wonder what all those trees look like. I still think that the little pineapple palm is the cutest."

"I agree," said Cass. "Now, can we think of something else, oh wondrous teacher?"

Vickie gave her a raspberry, but was happy to relax and watch the scenery.

The traffic on the coast highway was heavier than they had expected, so neither one had any reason to notice the big black pick-up truck, which had been following them relentlessly, from the time they left Edgewater.

Chapter Sixteen

It turned out to be a perfect day. There were some great antique shops, fancy boutiques, and funky little eating places, so they shopped, they walked, and they ate. They spent an inordinate amount of time in Grady Market, which had very trendy clothes, as well as some unusual gift items. Vickie bought a scarf in navy, yellow and white. It was perfect with her outfit, and she decided to wear it. As it turned out, that was a good idea.

After spending time in every little shop they could find, they decided to have lunch at Caroline's. It was an interesting eating place right on the water. They enjoyed the lavender linen tablecloths, which matched the gray and lavender wallpaper. Their window table afforded them a great view of the bay. Right outside the window were many pier posts on which perched seagulls and pelicans. It was a totally different Florida from the elegant Edgewater Beach Resort in Panama City Beach, but they decided that both places were charming in their own special ways.

They were enjoying themselves so much, that they lingered over lunch longer than intended.

After lunch, they wandered back to one boutique which they had missed, and they each bought a pair of earrings.

Next they headed to the famous old Gibson Inn, just to have a look around. It was a perfect example of Victorian architecture, and a very popular place for tourists. They sat on the old fashioned veranda, and rocked in the high backed rockers.

They couldn't leave without a quick tour of the interior. They were both hoping that they might spot the ghost, old Captain Wood, who died in room 309 about fifty or sixty years ago. The local lore says that old Capt. Wood likes to play tricks on anyone in that room. Pictures sometimes fall off the walls for no apparent reason, and small items tend to be moved around when no one is looking. Some staff members insist they have seen him, but Vickie and Cassie had no such luck. Apparently the captain was not performing today.

They were totally charmed by the old hotel, however, and wished they had more time to explore it.

It was just as they were leaving, and heading back to their car, when Cassie stopped, and put her hand on Vickie's arm.

"You're going to think I'm nuts, paranoid, but,"

"I already do," grinned Vickie affectionately. "What now? I suppose you've just seen old Captain Wood, or maybe even the killer stalking us," she joked.

"Yes, I think I have," replied Cassie, in a serious tone. "I think I saw the killer across the street, looking right at us. I'm sure it was the same guy. He was big and brawny, and I think he has one of those stupid soul patches on his chin now. He was wearing a hat, so I couldn't see his hair, but my scalp has started tingling."

Vickie knew better than to argue with Cassie when her scalp started to tingle. It almost always presaged something bad. She looked around carefully, but could see no one who looked anything like the killer.

"Look, Cass. I've learned that we should always pay attention when your scalp tingles. It's like an early warning sign. On the other hand, it just doesn't make any sense that it would be the killer. How in the world would he have found us in Apalachicola? You're making this guy seem like Superman. He's everywhere we go. I'm sure he's in hiding somewhere, so let's not allow your omens and presentiments to spoil our nice day."

Cassie didn't take offence at this. She knew her friend too well.

"Vic, I swear he was watching us. I felt his eyes on us before I even saw him. I know you think I'm being paranoid, but let's get out of here. Let's get back to Panama City Beach as fast as we can. I don't feel safe here now."

As she was saying this, she was speeding up, so that Vickie had to hurry to keep up with her. Vickie just shook her head, and didn't offer any more protests. She'd known Cassie for a very long time, almost all of their lives, and if Cass was suddenly feeling scared, then there was likely something wrong. She was now as anxious to get out of there as Cassie was.

Unfortunately, when they reached their rental car, they saw to their dismay, that the rear tire was flat. They had either picked up a nail, or someone had deliberately let the air out.

"How could that be?" asked Vickie in disbelief. "That thing's as flat as a frisbee. We haven't been anywhere off the beaten path. How could we pick up a nail on the highway?"

"That is weird, isn't it?" mused Cassie. "You know darn well that it likely wasn't a nail. I'll bet we'll find that the tire is either slashed, or the valve stem is gone."

"Since when did you know so much about tires?" asked Vickie, crossly. She was now convinced that Cassie was right, and that the killer had done something to their tire to keep them in this little village, far from the safety of their condo.

"Come on, let's find a garage and get the heck out of here. I won't feel safe till we're back in PCB."

After a bit of looking and asking, they were able to find a garage which was just closing up, and persuade the man to fix the tire for them. Of course, because this was a charming little Southern village, they should have expected that the mechanic would be slow. They didn't expect, however, that he would be slower than a donkey with two broken legs. In disgust, they called Steffie and Kitty, to let them know they would be late. They didn't say anything about their suspicions. There would be time enough for that once they were safely home.

The mechanic, whose middle name must have been "Molasses," could find nothing wrong with the tire, except that it had no air. There was no nail, there were no slashes, and the valve stem was still tightly in place.

"Can't figure this one out," he said, scratching his thinning hair with a greasy finger. "There ain't a darn thing wrong with this tire. It's just as if someone had let all the air out of it, then tightened it up again. No one around here would do a thing like that, except maybe some smart ass kid." The greasy finger returned to his balding pate, and continued its scratching.

The women were pretty sure they knew what had happened, but they didn't say a word. All the time he was working on the car, they kept looking around for any signs of the man who was stalking them. They didn't see him, yet they felt his presence. Were their imaginations getting the best of them? They didn't think so.

Before paying him, Cassie asked him to look under the hood, and see whether everything looked okay. He seemed puzzled at the request, but was obliging. He assured them that everything was "hunky-dory."

To their dismay, it was just getting dark, by the time they finally set out for Panama City Beach.

Frustrated and tired, they were in no mood for dawdling, and were driving along at a good clip. Since Cassie had driven over, it was Vickie's turn to drive back. They were somewhere between Apalachicola and St. Joe, when Vickie noticed bright headlights coming up quickly from behind.

"We've got some kind of a jackass on our tails," she said, mildly, trying not to alarm Cassie, and keeping an eye on the rearview mirror.

"What the heck is he doing?" she said suddenly. The words were barely out of her mouth, when their car was rear-ended. She grabbed the wheel tightly, while the car tried to spin out of control.

"That was deliberate," she squawked in disbelief, just as they were hit again, harder this time.

"Oh Gawd. He's trying to run us off the road. You were right. It must be the killer."

Cassie was turning around, trying to see the vehicle behind them. With its blazing lights, it was impossible to see it clearly, but she got the impression of a big vehicle – likely a pick-up truck or a van. She realized that they were in the area where there was a fall-off on the left side, and dense woods on the right. At the moment, there were no other cars in sight in either direction.

"Hug this side of the road, Vic. We don't want to get near the edge, or that goon will push us right over." Cass couldn't believe she was even saying such a thing. This only happened in the movies.

"Hold on, he's coming again," cried Vickie, as they were hit on the right rear corner. This caused the car to head diagonally across the road. He came up behind them one more time, and gave them one final push. There was nothing Vickie could do. She was pumping the brakes, and was steering away from the edge, but the vehicle pushing them was much heavier and more powerful. The next thing they knew, they were going nose first down the incline. It wasn't steep, but it was just enough for the car to land with a thump on its side. It teetered there, as if it wanted to roll right over, but it finally settled, with two dazed women trapped inside.

Chapter Seventeen

Everything seemed to happen in slow motion. It was like some crazy carnival ride gone awry. Because it was likely no more than six feet down, the car bumped and swayed, but did not roll right over. That was a piece of luck. It did, however, leave Cassie hanging from her seat belt right over Vickie, who was flat against the driver's door. There was no way out on that side.

The world was silent, except for a hissing sound. Both women were alive, but stunned.

"Are you okay?" Cassie asked this as she was fumbling with her seat belt. Hanging sideways in the dark was a strange feeling. She was totally disoriented, but she knew they had to get out of the car. It could explode at any moment.

"Yah, I'm okay, I think. "Is it pitch dark in here, or have I gone blind?" asked Vickie.

"It's dark," was Cassie's terse reply. Her belt finally unlocked, and she fell unceremoniously against Vickie. Their heads bumped, and they both let out a yowl. Vickie felt something trickling down her forehead, and took a swipe at it. It was too dark to tell in the car, but she was pretty sure it was blood. She must have hit her head on something before Cassie fell on her.

Cassie found that it was difficult trying to lift herself off Vickie, in order to get at Vickie's seat belt buckle. Their hands were both fumbling with it, when it finally gave way. The next challenge was to get the door open. It was now directly above them, and it seemed impossible to get it unlocked and push it up. Cass had no place to put her feet, except on Vickie, who was still squashed against the driver's side door.

It seemed to take forever, and they were both surprised at how calm they felt. A sudden shock, or just plain fear, can sometimes anesthetize a person, and put them in a temporarily calm or almost catatonic state. This seemed to have happened. They were both much more calm than they should have been, even though they wondered whether they were going to die on this lonely road.

There was no telling where the killer was. He could be standing right outside the car, waiting for them to come out, waiting to see whether they were alive or dead.

"What if he's out there with a gun?" whispered Vickie.

"I know. I'm thinking the same thing. I'm afraid the car might explode though, and we'll be trapped in it. We've got to take our chances," reasoned Cassie.

"Wait. When you can get your head out the door, try to see the ground. You don't want to fall into water, or land on a sharp stick."

"Thanks for those encouraging words," grunted Cassie, as she hoisted herself up and partially out the door.

It was a dark night, and difficult to see much of anything. The headlights were still shining, but they weren't pointing anywhere useful. She couldn't detect the form of a man, and she couldn't hear anything, so she told herself that the killer wasn't close to them.

"Here goes," she muttered, as she scrambled out and fell to the ground.

"Yuck. Be prepared, Vic, because it's squishy and wet."

Vickie finally managed to make it out the door, and fell down beside Cassie. They realized they were in some kind of a ditch, which contained about three inches of water. Neither wanted to think that there might be snakes in it too. After all, this was water moccasin territory.

"I think he'll come back to make sure we're dead, or to finish us off. We've got to get into those woods across the highway, and hide. Somehow we've got to climb this embankment, and get across before he sees us. Come on." Vickie was half pushing, half pulling Cassie, as she said this. In their haste, neither woman thought to take her purse, or the flashlight, or the two bottles of water, which they usually carried in the car.

When they reached the top of the incline, they peered carefully up and down the dark and seemingly deserted highway. If only a car would come along and rescue them, they wouldn't have to run into those dark, foreboding woods to hide. They were both thinking that there might be swampland in there. For all they knew, it could be another Everglades. The unwelcome thought made them shudder, but there was no choice.

It was only as they ran across the highway and into the trees, that Cassie realized she had lost one sandal. Well, that was an inconvenient, but small price to pay for having survived the accident, which, of course, was no accident at all.

Just as they reached the edge of the highway, Cassie cried, "Oh shit. I think he's just up there to our left, watching for us."

As she said this, a large, dark pick-up truck started up, and headed toward them.

The friends darted into the woods, but knew that he had seen them. He had been waiting and watching, just in case they survived the fall. Vickie pictured a hyena lying in wait for its innocent prey.

They moved as quickly as they could in the dark, but the trees were thick, and there was a lot of undergrowth. With one sandal off, and the other sandal sporting a two inch heel, Cassie was at a serious disadvantage. She was afraid of impaling her bare foot on a sharp stick, but they had to keep moving. She tried to hang on to the back of Vickie's jacket, so that they couldn't get separated in the blackness.

They heard the truck door slam shut, and knew that he was close behind. This guy just didn't give up. He wasn't going to quit until they were both dead.

"Yuck" Vickie muttered, as she stopped in her tracks, frantically wiping her face.

"What's the matter?" hissed Cass, slamming into her back.

"I've either run right into a giant spider web, or it's that Spanish moss which is hanging from the trees. It's all over my face and hair."

"Come on, we can't stop yet. Just be quiet," Cassie urged her friend. There was no time for sympathy.

Vickie could feel blood trickling into her right eye, and she kept trying to wipe it away.

Their only advantage was that they were slight, and he was a big, heavy guy. They hoped that this would slow him down a bit. On the other hand, he sounded like a bull plunging through the trees and bushes. Nothing was stopping him. He was on a mission, and they were the target. Cassie pictured a huge army tank rolling along towards them.

"Stop slapping at those mosquitoes. You're making too much noise," hissed Vickie, sotto voce.

"They're eating me alive," groaned Cassie, in an equally low voice. "If this guy doesn't kill us, the mosquitoes will," she declared crossly, as she gamely limped and hopped along behind Vickie.

Vickie was still concerned that they might both plunge into a swamp populated with alligators and water moccasins. She didn't have the breath to mention this to Cassie, but Cass was thinking the same thing. They were trying to feel the ground in front of them with an experimental foot, be as quiet as possible, and move as quickly as they could. It was an impossible task. They weren't sure which way they were going, which was another impediment to progress. Was it smart to go as deeply into the woods as possible, or should they be trying to circle back and find the highway?

There was no time to stop and confer. They just had to keep struggling along. Finally, they were both so out of breath, that they had to stop and take a few painful gulps of air.

"We can't just keep running," whispered Vickie. "We have to find a place to hide."

"What do you suggest, climbing a tree?" asked Cassie sarcastically. She was quickly losing heart, and had already hurt her foot on a rock. She had bitten her lip to keep herself from crying out. It hurt like the devil, and she suspected that it was bleeding.

They could still hear him blundering through the bushes, but now the sound seemed to be coming from their right. Instinctively they turned to their left, and started moving quickly again.

At just about this time, the fates decided to give the women a little help. Vickie stumbled over a bush, and fell to her knees. It was then that she barely discerned the outline of a large boulder. If she hadn't been on her knees, she would never have seen it in the dark. The boulder had an opening to the side of it. The opening faced another two rocks, almost buried in the bushes. "Cass, let's hide here," she whispered in desperation.

Feeling their way, they realized that they had stumbled upon a small cave. Well, cave was a pretty pretentious name for this little indentation, but, any port in a storm, so to speak. Behind it, the land rose to a different level. Beside it, were a few more large boulders, and in front of it, were several small prickly bushes, which pretty well covered the entrance completely.

They blindly crawled their way into this small haven. The bushes stabbed them, and tore at their skin, but they barely noticed. It was too small for them to stand up, but it was wide enough for them to crouch side by side. It was deep enough that their stalker would have to get down on his knees and peer in to see them.

For the moment, they felt safe. At least this would give them time to catch their breath and plan their next move. Neither one wanted to think about the fact that caves and rocks were the favourite sleeping places for snakes.

Chapter Eighteen

By mutual silent agreement, they didn't make a sound for at least twenty minutes. By then they could no longer hear their stalker making any noise. He had either gone the other way, and was far away from them now, or he was being cunning, and was standing quietly, just listening.

The silence gave them a chance to assess their situation. Both were badly scratched from the brambles and sharp branches and stones along the way. Vickie's head didn't feel as if it was bleeding as much, but Cassie's foot was stinging and throbbing. She was sure it was bleeding, but was afraid to find out.

They both jumped when they heard the rustling of leaves very close to them. It was a raccoon, who had no interest in them. They could barely see him in the dark, although the moon was now beginning to peek out from behind the clouds. They hoped that the night would remain cloudy. The darker it was, the less chance Monster Man had of spotting them, unless, of course, he had a flashlight.

"Oh man, I wish Jack was here with us right now," moaned Cassie.

"Oh, for heaven's sake, forget Jack," hissed Vickie in a low whisper. Your husband's name is Dave, not Jack, and Dave is a great guy who happens to love you. Just get over this romantic fantasy you have about Jack. You've both gone your separate ways, and that's the way it should be."

Vickie was not a fan of Detective Jack Willinger of the Niagara Regional Police Force. They had, however, reached an amicable truce over the past three years, after Vickie and Cassie had saved Jack's life.

At the moment, Vickie was scared, and wasn't in the mood to indulge her old friend in her romantic flights of fancy.

"Well, Jack's the kind of guy who just naturally takes charge in a situation," explained Cassie, trying to defend her remark. "He'd get us out of this mess." She and Vickie often had this same argument. Vickie thought that Dave was a terrific man, and claimed that Cassie wasn't sufficiently appreciative of him.

As they sat huddled in the tiny cave, Cassie whispered, "Shh, did you hear something?"

Vickie couldn't hear anything.

"You know, I read that the Florida black panther is gradually making its way up north from the Everglades," whispered Cassie.

"Oh great! Now we have a panther chasing us, as well as a killer. What next, a giant scorpion or a tarantula?"

"Shh. There it is again." Cassie clutched Vickie's arm, and this time Vickie heard it too.

They crouched in silence, as the sound became louder. They couldn't tell whether it was human or not. Their hearts were pounding like jungle drums, as they tried to squeeze further back into the little rock indentation. If it was the killer, and if he had a flashlight, they were done for. If, on the other hand, it was a panther, or a black bear, they were equally in trouble.

Cassie remembered that Kitty had once sneezed in her boutique, while she and Steffie were being robbed. That sneeze had scared the robber, causing him to spin around and shoot Steffie. She silently prayed that neither she nor Vickie would have the urge to sneeze or cough.

It seemed forever that they crouched there, listening to the approaching sounds. Finally, by the watery moonlight, they could see a large shape coming towards them. They froze in place, afraid to even breathe. He was moving slowly, looking right and left, and he walked right past the prickly little bushes guarding their hideout. He stopped about six feet away, and stood with his back to them, looking around as if wondering which way to go. Because it was such a dark night, with only a hint of moonlight, they could barely see him, but they knew he was there.

"Please don't let him look back over his shoulder," both women were thinking, "and please don't let him have a flashlight."

Their prayers were answered. He stood there for a long time, just listening. Finally making a decision, he turned to his left, and immediately disappeared amongst the trees.

They stayed crouched in their hiding place for what seemed like another hour, just in case their stalker returned. They were afraid to even whisper, in case he was hiding behind a tree within hearing distance. Finally they couldn't stand it any longer. Dangerous or not, they had to move. Slowly they crawled out, and stretched their legs. They were so stiff that just standing up was an accomplishment.

"He went left, so we should go right," whispered Vickie.

"Maybe we should just stay here until morning," suggested Cassie.

They were both speaking so quietly, that they had to lean towards each other in order to hear what they were saying.

"I just don't know. We've got to get back to the road though. Steffie and Kitty might come looking for us, and they'll find the car. They'll have the police out looking too." She said this with more conviction than she felt. She really had no idea as to what Steffie and Kitty would be doing.

Victoria Craig, the one who was always pretty positive about things, the one who usually saw the bright side, was feeling strangely helpless. She knew that the killer wouldn't give up now. If he had followed them all the way back from Cozumel, and had followed them all the way from Edgewater to Apalachicola, he meant business. He would stalk through these woods until he found them.

They had to make a run for it. There was no choice, but travelling through the woods in the dark was not a quiet undertaking. Would they be better to wait till dawn, when they could at least see their way, and not make as much noise crashing around? Yes, likely. "Okay, we'll wait till it starts getting light," she agreed.

"He's going to be making his way back to the road too. He knows we have to come out eventually. Maybe he'll just hang around the car till we appear. That means that when we do reach the road, we have to be sure that we don't come out too near the car."

"You're right. Somehow we have to make it to the next town, but if he's lurking around the car, we're screwed."

"Look, he can't know whether we'll go back to Apalachicola or head for St. Joe. Between the two of us, we must be smarter than he is. We've got to out-think him." Cassie loved a challenge, but this one was a doozy.

"What if, instead of trying to find our way back out to the road, we were to go the other way, further into the woods. Do you know whether there are any little towns back further inland? He wouldn't expect us to go that way."

"Are you kidding? For all we know, it's just miles and miles of bush or swampland. It's bad enough dealing with the Spanish moss, and maybe bears and whatever, but can you imagine falling into swamp water in the dark? We could fall right on top of an alligator or a water moccasin. No thank you. I think we have to stick to these woods near the highway."

"I do remember seeing on the map that there's a 'Dead Lake' somewhere back in there, but I don't know how far," said Vickie thoughtfully. "Dead Lake doesn't sound promising, does it? It's probably a swamp. I just wish I'd paid more attention to the map. You're right. I can't remember seeing any other little towns in this area, but I wasn't really looking for them. There's likely no civilization for miles and miles, except along the highway.

I do remember from the map, that there's a national forest park or something, but I have no idea how far away it is. There could be people camping in it, and they could help us, but I guess we can't take that chance. It's likely miles away. I vote for getting out of the bush as soon as we can. I'm thinking that your feet can't take much more, not with one shoe off and one shoe on, hi diddle diddle, my son John."

Vickie was getting panicky. She felt like crying, but was acting silly instead.

"Okay, here's what we'll do," said Cassie, with newly found determination. First we have to figure out which way to head. When the sun comes up, well, if the sun does come up, we'll know which way is east. We'll head southwest till we hit the highway. Then, we'll stay hidden just inside the woods, watching for the killer, and watching for the first car going by. If it looks safe, we'll dash out and stop any car or truck."

"Sounds good," agreed Vickie. "Of course, if this was a movie, the first car to come along would have the killer in it."

Cassie grimaced. "I know. I've thought of that, but I can't see what else we can do. We know he's driving a big truck, so we'll stay well hidden if any pick-ups come along. We'll only show ourselves for a car or a big rig. There might be one or two big lumber trucks coming by, and those guys would help us for sure. Of course, with our luck, we'd stop the only truck driven by a serial killer or a rapist," she added gloomily.

"Before we get back into our little hideaway, let's pick up a couple of good strong sticks. If he attacks one of us, the other can beat him around the head with the stick."

The idea was a good one, but in the dark it was almost impossible to find any loose sticks which might do as a weapon. They were afraid to venture far from their little rock haven. They finally found one fairly decent one, and huddled back in the cave. They were too tired and discouraged to talk, but neither one dared close her eyes, in case she drifted off to sleep.

When the sky was just beginning to lighten up, they headed out. Just standing up was a painful and tricky operation. They were so cramped from huddling for so long, that their legs were wobbly. They also had to go slowly, because of Cassie's bare foot. It was now throbbing steadily. She still hadn't checked to see whether it was bleeding. Since there was nothing she could do about it, she really didn't want to know. She couldn't help thinking about blood poisoning, though, as she tramped along over dirt and sticks and rocks. They constantly checked behind and around themselves, to be sure that the killer was nowhere in sight.

What a sorry looking pair they were. Vickie's head had stopped bleeding, but there were red streaks of dried blood down her cheek. She looked like an Indian with war paint on one side of his face.

Her one eye was swollen, and was beginning to turn black.

One sleeve of her jacket was torn, from catching on a sharp branch, and the front of her yellow top was a dirty gray, from crawling in and out of the cave.

Cassie didn't look any better. She had a puffy eye as well, but hadn't realized that she had bumped it on anything. Her lovely pink skirt was streaked with dirt, and had a rip in it. Her bare foot was filthy. They would be lucky if anyone would stop to help them.

Finally, Vickie, who was walking slightly ahead of Cassie, turned and put her finger to her lips. They both stood listening, and were sure that in the distance they could hear a large truck speeding along. They must be near the highway! They grinned at each other, as they tried to pick up the pace.

It was likely because they were trying to hurry, that the accident happened.

Later, Cassie would try to remember just how it had all occurred, but her recollection was blurry. She had thought that she heard something, and was turning to look over her shoulder, just as she took another step with her bare foot. The something she had heard was not behind her, but directly in front of her. It was the rattle of an angry snake, as she unwittingly almost stepped on it with her unprotected foot.

The snake struck quickly, and with deadly aim. He got her a few inches above the ankle. Cassie yelped, and staggered back a bit. She watched in disbelief, as the large rattler slithered away between two rocks.

Vickie turned just in time to see the last half of him disappear. He was a big one, and there was no mistaking the rattles on his tail, and the diamond pattern on his back. The diamonds were dark, with brown centers and cream coloured borders. Vickie's heart sank, as she realized that Cassie had just been bitten by a large diamondback rattlesnake, the deadliest of all pit vipers.

Chapter Nineteen

"Shit, oh shit, Vickie. He bit me. That damn rattler bit me," Cassie exclaimed, as she stared at her leg in total disbelief. This couldn't be happening. What had they done to deserve all this trouble?

"My God, Cass. It looks as if Dracula bit you." Vickie was looking at the two bites, and the blood trickling down Cassie's leg.

They stared at each other in dismay. This was possibly even worse than coming face to face with the killer. They were on their own in the woods, well, in one way they hoped that they were on their own. They were hoping that the killer was far away by now.

Unfortunately, there was no telling how far from help they were. They had absolutely nothing with them, no phones, no pocket knives, no bandages, no water, and certainly no anti-venom drugs. It was not a good scenario. There was definitely something wrong with this picture.

Vickie remembered reading that, contrary to popular belief, you do not try to cut open a rattlesnake bite and suck the venom. Thank God for that, since she had no knife, and didn't relish the idea of sucking snake venom, although she would have done it for Cassie. She also remembered that you keep the bite area lower than the heart, so that the venom doesn't reach the heart so quickly. Other than that, she didn't have a clue what to do.

Cassie was looking appalled, as she inspected the blood, and the double puncture marks on her leg. "Shit," she said, "this just can't be happening. After spending the night squatting in that little cave like a couple of aborigines, what were the chances of getting bitten by a rattler! Someone up there doesn't seem to like us at the moment. If this was in the movies, we wouldn't believe it." She shook her head in dismay, as she looked at Vickie for help.

"Okay, we've got to get out of here as fast as we can," said Vickie. "Here, lean against this tree. Come on, hurry up." She got bossy when she was scared, and she was scared now. "I'm going to wrap this scarf around your leg like a tourniquet. I think that's the right thing to do, but I'm not sure."

"Oh, Vic, that's the lovely new scarf you bought in Apalachicola yesterday. I promise I'll buy you ten new ones to replace it."

"Phooey, just be glad that I did buy it. It's the only damn thing we have. If only we had some water. I know you're supposed to drink water to flush the venom from the kidneys. You need to be hydrated, and we should have some ice to put on it," she added forlornly, looking around, as if she expected to see a refrigerator appear miraculously in these unfriendly woods.

Cassie was silent, as she watched her friend wrap the elegant scarf above the puncture area, between the bite and the heart. Vickie wasn't sure just how tight she should make it, but she had a vague recollection that you leave it loose enough to be able to insert one finger between the bandage and the skin. She was flying by the seat of her pants here, and just hoped that she wasn't doing anything to make matters worse.

"You know, Cass," said Vickie, as she worked on the tourniquet. "It seems to me that in the past few years, you've had one foot on a banana peel. A lot of major and minor disasters have happened in your life. I mean, what do you think are the statistical odds of you and that snake coming toe to toe, when we're trying to run from a killer?"

She was muttering as she worked on the dirty leg, which was quite likely to become infected. Unfortunately, there was no water to clean it. She continued without looking up from her efforts. "It's getting to be like the trials and tribulations of Job. What the heck does the Almighty want from you? What's He trying to tell you?"

"Oh, Vic, don't make me laugh. It'll get my blood racing, and will spread the poison faster. Maybe He's just punishing me for wanting more excitement in my life."

"Yah, well, enough's enough. He's punishing me too every time He gives you another slap in the face. "Hey, up there," she said, turning her face towards the sky. "We've had enough. How about a break now?"

Cassie gave her a half-hearted grin, and squeezed her hand. "I'm sure He's heard you, and will take that heartfelt plea into consideration," she laughed.

Finishing with the tourniquet, Vickie now took off her left sandal, and worked it onto Cassie's bare foot. "Don't even think about saying 'no'. We have to get out of here as fast as we can. Lean on me, and try not to put your weight on that leg. You'll be walking like a drunk, with one heel higher than the other, though. Damn, that's not going to work. Here, take both my shoes, and I'll wear your one."

Cassie didn't say a word, but she realized just how fortunate she was that Vickie was here with her. They had been in a lot of sticky situations together, and this one might just top the charts.

She thought of the night they had been knocked unconscious, then left to die in a burning building. The time they were attacked by the bees in the car had also been scary, since Cassie was very allergic to bees. She remembered the night they had been caught by Jordan when they were sneaking around his house, looking for clues. Together, they had managed to talk themselves out of that one.

Then, of course, on their wonderful cruise, she had nearly been pitched over the side of the boat, while Vickie was chased and almost cornered by Zorro. She was just thinking about their encounter with last year's serial killer, who called himself the Black Sheep, when Vickie said, "There, that's the best I can do."

The scarf and sandals were in place, but they both noted that the area of the bite was beginning to swell and discolour. It was turning a strange greenish-purple.

Well, that didn't take long, thought Cassie grimly. Then, to her dismay, she realized that she was also starting to feel a bit queasy. Was it just her imagination, or was the poison already travelling through her system at a fast pace?

How ironic that she might die here in the woods, somewhere between Apalachicola and Panama City Beach. All her money might not be able to save her now. Life was full of little ironies, but this one was a stinker.

She wondered whether some evil fates were sitting up there in space, taking pleasure in toying with these lowly earthlings. They were being played like violins, moved like chess pieces. She and Vickie just couldn't catch a break.

Subconsciously, she was aware of a little red ladybug sitting primly on a very green leaf. What a pretty picture. That ladybug didn't care a fig about Cassie's predicament. Well, why should she? She wasn't the one who had been bitten by the vicious snake.

Then, shaking her head to clear it, (this was no time to let her mind wander), she pushed away from the tree, and gamely set out, holding onto Vickie for a bit of support.

Most people survived snakebites, she assured herself. It was basically a matter of time. If she could get to the hospital in time, she would be fine. She knew, however, that it was a bit chancy. They had to make it out of the woods, make it to the highway, and find a friendly driver to take them right to the hospital. They had to do all this before the killer found them. Time was of the essence, and at this point, time did not seem to be on their side.

Chapter Twenty

Vickie kept looking at Cassie to see if she was turning pale. That was one of the signs of shock. So far she looked okay, although there was sweat starting to appear on her forehead. Vickie knew that a snake bite victim was supposed to be kept calm and immobile till help came, but here they were, blundering along through the woods, over rocks and logs.

Victoria Craig was praying that the vicious snake had already bitten someone or something else that morning. She knew it wasn't likely, but if it had already attacked someone else, it wouldn't have had much venom left for Cassie. In that case, the bite would not be too serious. Talk about a faint hope, she thought to herself, as they stumbled on.

They were both too tired to waste their breath on talking. They were watching carefully for snakes, and were being as quiet as possible. Being quiet was a necessity. They had to be able to hear the warning rattle of another diamondback, and they had to be able to hear the sounds of their attacker approaching from any side. The worst part was that Cassie had to walk on that darn leg, when she should be lying quietly.

"Dammit, I just can't take the chance of leaving you here while I go for help," said Vickie apologetically. "I know you're supposed to be kept quiet, but if I left you, you'd be totally helpless if Monster Man found you."

"I know that, Vic. Don't you dare even think of leaving me. I'll keep up, I promise, but just now I need to stop for a minute. I'm getting a little dizzy, and my leg feels sort of numb." Actually, she was getting very dizzy, and her leg felt like a big soggy tree stump. The more she moved, the faster the poison was travelling through her body.

Vickie helped her to a rock, where she sank down gratefully. Her friend tightened the tourniquet, which had slipped down uselessly around her ankle. Then she looked in despair at the swelling and discolouration. That snake had really done a number on Cass.

"Well, the good news is that it certainly didn't look like a young snake. It was too big. Young snakes have much more concentrated venom. You might say that they're full of piss and vinegar. I know that from the Animal Planet channel. Thank goodness I watch a lot of television."

She had to try to keep things light, and not let Cassie know how helpless she was feeling. The bad news was, that older, bigger snakes, have longer fangs, so their bites penetrate further. Unfortunately, that guy had looked awfully big, at least the tail end of him did. She wasn't about to share that thought with Cassie, though.

"Look, old pal. I'm getting a bit fuzzy headed. In case I pass out, I just want you to know that you're the best friend anyone could ever hope to have. You know that I love you. Thank you so much for always being there for me."

"Oh Gawd. Don't talk like that, you'll make me start blubbering. Get a grip. It's only a little snakebite. It's not the last act of "The Death of Camille.""

Vickie was scared, so she was trying to keep joking.

It was impossible to fool Cassie, though. She knew her friend too well. She wondered whether it might turn out to be the final death scene, but quickly discarded the unpleasant thought. Somehow she and Vickie would get themselves out of this mess. They always did.

"Cass, do you think I could carry you?" asked Vickie, without much hope.

"Are you kidding?" giggled Cassie. I weigh just about the same as you do. There's no way."

"Don't give me any lip, girl. We've got to get you out of here, and I don't know how much time we've got. Come on, let's give it a whirl. You stand on this rock, and I'll scootch down, then you climb on my back. I'll piggy-back you."

"Shoot, if I'd known you were going to try to carry me, I wouldn't have had that piece of key lime pie for lunch yesterday," joked Cass.

"I just wish I knew how much poison that snake in the grass gave you," groaned Vickie, bending her knees.

Cassie didn't have the energy to argue, but she mumbled under her breath, "I think he gave me quite a bit." Then, pulling up her tattered skirt, she obediently climbed on her friend's back, wrapped her arms around Vickie's neck, and Vickie staggered off. She, of course, was only wearing one shoe, which put her slightly off kilter. She managed to take about twenty steps before losing her balance and falling sideways, as she tried to step over a fallen log.

"I'm sorry, Cass. Come on, get back up here. I've got the rhythm now. We can do this, but you sure as hell are a lot heavier than you look."

Cass wasn't sure whether Vickie was just trying to convince herself that they could do it, or whether she was trying to convince Cassie, but she gamely climbed up again on her friend's back. She didn't want to admit that her hands were tingling, and it was difficult to hold on. They went a bit further this time, but Vickie was staggering all over the place, and suddenly they both fell.

"Well, that was fun," said Cass, attempting a grin, so that Vickie wouldn't feel badly. Her friend was trying so hard. They both started to laugh, as they looked at each other in despair.

"The last time you carried me on your back was in that crazy church race when we were in Grade 7 or 8. Do you remember?"

"Yep. You were a lot lighter then," grinned Vickie, "and I think we came in second that time."

"Well, you're doing a great job, but I think we'd be better off if I put my arm around your shoulder and try to hop a bit. I can still step on that leg, although it's really tingling now. I'll hop and step as lightly as I can. We must be near the highway, because I can hear the occasional car."

She was acting cheerful, but actually, she was feeling quite queasy, dizzy, and terribly thirsty. There was a strange metallic taste in her mouth now too. She knew that she had to get help soon, or she was in way more trouble than either of them could handle.

Within ten long and tortuous minutes, they were at the edge of the highway, but still hidden in the woods. Vickie leaned Cassie against a tree, and cautiously poked her head out to look up and down the road. The curve where their car had taken its plunge, was nowhere in sight. Thankfully, neither was the killer. She had no idea where they were, but was grateful that their stalker didn't seem to be around.

"Don't you worry, Cass. We'll get a ride." Vickie knew it would be tricky watching for the killer, and at the same time, trying to get someone to stop and help them. The way their luck was going, it was likely to be the killer who would stop to pick them up.

Vickie was talking again. "Remember we passed a little clinic on our way over to Apalachicola yesterday. They'll be able to help us. I just can't remember exactly where it was, can you?"

"No," said Cass, shaking her head and looking down at her leg again. It certainly wasn't looking any better.

The first vehicle to come along was a car, which sped up past her, as she frantically waved her arms. Vickie realized that she must look a real sight, but hoped that someone would be kind enough to stop and help.

"Thanks a lot, you shithead," she mumbled under her breath, watching it disappear in the distance.

The next vehicle was a pick-up truck. The way their luck was going, it was likely the killer's truck. She quickly hid back in the woods beside Cassie, who was now extremely pale, and very sweaty. All this movement wasn't doing her any good, in fact, she might be gradually killing Cassie by dragging her through the trees. She was determined that they were going to get out of this latest disaster, but she surely could use a little help.

Finally, they got a lucky break. A small moving van came along, heading northwest towards Panama City.

"What's happened here, darlin'?" asked the driver, as he exited his truck, and followed Vickie towards Cassie, who was still propped against the tree.

"My friend's been bitten by a rattler, and we have to get her to the nearest clinic," said Vickie, trying not to notice the fact that their would-be benefactor had only three teeth in front, and a very greasy ponytail. "Well, beggars can't be choosers," she muttered to herself, as they helped Cassie into the back of the truck. It was only partially packed with furniture, and the driver put an unused mat on the floor for her. He wanted Vickie to sit up front with him, but she chose to sit beside Cassie, who was now very quiet.

"We'll take her to the hospital in Panama City," he told Vickie, spitting tobacco juice onto the ground at her feet. "Don't you worry, little darlin', your friend's gonna be just fine."

"No, we'll take her to the clinic. I think it's just up the road," said Vickie firmly. The sooner Cass got some help, the better.

The truck driver looked doubtful, but he wasn't about to argue with Vickie. She looked formidable when she got herself wound up, and right now she was on the edge.

The clinic came into view sooner than expected. Vickie ran in and told the receptionist she had a very sick person who had been bitten by a rattlesnake.

The receptionist looked interested, but said that they had no antivenom there, and no way of treating snakebite. "You'd better get her to the hospital in Panama City as fast as you can," was her advice.

Vickie couldn't believe the bad luck. Would they never get a break? She raced back to the truck and told the driver to get going. Good manners were long forgotten. He was doing them a tremendous favour, but she had no time to be polite. When she was scared, she became bossy, and Victoria Craig had never been as scared as she was right now.

Cassie rolled her eyes at Vickie, but didn't say anything. She was trying to conserve her strength, and think about other things, to keep her mind off the throbbing, tingling, swollen mess, which was her leg.

Chapter Twenty-One

Cassie was semi-conscious by the time the old rattletrap truck raced into the emergency entrance of Bay Medical. They had endured a hair-raising ride. The toothless wonder at the wheel had done his best, and had kept the pedal to the metal as much as possible. The old truck shivered and quivered, the furniture shifted a bit, threatening to fall on Vickie and Cassie at any time, but he got them there all in one piece.

Vickie slipped a twenty dollar bill into his hands, as she thanked him, and said good-bye. It had been tucked in the pocket of her bell bottoms, and she found it when she pulled out a Kleenex. Cassie was conscious enough to thank him, but she was now biting her lips to keep from moaning with the pain. He went on his way, feeling quite heroic, and with an interesting tale to tell his friends and family. No doubt it would be highly exaggerated by the time he had told it to anyone who would listen.

Before he left, Vickie had run into Emergency, grabbed a nurse, and told her the situation. The nurse stopped an orderly, and they ran out, pushing a gurney. They got Cassie onto the gurney, and whisked her away, with Vickie lurching along behind. She finally gave up on the single sandal she was wearing, and pitched it into a trashcan. Going barefoot in a hospital likely wasn't allowed, but if they didn't like it, they could get her a pair of slippers.

Long afterwards, Vickie would still be talking about the excellent and professional care which Cass received that day, and all that following week.

She didn't want to be separated from her friend, but she wasn't allowed to stay with her. Cass, at this point, was not looking good.

Even her face was swollen now, and her eyelids were drooping. She was having some difficulty breathing, and seemed incoherent.

The emergency doctor and the nurses quickly assessed her condition, examined the puncture marks, and attached a blood pressure cuff. They gave her something in an IV bag, slipped an oxygen mask on her face, and questioned Vickie extensively about what kind of snake it had been. Because she was able to describe the snake so clearly, and after inspecting the puncture marks, they agreed it had more than likely been an Eastern diamondback rattler.

Vickie had assumed that they would give Cassie an anti-venom shot immediately, but realized that they had to verify what kind of snake it was, before giving any medication.

The nurses marked the leg around the puncture with a magic marker. This allowed them to see how much swelling was occurring, and how quickly it was happening. By now, the usually calm and quiet Cassie, was crying with the excruciating pain. They gave her a shot of something, which Vickie guessed was either Demerol or Morphine. Whatever it was, it seemed to work quickly.

Once the assessment was complete, they put the anti-venom into a saline bag, and started the intravenous. Vickie, who was pacing in the emergency waiting room, caught a passing nurse, and asked as many questions as she could. The nurse took a good look at the cut on her head, and suggested that she go and wash some of the blood off her face, wash her hands well, and come back to emergency. It looked as if she would need one or two stitches in the cut on her forehead.

Vickie reluctantly took the advice, and headed to the washroom to repair the damage to her appearance. She did a double-take when she saw herself in the mirror, then began to laugh. No wonder the nurses had eyed her with distaste.

She had forgotten all about the car accident, which seemed to have happened a long time ago. The cut on her forehead had stopped bleeding the previous night, but there was dried blood on her one cheek, and down onto her yellow top.

The lovely new yellow and white scarf, which had looked so pretty on her outfit, was now a dirty, bloodied mess lying in the back of the moving van. She had taken it off Cassie's leg in the truck, when she saw how quickly the leg was swelling. She was very grateful that she had removed it, because when the doctor first looked at Cassie's leg, he had turned to Vickie, and said, "Good for you for not putting a tourniquet on her. That's a mistake most people make."

Her heart had sunk at that, and she didn't have the nerve to confess that she had, indeed, wrapped her lovely new scarf around Cassie's leg. Well, there was nothing she could do about that now. She had done her best, the scarf had been pretty loose, and she just prayed that she hadn't done any damage.

It was so unfortunate that they had been so far away from help, and that Cassie had been forced to run on the bitten leg, instead of lying quietly. Vickie knew enough about venomous snakebites, to know that the skin and tissue around the bite area would deteriorate very quickly. She prayed again that she had managed to get Cassie to the hospital in time.

With a sigh, she took another look at herself in the mirror, and saw that she now had a black eye, which made her look tough, and her auburn hair looked like a fright wig, standing out in all directions. The tear in the sleeve of her jacket did nothing to enhance her appearance. Most bag ladies looked a heck of a lot better than Victoria Craig did at that particular moment. No wonder the nurses had eyed her with suspicion.

Since her purse, brush and lipstick were still back in the car, she could do nothing but wash her face and hands, and run her fingers through her hair. It didn't help much, but at least she was able to return to emergency looking somewhat more human.

A kind nurse put four stitches in her head, and assured her that Cassie had a very good chance of making it, in spite of how long it had taken to get help for her. That made Vickie feel much better. Cass had already gone to intensive care, so Vickie headed for the public phones, to call Steffie and Kitty.

There was no answer at the condo, so she left a long, involved message, and finished with a plea for them to meet her at the hospital. She suspected that they were somewhere on the highway between Panama City and Apalachicola, looking for their missing friends, but there was nothing she could do about that. If they didn't show up soon, she would take a taxi back, and have the driver wait, while she ran up to the condo to get some money.

Thinking of money, made her think of their purses, still lying in the car. She wondered whether the police had taken them to keep them secure. She wondered whether anyone had notified the rental people that one of their cars was totalled. She wondered whether the killer had searched the car and had taken their wallets. There was so much to consider, but all she wanted to know was that Cassie was going to be okay.

She finally made her way to the ICU, and spoke with a nurse. They wouldn't let her in to see Cass, likely because she looked so dirty and dishevelled. They were very interested, however, in how Cassie had come to be bitten. Vickie went through most of it, downplaying the part about them being chased, and even to herself, it sounded far fetched. She was able to assure them again, however, that it was definitely an Eastern diamondback rattler. She had no doubts of that, and it was valuable information for the nurses and doctors.

She had faith that they were taking good care of her friend, so, when they told her that she wouldn't be allowed in to see Cassie until the next day, there was nothing for her to do, but to head back to the condo. At this point she was faint with fatigue and hunger. All she wanted was to have a long, hot shower, and a strong cup of tea, before falling into bed.

As she stood in front of the hospital, waiting for the taxi, she realized that she had been awake for about thirty hours, and hadn't eaten for twenty-four of them. During that time, she had been driven off the road, suffered a good wallop on the head when the car went over the embankment, had been chased through the woods by a madman, had spent the entire night squatting in a cave, and had half carried her friend to safety. She felt justifiably giddy and lightheaded, but also felt sure that she had done her best.

The taxi finally arrived, and Vickie gratefully sank into the back seat. Looking over her shoulder, she wondered fearfully whether she would ever see Cassie again.

Chapter Twenty-Two

They were halfway across the Hathaway Bridge, heading for Panama City Beach, when Vickie suddenly sat bolt upright in the back seat of the cab, and cried out, "Oh gawd, I'm an idiot. Turn around, you've got to go back to the hospital."

The cab driver was startled by her outburst, and veered slightly into the next lane. Getting the taxi back under control, he looked at her in the rear view mirror. "What's wrong?"

"It's a long story. Just please, turn around as soon as you can, after we get off this bridge. I need to get back there right away."

She had suddenly realized that Cassie was still in grave danger from the murderer. He would read about the snake bite victim in the paper, or hear about it on the local TV channel. She had seen enough movies, and read enough mystery novels to know just how easy it would be for this monster to slip into the hospital and get at Cassie. He seemed very good at disguises, and had proved how tenacious he could be. Cassie, lying helpless in a hospital bed, could become a very easy victim.

She gave the cab driver her phone number and address at the condo, and promised to pay him later for the fare. Fortunately, he seemed quite willing to trust her. Well, there was nothing that he could do about it, because she definitely had no money with her.

She rushed into Emergency once again, and searched out the doctor who had attended Cassie. She found him giving orders to a nurse, and tried to explain all about the killer, and the danger in which Cassie found herself.

Unfortunately, the young Dr. Jim Barker was overworked and underpaid, and he really didn't have the patience to listen to this semi-hysterical woman, who looked as if she had had too many drinks the night before.

Vickie overheard one nurse say to another, in a sarcastic tone, "Is she afraid the snake will come back and finish off her friend?"

At that point Vickie lost her cool. "You idiots," she shouted. "Don't you realize a woman's life is at stake here? She needs a guard on her door. There's no doubt that the killer will come back for her. Please listen to me. She's in serious danger. You've got to help her."

"Now, now, calm down," said the doctor, laying a hand on her arm. Then he turned and murmured something to a nurse. Vickie suspected that he was ordering them to give her a shot of something to quiet her. That was the last thing she needed.

Realizing that she was getting nowhere with the doctor, she grabbed the nurse who had done her stitches. She had seemed a reasonable and caring person.

Slowly and carefully she began her tale again. "Honestly, I'm not crazy or delusional. There is definitely a killer after us. He ran us off the road, and he chased us through the woods last night. That's why we were in there, and that's why Cassie was bitten. My story is easy to check, because the police should have found the car by now. If you would just call Detective Davidson in the PCB police department, he'll verify what I'm saying about the killer."

Fortunately the young nurse believed Vickie. She called the police station, and was able to locate Detective Davidson. He asked her to keep Vickie there at the hospital, and said he would be there in half an hour.

By the time he arrived, Vickie greeted him like a long lost friend. He took one look at her, and was sure that her story was true, unbelievable, but true.

It was another hour before they got things organized, but by the time Vickie was ready to leave, there was a policeman sitting on guard right outside the door of the intensive care unit.

Vickie asked the detective if he could give her a ride back to the condo. She was too tired, and too weak from hunger, to care about how she looked, or whether she might be inconveniencing him.

Luckily, Steffie and Kitty arrived just at the right time.

"I know what I look like," she laughed, as they gazed at her in shocked silence. Just wait till you hear my tale of woe, and you'll be surprised that I'm still standing. I've had one hell of a couple of days, but Cassie's in a lot worse shape. She's in serious trouble, guys. Right now she needs our prayers."

Steffie was particularly solicitous, as she tucked Vickie into the car. She remembered very well just how wonderful these three friends had been to her, when she had been shot the previous year. Boy, we do lead exciting lives, she thought to herself, as they headed back to the condo.

While Vickie showered, Steffie made a big pot of tea, toasted some bagels, and cooked a couple of slices of Canadian bacon.

As she snuggled into bed, and devoured the wonderful food, Vickie told them the entire story, starting with the mysterious flat tire. Kitty and Steffie were appalled at all the problems they had experienced, but the worst of all was Cassie's snakebite. They promised Vickie that they would call the hospital every hour to get an update on Cassie's condition, and then she finally slept.

"I can't believe that all this has happened," said Kitty, shaking her head. "And it's all because Cassie saw that monster throw the woman off the balcony. What a lousy piece of luck that was."

"Yep, and it wasn't so good for the woman either," replied Steffie, with an attempt at a grin.

"Well, we'd better call Dave, and then I'll call my mom and dad. I don't know how long they'll be able to stay and mind the boutique for us. Maybe we should think about going home tomorrow as planned. Vickie will want to stay, but there's not much we can do, except to lend moral support."

"We're almost packed anyway, so let's wait and see how Cassie is by tomorrow. Then we can decide whether to take our flight home or cancel it. Dave will catch a flight tonight or tomorrow, so they really won't need us. He'll likely be here before we leave."

"Okay, let's make all the phone calls, including one to the hospital, then we'll go out for an early dinner while Vickie's sleeping, and we'll bring something back for her."

"Sounds like a plan," agreed Steffie.

She made the call to Cassie's husband, Dave, and kept it as brief as possible. Cassie hadn't wanted him to know anything about seeing the woman thrown off the balcony, and being chased by the murderer because she was a witness. She had planned to tell him everything when she got home. Steffie simply said that Cassie had been bitten by a rattler on her trip to Apalachicola, and left it at that. They could fill him in when he got here.

Kitty called her dad, who was staying in her home while she was away. Her parents had come from Toronto to look after the boutique for her and Steffie, and even more importantly, to look after Kitty's two little cats. Her dad was upset to hear about Cassie, but assured Kitty that the shop was fine, and that he and her mom would stay as long as necessary.

"How are Rosie and Petie?" asked Kitty, suddenly missing them very much.

"They are two spoiled little felines," laughed her dad. "Petie sits on the piano every night and wails for you. He sounds like a singer with his finger caught in the door. Rosie is a real little flirt. She follows me around the house like a shadow. When I sit down, she sits down, right on my lap! Your mom dances attendance on them as if they were royalty."

"Well, they are as far as I'm concerned," grinned Kitty. She felt much better after talking to her dad. They had a very special relationship.

"Mitch called the other night to see how we're doing. He sounded lonesome for you. He was in Montreal on another book tour. You likely know he's going on to Halifax before he gets back to Toronto. Maybe he'll be able to use all this stuff about the killer in his next book. He's a great guy, Kit Kat. Don't let him get away on you."

"I won't if I can help it, Dad. Listen, I'll call you tomorrow, and let you know when we're coming home. In the meantime, give my love to Mom, and hug those two furballs for me."

Chapter Twenty-Three

Vickie went to the airport to pick up Dave. They had been good friends ever since Cassie married him. Actually, at one low point three years ago, Cassie had wondered whether Vickie and Dave might be having an affair. She had soon come to her senses, however, and felt very ashamed of herself for doubting her husband and her best friend.

Vickie watched with pleasure, as Dave strolled down the concourse.

He was a tall, lanky man, with brown hair just starting to show some silver at the sides. He always seemed to have an amused look on his face. He had a lot of laugh lines, and a small cleft in his chin. He wasn't really handsome, but he gave the appearance of an honest, intelligent man, who felt good about himself, and about the world around him. He was quiet and laid back, and seemed to take things calmly.

He was wearing jeans and a light blue sweater, and his face lit up as he spotted Vickie.

As she watched him approach, his carry-bag slung carelessly over his shoulder, she mused at how different he was from Cassie's former love, Jack Willinger. Jack was a really handsome guy, in spite of the long scar, which stretched down one side of his face. He had such sex appeal that women turned to look at him when he walked by.

His piercing blue eyes were like Paul Newman's, and he strode through life with that certain arrogance typical of detectives. There was electricity in the air when Jack came into a room. Vickie had known him since she and Cassie and Jack were little kids, and she had never liked him. She and Jack had always fought for Cassie's attention, especially once they got to high school.

Cassie, however, saw a totally different side of Jack. She saw the charming, loving, very sexual being. For Cassie, Jack was pure excitement. Her heart started pounding and her breath became ragged just when she saw him approaching. It had always been that way. She liked to say that Dave was her security blanket, always there for her, always promising love and warmth. Jack was her night out on the town, always promising action and fun, and wild wonderful sex.

Vickie just couldn't understand the attraction. She felt that Jack was trouble, and wished that he hadn't dropped back into their lives. A few years ago, however, Vickie and Cassie had saved Jack's life, by attacking a knife-wielding man, determined to kill him. Since then, she and Jack had enjoyed an amicable truce. As long as he didn't do anything to hurt Cassie or her marriage, Vickie would tolerate him. She was very protective of Cassie, who still seemed to be in love with Jack, as well as Dave.

The interesting thing was that Dave knew next to nothing about Jack. He knew that Jack and Cassie and Vickie had been kids together, but had no idea that Cassie and Jack had been lovers for years before he met Cassie.

Vickie threw her arms around Dave, and gave him a friendly hug. "It's so good to see you," she cried. "Our gal's in a bit of a mess this time."

"How's she doing?" asked Dave, as they strolled toward the baggage arrivals.

Now that she looked at him more closely, she saw that he looked frazzled and nervous. He really loves her, she told herself. If only Cass could get Jack out of her head once and for all. This guy was a real keeper.

"It was a pretty bad bite, Dave. It would have been a lot better if I could have managed to get her to the hospital sooner. I did the best I could though. We were pretty deep in the woods when she was bitten."

"What the hell were you doing in the woods?" he asked, "and what the heck happened to you?" He was looking at her black eye, and the stitches on her forehead.

"Wait till we get into the car, and I'll tell you the whole story."

Dave could barely believe that they had got themselves entangled in another murder situation, this time through no fault of their own. Trouble just seemed to follow those two around like a bad genie waiting to pop out of the bottle.

They were reassured to see that there was still a guard sitting outside the intensive care unit. They were disappointed, however, to see that Cassie was still being kept in that unit. They had hoped that she might have been well enough to have been transferred to a private room by now.

Dave was allowed in first, and he was horrified at what he saw. Cassie had IV lines snaking into both arms, a monitor was beeping quietly behind her, and oxygen was being pumped up her nose. Dave's heart sank when he saw all those machines, wires and tubes. Somehow, they looked like alien beings with long sinewy fingers, launching an attack on Cassie, rather than the best medical equipment money could buy, trying to help her.

Her face was swollen, as were her hands and legs. There were strange red mottled looking splotches on her face and neck, and even her eyelids were swollen. She looked like a monster, not his beautiful, classy Cassie.

She seemed to sense his presence, and opened her eyes, which now looked like slits in her face. She gave him a welcoming smile, which was more like a grimace, and it just about broke his heart.

"Hi kiddo. Looks like you lost this round. You must have really pissed off that old snake."

"If I'd had my shoes on, I would've kicked the shit out of him," she muttered.

"That's my gal," he laughed, patting her hand gently.

"Where's Vicky?" she asked.

"She's right outside, pacing around. I think they'll let her in for a minute when I leave."

"She saved my life, you know. That crazy gal even piggybacked me a bit. She did everything she could possibly do, and I'd be deader than dead if she hadn't been with me. I really owe her big-time now."

"Don't worry, we'll do something special for her as soon as you're better. By the way, Sugar Plum and Muffin have really missed you. They can't wait for you to come home. I've got Mrs. MacDonald looking after them for us. Have the doctors said when they think you can get out of here?"

"No," she said, groggily. I hardly know where I am. Do I look awful?"

"Yes," he laughed. "Just don't ask to see a mirror for a few days. The good news is that you're going to be fine." He didn't know this for a fact, but couldn't conceive of any other possible outcome.

He realized, with disappointment, that he would have to postpone his trip to Europe, at least for a while. Why the heck was Cass always getting herself into these situations? Why in the world was she being chased by a killer she didn't even know? She seemed to bring these things on herself, he thought with resentment. Still, he loved her, and all he wanted to do, was to get her home at this moment in time, and start taking care of her, at least for a little while.

When Vickie was finally allowed in for a short visit, the two old friends simply looked at each other, and started grinning. Vickie looked a lot better than Cassie did, but she still looked funny with her yellow and green bruises around her swollen eye, and the black tracks of stitches on her forehead.

It made her feel sick to see how swollen Cassie's leg was, and she wondered whether her friend would ever dance arabesques again. She remembered so clearly the day that Jack Willinger had come back into their lives. That day Cassie had done a little bump and grind right down the hall and into the kitchen, just to show her excitement and delight to have found "her" Jack again. Would she be able to dance so joyfully like that in the future?

"Well, what do you think we should try next, kiddo?" Vickie joked, kissing Cassie lightly on her forehead. "How about jumping out of a plane without a parachute?"

Cassie tried to grin again, but with her swollen lips, it created a frightening picture. "I sure as hell don't feel like another walk in the woods," she said weakly.

Vickie and Dave hung around the hospital for almost an hour, then went back in to see Cassie, before going home. She seemed in good spirits, considering what had happened to her. It was likely the painkillers they were giving her. She was happy to hear that there was a guard right outside the door. She certainly was in no condition to fight off the killer if he decided to show up now.

Dave and Vickie hunted down the doctor who was looking after Cassie, and were reassured that he thought she would make a full recovery. She had been given several vials of the anti-venom drug CroFab, which was made specifically to counter diamondback rattlesnake bite. At this point, she was definitely responding to it, and he was cautiously optimistic.

"The pain has remained pretty well localized," said Dr. Tillson. "There is still severe edema, nausea and vomiting, and there have definitely been some alterations in her blood, but she is certainly better now than when she came in. She suffered what we call 'moderate envenomation,' so it could have been much worse," he went on to explain.

"What exactly does that mean?" asked Dave and Vickie at the same time.

"Well, 'moderate envenomation' is not as good as limited, but not as bad as severe," said Dr. Tillson. "The snake could have injected a lot more venom into her body, or he could have put less. In this case, it was just a moderate amount, but since the diamondback rattler is such a venomous snake, even a moderate amount is way too much for someone the size of your wife. She was within half an hour of death when she arrived here," he added in a matter of fact way.

Dave and Vickie just stared at him with horror.

"She was really that close to dying?" asked Vickie, with disbelief, her stomach starting to do back flips.

"Oh yes. It's a very good thing that you got her here when you did. All that running through the woods didn't do her any good, but, on the other hand, I think you did a marvelous job getting her out of there. It must have been a tough call, trying to decide whether to leave her, and go for help yourself, or drag her with you. Under the circumstances I think you made the right decision."

The doctor then went on to explain that about ten days after the treatment was started, there was a danger of Cassie developing "serum sickness." That was a condition which resulted from the immune system trying to reject the serum. Not all people had this reaction, though, so they were hopeful that Cassie would be fine. Once they got her past that point, she would be in good shape.

Dave was insistent that he wanted to get her back to Canada as soon as possible, but the doctor was just as insistent that they were going to play the waiting game. It seemed to be a Mexican standoff.

As they left the ICU, they had no reason to notice a tall man, carrying a big bouquet of flowers, just getting onto the elevator. They would have been alarmed if they had realized that a few minutes earlier, this same man had stepped off the elevator, and started walking down the hall to the intensive care unit. When he noticed the guard sitting reading a magazine outside the ICU door, he had hesitated, then, acting as if he had mistakenly gotten off at the wrong floor, he had turned around and reentered the elevator.

He was tall and brawny, and was wearing a baseball cap over hair tied in a pigtail. There was a soul patch beneath his mouth, and he had small eyes, which were placed close together on his wide face. If anyone had been looking, they would have noticed the Rolex on his wrist.

Chapter Twenty-Four

It was ten long days before Cassie, Vickie and Dave, finally made it back to Niagara Falls. Steffie and Kitty had returned home earlier. Once they knew that Cassie was going to be fine, there was no need for them to hang around in Florida.

Cassie couldn't believe just how wonderful her new home looked to her. Dave had done a great job of supervising the workers, and the workers had done a great job of doing everything Cassie had wanted.

The library was even more terrific than she had hoped. It was twice the size of the library in her former home. Cassie had loved that cosy library, and had fashioned this one on it, just making it bigger. There were floor to ceiling shelves on every available wall. It would take her months to fill all those shelves with the books she wanted to buy.

One wall was almost all windows looking down onto the Niagara River.

Just as in the big sunroom, the windows had padded seats with thick cushions, so that the cats could sit gazing out at the world, or sleep, curled up in the sunshine. Another wall showed off a beautiful Muskoka stone fireplace, Cassie's small escritoire, and some good pieces of art. It was a bibliophile's dream, and Cassie knew that she would spend many happy hours here. She was finally coming to realize just how good it was to have money, lots of money. Whether she deserved it or not, she had it, and was learning to make the most of it.

Dave had been solicitous and loving during Cassie's week in the Panama City hospital. He had them put a cot in her room, and he slept there every night, in spite of the fact that the guard was just outside the door. He was taking no chances of the killer getting close to

Cassie again. He had started having nightmares about that madman throwing Cass off the cruise ship in the Caribbean.

Once out of the hospital, they had spent a couple of days at the Edgewater Beach condo, so that Cassie could rest and recuperate, before the flight home. Vickie, of course, had stayed as well. There was no rush for her to get back to Vancouver. Brian was coming home from Ireland, and she knew that Dave was planning to go back to Europe within a few days. There was no way Cassie was going to be left alone. Timewise, it worked well for everyone.

"Dave, I wish you didn't have to leave so soon," sighed Cassie for the umpteenth time. "Couldn't you catch up with that singer, whoever he is, later on?" She knew what Dave's answer would be, but couldn't stop herself from asking again.

Her husband shook his head. "Cass, I've been here all the time you were away on the cruise. While you were having fun cruising, I was working with the contractor, and then I spent another ten days in PCB with you. You have to be fair about this. I've delayed my trip long enough. If I go now, I can be back in about three weeks, maybe four. Doesn't that sound logical?"

"It may seem logical, Mr. Spock, but I don't have to like it," frowned Cassie. "What if this murderer finds me and gets to me while you're cavorting around Europe? Won't you feel guilty?" She was only half kidding.

"Cut it out. He's not going to follow you up here. He's likely far away by now. He didn't try anything at the hospital, so why would he traipse all the way up here?"

Dave was serious about his work. Now that Cassie had inherited such a lot of money, he certainly didn't need to work, but he loved it. He loved the excuse it gave him to travel all over the world on his own. It gave him a freedom he had never known.

Of course, he had travelled before Cassie inherited her fortune, but now, thanks to Cassie's generosity, he had the big bucks to go anyplace, and stay as long as he wanted. He couldn't get away fast enough, now that he knew Cassie was fine.

He knew it might be considered a selfish attitude, but he didn't care. He had been a good husband, father, and provider for many years, and now he was catering to himself. Maybe it was his own little mid life crisis, and, indeed, it truly was a crisis. He couldn't lay it on Cassie this trip, but next time he came home, he'd have to tell her. He sighed as he thought of how difficult it would be to share his secret.

The air bus picked him up early the next morning, and Cassie and Vickie were alone in the beautiful new house, with just Muffy and Sugar Plum for company.

Cassie's leg looked almost normal now, although it was still discoloured around the puncture marks.

"That snake really chewed you up," said Vickie, watching Cassie rub her leg. "I wonder how many people he's bitten in his lifetime, or whether you were the first. They say that a fully grown rattler will often simply bite without injecting any venom. That guy must have been in a really bad mood the morning he bit you."

"Never mind that old snake. I've got something really interesting to show you. I've been waiting for just the right time, and this is it. Come on up to my room."

They climbed the stairs to the elegant master bedroom, which was decorated in pale greens and cream, with touches of burgundy here and there. Cassie had a large walk-in closet, to which she led Vickie.

"Okay, kiddo. This is it. See if you can find anything unusual in this closet," she commanded.

"Well, what is it that you think I'm going to find?" asked Vickie, looking around in bewilderment. "Am I looking for new clothes, or fancy shoes or what?"

"I'll give you a little clue. Look down along the baseboard on the back wall." Cassie was enjoying this game immensely.

Vickie looked carefully, but couldn't see anything unusual. "I give up. What the heck am I supposed to find?"

"Watch this, oh unenlightened one," laughed Cassie, kneeling down to push against the middle of the baseboard. As she did so, the entire wall slowly swung back, and Vickie walked into a small, windowless room.

"What is this?" she inquired, looking with amazement at a couple of chairs, two flashlights, a big jug of water, and some cups. There was also a box of tissues and a bag of chocolate bars on a small shelf.

"It's a panic room. It was here when we bought the house. Apparently the guy who owned this place, was an accountant for the mob. You know that there are quite a few mafia in Niagara Falls, or so they say. Anyway, he kept two sets of books for them, and he had one set hidden here. I guess he figured that if things ever got bad, he could go to the RCMP and give them the real set of books. Or maybe he figured he might have to hide himself and his family some day.

Remember in the 80's a lot of the big homes in Toronto were putting in panic rooms, in case of home invasion. If you hear the intruders in time, and can get to the panic room, you're pretty safe. You can bolt this thing from the inside – see."

Vickie was duly impressed. "How long do you think you could hide in here?" she asked, plopping down on one of the chairs.

"Hopefully long enough to call for help. I'm going to put a cell phone in here, and keep it charged up. After all the crap we've been through in the past few years, I'm thrilled with this little room. You musn't tell anyone about it, though. Don't even mention it to Steffie and Kitty. The fewer people who know about it, the better. See, I've even got a litter box and some food here for the cats. If I ever had to hide here, I would take them in with me, so that an intruder couldn't hurt them."

"Wouldn't we have had fun playing in a room like that when we were kids?" asked Vickie, as they reentered the master bedroom.

"You've got that right. We would have spent all our time in it, making up wild stories about murderers and escaped convicts etc."

"I have to ask myself, how many friends do I have with a panic room in their home. The answer, of course, is ONE. You are something else, Mrs. Meredith. You never cease to amaze me with all your little tricks and ideas."

Vickie was laughing and shaking her head as she said this. She looked with affection at her old pal, and continued.

"Are you sure that a cell phone would work in there? If the walls are lined with steel, or whatever they use to make those panic rooms, it wouldn't be able to get a signal."

"Shoot. I never thought of that. Well, I guess you could punch 911, and leave the cell phone on, but outside the panic room. By the time the intruder found the phone, or noticed that it was on, emergency would have traced the call." She sighed as she sat down on her bed. "Trust you to find a fly in the ointment. I was so happy with that room. Now it doesn't seem so good, if I can't use the phone to call for help."

"Look, in the first place, I doubt that you'll ever need to use it. In the second place, it doesn't take long to punch in 911, and then leave the phone out here. That's a good idea. In the third place, I hear the doorbell. I'll run and get it. You take your time coming down the stairs. I don't want you taking a tumble with that weak leg." She was still taking good care of her friend, as she had since they were kids.

Chapter Twenty-Five

By the time Cassie reached the main level, Vickie was walking back from the front door, carrying a long box of flowers, tied with a big satin bow.

"Wow, lookee here. I'll bet Dave has sent you flowers to apologize for leaving so soon," she said, as she handed the box to Cassie.

"Oh I doubt that," said Cassie ruefully. "He was really cross with me when he left. He couldn't understand why I wanted him to stay a bit longer. I told him that I thought he was a selfish bastard, and he didn't like it. It's true, though, I think he's being very self-centered. He's got people working for him now, who could scout out this new singer just as well as he could. He just couldn't wait to get away."

"Come on, Cass, give him a break. He stayed home while we went on our cruise, and he flew right down to PCB when you got bitten. He delayed his trip until he was sure that you were recovering, and he knew that I'd be here with you, so he wasn't exactly leaving you all alone. I think you're too hard on the poor guy."

Vickie always took Dave's side in any discussion of his shortcomings.

"Oh phooey. You always stick up for him. You say nicer things about him than you do about your own husband."

Vickie laughed at that. "I guess you're right about that. My dear old Brian is such a boring stick-in-the-mud. Dave seems pretty exciting in comparison. Still, I wouldn't trade my old guy for anyone else, and look how much he travels. Shoot, he's always away in some dumb place doing boring research for another boring book. In my case, he's always begging me to go with him. Remember my disastrous trip to Scotland? No thanks. I'd rather stay home and talk to myself."

Cassie grinned. "Well, at least you don't have any worries about him having another dolly on the side. He always invites you along. In my case though, Dave promises that he'll take me on the next trip, but that never happens. You know, I still wonder at times whether he's got a mistress or maybe another family stashed away somewhere in Europe. He spends too darn much time over there. And now he's talking about maybe going to Australia to check out some of their entertainers. You don't suppose he could be a spy for the Mounties or something like that, do you?" She looked as if this idea had just occurred to her, and she seemed to like it.

"Oh please, I doubt it, Einstein. You can pull the plug on that silliness. Dave doesn't seem the undercover type of guy. It's more likely that he just likes to get away by himself for a bit, just to be free and have no bothersome duties such as looking after a house, looking after a wife, looking after kids. What guy wouldn't enjoy that freedom?

Anyway, let's take these flowers into the kitchen to open them. I think you said that all the vases are in there. We could use a lovely bunch of flowers to cheer us up today."

Undoing the box, they both gasped to see a dozen black roses.

"Oh, how ugly," cried Cassie. "Dave would never send anything like this no matter how mad he was. It must be a joke or a mistake."

"It's no joke," said Vickie, grimly. "I can guess who's sent them. Open the card, because I hope I'm wrong."

Suddenly she had an overwhelming sense of déjà vu. She remembered so well that day three years ago, when they had received a parcel from a delivery man. Just like today, they had gone to the kitchen to open it. Inside the box had been a dead rat. The message had been clear. If they "ratted" on the killer, they too would be killed, just like the rat.

If these flowers had been sent by their current stalker, and Vickie was sure that was the case, how coincidental that he had basically the same idea as the killer three years ago. He must have sent the roses to warn them that he was going to kill them. She knew that Cassie must be thinking the same thing.

Cassie opened the card, and mutely handed it to Vickie. It said "I'll Be Killing You," and there were little musical notes drawn around it.

"It's from that old song, I'll Be Seeing You," whispered Vickie in dismay, holding the card by its edges, just in case there were fingerprints on it.

"Do you think he's here in Niagara?" asked Cassie, as she sat down on a kitchen chair. The leg which had been broken in a skiing accident, and which had been chewed by the rattler, was still weak.

"I guess he could have sent these from anywhere," replied Vickie. "He's just trying to scare us into keeping our mouths shut. He's likely back in Mexico, and he sent them by internet or something."

She didn't believe it for a moment, but there wasn't much point in getting themselves too upset. That was just what this creep wanted. He was toying with them, teasing and taunting them. Well, they weren't going to let him get to them. They were smarter than he was, and they just had to stay calm and figure out a solution. They had both had enough excitement for quite a while.

"You know, Cass, at the moment, your life is like a damn train wreck."

She shook her head, as she looked at her friend, and she had no way of knowing just how right she was. If it was a train wreck now, it was about to completely jump the tracks in the near future.

Staring at the card, they realized that it was from a Niagara florist. Cassie called immediately. She asked for the manager, told her who she was, and explained the problem.

"I really need to know who sent these black roses. It must be some kind of a joke. Maybe it's someone I met on my recent cruise. Anyway, could you please check your records for me. I'm sure you don't get many orders for black roses."

The manager was very helpful, and said that she would call back as soon as she had checked the order.

Vickie poured a couple of glasses of wine, and they went to sit in the new library. Muffin, the affectionate little orange tabby, followed along behind. He knew there would be a lap for him, and maybe some ear scratching.

Sugar Plum, aka Sugar Plump, as she was called so affectionately, was already curled up on the window seat in a patch of sunshine. She looked like a fluffy little gray and black cushion lying there. Muffy apparently decided that he could forego the lap and the ear scratching, as he jumped up beside her, snuggling close, in order to share her patch of sun. Now they looked like two fluffy cushions.

When the phone rang, all four of them jumped.

"Mrs. Meredith, I'm afraid I really can't help you. The flowers were paid by cash, so we have no name for the sender. One of my clerks, however, remembers that it was a young man of about sixteen. She says that he was dressed in baggy pants, and had a cap on backwards, the way the young people like to wear them. She remembers him well, because he didn't look the type to send flowers to anyone. She says that he seemed nervous.

He simply told her what he wanted, gave your address, which he had written on a piece of paper, and paid in small bills. He had already written out a card, which he had in his pocket. Does that help you at all?"

Cassie could just picture the stalker writing out the card, and drawing the little musical notes around the words. She was angry when she got off the phone. "He's here in town, Vic. He knows where I live, and he hasn't given up. He's going to stalk me till he can kill me, and he'll go after you too. This guy isn't going to give up ever. He's like a dog with a bone. Somehow we've got to stop him."

Vickie agreed. "He must have picked out some kid off the street, given him fifty bucks or whatever to keep his mouth shut, and told him what to do. Even if we could find the kid, I'll bet anything that he doesn't know our killer, or anything about him. He'll be impossible to trace. Black roses. Shit. Somehow they seem more scary than the rat was." Vickie was frowning as she looked at her friend.

"I know you're not going to like this, but I think I'm going to call Jack," said Cass defiantly. "I admit I'm scared now, but I'm also damn mad, and after that demonic chase in the woods, and the poison snake, I don't feel ready to cope with too much more. Jack will know what to do. He'll help us."

Her heart was beating a little faster just thinking about seeing Jack again. She had tried so hard to stay away from him. She knew that it wasn't wise to see him in her present state of mind. She was angry with her husband, and Jack was now a free man. It wasn't a good scenario, but Vickie would be here to keep her on the straight and narrow.

She expected an argument from Vickie, and was prepared to do battle with her. To her surprise, however, her old friend agreed with her.

Sitting herself down on a kitchen stool, Vickie looked at the black roses again, and shook her head. "You're right, this has gone on long enough. It's time we got some help, because we're floundering here. It's time to call in the big guns. Let's get Jack and Bud to come over, and we'll kick some ass. We have to put a crimp in this guy's style before things go any further. Go call them, Cass, and see if they can come as soon as possible."

Cassie suddenly felt a whole lot better. She'd been moping around long enough. She and Vickie were a team, and with a little help, she felt sure that they could get this guy, before he got them, at least that's what she told herself.

Chapter Twenty-Six

Jack Willinger wasn't at the station when Cassie called, so she tried him on his cell phone. Fortunately, she caught him as he and his partner Bud Lang were returning from a trip to Fort Erie, finishing up details on a murder investigation. They promised to be there within the hour.

Her old friend and lover was looking more trim and handsome than ever these days, although there was a sadness around his deep blue eyes, which hadn't been there before. He had lost ten pounds after Darla's death, finding that food just seemed to stick in his throat. He never felt hungry, and didn't even enjoy sharing doughnuts with Bud at their favourite coffee shop. He would sit there with Bud, drinking cup after cup of coffee, while Bud managed to devour two or three doughnuts.

Bud always joked with Jack that if his wife Amanda had even suspected all the junk food he consumed in a day, she would take a stick to him. Bud lived in a totally female environment, with a wife and three little girls, all of whom adored him.

Jack was carrying around a whole load of guilt at the moment. Darla had been partly correct in her accusations. She had always said that he was too involved in his job. She was alone too much, and that was how and why she had started her secret drinking.

The several miscarriages she had suffered had contributed greatly to her depression. Jack knew he hadn't been a very supportive husband. He hadn't understood the depth of her devastation after the last miscarriage, and his mind had been more on Cassie than on his wife. Every time he thought of her sitting drinking alone, then falling down the stairs and dying alone, he was overcome with sadness, guilt, and a raging anger at himself. The feelings were gnawing at him like a ravenous beast.

His partner Bud was the only person alive who knew how he felt about Cassie, and Bud was a good sounding board. Jack had no idea that Cass was in any kind of trouble, but he couldn't stop thinking about her. He didn't know about the snakebite, or whether she was even back in town. The last contact he had with her was when she wrote him a very nice note after Darla died. Other than that, the last time he had heard anything about her, was when he ran into Steffie, and learned that the four friends were going on a cruise together.

Strangely, he and Bud had just been discussing her, when Jack's cell phone rang.

Cass didn't sound like her usual calm, take charge sort of self. She sounded angry, and maybe a bit scared. That surprised and worried Jack. Cass and Vickie were always getting themselves into some kind of tangle, or "adventure" as they called it, and he wondered what it was all about this time. Cassie didn't give him many details on the phone. She just told him about the black roses, and asked him to come over.

"We'll be there in half an hour, Cass. Don't worry, we'll fix it, whatever it is."

"What now?" asked Bud with resignation. He wished that Cassie would move to the South Pacific, or maybe Antarctica. He liked her very much, but felt that she was bad news for Jack. She seemed happily married, and Bud knew that she would likely never leave Dave, so that left Jack out in the cold. It was a sticky situation, and Bud could do nothing but be there for his friend.

Neither of them had been out to Cassie's new home on the Niagara River Parkway. They were suitably impressed, as they drove up the long driveway to the mansion on the river. The driveway was framed by tall king maples, and feathery fir trees, interspersed with colourful wildflowers, and the picture perfect landscaping around the house had obviously been done professionally.

Bud gave a long, low whistle.

"Looks like she's putting her money to good use," he muttered, as he unfolded himself from the car. In spite of his size, Bud Lang moved with a certain grace. He was big, but he wasn't threatening, not once you saw those mischievous brown eyes looking at you. His face was craggy and weathered, and he had crinkly lines around his mouth and eyes. You could tell that he laughed a lot.

Around the station, he was known as the "gentle giant," but crooks who mistook him for a tub of lard, got a rude awakening. There wasn't an ounce of fat on him. It was all muscle. In spite of his size, he was fast, and in spite of his good nature, he was nobody's fool. Bud Lang was an excellent detective, quiet, thoughtful, and perceptive. He was also a faithful and reliable friend.

Cassie was grateful that Bud had come along with Jack. She hadn't seen Jack for a long time, and she didn't trust herself alone with him.

"Come on in. We'll have coffee in the sunroom. Vickie's here too, just like old times," she laughed. She was referring, of course, to the fact that she and Jack and Vickie had grown up together, played together, and gone to school together. Actually, Vickie and Jack had lived on the same street as kids, but had never liked each other much. Jack had teased the girls mercilessly when they were young.

By high school, however, he had turned into the heartthrob they all wanted to date, everyone except Vickie, that is. Vickie resented Jack, feeling that he was going to break Cassie's heart. Jack resented Vickie, feeling that she led Cassie into too many scrapes. Cassie, caught in the middle, loved them both fiercely.

Now, so many years later, Vickie and Jack had agreed to disagree. They were working on a truce of sorts.

"Bud, it's so good to see you," said Vickie. "What have you been doing lately?"

"Oh, not much. There've been a few murders, some robberies, a lot of drug busts. There's nothing much new in this old town," he laughed, as he picked up Muffy, who had come to see who was making all the noise. Bud and Muffy had enjoyed their first encounter three years ago, and were still friends. Even though they didn't see each other very often, Muffy obviously remembered him. Bud had such a nice big lap for a little cat. Now Bud had two cats of his own, and Muffy sniffed him with interest.

Cassie served coffee and fresh date squares, which had been in the oven when the black roses arrived. They all chatted about inconsequential things until they had finished their coffee, then Cassie brought out the ugly roses and the card.

"It looks as if this guy isn't going to give up," said Vickie, launching into a recital of everything that had happened since the night Cassie saw the woman thrown off the balcony. Cass filled in any details which Vickie omitted.

The two detectives sat quietly listening, shaking their heads occasionally, asking one or two pertinent questions, and looking amazed as the story got longer and longer. Jack was really concerned when he heard how close Cassie had come to being dumped overboard. When Vickie told him about the rattlesnake bite, he ran his fingers through his hair in disbelief.

"Do you two ever go any place without getting yourselves into danger?" he asked, only half kidding. He was looking at Vickie as he said this. Somehow, in his mind, it was always Vickie who got Cassie into trouble, although that was totally untrue in this case.

He seemed truly annoyed, when he asked where Cassie's husband Dave was, and discovered that he was out of the country again. He had to bite his tongue, to keep from saying something derogatory about Dave's peripatetic ways. He knew it was none of his business, yet he hated to think that Cassie was being neglected.

He just couldn't understand a man leaving his wife alone, when he knew that a murderer was stalking her, and threatening her in such a blatant fashion. Actually, he couldn't understand any man leaving Cassie at any time, just to go wandering around some foreign country. If he was married to Cassie, he would never leave her side. Well, that was a road better left unexplored.

The two hours they were there gave Cassie plenty of time to study Jack. It broke her heart to see the hurt in his eyes. He didn't seem quite as self-assured, (Vickie would call it arrogant), as usual. He had lost weight too, and she thought he looked almost too thin. He was still tall and handsome though. She wanted to put her arms around him and hold him, but she knew she mustn't do it. He was too vulnerable right now, and she was all mixed up in her mind about Dave.

"Have you had any threatening phone calls, or calls where no one is there?" asked Bud, as he rubbed Muffy's ears.

"No, not at all. Remember the calls we kept getting three years ago before all hell broke loose?" asked Cassie with a smile. "That was an exciting summer."

"A little too exciting for my taste," said Jack grimly. "You don't want to get into a situation like that again. I assume that you've got a good alarm system throughout the house. Do you mind if I have a look at it?"

"Sure, I'll take you. Vickie can stay here and entertain Bud," said Cassie quickly.

It was a bit awkward at first, as they talked seriously about alarm systems, and double locks, but then Cassie stopped and took Jack's hands into hers.

His heart was hammering as he looked into Cassie's big blue eyes, so full of love and concern for him. It took great self control, and a sense of honour, to keep himself from putting his strong arms around her, and kissing her just the way she needed to be kissed.

Chapter Twenty-Seven

"How are you doing, Jack? I've thought of you so often since Darla died. It must have been dreadful for you."

"Oh, I'm hanging in there. It's strange with her gone, but she was very unhappy. I just wish I had realized sooner just how alone she felt. In her eyes, I was a terrible husband. No wonder she drank."

"Stop it. You mustn't beat yourself up with guilt. You were a good husband to her, and there was likely nothing you could have done differently." Cassie didn't really know what the situation between Jack and Darla had been, but she couldn't stand to see him hurting this way.

They chatted companionably, as they did a complete tour of the house. Cassie couldn't resist showing Jack the panic room. He was impressed with it, and pleased that Cassie had such a good hideaway.

"We would have loved a place like this when we were going together," he laughed. "Remember some of the crazy places we found where we could be alone?" He waggled his eyebrows at her, and gave her a leering grin.

Cass couldn't help but laugh too. It was starting to get pretty hot and steamy in that small room, but Jack's joking had broken the tension to a certain degree. Cassie still wanted to be in his arms, to smell his clean man smell, to run her fingers along that intriguing scar. She wanted to feel those sensuous lips on hers. She was breathing heavily as she turned away, and hurried from the tiny hiding place.

He was still so darn attractive, that Cass imagined every widow and divorcee in town would be after him. She couldn't resist asking, "Are all the women lined up to bring you casseroles these days?"

Jack just grinned and shook his head. "I must admit there've been a few, but I don't always answer the door. I didn't realize that there were so many unattached women around. They make me nervous."

Cassie felt the sting of jealousy, as she pictured one gorgeous woman after another ringing Jack's doorbell. She had no right to be jealous, but she was.

After returning to the sunroom, where Bud and Vickie were chatting amiably, they discussed the problem some more. Eventually, they reassured the women that they would get right on the intriguing case of Harold Johnston, aka John Duncan, aka Bill Gordon.

"We'll start with the Panama City Beach police, and go from there," said Bud. "Don't you worry, we'll get this creep, who's apparently making a career out of marrying rich women, and then killing them. He's going to make a mistake, and we'll get him."

Cassie and Vickie just looked at each other. They had heard something similar on numerous occasions during the past three years, and it didn't always prove to be true. The killers had always been caught with more than a little help from Cass and Vickie. They didn't place a lot of faith in the police, although they liked these two detectives very much, in Cassie's case, she liked one of them way too much.

"Meantime," said Jack, " you two have to be very careful."

Again they looked at each other and grinned. Where had they heard that warning before?

Holding up his fingers, Jack began to tick off some suggestions. "Always have the alarm on when you're inside. Don't stay here alone, either one of you. Carry your cell phones with you at all times, even around the house. I'm not going to suggest that you get a gun, because, knowing you two, you'd likely shoot yourselves, or each other." He looked at them seriously, but they could see laughter in his eyes.

"I don't think the killer knows what he's up against with you gals, but don't take any chances. Leave the police work to the professionals. I know we've given you this spiel before, and you've never listened, but this time you really must."

Bud jumped in at this point. "This Johnston character sounds dangerous, and pretty resourceful. If he's followed you all the way to Niagara Falls, then he's really anxious to finish the job. We can't stress enough just how important it is to stay alert. Stay out of crowds, and don't go any place alone.

A guy like this, who's been able to get away with murder in the past, feels that he's invincible. He thinks he can't be touched. He's sure that he's smarter than anyone else, and he's determined to get his own way. He focuses on anyone who could stop him, and he'll go to any lengths to get that person out of the picture. He'll even go beyond the point of good sense.

He's on a mission, and feels that nothing or no one can stop him. He'll start taking chances, and he'll make a mistake. That's when we'll get him."

Jack added, "From what you say, we know that he's good at changing his appearance. The only thing he can't change is his size, so that's what you keep in mind. Watch out, and beware of any man who looks to be big and brawny. It doesn't matter whether he has freckles on his face, or red hair, or a huge nose. It could be our guy, just using an imaginative disguise. Don't be taken in, and don't develop a false sense of security. We'll get him, but it may not be easy, and it may not be soon."

"Sounds like we're in for a pretty dull time, hiding in the house till you catch this fiend," complained Cassie.

"So what? At least you'll still be alive. You can barricade yourselves in this beautiful home and be totally safe. That's what I'd like to see you do. We'll keep in close contact, and you call us if anything at all scares you or makes you suspicious. Oh, and don't accept any more parcels. Just have them leave anything outside on the bench under the trees, and call us right away. Got it?"

"Jack, we can't live that way. Surely you'll catch him in a few days," said Cassie, hopefully.

"That's right, you guys. Who wants to stay cooped up for days or weeks? We aren't going to let him take away our freedom. We'll be careful, but we aren't going to become prisoners," declared Vickie, belligerently.

Jack sighed, and looked at Bud. Bud was not saying a word, but he was shaking his head.

"I've got an idea," he said, suddenly. "Cassie, do you still own that cottage in Muskoka?"

"Yes, of course, although we rarely go up there. It's been in the family a long time, as you know. Why?"

"Well, it's very unlikely that our mystery man would know anything about it, or be able to find out about it. That would be a perfect place for you to hide, if you aren't happy about staying here. Why don't you and Vickie sneak out and go up there? We could think of a way to get you out of the house safely without him seeing you, just in case he's watching."

"That's a great idea," added Jack. "Let's talk about it for a minute."

Cassie was happy to have any excuse to keep Jack there a little longer. Just looking at him, and thinking of days gone by, gave her a certain bittersweet pleasure.

What a fool I am, she told herself, as she tried to concentrate on the conversation.

"You could go boating, and lie in the sun, relax and enjoy yourselves, just as long as we can sneak you out of here. What do you think?" Jack felt like saying that he would move in with the two of them, but knew that wouldn't be a viable solution.

"That's a real possibility, Jack. We could have a wonderful time up there, and we could stay until you catch him, provided it doesn't take you more than a week or so. I don't want to leave Sugar and Muffin for too long, although I could get someone from the cattery to stay with them. No, actually, I think I would want them out of the house too," Cassie added thoughtfully. "If he broke in, he might be so angry that we weren't here, that he could take out his anger on Sugar and Muff."

"I wonder whether Kitty and Steffie could get away for a few days," suggested Vickie, suddenly very enthusiastic. "There's always safety in numbers. I'd feel a whole lot better if there were four of us up there. They could come over here, ostensibly to visit us. We could sneak into their car in the garage, and hide in the back under a blanket or something. If the murderer was watching the house, he would just see the two of them driving away again after an hour or so. That wouldn't be suspicious at all."

"Yes it would," Cassie disagreed. "We have a three car garage, and there are only two vehicles in it. It would look too suspicious if Kitty and Steff just came for an afternoon, and put their car in the garage. It would be more normal just to park it on the driveway. But, if we had them for a sleepover, a regular old hen party, it would be normal for them to use the garage.

They could stay a couple of nights, and we would take their car back and forth out of the garage. If the stalker is watching, he wouldn't think much about it. Then, when we want to get out of here without him knowing, we could have them over, and while the car is in the garage, we could sneak into it from the house. We'll hide on the floor in the back seat, and ride right on out of here. He won't suspect a thing."

Cass was delighted with the plot. She loved mysteries and intrigue as much as Vickie did, and would welcome an excuse to go up to the cottage in some secretive way.

"They could drive us up to the cottage and stay for a few days, or as long as they wanted," said Vickie. "I'm sure he wouldn't follow them, because he would think that we were still here in the house, and obviously, we are the ones he wants. Yes, it could really work. It sounds plausible."

"Wait a minute, though. If Kitty and Steffie wanted to come back, that would leave us stranded up there without a car. I'm not sure that's such a good idea," she admitted. Vickie loved excitement even more than Cassie did, but there was also a pragmatic and practical side to her nature.

"If you want to do this," said Jack, "we can work out all the logistics. Frankly, I'd feel much more comfortable if I thought you were right here, locked up in the house. Since, however, I don't trust that you'll stay locked up, then Muskoka is a good alternative. I think it can be done. You can always rent a car up there, or better still, we'll get you a car. We'll borrow one from someone who has no connection to you. Do you think that Kitty and Steffie would go for it?"

"Yes, I'm sure they will. Kitty's mom and dad love to come over from Toronto to look after the boutique and her cats. Kitty and Steffie love it up in cottage country. Kitty's parents have two cottages up there on a different Muskoka lake. Actually, that's where she met Mitch. The four of us could have a great time. We'll talk to them tonight and see how soon we can go."

"Well, don't talk on the phone, just in case this guy has managed to tap it. We'll send someone over to sweep the place for any bugs, although I doubt he would have gone that far. Anyway, invite the gals over for a drink or something, or for the "hen party." Just be careful not to tell anyone else."

"Of course I'll have to tell my cat sitter," said Cassie, frowning.

"No, don't even do that. You can tell her you're going to Toronto or Montreal. Don't even suggest cottage country."

"But what if something happened to one of the cats while we're away? She wouldn't be able to get in touch with us."

"I would get in touch with you if anything happened to the cats. We're going to put every man available on this, and hopefully, the perp will be in custody within a few days."

"Okay," agreed Cass, reluctantly.

Just then, she gave a little gasp. "Guys, I know what's been bugging me all day. It finally came to me. We described how the killer looked that night we saw him getting off the elevator, but I forgot about how he smelled. He had a very distinct lime smell about him, as if he had put on too much lime scented after-shave. I never thought to tell the Panama City Police about that. It might be something he wears all the time, and I remember now that I smelled it the night he tried to throw me overboard. Did you smell it too, Vic?"

Vickie shook her head, slowly. "You know me, Cass. My nose is always stuffed up with one allergy or another. I really don't remember smelling it."

"Well, that's a help," agreed Jack. "Anything else you can remember, no matter how seemingly insignificant, you call us."

"In the meantime," cautioned Bud, "you really have to stay here with the alarm on. Just make the most of this beautiful place, until we can get the plans all settled. Can we trust you?"

Muff was now sitting on Bud's shoulder, and seemed to enjoy surveying the world from this new height.

Both women laughingly agreed that they would behave, and stay cooped up here till they could discuss plans with Kitty and Steffie. They weren't laughing, however, as they bolted the door, and put on the alarm. They suddenly felt like a couple of prisoners, who couldn't wait to make their escape.

Chapter Twenty-Eight

Everything fell into place quite easily. A trip to the cottage seemed a great idea. Kitty and Steffie loved the thought of another vacation, and were able to make all the arrangements for Kitty's two little cats, and for the boutique. Kitty's parents were always there when she needed them. Her boyfriend, Mitch, was away on tour with his latest book, so that worked well.

Cassie and Vickie had a lot of laughs, trying to sneak Sugar Plum and Muffin out of the house, to take them to their sitter. Cass thought of putting them into a cat carrier, then into a big cardboard box. They were in the back seat, with some folded clothes over the top. It just looked like an innocent big box of clothing. Even if the killer was watching them, he wouldn't suspect anything. Actually, they were pretty sure that he wasn't watching them. Besides, they did all this undercover finagling within the confines of the garage, so it was unlikely that he could see anything.

Because Cassie's new home had a long driveway, he would either have to be staked out on the Niagara Parkway, waiting for them to come out, or he would have to walk down that driveway, and hide in the bushes near the house. It all seemed too complicated, and very unlikely. The guy was too clever to do anything amateurish.

The day they actually left for the Muskoka cottage, they were all laughing, as Cassie and Vickie crouched down in the back, under a couple of blankets. It seemed so ridiculous, and so unnecessary, but they had promised Jack and Bud that they would be really careful getting out of the house without being seen. The tinted windows in Steffie's car helped too. It was difficult to see into the back, unless you were right up to the window. There seemed absolutely no way that their stalker and would-be killer could be spying on them, yet they took every precaution imaginable.

They drove down to the boutique, "just in case". They were hoping that, on the far-fetched chance that he was indeed following them, once he saw that Kitty and Steffie were going back to their shop, he would give up, and go back to watching Cassie's place, which would now be empty. It was all speculation on their parts, but it was fun in a silly sort of way, and they made it into a game.

Mid morning traffic wasn't too bad, and they waited until they were onto the highway before Cassie and Vickie emerged from their cramped positions on the floor of the backseat.

"That was one of the silliest things we've ever done, and we've done lots of silly things," laughed Vickie, trying to smooth her ruffled hair.

"Hey, we're pretty good at this undercover stuff," grinned Kitty.

The others groaned at her pun.

The four hour trip was uneventful. They sang, they chatted, and they were just four good friends, out on another adventure.

When they drove down the cottage lane, they were pleased to see the borrowed car which Jack had provided. It was parked under a tree, waiting for them.

"Good old Jack came through," said Steffie happily, as she stepped from the car. She had a soft spot in her heart for Jack. He had been extremely kind and helpful, when she had gone through a devastating crisis involving her brother, the previous summer.

The old Muskoka cottage seemed to welcome them. Cass felt guilty at how seldom she managed to come up for a week or even a week-end.

It was a beautiful old cottage, one which she had inherited along with all her money. It had been in her family for years, and could have told some intriguing stories. Although she had spent many wonderful summers here as a little girl, once she had actually inherited it, she felt strangely uncomfortable, thinking that she really didn't belong here.

It was supposed to be Jenny's cottage, but Jenny was dead. Was Jenny haunting it? She could be. She had certainly hated Cassie enough, when Cass got all the money. Well, Cassandra Meredith was not going to let her occasional moments of doubt spoil this unexpected vacation. She and her three pals were going to make the most of their time here.

The five bedroom cottage was built of Muskoka stone and cedar, and stood alone on a bit of a hill, looking out into the main part of the lake. With a thousand feet of shoreline, there were no cottages on either side. In a way, it was a lonely place, but in another way, the solitude was very soothing.

One year, a Hollywood movie company had tried to dicker with the family, because they wanted to shoot a movie there. It was to be a scary thriller, but the family had refused. They had all loved the cottage, and hadn't wanted to give it up for a full summer and fall, but it would have been interesting.

Cass noticed that the perennials planted around the cottage were all in bloom, along with the wildflowers, which grew in abundance in all directions. There were many big granite outcroppings, and Steffie was already planning some serious sketching sessions. She sighed with pleasure as she stood gazing around. What a beautiful place to spend a few happy days.

It didn't take them long to unpack the car, open all the windows to air the place, and choose their rooms. Three of the bedrooms faced the lake, with the other two facing back down the trail, which was bounded by maples, evergreens, and tall white birch.

The bedrooms facing the lake, opened onto a big cedar deck, which ran right across the front of the cottage. Everyone wanted to be on the lakeside, so Kitty and Steffie took the room with the two double beds. That left a room each for Vickie and for Cassie.

Getting into their bathing suits was next on the agenda. This unexpected holiday, whether it was a few days or a couple of weeks, was going to be fun. They planned to put all thoughts of the killer right out of their minds. They would stay alert to danger, but would not let it spoil their fun. That, at least, was the plan. Unfortunately they had forgotten that fate sometimes steps in at the most unexpected times, just to stir things up a bit.

Taking a small cooler full of drinks and snacks, and a big bag of peanuts for the friendly little chipmunks, who spent their days scampering back and forth, they headed to the dock.

Cassie busied herself getting one of the boats out of the boat house, while the others unloaded their sun tan lotions, visors, beach towels, and books, from their beach bags. They were ready to spend the afternoon in the water, on the dock, and in the boat. It was glorious.

"Cass, when you were little, did you come to the cottage often?" asked Kitty, rubbing lotion onto her legs. With her fair skin, she had to be careful out in the sun.

"Oh ya. We spent entire summers here. You know how much fun that can be, Kitty. You grew up spending every summer at your cottage too, didn't you?"

"Yep. We were cottage bums. My sister Lacey and I thought it was the most magical place on earth. I still love it there. That's where I met Mitch, you know."

"And that's where you almost drowned in that freak canoe accident," added Steffie, settling her big floppy hat on her head.

"That was a night I'll never forget," said Kitty, shaking her head. "It was scary, but Mitch turned out to be wonderful. We took shelter in a tiny old cabin with virtually nothing in it, and we spent the night wrapped in a scratchy old blanket, sitting in front of a lovely fire. Our clothes were soaked, so we were naked under that blanket. What a feeling that was!

At that point we didn't really know each other at all, and it was his fault that we had found ourselves in that situation. He had been so stubborn about going out for a canoe ride, even though I was sure that there was a storm brewing. We were both dumb, but it turned out well," she added, with a satisfied grin.

"There were mouse droppings all over, and big spider webs, but we sat there drinking rot gut whiskey to warm up, and it seemed romantic in a scary sort of way. We often laugh about it."

It soon got too hot on the dock, so they piled into the boat, and went for a cooling ride. There were many boats out on the lake, and they waved at all of them, as they flew past.

"Darn it," said Cassie, slowing the boat down, and turning to her friends. "We could have gone over to Clevelands House for a drink on their deck, but I never thought to bring any money. What a dork."

"You are the dork of dorks," agreed Vickie, with a laugh.

"You are the Queen of dorks," grinned Kitty.

"You are the biggest dork who ever came around the corner," asserted Steffie, punching her lightly on the arm.

"Well, did any of you bums bring money or credit cards?" inquired Cass hopefully, ignoring their slanderous jibes.

"No," they all chorused at once.

"Never mind, we'll do it tomorrow. Right now, we'll go back to our own dock and have something cool and delicious. Later, if we feel like it, we'll do some canoeing."

Cassie was thinking about Jack, and about how lovely it would be to come here some time with him. That made her cross with herself for being so ridiculous. She was a married woman with a perfectly good husband of her own. Why couldn't she get Jack out of her heart and head?

Now that Darla was dead, Jack was available, and the tempting thoughts were driving her crazy. Somehow she had to put him out of her life forever, but she knew there wasn't much hope of that. He was as much a part of her as anyone in her life, as much as her husband, and as much as her children. She sighed, and tried to think of something else.

Suddenly an errant and unwelcome thought crossed her mind, as they cruised back to the cottage. If, by any chance, the killer managed to track them here to Muskoka, they would be sitting ducks. The only way out was through the heavy bush on either side, across the lake by boat, or back down the winding road behind the cottage. Not one of the choices was really feasible. She wasn't about to go running through the bush again, as she had done in Apalachicola. Besides, this northern bush was much thicker, and, for all they knew, it could be full of black bears, or even snakes. Cassie was not interested in any more snake encounters.

Getting away by boat might be the best choice, but it would take time to get all four of them down to the boat house, get the boat started up, and make a getaway. The killer would have shot all of them by the time they did all that. Taking the winding road route would be useless. Presumably, he would have them blocked off with his vehicle.

Well, they should talk about it tonight, and devise some sort of plan. What she did know for sure was that they would have to stay pretty close together at all times, and they should each keep a cell phone handy. It could be fatal if they were scattered all over the property, each one doing her own thing, if and when Harold Johnston did show up.

Wicked or not, Cass knew she would feel a lot safer if Jack could be here beside her. This trip to the lonely cottage might not have been such a good idea.

Chapter Twenty-Nine

Two nights later, the women were feeling relaxed and happy. Niagara Falls seemed far away, and in their minds, the murderer was even more remote. With the peace and tranquility of Muskoka working its magic, it seemed impossible that some stranger could be plotting to kill Cass and Vickie. It simply made no sense.

In cottage country, their thoughts were more likely to turn to the sounds of the deep blue water lapping against the dock. They thought of the warmth of the sun, radiating on their wet bodies, as they climbed out of the water. They relived the invigorating feeling of the wind in their hair, as they had cruised the lake in the big inboard/outboard bow rider. Stalkers, killers, people who sent black roses, just didn't exist in Muskoka, or so they told themselves.

They were sitting in the gazebo down by the water's edge, and asking each other questions from the Trivial Pursuit cards. They were using a flashlight to read the cards, and were doing more laughing and wine drinking than actual thinking about the answers.

"Sh, what's that noise?" asked Steffie, peering out the screen. "There's something in the bushes."

She turned the flashlight on the bushes, and sure enough, even as she was speaking, two big raccoons, the masked bandits of the night, emerged from the trees, and wandered onto the dock. They were obviously unconcerned about the women sitting in the gazebo, and were busy looking for food.

Tonight they were in luck. Earlier in the afternoon, the four friends had been drinking cokes and eating chips and Oreo cookies. When a short rain shower had taken them by surprise, they had gathered their things and made a run for the cottage. Inadvertently, the bag of cookies had been left behind on the table.

The raccoons knew they had hit the mother lode. With their very dexterous fingers, they managed to open the package and help themselves.

The women sat silently watching. Contrary to popular belief, raccoons do not always wash their food before eating it. They sat there, taking one cookie at a time from the package, as if they were two old friends in a coffee shop. It was funny to watch them.

Kitty wondered whether she could get them to eat from her hand. She did it all the time at her cottage. There were always a few daring enough to come right up to her, if she was offering food, and she had found their long, relatively soft fingers very gentle. There was a bag of pretzel sticks in the gazebo, so she took a few as quietly as possible, and walked very slowly onto the dock.

The raccoons paused in their munching, and looked at her with a certain cautious interest. She was holding out a pretzel stick in each hand, and talking very quietly to them. They could smell the food, and whatever fear of her they might have had, was overcome by the interest in the pretzels.

The smaller of the two took a few tentative steps towards her. Kitty kept on with her tentative steps towards him. They met in the middle, and the raccoon very gently took the pretzel from her hand. In doing so, his paw touched her fingers, and that little paw with the long slim fingers, felt like soft rubber.

The second raccoon, not to be outdone, moved to her more quickly, and grabbing the pretzel, he waddled a few feet away to eat it.

Kitty had taken several pretzels with her, so she repeated the actions, until all the treats were gone. She knew that, for several sound reasons, it was bad to feed wild animals, but it had been so tempting to get close to these lovely creatures. It was always a magical experience for her, when she could feed raccoons or chipmunks from her hand. Her three companions in the gazebo were quite mesmerized by the little tableau.

"Oh, Kitty, that was great. I wish I'd been able to take some pictures," cried Steffie, as Kitty returned to the gazebo.

"Good for you, girl," said Cass. "You've just made two new friends. If we're down here again at night, they'll be back looking for more treats."

"Well, come on gals, it's getting chilly. Let's go back to the cottage, put on a nice fire, and talk dirty about men," suggested Vickie, with a grin, which no one could see in the dark.

The stars were gradually appearing, so they stopped to gaze at them, make some silent wishes, and point out the ones they could recognize. Unfortunately there were as many mosquitoes as there were stars, so they cut short the stargazing, and headed inside, totally unaware of the excitement which lay ahead.

Kitty was the most domesticated of the group, and she loved to bake. She had brought all the ingredients for some butterscotch brownies, and chocolate chip cookies. Although it was late, while her three pals made a fire, and poured some wine, Kitty headed to the kitchen to bake the treats.

The outside back light was on, and it illuminated the parking space behind the cottage, as well as a little way down the road. As Kitty was mixing the brownies, she looked out the window, and was startled to see something or someone disappearing into the bushes.

She wasn't sure just what she had seen, so she stood there quietly, staring down the road. Nothing moved. What could it have been? Had she really seen anything? Was it just a shadow made by the wind blowing tree branches? Maybe, but not likely. Should she mention it to Cassie? No, probably not. She must have been mistaken.

She kept glancing out the window, as she finished the baking, and cleaned up the counters. There was no further movement out there, so she decided that it had been nothing. Setting the timer for the oven, she turned out the kitchen light and went to join her friends.

By the time that the brownies and cookies were baked, it was time for bed. Kitty had finally mentioned her little fright to her pals, and they all trooped into the kitchen to stand looking out the window. There was nothing out there, not even a skunk or a rabbit.

"You were seeing things, Kit Kat," laughed Steffie. "If it was our Monster Man, he'd be eaten alive by mosquitoes by now, and he'd be running out of that bush."

Kitty had convinced herself that she hadn't seen anything, so she changed the subject. "These things are too hot to pack away in a tin yet, so I'm going to leave them here on the counter over night. I'll just cover them lightly with some foil, and I'll ice the brownies in the morning."

They had all done some water skiing that day, and were feeling the effects of the muscles which hadn't been used for a while. The combination of the sun, the wind, the exercise, and the wine, had made them sleepy, and they were happy to check all the locks, and head for bed.

Unfortunately, no one noticed that the kitchen window was open about eight inches.

Before going to sleep, Cassie went out onto the deck, just to look at the stars again, and to enjoy the beautiful night. She also wanted to make sure that there was nobody skulking around. She was a bit concerned as to whether Kitty had really seen someone out at the back. Surely the killer couldn't possibly have tracked them all the way up here.

She had no way of knowing that Jenny Wainwright, the strange young girl from her family, who had tried to kill her three years ago, had also stood on this deck one dark and velvety night, before carrying out her Machiavellian plans. Cass had no way of knowing that the very bed in which she intended to sleep, was the bed on which Jenny had lain, plotting against her brother. Cass didn't know the details of what had happened here, and she never would know, but she had an eerie feeling that Jenny's ghost wasn't far away.

Jenny had hated and resented her, and she certainly wouldn't like to know that Cassie was now enjoying the cottage which was supposed to be Jenny's.

Cass shivered as she returned to her room. It was as if someone had just walked over her grave. She wished she had Sugar Plum and Muffy to keep her company tonight. She also wished that she and Vickie had taken the double room. This was a night for company, not for sleeping alone.

She realized that maybe it had been foolish of them to come all the way up here, so far from help. She wished she was back in her lovely new home, with the secure alarm system, and that reassuring little panic room. They were way too isolated, and calling 911 would be next to useless. By the time the police could get out here, the killer could have done away with all of them, and made his escape.

While Cassie was thinking these scary thoughts, Kitty and Steffie were giggling like schoolgirls in their room, and Vickie was already sound asleep in hers.

Kitty had no idea what time it was when she wakened from a sound sleep. She lay very still, listening to the sounds of the night. What had she heard? What had wakened her?

Suddenly, she sat up in bed. She had definitely heard something coming from downstairs. Was it just the trees slapping against the windows? There didn't really seem to be a breeze tonight, so that wasn't it. Maybe it was a bear up on the back porch. She remembered the bear at her cottage last year, when she had been alone in the gazebo. Yes, it was likely a bear. Should she get up and go downstairs? "Not a chance," she muttered to herself.

As she was trying to decide what to do, Steffie sat up and said, "Did you hear something just now?"

"Yes, I did. It must have been an animal out on the back deck. It sounded as if it was coming from the kitchen area," she whispered.

"There it is again," said Steffie, reaching for the flashlight. Somehow, it didn't seem right to turn on the lights. "Come on, we'd better waken Vic and Cassie. If the killer has found us, we need to be together and get out of here. Bring your cell phone, and let's go."

Chapter Thirty

The tone of Steffie's voice startled Kitty. Steffie really thought it was the killer! That shadow Kitty thought she had seen out the kitchen window, must have been their stalker. How had he been able to find them way up here in Muskoka? More importantly, how were they going to get out of this jam?

It was easy to waken Vickie. She got up quickly, not making a sound. She also grabbed her flashlight, and stopped to put on her running shoes. Vickie was thinking ahead. If they had to make a break for it, slippers would be useless. She went to waken Cassie, while Kitty and Steffie went back to their room to find their shoes.

Cass was a very sound sleeper, and Vickie had to shake her shoulder and put her hand over her mouth momentarily, to keep her from calling out in fear. Cass knew right away what was wrong. "Is he here?" she asked, slipping into her runners, and grabbing her flashlight. She had made sure that there was a flashlight with fresh batteries in each bedroom, just in case the power went out.

"We don't know. We've all heard some sounds coming from downstairs, but maybe they're coming from some animal out on the back deck off the kitchen. We need to decide what to do, and we don't have much time."

"Okay, let's go out on the balcony, and we'll make a plan."

The four of them glided softly out the door, and onto the long deck which covered the front of the cottage on the second floor.

"Look," whispered Cassie, "if it's our guy, I think our best plan is to try to get down to the boat. That means we have to get off this deck somehow. It's too high to jump, but maybe we could tie the sheets together and lower ourselves."

"Are you joking?" interrupted Steffie. "By the time we strip the beds and tie sheets together, our friend will be up here having his way with us. No, we need to arm ourselves with something or other, and sneak downstairs. If we're really quiet, we might be able to get out the front door and down to the boat before he realizes what we're doing."

"That sounds pretty good," said Kitty, "but I don't think we can do it without alerting him. What the heck do you think he's doing down there? Could he be pouring gasoline all around? Maybe he plans to burn us up while we sleep." The thought was terrifying.

They stood looking helplessly at each other. Vickie was peering over the balcony, to see whether there was any way they could jump. That didn't look possible. There was, however, one old oak tree, whose branches came pretty close to the deck. Cass wondered whether they could reach a sturdy branch, and shimmy down the trunk. It always looked possible in movies, but she didn't think there was time to give it a try. If he was in the cottage, he'd be upstairs momentarily.

"Okay," said Cassie, after a moment's gloomy silence. "Get whatever weapon you can find – scissors I guess, or maybe curling irons. We could hit him with those. We could also use the flashlights to hit him. If he has a gun we're royally screwed. If, however, he planned to burn us out, or maybe suffocate us with pillows, we've got an advantage. There are four of us and only one of him. Whichever one he attacks, the other three jump on his back and stick him in the eyes with the scissors, and hit him on the head with the curling irons. Even though he's big and brawny, he can't fight all four of us at once."

"Unless he has a gun," they all said at the same time.

No one had any other bright ideas, so they decided to tiptoe downstairs, and try to find out where he was, and what he was doing. There wasn't much point in hiding upstairs and maybe being roasted alive.

As they moved quietly along the hall, Vickie asked herself what she was doing here. She and Cassie had been in so many tight places over the past few years. What was it about Cass that seemed to draw trouble? Cass was the best and dearest friend she had ever had, and she loved her more than a sister, but she did tend to get them into trouble time and time again.

Vickie wondered whether she should just pack up and go back to Vancouver, if they got past this little bump in the road, that is. Then she came to her senses. She and Cass were in trouble. They would get through this together or not at all. Now was not the time to bail out on her life long friend. She wished, however, that one of them had a gun. That would even the playing field a bit. At least they might have a chance against this wife killing madman. Sighing, and shaking her head, she realized that giving a gun to Cassie or Vickie would be like giving a lit stick of dynamite to a baby. Somehow she knew that they would likely manage to shoot themselves in the foot.

Steffie decided that she would go first. "Let's not fool ourselves," she said, in a practical manner. "No matter who goes first, he's going to try to kill all of us, so it doesn't much matter. Maybe he'll be so surprised to see me instead of Cassie, though, that it will give us a moment's jump on him. Cass should go last. We'll give her as much protection as we can. Vickie, you go right ahead of her, and Kit-Kat, you follow me."

"Well, on that happy note, let's go," said Vickie. Cass didn't argue about being last, but she kept checking behind her, in case he had crept up the stairs while they were out on the balcony, and was planning to attack them from the rear.

Four women being totally silent is an impossible task, but they did very well. There might be four lives on the line here, and they understood the danger.

They made it to the foot of the stairs with no problem. Now what? They were tempted to make a run for the front door, but didn't think they could do it quietly enough. They were trying not to use the flashlights in case it alerted him, and it was pretty dark in the cottage. A welcome bit of moonlight was coming through the windows, enough, at least, to help them find their way.

As they stood there, undecided, there were more strange bumping and shuffling noises coming from the kitchen. Vickie had the wild idea that maybe he was bringing in luggage or trunks to use for hiding their bodies.

They slunk down the hall towards the kitchen, Cassie still looking over her shoulder, in case of a rear attack. Steffie was still in the lead, and she stood quietly at the kitchen door, just listening. Her heart was pounding, and she wanted to be anywhere but where she was.

As her eyes adjusted to the darkness, she couldn't believe what she was seeing. Letting out a whoop, she reached for the wall switch, and turned on the light.

Everyone crowded around to watch in disbelief, as two very naughty raccoons looked up, then scurried back out through the tear in the screened window, through which they had entered. They had been sitting on the counter, having a butterscotch brownie and chocolate chip cookie party. The treats were half gone, when the bandits were so rudely interrupted. A loaf of bread had been knocked onto the floor, along with a plastic butter dish and a knife. Cutting through the screen with their sharp and clever little fingers, knocking things off the counter, and huffing and snuffing while they devoured the cookies, were the noises the women had heard.

Weak with relief, they laughed until they cried. The joke really was on Kitty. She had gone to all the trouble of baking the goodies, and the two pretzel eating raccoons with whom she had felt a certain rapport, had invited themselves in to gobble up her efforts. It was hilarious.

"Oh, I wish we had been able to take some pictures," cried Vickie, wiping tears from her eyes. "I don't know which was funnier, the raccoons on the counter eating brownies, or the look on your face, Kitty."

They decided they might as well have a cup of tea while they were so wide awake. They could always sleep in the next day. Unfortunately, they couldn't enjoy any of the fresh goodies, as the raccoons had walked all over the ones which were left. What a mess they had made!

Kitty was a good sport about it, and laughed with the others. She said maybe Mitch would write the misadventure into his next book, four idiotic women preparing to do battle with two little raccoons. That made them laugh some more.

Vickie bemoaned the loss of the treats. She was the one with the sweet tooth, and she had been looking forward to a few brownies for breakfast.

"Well, your heart was in the right place, Kitty," soothed Cassie, as she gave her a hug. "They smelled delicious, and at least we all had a taste right when they came out of the oven.

Come to think of it, I should have known it wasn't the killer. My scalp always tingles when we're in danger, and it wasn't tingling at all. That was stupid of me. I could have saved us a very scary time. Besides that," she added, with a frown, "I can't believe that we were so careless that we left that window open. Jack would cut out our hearts if he knew."

"Let's forget Jack, and the cup of tea, and have a glass of wine instead," suggested Steffie. "You know, the one thing that this little episode has pointed out, is that we aren't the least bit prepared, if this guy shows up. We really aren't safe here. As a matter of fact, I think we're a bunch of morons to have left the safety of the house. In spite of all the fun we've been having, maybe we should just pack it in and go home. We'd all feel safer there."

Chapter Thirty-One

When Jack heard their story about the raccoons, he and Bud had a good laugh. It did, however, point out the fact that the women weren't nearly as safe there as they were at home. They were safe as long as the killer didn't know where they were, but on the outside chance that he could find them, Jack knew that they would be much safer back in the city.

Their safety, however, would depend on them staying inside Cassie's house, with the alarm on at all times. It wasn't a very tempting proposition, but they half-heartedly consented. Their few days at the cottage had been wonderful, but they all agreed reluctantly that they needed to get back to the safety of the house, before the stalker found them.

Everything appeared fine back at the beautiful home on the Niagara River Parkway. Sugar Plum and Muffy were returned safely, and were once again ensconced in their familiar setting. They spent the first hour or so, inspecting and sniffing everything in sight. Finally satisfied that things were back to normal in their little cat world, they were now sitting in the window of the library, looking out at Cass and Vickie.

The two friends had snuck out to sit on a double swing in the backyard, overlooking the Niagara River. From where they sat, the river looked calm and cool. It was flowing along in a deceptively gentle manner. The women knew, however, as did all Niagara residents, that the lower river could be cruel and duplicitous, as it meandered down to the treacherous whirlpool, before spilling itself into Lake Ontario.

The fact that they shouldn't be sitting out there on that sunny, hot afternoon, made it all the more enjoyable. Poor Jack didn't have a hope of keeping them locked in that house. It was a good idea on paper, but that was as far as it went. It was just too nice a day to be cooped up inside, and what Jack Willinger and Bud Lang didn't know, wouldn't hurt anyone, or so they told themselves.

"Miss Vickie, I think that we could slip into the car, and drive over to St. Catharines for a while. There are two new stores which have opened this summer, and I'm interested in buying some really spiffy patio furniture," said Cassie, with mischief in her eyes.

"You know exactly what Jack would say about that," replied Vickie, standing up and ready to go. She wasn't about to argue. Vickie was a free spirit, and she loved a challenge. If Cass was ready to "fly the coop," then Vickie would be right there beside her.

"I know the guys wouldn't like it if they knew, but we'll go crazy if we have to stay cooped up here too long. I suspect that murdering twerp is happily hidden away in Mexico. Why would he risk getting caught, by coming across the border just to kill us? It doesn't really make a lot of sense. We've likely blown this all out of proportion.

Come on, let's get changed and go. We'll be there and back before Jack and Bud have any idea that we aren't languishing in the house."

Within half an hour, they were on their way to St. Catharines. Cassie was driving, and Vickie kept turning around to see if they were being followed. As far as she could tell, they weren't, but Vickie couldn't really tell one car from another, so she wondered whether she would even notice the same car trailing along behind them.

"How's your scalp, pal?" she asked, looking at Cassie, with a grin on her face.

"My scalp is fine, no tingling," laughed Cassie, as they drove into the small lot behind their first destination.

They had a great look around the new store, but Cassie didn't see anything which took her fancy. Vickie saw some outdoor placemats which she loved, so she bought them, along with the glasses and plates to match. "I'm hardly ever home long enough to use these," she admitted, as they got back into the car, "but I couldn't resist. I guess that's what having money does for a person. You can indulge yourself with impulse buying, and never worry about the price.

By the way, I didn't tell you how nice you look in that outfit. You should have had that on the cruise."

Cassie was wearing a pair of beautifully tailored white slacks, a sleeveless white silk turtleneck top, and a navy blue summer blazer. For fun, and in an attempt to disguise herself a bit, she was wearing sunglasses, and a floppy white hat. Vickie thought she looked like an elegant movie star.

Cassie found two sets of patio furniture which she loved, and couldn't make up her mind which one to buy.

"Oh, you've got to buy this turquoise and white redwood one, Cass. It's gorgeous. Do you know how good I would look lounging on this in my little white bikini, with a drink in one hand and a book in the other!"

"Vickie, you'd look good lounging on anything, but I've never in my life seen you in a little white bikini. Do you really have one?"

"No, but I might get one if you buy this furniture," joked her friend.

" I think you're right. I do like this one best. Just let me look a little more, in case there's anything better. If not, I'm going to buy this one."

As she was comparing one set to another, Cass gradually became aware that her scalp had started tingling. Wait a minute. Was that the faint aroma of lime she could detect?

She stood there, sniffing the air like an old hound dog, while looking around the store. As far as she could tell though, there wasn't anyone who looked like the stalker. Wait, had she caught a glimpse of a tall, well built man just disappearing behind those ficus trees? No, she was just imagining things. She had to stop being so paranoid. Her scalp was likely tingling because she wasn't used to wearing a hat. She decided not to mention the tingling scalp to Vickie, at least not right now.

Vickie had wandered away to look at something else, but caught up with Cassie, who had found another set which she quite liked.

"Cass, you won't believe this, but, there's a woman over in the picnic section who is dressed almost identically to you. She's wearing white slacks and top, and a navy blazer. She even has on a floppy white hat. I thought it was you, and I started talking to her. What a coincidence. Up close her clothes aren't nearly as nice as yours, but at first glance you really can't tell the difference. From a distance you could pass as twins."

"Shoot, and I thought I looked so smart in this outfit. Well, I'm going to take this turquoise and white redwood set, and then we'll head home. Keep an eye on her, and tell me if she comes this way. I don't want to come face to face with her. I'll get that clerk over there, and make arrangements for this to be delivered."

Vickie looked carefully around the store, but didn't see the other woman who could have been Cassie's twin. Then she noticed her just leaving through the front doors. If Vickie hadn't turned away so quickly to follow Cassie, she might have noticed the heavy set man who followed the other woman out.

Cass was just paying for her new furniture, when they heard the squealing of brakes, and several screams from outside.

They rushed out, along with just about everyone else from the store. A big city bus was stopped two stores away, and a crowd was gathering right in the middle of the intersection.

"What's happened?" Cassie asked a short, pudgy bald man who was standing in the crowd.

"The bus hit a woman. She just flew off the sidewalk, right in front of him. He didn't have a chance to stop."

"She flew because she was pushed," asserted an elderly woman, who was pulling a small shopping cart behind her. She was so upset that she was almost in tears. "There were quite a few people waiting to cross with the green light, and a tall man just pushed her. I saw him. He put his two hands right on her back, and he pushed. I screamed, but no one else seemed to notice. They were all looking at the woman. The bus hit her, and she flew right through the air. He hurried down that side street and disappeared. Oh look, there's her white hat lying in the road. Oh, that poor woman. I wonder whether she has children at home."

Cass and Vickie looked at each other in distress. Vickie recognized the hat, and Cassie's scalp was really tingling now.

"Cass, it was the woman who was dressed like you. Are you thinking what I'm thinking?"

"Let's not jump to conclusions. See if we can get closer, and get a look at her. There could be lots of women wearing a white floppy hat today," she said without much conviction. In her heart she knew that it was the lookalike woman, and she also knew that it was no coincidence. The murderer had followed them, and had somehow mistaken the poor woman for Cassie. It was a lucky break for Cassie, but a dreadful turn of fate for the other woman.

Chapter Thirty-Two

They got back safely to Cassie's house, and with relief, they locked themselves in, and turned on the alarm system.

The events of the afternoon seemed incredible. They were feeling guilty and somewhat ashamed, because of what had transpired. They knew without putting it into words, that if they had stayed home, minding their own business, and doing what Jack and Bud had asked them to do, none of this would have happened.

Because they had been stubborn, because they hadn't taken things seriously, because they were bored and looking for some fun, they had gone out to shop, and now a woman was dead. The chain reaction seemed unbelievable, yet there it was.

"We've got to tell Jack and Bud that we now know for sure that the killer is in town," said Vickie, sipping her glass of wine, while they sat in the sunroom.

"I was thinking of not telling them at all," said Cass, "but I guess we have to." Part of her was very reluctant to admit that they had been foolish, had gone out against direct orders, and had been the cause of an innocent woman being killed.

It was dinnertime before Jack and Bud drove up the long driveway.

"Sorry we couldn't get here sooner, ladies," said Bud, as he ambled down the hall to the library, following close on Cassie's heels. He seemed to have deliberately placed himself between Jack and Cassie. He didn't want to see any more sparks flying than necessary. The air was always supercharged when these two were in the same room.

"We're being run ragged here," stated Jack, blowing out a big breath, as he stretched back in a comfortable chair. "All hell seems to have broken out in our usually quiet Niagara region. We've had a woman murdered out in Chippawa, and her husband has disappeared. There was a robbery in a jewellery store down on Queen St., and there are no clues whatsoever, and a woman was mugged coming out of the casino, after winning a thousand dollars." He was holding three fingers up now, counting the crimes around the area. Then he put up the fourth finger, and added, "The worst of all is that a little girl has disappeared from her back yard in St. Catharines. Every available man on the force is out on that one."

Vickie knew he was leading up to something, and she knew it wasn't good.

"We were hoping that after he sent you the black roses, the killer had left town. Now, of course, after what you've told us, we know he's still here. The timing is rotten, we're so damn short of men at the moment. We can't even leave anyone on guard outside."

"We've had alerts out with every hotel, motel and B&B in the area," said Bud. "They're all looking for a tall, well built guy, likely travelling alone. So far, there've been seven or eight hits, but the big guys all checked out to be legit. Do you realize just how many tall men there are around at any one time in any one place? Talk about a needle in a haystack!

Anyway, we're thinking that he's either sleeping in his car, or staying with friends, or he's keeping a really low profile by staying in Toronto, or Hamilton, or some other city. He's crafty and lucky, but he's getting careless. That stunt this afternoon was absolutely mad. Anyone could have seen him push that woman. Anyone could have stopped him. He must be getting a bit desperate to take such a chance in the middle of the day. Desperation leads to mistakes, and in a way, that's a hopeful sign for us."

"I just don't understand how or why he mistook me for that other poor woman. I know we were dressed alike, but we didn't really look alike," said Cassie, frowning.

"That's easy," said Bud. "I suspect that he followed you, and saw you and Vickie go into that store. By the time he parked his car and went in, you two had separated, he saw your double, and never looked any further. Why would he? What were the chances of two women almost the same size, being dressed almost identically, and shopping in the same store at the same time? That's material for a book," he snorted.

Bud was talking it all out, trying to get it clear in his own mind. "He just waited, followed her out, and when he saw her standing on the curb, waiting for the bus to go by, he made his move. Obviously, he didn't stop to wonder why Vickie wasn't with you. He just saw the woman, thought it was you, and went for it. That shows that he really is getting careless, and likely very frustrated."

"He still remains a vicious, relentless, and determined killer, though," added Jack. "If he's getting careless, that's good, but I don't know how we can make you understand that you have to stay safely locked inside for a short while. There's no other way.

I'm really disappointed in you Cass. I thought you had more sense. Going out there this afternoon was a bonehead move. Since when did you get so damn silly?" He was staring at her, as if trying to emphasize his point, and there was true concern on his face. He ran his fingers through his hair in a gesture of frustration.

"I can't believe there's so much crime all of a sudden," said Cassie, choosing to ignore his admonition. "Our beautiful Niagara Peninsula has always been such a quiet, comfortable place to live. Now there seems to be danger at every turn."

"It's still a very safe and quiet place to live, but you know how it is. We've had a long spell with no serious crime at all, no killings, no robberies, no kidnappings. Now it's catching up with us. The heat and humidity always bring out the worst in people."

He added, "Bud and I have been doing fourteen hour shifts the past couple of days, and that's going to continue, at least until we find the little girl. She's our top priority. We were discussing it in the car, and what we thought we might do, is take turns staying with you overnight, just until we can spare the manpower again. How does that sound?"

Vickie and Cassie just looked at each other. Cassie had secretly been wishing that Jack could come and stay here with them, but now that it was a possibility, she knew that it wasn't a good idea. Jack's proximity could only lead to trouble.

Vickie was thinking that Bud staying here would be fine, but she'd have to keep a close eye on Jack and Cassie. They were like two high school kids when they got together. The sparks could have set the house on fire. The chemistry was almost palpable.

"We would nap on the couch either here or in the living room, and with the alarm system on, you should be perfectly safe. Hopefully, we'll only need to do it for a couple of nights, till things settle down a bit. That's really the best we can do," added Bud apologetically. "If you weren't friends of ours, we wouldn't even be doing that. My wife will put up with it for about two nights, and then I'll be up shit creek," he laughed.

"No, we can't put you to that trouble, guys," said Cassie emphatically. "We're fine here. With the alarm, and with the panic room, we'll be okay. That monster can't possibly get in, and we'll promise to stay inside. You need to get real sleep, not just naps on some uncomfortable couch. Besides, Bud, I don't have a couch big enough for you," she added with a laugh.

She finally looked at Jack, and saw a mixture of relief and disappointment on his handsome face. He looked so tired. She wanted to put her arms around him, and just hold him, but hastily looked away, and offered to make them some coffee, and a bite of dinner.

"That sounds great, Cass, but we don't have time for dinner," answered Bud, before Jack had a chance to speak. "Maybe, when this is all over, you can treat us to a good meal, but at the moment, we're subsisting on Harvey's and good old Tim Horton's. Thank God they still make the best coffee available. That's what keeps us going."

"Yes, and don't forget the doughnuts, old pal," grinned Jack, as he patted Bud's stomach. "Amanda's going to be sending you to the fat farm when this is all over," he added.

"That's considerably better than the funny farm," answered Bud agreeably.

"Promise me you'll stay in and set the alarm?" asked Jack, as he walked to the front door with Cassie. "It would be so much easier for us if we didn't have to worry about you two." In his mind, he knew that he couldn't stop worrying about Cass till they caught the killer. She was his first priority, but he mustn't let her know that.

"I can't promise, Jack, but we'll really try. Just don't leave us cooped up here for too long."

"Okay, we'll get him, kiddo. In the meantime, stay safe. You too, Vickie. Just think how lucky you are to be confined to this gorgeous house. It must be like a vacation every day. A lot of people would change places with you in a heartbeat. Now, are you sure you don't want me to come back and sleep on the couch later tonight?"

"No way. Go home and get a good night's sleep. We'll be fine," laughed Cassie, pushing Jack towards the door.

He leaned over and kissed her lightly on the forehead, then was gone. Cassie's heart began beating like a bongo. She felt the touch of his lips on her forehead long after the door was closed.

Chapter Thirty-Three

Cassie stood there for a moment, until her heart calmed down a bit. It was like this every time Jack touched her. She felt totally foolish, acting like a teenager with her first big crush. What an idiot I am, she chided herself.

Vickie was just standing watching her. "Okee dokee," she laughed. "Good for you, pal. I'm glad you saw the light, and sent him on his way. I had visions of having to patrol the house all night, or locking you in your room, if he'd been staying over," she grinned.

"I must admit it was very tempting," agreed Cassie. "I've got to get him out of my head. If only Dave would come home and stay put for a while, it might be easier. With him away so much, there are days when I almost forget that I have a husband. It's sad, but true. The trouble is, I'm starting to enjoy it when Dave is away. I can do whatever I want, when I want. Damn, what an emotional mess I'm in. I'm just so glad that you're here with me. Promise you won't even think of leaving for a while."

"I'll stay as long as you need me, you know I will," agreed Vickie, giving Cassie a hug. "As usual, we're in this together," she laughed. "We're like the three musketeers, except that there are only two of us." She settled herself into the big recliner. Muffy immediately jumped into her lap and started purring loudly.

Vickie loved this grand new library in Cassie's beautiful home. She was already starting to think of changes she wanted to make in her house, when she returned to Vancouver. She wondered when that would be. At the rate things were going here, she might be away from home for quite a while. Oh well, who cared? There was no one waiting there for her now anyway. Brian was in Ireland, and her two kids were away doing summer jobs. Her neighbour loved keeping Vickie's two dogs, so there was no problem about staying as long as Cassie wanted her.

"Great," smiled Cass. "I knew I could count on you. I've always been able to. You seem to be the anchor in my life, kiddo. Don't ever change."

Then, feeling herself getting a bit maudlin, she hastily turned to a new subject. "Now, here's what I'm thinking. We'll play Jack's game for a few days. We'll stay in and watch television, and read and drink wine. We'll play with the cats, and talk till our tongues are swollen. We'll try on each other's clothes, and we'll bake brownies and tarts. We'll watch out every window, front and back, for any sign of the killer. There's plenty to keep us busy.

Let's see now. This is Thursday. If we don't see or hear anything that leads us to think that the killer is still around, we're going to go out on Sunday. We'll go to church as usual, then we're going to the Jazz Festival at Willowbank."

"Hey, I love it," enthused Vickie. "We could even kick it up a notch. We'll be watching for him in the crowd, and maybe we can trap him. There'll be plenty of people at the Festival, and wouldn't it be great if we could catch him ourselves. All we have to do is spot him. Then one of us will try to keep his interest, while the other one calls 911.

With a crowd around us, we can scream if we get into any trouble, so we should be totally safe. It's a great idea. If he's still hanging around and watching us, he'll definitely follow us there. This is going to be perfect."

Vickie was getting carried away now. She had great faith in what she and Cassie could do. Cass looked at her affectionately, and remembered how Vickie had piggy-backed her out of the woods, and virtually saved her life. She owed Vickie a lot, and she wouldn't forget it.

"Don't get too excited, now," she laughed. "We're not Starsky and Hutch, or Jessica Fletcher, or any of those television heroes. We're just two middle-aged women who seem to go from one potboiler to another. We've been really lucky so far, so don't push it. On the other hand," she added with a mischievous grin, "I agree that it would be really great to catch the bugger all by ourselves. As usual, it appears that the police could use a little help. Let's give it a try."

"That's the spirit. It's a win-win situation for us. We'll have a lovely afternoon of jazz, and if he doesn't show up, we can figure he's gone out of our lives, and if he does appear, we'll catch him somehow." The catching him part was very fuzzy in her mind, but she had faith that they could do something to bring him down, or hold him till the police arrived.

"That yearly jazz festival at Willowbank has turned into a pretty big affair," said Cassie, going to her desk to find the advertisement. "Peter Appleyard is performing again, and so is John Sherwood. There's always great food and wine, and there's a silent auction, which can be fun. I went the first year they had it, but haven't been able to make it since.

We bring our own lawn chairs, and sit out under the trees, or under the big tent if it should dare to rain, and we just hang out and listen to all the groups. It's a great outing, and goes on all afternoon. You're going to love it."

"Oh I know I will. You know that I've wanted to get in to see Willowbank for a long time. They do let you get inside, don't they?"

"Sure. You can't go through the whole mansion though. It's in the very lengthy process of being restored to its former glory, and I suspect that some of the floors upstairs may not be safe yet. It was in a terrible state of disrepair and neglect when the Willowbank School of Restoration Arts took over. This Jazz Festival is one way for them to raise money. They are so dedicated to the cause, and they've certainly raised the interest level of people in the community."

"It's so beautiful and interesting from the outside. I love those Grecian columns. Have there been many different families living there over the years?"

"Honestly, I don't know. It has a fascinating history, though. It was built way back in the 1830's for the first postmaster, Alexander Hamilton. They had a little post office right on the property, which is about 12 or so acres. My history is very sketchy, but I'm sure I read that while they were building Brock's Monument, the one which stands so tall and proud today, his body was temporarily buried on the

Willowbank property. His first monument had been burned by some radical, I think."

"Well, when we drive past it, it reminds me of the old southern mansions you see along the Mississippi. It's so evocative of a totally different age. I'll bet it has lots of ghosts in it," grinned Vickie, who loved the idea of ghosts in an old house. She was thinking of the old mansion up on Lake Erie, where Kitty and Steffie had slept one stormy night the previous summer. Steffie had apparently seen a ghost there, and was hoping to go back some time to get another look at it. Vickie thought she would love to spend a night in Willowbank, and see what she could see. Of course, thinking about it, and doing it, were two very different things. "Tell me some more about it," she coaxed.

"I really don't know much more about it. I think it's supposed to be in the style of a Greek revival country home, and it looks a bit like the Parthenon, with its eight great Grecian columns. I know that it's been declared a National Historic Site of Canada. The man for whom it was built, was the brother of the man who founded the city of Hamilton. They must have been real movers and shakers. There's a lot of history there in that old place. Thank heavens they saved it from the wrecker's ball, and decided to restore it."

"Well, who's been living there all these years, and how did it fall into such disrepair?"

"Stop asking me questions for which I have no answers," grinned Cassie, shaking her head. She had just picked up Sugar Plum, and was giving her a little massage. "I think it was a school for boys at one time, and a nun's retreat or something like that. I know of one family who lived in it for many years. Actually, I think that a couple of their kids still live in the area. Of course they're adults now.

Vic, can you even imagine growing up in a mansion like that? The grounds are so wonderful. Can't you just see little kids playing hide and seek in amongst all those bushes and gorgeous old weeping willows? That's where it got its name, of course, from the willow trees.

Dave and I went to a fundraiser there a couple of years ago, and the tables were all set outside on the front lawns. It was a balmy June night, and it was simply wonderful sitting out there. There was someone playing the piano in the main entrance hall, and it was truly a magical evening. I felt as if I had been transported back to some other era, a gentler, easier time. Actually, I felt like Scarlett O'Hara sitting out on the lawns of Tara. All I needed was the hoop skirt, and Mammy fussing over me in the background."

"Gone With The Wind" had been one of their very favourite books when they were in their teens, and they oftened got out the movie and watched it again.

Vickie seemed totally entranced with Cassie's history lesson, so Cass continued sharing her little fund of knowledge.

"Last year they held a Harvest Moon Ball in August, but, as usual, Dave was away, so we couldn't go." At this point she rolled her eyes at her friend.

It just seemed that Dave was always away, and she was sick of it. Somehow, this summer, it was bothering her much more than usual. She resented the fact that he had gone rushing off, even though she was just now recovering from a near fatal snakebite. She also wondered whether any other husband would go jaunting off to Europe, knowing that a wanted killer was stalking his wife. She was positive that Jack would never have left her under such dangerous circumstances. The more she thought of it, the more resentful she became.

Sighing deeply, she got back to the subject of Willowbank.

"Apparently the ball was really special, and turned out to be a huge success. They had moonlit carriage rides, which must have been fun. There was dancing, and wonderful food, and people went in formal clothes, or period attire. If I went, I'd go in costume for sure. I get excited just thinking about it."

Then Cassie started to laugh. "Vic, remember the time in Grade 9 that neither of us had a date for that Sadie Hawkins costume party, so we went as a couple. You were so mad that I made you play the man, because at that time you were a bit taller than I was. We went as Anthony and Cleopatra, and we wore our masks the entire night."

"I remember it well. We had a ten o'clock curfew, so we left before anyone had to take off their masks. No one figured out who we were."

"The best part was that we danced together the entire evening, and had a wonderful time. We always threatened to do it again, but never did. Well, I'm telling you, if Dave is home this August, and if they hold the Willowbank Harvest Ball again, we're definitely going. I'm going to drag him there whether he wants to go or not. He owes me bigtime for running off again so soon."

"Oh, give the guy a break. You know you love him. Anyway, the Harvest Ball sounds like fun. You're making me jealous. I'd never get Brian to go to anything like that. You know what he's like. He doesn't like to dance. Actually, there are a lot of things he doesn't like to do. He can be so dorky at times, but he's my dork, so I have to put up with him," Vickie grinned.

"He might go to it just for its historic value," suggested Cassie. "He's such a history buff, and Willowbank oozes stories of the past. The two of you could fly down for a week and we could do a lot of fun things, including the Harvest Ball."

"You know that's not likely to happen, but you and I will definitely go to the Jazz Festival on Sunday. Not only will we be able to enjoy touring the house and sitting out on the beautiful grounds, but we just might catch ourselves a killer. I can hardly wait!"

Chapter Thirty-Four

Thursday, Friday and Saturday went by quickly. The two friends found they had lots to do to keep themselves busy. It rained most of Friday, so it was a perfect opportunity to curl up in the library, read, talk and cuddle the cats. The cats, of course, were delighted to have so much attention.

They had a bit of a scare Friday night, when Muffy jumped off Cassie's bed, and started growling at the window. Cass got up, and went to look out. Because it was rainy and windy, and very dark, she couldn't see much of anything outside. She went to Vickie's room to waken her, just for moral support. Something had definitely wakened Muffy. Had he just had a bad dream, or had someone been trying to get in?

The situation reminded Cassie of the night three summers ago, when something had wakened Muffy. That was the time he had heard someone on the driveway. It turned out to have been two people who were putting a box of bees in Cassie's car, knowing that she was highly allergic to them. That was partially why she was being so careful tonight. If Muffy was growling at the window, there was likely someone out there.

Vickie very bravely, or maybe in a foolhardy manner, went downstairs to check that the alarm was still on. She was holding a pair of sharp scissors, the only weapon she could find. After checking the alarm, which was set, and functioning properly, she circled the inside of the large house, looking out each window. She couldn't see anything or anybody. It did seem the kind of night that a murderer might choose to break in, but she felt pretty secure, as long as the alarm didn't get shorted out by lightning.

Upstairs, Cassie was checking out each window as well. She also got her cell phone, and opened the door to the panic room, just in case they had to rush into it.

They finally decided that it might have been a dog or another cat, although an animal wouldn't likely be wandering around in this rain.

Eventually, they made themselves a cup of tea, then headed back to bed, telling each other that there was no killer on the loose.

"Well, that should give us confidence that everything's fine," laughed Cassie, as she entered her bedroom. There, on the bed, cuddled in a heap, were Sugar Plum and Muffin, both fast asleep. "Whatever Muffy heard, he's not worried about it now," she grinned, as she said goodnight to her friend.

Saturday morning the rain was gone, the sun appeared, and it promised to be a hot, sultry day. Cassie went out to walk around the house, looking for footprints, or any evidence that someone had been there the night before.

They had decided that Vickie should stay inside, watching out the windows, cell phone in hand. She was ready to call the police if anyone attacked Cassie.

They knew it was foolish to go out, but they didn't think that anything was likely to happen. This business of hiding in the house like a couple of mice, seemed so ridiculous. The murderer likely thought he had killed Cassie, when he shoved the woman in front of the bus, and was on his way back to Mexico, or maybe even South America by now.

Hopefully he had left town right away, without watching any television, or reading any newspapers. It would be to their advantage to have him think that Cassie was now dead.

Cass didn't find anything outside to make her suspicious, which was a relief. They could now look forward to going out on Sunday. Of course, they hadn't told Jack and Bud of their plan. One or the other of the detectives had called two or three times each day, just to be sure that they were staying in, and behaving themselves.

Cass knew that Jack would be really angry with her, if he discovered that she and Vickie were sneaking out. On Sunday morning he called fairly early, before they left for church, and Cass hoped that they would be back home before he or Bud called again. All systems were go for their adventure.

They felt like two escapees, as they drove down the Niagara Parkway, towards the church in Niagara Falls. The skies were blue, the sun was shining, and there were no clouds to be seen. What a perfect day for an outdoor Jazz Festival.

Cass met several friends at church, and chatted amiably for a few minutes. Next they headed to the Whirlpool Restaurant for their Sunday lunch. It was so good to be free again. Although the house was luxurious, and afforded them lots of space, in case they got tired of each other's company, it was still annoying to be forced to stay inside. Jack had been dreaming if he really thought these two would remain voluntary prisoners for any length of time.

The restaurant was crowded as usual, but they got a good window seat, and watched the golfers finishing up on the ninth hole. It was a lovely restaurant with a million dollar view.

Next on the agenda was a quick trip to the cattery, which was located just outside the quaint little village of Queenston. Cassie tried to visit there every day, and it had been a real hardship to be locked in the house, and unable to visit her furry little charges. She loved every one of the cats living there, and found it difficult to give up any of them for adoption. Her friend Ginny was in charge when Cassie wasn't there, and Ginny brought her up to date. There had been no additional feline guests for a few days, which was always good news.

Just as in the Hemingway cat retreat in Key West, the little cats, who were strays, or victims of abuse and neglect, now lived a life of luxury. They had full run of the big old house on the property, and had full run of the property itself, which had been totally fenced in at great expense. This was the first project Cassie had undertaken, after receiving her inheritance. A full-time veterinarian lived on site, and every cat was nursed back to health, with good food and much love.

From the cattery, they headed back to Cassie's house, which was just a couple of miles up the road. They wanted to pick up a few things, leave fresh food and water for the cats, and make sure that there were no signs of an intruder. Finally they headed to Willowbank, which was located right in Queenston.

The first people they met were Kitty and Mitch. Mitch had come over from Toronto just for the day, and Kitty was beaming. She was so proud of her "fella," and it was obvious that Mitch had really fallen for Kitty.

Mitch Donaldson was tall and lanky, with a rugged face and a strong chin. His brown eyes were serious, but there were plenty of laugh lines around his mouth. He was a very successful writer of mystery novels, and he and Kitty had met the previous summer, when he had rented the smaller of the two cottages on her family property in Muskoka. They had started off on the wrong foot, but were now serious about their relationship.

"Where's Steffie?" asked Vickie, as they stood chatting.

"She's gone over to Toronto to see Brad Butler, her cruise buddy. This is the third time he's invited her, so she finally decided to go. You know what Steffie's like. She's just not interested in getting into a serious relationship, but she really enjoyed Brad on the ship. He seems like a fun guy, so I hope it turns out well."

"Here's a good spot," suggested Cassie, finding a nice area under a big tree. They set up their lawn chairs, bought some wine, and settled down to listen to the first jazz band, which was playing Dixieland, Cassie's favourite.

"This is so great," sighed Vickie, looking around with pleasure. She had forgotten that part of the reason they were here was to look for the killer. This was just the loveliest way to spend a Sunday afternoon.

Cassie was thinking that Jack would be disappointed and cross if he could see her now. As usual, he would blame Vickie for leading her astray. She was also thinking how nice it would be to be sitting here with Jack, enjoying the great outdoors, the beautiful lawns, and the jazzy music. Thoughts of her husband never entered her mind.

They sat there most of the afternoon, chatting, listening to the music, and wandering the property during the intermissions. Finally, they realized that the afternoon was almost over, and they still hadn't done what they set out to do. It had been such an agreeable afternoon, that the time had flown by, and they had basically forgotten about the stalker, who just possibly might be here.

Kitty and Mitch were over talking with Peter Appleyard, who was about to perform. Mitch had known Peter in Toronto for several years.

Kitty was excited to meet the famous and beloved Canadian icon. Once Peter performed, the festival was over. People were already gathering their things, getting ready to leave as soon as they heard the last melody. The sunny afternoon had turned cloudy and dark. It was obviously going to storm.

Vickie left Cassie sitting quietly, just enjoying the entire scene, while she went to get another plate of goodies, before everything was cleaned up and put away. Vickie, with her sweet tooth, could never resist the goodies.

As she wandered back to where Cassie was sitting, she glanced across the lawn, and stumbled, as she saw a tall, heavyset man, standing halfway behind a tree, and looking towards Cassie. She almost spilled her whole plate of treats, as she hurried to Cassie's side.

"Cass, he's here. He's followed us," she hissed, leaning over her friend.

"Where?" Cassie jumped up quickly.

"Don't let him see you looking at him. He's standing right over there half behind that tree," said Vickie, not wanting to turn around and stare at him. She didn't want him to know that she had spotted him, so she simply nodded her head in his direction.

Cassie, with her floppy hat and sunglasses, turned casually, as if she was just surveying the entire scene. "Where is he? I don't see anyone behind any tree," she said, moving her gaze slowly from tree to tree.

Vickie turned around, and was dismayed to realize that the big man was nowhere in sight. "Well, he won't be hard to spot, he's so tall," she muttered, now openly staring at everyone.

"Are you sure it was the killer?" asked Cassie, doubtfully.

"No, I'm not sure, but he was big enough, and he seemed to be looking at you," said Vickie defensively. "Besides, he was sort of standing halfway behind a tree, as if he didn't want to be noticed."

They kept looking around, through the trees which bordered the property, and into the crowd, but with no success. In frustration, they sat down again, to hear the end of the concert, when Vickie suddenly cried. "There he goes. He's just gone into the house. Come on. We'll follow him."

Chapter Thirty-Five

They didn't stop to think that they should tell Kitty and Mitch where they were going. They didn't stop to think that people would be leaving momentarily, and the big mansion would be locked up. They didn't stop to think that they should call Jack before entering that huge old house. In typical fashion, they just didn't stop to think.

They had seen the hefty man enter one of the doors on the bottom level, so they went through the same door. Peter Appleyard was now playing his heart out, to the delight of the crowd, and they were going to miss the rest of his concert, but they were on a mission.

After all the bright sunshine, the house seemed dark.

A woman was just coming out of the washroom, so they asked her whether she had seen the big man, and which way he had gone. The woman had not seen anyone.

"Cass, why don't you go upstairs, and I'll cover this floor. If you spot him, come back and get me. What I'm afraid of, is that he might have gone upstairs and right out the front door." Vickie was all revved up now. She wanted to corner him and finish this uncertainty. Again, she didn't stop to think of just what danger they might find.

Cassie wasn't really interested in going down any dark corridors, or looking into any empty rooms all by herself. She firmly believed in "safety in numbers," but she reluctantly agreed. With her cell phone in one pocket, and her trusty scissors in another, she headed up to the main level.

The front door opened onto the balcony and the elegant stairs, which, in turn, led down to the extensive lawns. Cass noticed that the extra wide door was open. Had their quarry gone out the front way?

Was he locked in the washroom? Was he hiding behind one of the large pieces of furniture, such as the gorgeous old piano, which sat in the vestibule? She peeked behind it, before going out onto the balcony to survey the property. It was a relief to verify that he was not hiding behind the piano, ready to spring out at her.

There were a few people milling around on the front side of the mansion, but no large man. Re-entering the house, she proceeded carefully from room to room. This didn't seem such a good idea in the twilight. On a sunny morning, or a beautifully bright afternoon, the mansion would have been charming and delightful. This early evening, however, the approaching storm had turned the skies dark and foreboding.

With darkness, the ghosts were bound to come out. Nighttime was their time, and Cassie didn't want to interrupt whatever ghosts liked to do in the dark of night. She was fairly sure that the big man wasn't here, and that they were wasting their efforts.

Coming back through the lovely front entrance, Cassie tried a door to the right. It opened onto a small room, which might have been a den at one time. Now, in the middle of the room there was a long table, surrounded by chairs. At the end of the room was an intriguing old fireplace. It was likely being used as a meeting room now, she guessed.

It was obvious that the stalker wasn't hiding here, unless he was in the large armoire standing against one wall. Cass, however, was intrigued by the mansion, and felt it was an excellent opportunity to get a look at each room, while supposedly searching for the killer. She was particularly interested in the fireplace, and walked over to have a closer look. After examining it, she turned to see the full room again, and casually put her hands on the back of the end chair. It was vibrating!

Her hands flew off it, as if they had been burned. Gently, she once again placed them on the back of the chair. It was definitely vibrating. There was nothing under it, and there was no motor of any kind anywhere in the room, at least not that Cassie could see.

Forgetting all about the big man she was supposed to be following, she walked around the table, putting her hands on the back of each chair. Now there were no vibrations. What was going on?

Could there really be a ghost here, a ghost who was somehow warning her to get out? Anything was possible, but Cass couldn't accept that explanation. She tiptoed to the armoire, and carefully opened it. She had left the door to the room open, so that she could make a hasty exit if anything or anybody jumped out at her.

To her relief, the armoire seemed to be used as a simple storage cupboard. No big man was hiding there, and no ghost floated out at her.

She took one more turn around the table, feeling the back of each chair as she went. Only the end chair in front of the fireplace was vibrating. This was indeed a mystery. She had to finish her search for the killer, then get Vickie up here to feel the vibrations. She was partly convinced that it really was a ghost either threatening her, or trying to make contact with her.

Reluctantly, she exited the mysterious room, looked around the wide hall for lurking figures, and entered the large living room. Immediately she had the feeling that someone was looking at her. Turning quickly, she thought she saw a shadow disappearing into the room across the hall. Holding her breath, she tiptoed to the door of the offending room, but saw no one there.

Had she just imagined it, or had it been a ghost? Or, what if there was a secret panel behind one of these walls? Maybe it led to a tunnel, which went right down to the river, or out to the road. The more she thought about it, the more reasonable it seemed. Maybe her stalker had been here watching her, but had made his escape through a secret tunnel or room.

Feeling foolish, she tried pounding on each wall to see whether it sounded hollow. She wasn't sure that she would recognize a hollow sound, but it was worth a try. To her embarrassment, a woman appeared in the doorway, and said, with a puzzled and annoyed look on her face, "Can I help you with something?"

"Oh, forgive me," laughed Cassie. "I was just imagining this house in years gone by, and wondering whether there might be a secret tunnel used by bootleggers, or runaway slaves, or ghosts. I guess I got carried away with my wild notions."

Fortunately, the woman laughed with her. "We've all looked for secret rooms or tunnels, but haven't had any luck. I admit though, that it would be exciting to find something like that. Anyway, we're about to close, so I have to ask you to go back downstairs and use the rear door. Thanks so much for coming. Did you enjoy the afternoon?"

"Absolutely. It was a lot of fun." Cass, however, wasn't about to be rushed out. Now that she was here, she wanted to see the entire mansion, more out of curiosity than a belief that she would find the killer. Actually, she had pretty well forgotten about the killer, in her excitement over this old, and pitifully neglected home. She kept imagining how it would look when it was fully restored. What a gold medal day that would be, but at the rate they were going, it might not be in her lifetime. They really did need a financial shot in the arm.

Chapter Thirty-Six

The woman with whom she had been speaking, had walked away quickly, and Cassie hesitated, wondering what to do. The stairs to the top level were closed to the public, but it looked very inviting up there. Should she sneak up anyway, just for a quick peek, before looking for Vickie? Thinking it out carefully, she reasoned that if, indeed, the killer was here, and if he had come specifically to kill her and Vickie, there would be no reason for him to be hiding upstairs. It should be safe for her to go up and have a look around.

Not giving herself the chance to change her mind, she headed up the stairs, ignoring the sign which said the upper level was closed to the public, and that the stairs and floors were unsafe.

She was very careful, walking gently on the floorboards, picturing herself going right through at any moment. She was dismayed to see the derelict condition of these upstairs rooms. They had large windows, affording wonderful views in all directions, but oh, what a lot of work had to be done. These restoration people would be at it for years, in order to restore this beautiful old building to its former glory. She really admired their love and determination, and she decided that she should give them a large donation. She had more money than she could ever possibly use in one lifetime. Perhaps a million dollars would give them a good boost.

She was about to go back down the stairs, when she noticed one more door which seemed inviting. To her surprise and delight, she saw a narrow, spiral staircase, leading up to what must have been an attic, or possibly servants' quarters. Almost every scary book she had ever read, had a spiral staircase in it. Hesitating only momentarily, she headed up.

It was quite dark in the narrow passage, and she didn't dare step off the stairs and onto the floor up there. Her feet might go right through it. She was standing, peering into the darkness around her, when she heard a noise. It was a sort of shuffling noise, and she didn't wait to find out what it was. She turned and flew down those narrow, winding stairs as if the devil himself was after her. Maybe he was.

She made it down to the main floor, and was just trying to catch her breath, when a woman came around the corner and frowned at her.

"I'm sorry, but the house is being closed now for the night," she said, with authority. "I didn't realize there was anyone left up here. Please go downstairs, and out the backdoor." As she said this, she locked the big front door, and turned out some lights.

Cassie was happy to oblige, but first she asked the woman whether she had seen a tall, brawny man in the house.

The woman looked at her strangely, but said she had not, so, giving up, Cassie hurried back down the stairs, to find Vickie.

It had occurred to her that Vickie might be foolish enough, or brave enough, to go looking for the basement of this place. Surely she wouldn't be that silly, but then, look how silly Cassie had just been. Vickie wasn't always known for her good judgement when she got into one of her sleuthing modes, and Cass could certainly understand that.

As she reached the bottom level, she heard a booming laugh, followed by some low murmuring. She was surprised and relieved to see her friend standing at the door of a room, which was obviously used as an office. She was talking to a woman and a very big, very tall man!

When Vickie saw Cass, she turned to her and said, "Cass, this is Evelyn Lane, and this is Charles Edwards. Evelyn is on the Restoration committee, and Charles helped put this lovely festival together today." As she said this, she rolled her eyes at her friend. They had really made a mistake this time. "And this is my friend, Cassandra Meredith," continued Vickie.

"Lovely to meet you," murmured Cassie, staring up into the face of Charles Edwards. She saw that his arms looked like two tree trunks, and she shuddered a bit at the thought of how easily he could lift a woman and throw her off a balcony, or off a cruise ship deck.

His hair, what there was of it, looked real, and so did his nose. He didn't seem to be sporting any disguise. Covertly, she sniffed the air, to see if she could detect a hint of lime. I really am like a damn bloodhound, she scolded herself silently, as she sniffed surreptitiously. She had great faith in her own powers of nasal detection, so she just kept sniffing, but she could discover none of that clean, cutting smell of lime.

Since her scalp was not tingling, and she could detect no limey aroma, and since Vickie seemed quite relaxed with him, she decided that this was not the killer. Besides, he was really too big, and his eyes were very nice, not at all close together. No, this wasn't the right guy. Their killer was tall and strong looking, but he wasn't enormous. "Didn't we see you standing outside behind a tree a little while ago?" she asked.

"Oh you saw me, did you?" His booming laughter was rather unnerving.

"Yep, that was yours truly," he admitted. "I was just having a good look at the crowd, to see whether they were enjoying themselves. I was also keeping an eye out for people who bring their own booze, and drink it openly on the grounds. That's a real no-no. Being as big as I am, it's pretty hard to be inconspicuous, so I hid half of myself behind the biggest tree trunk I could find. A lot of people here know me, and they don't like to see me around. I sometimes put a crimp in their fun. I understand that they call me The Enforcer behind my back." Again he laughed the big resounding laugh.

I guess someone that big can't laugh quietly, thought Cassie, and he seems very jolly. She couldn't picture him throwing anyone off a high-rise balcony, but it was a bit disappointing. It would be so nice to catch the damn guy, and finish all this waiting and hiding. "Well, it certainly was a splendid festival," she said. "All the bands were great, but I must confess, I liked the Dixieland best of all." Cass was now at her sociable best.

"Well, thank you for coming, ladies," said the woman, who had been standing quietly in the office. She was obviously anxious to get them out of there, so that she could lock up for the night. "We hope you'll come for our next gala. We do appreciate the wonderful support from the public."

You're going to appreciate it a whole lot more, thought Cass to herself, thinking of the million dollar cheque she was going to write. There were times when it was really fun to have all that inheritance at her disposal.

Aloud she said, "You're certainly doing a good job. It must be overwhelming though, to realize how much work you have ahead of you."

The woman only nodded. Clearly, she was not interested in any more small talk.

Making their good-byes, they hurried out the door, to a parking lot which was almost empty. Kitty and Mitch were nowhere to be seen. They must have given up waiting, and had gone on their way. Vickie and Cassie had spent more time in the house than they had realized.

"Well, that was a fizzle," complained Vickie, as they gathered their chairs and tote bags from the lawn, and headed to the car, just as it started to rain.

"Not exactly," answered Cass. "Wait till I tell you what happened up there. You and I have got to come back and get into this place for a better look around. I think it really does have a ghost, maybe more than one."

Chapter Thirty-Seven

The friends were happy to get home and lock themselves in for the night. It had been a wonderful day, and they were very pleased with themselves. They had been to church, to lunch, to the cattery, and to Willowbank, and nothing bad had happened. They were more convinced than ever that the man who threw the unfortunate woman off the balcony, was long gone. It was a shame that he would likely get away with his crime, but it was good to feel that they were off the hook.

Cass was throwing together a nice Greek salad for them, while Vickie made some garlic toast, and poured the wine. They had decided they would eat in the family room and watch a little television.

Sugar Plum and Muffin joined them. Cassie had cut up some cold chicken for them, and after cleaning their plates, they sat washing their paws and faces.

"I love to watch them cleaning themselves," laughed Vickie. "Cats are the cleanest little creatures. They're so fussy and fastidious about their coats. No wonder their fur shines the way it does."

"I know," laughed Cassie, looking at them fondly. "They're the most wonderful pets. I can hardly remember what life was like without them."

"Well, I'm proud of the part I played in helping you start the cattery. Remember what fun we had flying down to Key West to study Hemingway's property? I just wish we had a couple of polydactyls here. I wonder whether any will ever show up."

"I doubt it. They're just rare enough that anyone who owns one would likely take good care of it, and never abandon it, or let it run loose."

Just then the phone rang. "I'll get it," said Vickie, jumping up. She was full of energy after the lovely day they had shared.

A few moments later, she returned to the family room. "That was Jack. He and Bud are on their way home, and they want to drop in for a few minutes."

"Do they have some news about the killer?" asked Cassie, hopefully.

"He didn't say."

When the two detectives arrived, Vickie turned off the alarm and opened the door.

"How's it going, gals?" asked Bud, as he ambled into the room behind Jack.

Cassie noticed that Jack looked grim. That arrogant sort of strut he had just wasn't there. He barely glanced at her as he sat down.

"Oh, we're doing just fine," she answered, a little guiltily. She hoped that they wouldn't find out that she and Vickie had been out roaming around all day.

"Been to any good Jazz Festivals lately?" scowled Jack, glaring at her.

Cass and Vickie just gaped at each other. How had he discovered their secret? Was there a policeman keeping an eye on them?

"Don't be mad, Jack. We were going crazy cooped up here, and we were very careful," said Cassie, giving him her sweetest smile.

"You were very stupid," said Bud, shaking his head. "We can't keep you safe if you're out wandering all over the place. You gals aren't taking this seriously."

"But if he was after us, he would have made a move before now. We've been here all alone in this house for days. Surely we would have heard from him or seen him. He must be gone," asserted Vickie.

"That's just what we've come to tell you," frowned Jack, ignoring Vickie, and looking at Cassie. "We've learned quite a bit more about this Harold Johnston, aka John Duncan, aka Bill Gordon. He's an odd character, but very smart. He's charming enough that he's been able to woo and marry three different very wealthy women. The police in

Florida and Missouri are now trying to tie him to another couple of accidents, which may have been murder. He seems to be making a career of killing wealthy women."

Bud was massaging Muffy, who had jumped into his lap as soon as he sat down. At this point, he took over from Jack. "Apparently he waits till the new wife has named him beneficiary of her will and her insurance policies. Once that's done, he spends a little time teasing and taunting, and driving the poor woman crazy, before he actually kills her. That's how he gets his jollies. For some reason, the women have seemed too stupid or too scared to cut him out of their wills, or to go to the police. Don't really understand how he accomplishes that."

Jack cut in again. "The first woman knew him as John Duncan. They had been married about a year, and her sister says that towards the end, she was terrified of him. She told her sister that she was afraid he was going to kill her, but he was so well liked by everyone, that no one believed her.

According to the sister, he was gaslighting her. You know what that means, don't you?"

"Yes, Jack," said Vickie, dripping with sarcasm. "We like old movies too, and we've both seen 'Gaslight' with Ingrid Bergman and Charles Boyer. He tried to make her think she was going crazy, and he really was driving her crazy. It's a wonderful concept for a story. Imagine our killer trying it out on his wives."

"Well, the sister says that he was doing a pretty good job of it. Then the wife supposedly fell off a cliff on a camping trip, and there was no way they could prove it was murder. The surviving sister is sure that it was, however, because her sister didn't even like camping, and wouldn't have gone willingly on a trip with him. Now, apparently the police in Nevada also think it was no accident."

It was Bud's turn to go on with the story. "He got all her money, and just disappeared. He left Nevada, and then popped up in Texas, calling himself Bill Gordon. Forensics now prove that it's the same perp.

It wasn't long before he met another rich woman at the country club, and they married. He took out a huge insurance policy on her, with himself as beneficiary, and somehow talked her into changing her will, again with himself as sole beneficiary.

Shortly after that, she told her mother that she was scared of him, and thought he was planning to kill her. When she drowned in the bathtub, her mother went to the police, and made such a fuss that they looked into it. It went to trial, but the jury let him go. They said the evidence was all too circumstantial. Besides, no one liked his wife very much. She had flaunted her wealth, and had stepped on a lot of toes in the community, so no one really cared that she might have been murdered. You know what they're like in Texas."

Vickie and Cassie were absolutely fascinated by all this information. They were beginning to form a much clearer picture of the man they had seen coming out of the elevator that fateful night.

"What about the woman in Florida?" asked Cassie.

"The details on her are pretty sketchy," said Jack. "By now he was calling himself Harold Johnston, and he apparently met her at a church in Pensacola. What they were doing in Panama City Beach is unclear. They had booked in for two nights, but that's all we know. It doesn't appear that he intended to kill her at Edgewater. She must have made him angry, or threatened to cut him out of her will, there's no way of knowing what happened that night to set him off.

"It wasn't carefully thought out though, the way the other two were. He took a huge chance of someone seeing him throw her off that balcony. The other murders were done secretly inside the house, or out in the woods, and made to look like accidents. This one was careless. It was likely done in a fit of rage.

The point is, that he is one smart cookie, and he has lots of money. He can afford to bide his time, up to a certain point. The fact that he pushed that poor woman in front of the bus, when there were a lot of people around, shows that he's getting careless, and anxious to get the job done, and get out of here. We think he'll make another attempt very soon. The part about sending the black roses was just his way of teasing you a bit."

Bud added, "He's a dangerous, clever, and determined killer. There have never been witnesses before, so this time he has to take chances which he hasn't had to do in the past. He feels he's got to get rid of you.

The one thing in our favour is his size. Even with disguises, he's hard to miss. He can't make himself smaller, so he always stands out in a crowd. That will help us a bit, unless he comes in the night. Of course, there are plenty of tall men around, and this guy doesn't really have anything to distinguish him from the rest. It's like looking for one red Smarty in a whole box of them.

He's definitely getting careless, but he's still a threat, and it's obvious that you're not taking this seriously. The fact that you were out running around all over the place today proves that."

"We're pretty sure that he just wants to finish it, and get himself out of town, so we're expecting some kind of attempt any day now. The big question is, are we going to have to put you two in jail to keep you safe?"

Jack was kidding, of course, but the friends could see that he was trying to impress them with the seriousness of the situation. He was making a point. They were in danger, and it was no time to be stupid.

They could tell by the way he was glaring at them again, that he was furious. He was doing a slow burn. He was obviously fed up, and had lost all patience with them.

Without even glancing at each other, Cass and Vickie knew that they were both thinking the same thing. There was only one way around this now. It was imperative that they catch the killer before he caught them, and it was just too bad if Jack didn't like it. That's why they wouldn't tell him what they were going to do. They would play it sweet and stupid. That little ploy always worked.

Chapter Thirty-Eight

The motel room was pretty shabby, being furnished in pieces which looked like "Early Depression." It did, however, have some pluses. It was far out Lundy's Lane towards the west end, and was only moderately busy. That was good. There weren't too many nosy people around. That was very good. The motel manager seemed a decent sort. He wanted to be paid promptly, and wasn't too interested in anything else. He likely got a lot of rough trade and undesirables out here, and that suited John. He liked people who minded their own business.

John Mason, aka Bill Gordon, aka John Duncan, aka Harold Johnston, lay on the bed (which was too short for him), and, hands behind his head, he stared at the ceiling. He had a problem which needed solving, and he was going at it from different angles.

He stared unseeing at the dingy yellow curtains, which had some strange, spider-like pattern on them. The small window air conditioner was noisy, and seemed to be coughing out its final death rattle. Someone had kicked a couple of good-sized dents in the bottom of the door. The room spoke of loneliness and despondency, but John, who had a cool eight million tucked away, barely noticed.

He loved his life. He loved the excitement, he loved the chase, and he loved the rewards. As John Duncan, he had inherited a good pile of money from his first wife in Nevada. Pushing her off the cliff had been easy, and tormenting her first had been fun. His sister-in-law had been sure that the fall had been no accident, but she and the police hadn't been able to prove a thing. The day he got his hands on the money, was the day he left for Texas, and became Bill Gordon.

With a lot of money at his disposal, he had joined the country club, and soon met his second wife. Teasing and tormenting her had been a great pastime, but as it turned out, it had not been a good idea. He should have just drowned her in the tub without giving her any warning. How was he to know that she would tell her mother she was afraid he was going to kill her? Hell, the sneaky bitch had told him that she had no family at all. Who the heck would have expected a suspicious mother to appear on the scene?

The police felt they had enough evidence to arrest him, but lucky for him, he had a good lawyer, and a great jury. They just couldn't believe that this decent looking, well spoken, well dressed man, could possibly have killed his wife. He eventually got the money from the insurance policy, and from her will, and he got the heck out of Dodge.

Florida was his next stop, and it hadn't taken him long to find himself a third victim. The country club hadn't turned up any good possibilities, but he knew that churches were always a good place to find lonely women, and before long, he had found himself a new wife. She was actually heiress to some big national chocolate company, and things were going well, when he made his first serious mistake.

She had very happily changed her will, making him the beneficiary of that huge estate. Unfortunately, following his old pattern, he began teasing and taunting her, treating her with disdain and disrespect. It was dumb, but it was also fun. He loved to feel the power he had over women, stupid women. He just couldn't resist letting them know how smart he was, and how much power he had.

They had driven over to Panama City Beach for a couple of days, just to see the place. His wife was talking about maybe buying a new penthouse condo in that vacation playground, which was in the middle of a huge growth spurt.

That night he had been teasing her about how he could have an affair any time he wanted, and she would never even know it. He had totally underestimated her, and misread her character. She had surprised him by flying into a rage, grabbing a kitchen knife, and stabbing him in the arm.

What really angered him was that she had obviously been aiming for his heart. Who would have guessed that the skinny little bitch would have the nerve?

His quick temper got the best of him. Without thinking, he had scooped her up, and thrown her over the balcony. Right away he knew that he was in trouble. As he had stood on that dark balcony, back lit by the living room lamps, he had heard a woman make an aborted scream or squeal. Looking down at the hot tub, he had seen a woman looking up at him, then rushing to get out of the tub.

In a panicked frenzy, he had grabbed his wallet and keys, jumped into his clothes, wrapped a makeshift bandage around his arm, and headed out. It had been plain old bad luck that he was getting off the elevator, just as the hot tub woman and her companion were getting on the other elevator. They got a really good look at him, and there was nothing that he could do about it.

It had been pretty easy to find out who the woman was, since she had conveniently dropped her gold bracelet with her name on it. With plenty of money at his disposal, it wasn't too difficult to track the women to the cruise ship, and Key West.

Luck had been against him there, but he wasn't discouraged. He loved living on the edge, and flirting with danger. He loved being the hunter, and knowing that it was just a matter of time before he caught up with his prey.

He had made a second mistake when he pushed the woman in front of the bus. How lucky he was that no one had noticed him. Well, maybe someone had seen him, but he had made his escape very quickly.

Now, he was glad that he had made that mistake. He didn't want Cassandra Meredith dead just yet. Once he found out just how wealthy she was, he put aside the idea of killing her right away, and tried to figure out how he could get his hands on some of that money first.

The police were really a non-issue. He wasn't worried about them. He had kept ahead of them for years, and the more money you had, the easier it was to evade them. No, the police weren't really a problem, but devising a foolproof plan might be.

Shaking his head, he got up from the bed, and poured himself a tumbler full of scotch. He didn't have any ice, and didn't want to draw unnecessary attention to himself by going to the icemaker, which was stationed just outside the motel office.

He was cleanshaven now, and was letting his hair grow back. A bald head was handy for slipping on a wig, and changing his appearance, but he hated how it looked and felt. It made him feel naked and vulnerable.

Pacing around the room, and sipping the scotch in noisy slurps, he tried to get his thoughts in order. He was remembering an old movie he had seen with Joseph Cotton and Theresa Wright. His last wife, Gloria, had loved the old movies, and insisted that he watch them with her. In this particular one, Joseph Cotton was the "Merry Widow" killer, and in it he had made some comment about how rich widows were generally lonely and foolish – a wonderful combination. John agreed.

In this case, however, Cassandra Meredith was not a widow. She wasn't lonely, and she wasn't foolish, at least he didn't think she was.

Unfortunately she was married, so he couldn't go the usual route, but there had to be a way to get money out of her. Suddenly he stopped, stared into space, swallowed the last gulp of the golden liquid, and laughed delightedly. He had already mailed her something which she should get tomorrow. He wished he could be there when she and that friend of hers, Victoria Craig, opened it. That was fine. It would put her on edge, maybe cause her to make a mistake. She had been lucky so far, but he could tell that she was carefree, and she was going to play right into his hands.

This new, inchoate idea was daring, and it would be difficult, but he thought he had the answer. He was going to get a lot of money out of the very attractive Mrs. Meredith, and he was going to have a lot of fun doing it.

Chapter Thirty-Nine

As Cassie walked past the open bedroom door, she saw her friend looking at her derrière in a three way mirror.

"Gawd, Cass, look at this. My butt looks like the backside of a barn," she groaned indignantly. "Those butter tarts are coming back to haunt me. I know these shorts weren't this tight two weeks ago. How bad do they look?"

"You're just looking for compliments, Mrs. Craig," grinned Cassie, as she entered the bedroom and plunked herself down on the bed. "You know and I know that you have a great butt. For an old bag in her mid to late forties, you ain't bad."

"Oh you silver-tongued devil," laughed Vickie. "You do have a way with words."

They sat there companionably, talking about clothes, diets, and hairdos, before getting around to the subject of the killer. Having made up their minds that they should be trying to catch him before he caught them, they began making themselves laugh with their crazy schemes and scenarios. So far, they had no sensible ideas, but many silly ones.

"Look at my leg, Vic. Do you think I'm always going to have those two puncture marks, or are they fading?" Cassie stretched out her leg for Vickie to inspect.

"I think it's looking good, Cass. You can see that they're fading. You may always have them, but they'll be very faint. Just think of them as battle scars," laughed her friend.

"When I think of that whole adventure, I can still hardly believe that you actually piggy-backed me for a while. Talk about superwoman. I'll bet you could lift a car if it fell on me."

"Don't know about that," grinned Vickie, "but I do know that I was very glad I had read about not sucking the poison from a snake-bite. You might have been dead by now if that old snake had bitten you on your ass! I have to draw the line somewhere."

They laughed so long and so hard at that picture, that both cats got up and stalked out of the room. Their sleep had been disturbed, so they headed for the kitchen, just in case there were any treats available.

"I don't suppose you'd like to go for a walk down in the Niagara Glen?" asked Vickie, with mischief in her eyes.

"You fiend," replied Cassie, with fake dismay. "You know darn well that there are Mississauga Rattlers down in that glen. What are you trying to do, kill me off before the killer can get me?"

"Getting back to the killer, what in the world do you think would cause a man to make a career of killing women for their money? Is he a sociopath, and if so, was he born that way?" Vickie had moved over to the window, and was looking out at the green Niagara River, as she talked. There was a certain fascination about it, and she loved to gaze at it. It was mysterious and dangerous, and therefore intriguing. From this distance it had such a seemingly smooth surface, yet in reality, there were hidden whirlpools, eddies, and currents, which could suck you down in an instant. She wondered how many bodies it might give up, if they could ever drain it.

In a way, that river is like life, she thought to herself. Everything seems to be going along smoothly on the surface, when suddenly, you can be sucked right into a morass of trouble and danger.

Turning around to look at Cassie, Vickie repeated her question. "Do you think he's a sociopath, or just a stupidly greedy bad guy?"

"I definitely think he's a sociopath. Just the little bit we know about him leads to that conclusion. He must have a superficial charm to be able to get all these rich women to marry him, and he obviously has no shame or guilt about it." Cassie was starting to tick characteristics off on her fingers.

"He's manipulative and able to con people, and he's likely a pathological liar. I've read that they can even pass a lie detector test."

Vickie stretched, then looked again at the river before adding her bit of knowledge to the conversation. "I was reading an interesting psychology book in bed last night. I got it from your gorgeous library right here in the house. That library is so neat. I'm really envious that you have all those books right at your fingertips. The little library I have in Vancouver fades in comparison, but I spend hours in it. Remember how much fun we used to have in the attic of my house? My dad had so many great books up there. We used to get so mad at my mother, when she would chase us outside to get some fresh air. All we ever wanted to do was play library or book store."

"Oh, I remember it so well. Some of my very happiest days were spent in your attic. As I think about it, it was really hot and stuffy, with no windows, but we didn't care. I was so envious of you having all those books right in your own home."

"Well, now I'm envious of you with your beautiful new library," laughed Vickie.

"Anyway, back to our killer. The book says that sociopaths love the excitement of always living on the edge, and they have no empathy for anyone else's feelings. They usually have no friends, just victims, and sometimes accomplices, who eventually turn out to be their victims."

"They call it the 'anti-social personality disorder,' and I think that's what this killer has," added Cassie, who had been researching the condition on her computer. "They're impulsive, and they change their image and appearance easily just to avoid getting caught. This guy fits all the criteria. Did the book you were reading say anything about whether it's in the genes, or whether it's caused by their environment?"

"Actually, it talked about that quite a bit, but the experts can't make up their minds. They think it may be in the genes, but mostly, they think it's a combination of both. Environment has a huge part to play in it. Apparently there are lots of warning signs. These kids start being cruel to animals at a very young age. They have no real friends, have no concept of right or wrong, and are juvenile delinquents."

"I imagine that they're abused as little kids. Everyone knows that abusing a child in its formative years does huge psychological damage."

"Cass, talking about child abuse, do you remember years and years ago, you told me something about a neighbour of yours who tried to lure you into his basement. What was that about? I've forgotten the details."

Cassie frowned as she thought about that long ago incident. "I think that old guy was just a pervert. I never heard of him doing it to any other kids, although maybe they would have kept it a secret, just as I did. Anyway, I was out in the front yard playing with my dolls, when he came across the road and started telling me about the new kittens which he had at his place. He asked if I wanted to see them. Well, you know me with cats. Even then I was crazy about them. I think I was about five.

He took my hand, and led me across the street. My mother had forbidden me to cross the street alone, but I figured it was okay if I was with a grown-up. He took me around the back of his creepy old house, and into a stone or concrete cellar, which had a wooden door to the outside.

I can always remember that we went down three stone steps, and it was dark in there. He must have been very sure that no one would come and bother us, because, lucky for me, he didn't shut the door all the way. I remember that his backyard had big hedges all around it, so no neighbours would have been able to see us.

I was busy looking around for the kittens, when he told me that first he wanted me to lift up my skirt and pull down my panties. He was holding up a shiny new quarter. He said he would give it to me if I was a good little girl, and did what he asked. Then he would let me play with the kittens. He was a very tall man with a shock of white hair, and his hands were like skeleton claws. I can still see his skinny fingers holding that quarter.

Suddenly I realized that there were no kittens, and that this was a bad man. I was afraid of him, though, and afraid not to do what he asked. I almost started to lift up my skirt, but there must have been an angel on my shoulder that day.

I was terrified by then, and made an end run around him. I shot out the door and across the street without looking either way. It's lucky I wasn't hit by a car, but it was a pretty quiet, residential street. Anyway, I kept expecting to feel those bony hands on my shoulders.

For some reason he didn't follow me. I guess he was afraid that someone would see him, or that I would start yelling. When I made it into the house, I just grabbed onto my mother, and wouldn't let her go. I was crying, but was afraid to tell her what had happened. I said that a big dog had scared me, and she went out looking for the dog. I just kept thinking that I would be in real trouble if she found out that I had crossed the street. You remember how strict my mother was."

"Shoot, that's a terrible story. I can just see you, a little wee girl, toddling off to look at kittens. Did that old fellow live alone?"

"Heck no. He had about a zillion kids, nine or ten at least. They were all bad kids, the neighbourhood scourge. I guess they were all at school that day, and maybe his wife was out. I've always been so thankful that he didn't take me into the house, because I would never have managed to get away. It was a big old three story house which was dilapitated, and looked haunted.

It was so weird that he took me into the fruit cellar, and then left the door partially open. I guess, though, because there were no windows, he had to leave it open a bit to get some light. Lucky for me that he didn't have a lamp or a flashlight, or else he would have shut the door and locked it. It was like a concrete bunker, so it was likely soundproof. No one would have heard a little girl yelling or crying."

"I'm just glad that shiny quarter didn't tempt you. Who knows what you would be like today if he had actually molested you."

"I'd likely be dead. He would have had to kill me, and maybe bury me right there under the dirt floor.

Hey, we're way off the subject of our sociopath. Maybe he was molested as a little kid, and that's why he's turned out to be so bad. Guess we'll never know. In the meantime, we have to be careful that he doesn't prove to be smarter than we are."

"Phooey, there's not much hope of that," laughed Vickie. "There's a lot of brain power there when you and I put our heads together."

"You've got that right, kiddo," agreed Cassie. "You know, we need to lure him someplace where the police are already waiting. I don't think he would use a gun or a knife. He seems to like the 'non-weapon' crime. He pushed the first wife over a cliff, drowned the second one in a tub, threw the third one off a balcony, tried to throw me off the ship, and pushed that poor woman in front of the bus."

"Wait a minute. What about me? In Key West he hit me on the head with something," protested Vickie, recalling that experience with a chill. It had been scary waking up all alone, so dizzy and disoriented on that deserted street.

"It was likely just his fist," replied Cassie. "He's so big and strong that one of his fists would be just as good as a weapon. No, I really don't think he carries a gun or a knife, and that should work in our favour. He couldn't attack both of us at the same time. If we could just get him alone someplace where the police are close by, we should be okay. If he attacked one of us, the other one could jump on his back and stick scissors in his eyes." Even as she said it, Cassie knew how lame it sounded.

What were they thinking? They were two middle-aged women, scrawny in comparison to that brute. He could knock one out with his fists before the other one could do anything. No, so far they were on the wrong track. This wasn't going to be easy.

Shaking her head, she frowned at Vickie, and said, "Maybe it's time for a reality check. You and I love fun and adventure, and we both feel somewhat indestructible because of all the close calls we've had the past few years. What we definitely are not, however, is stupid. I'm thinking that maybe there's no way we can lure him out, without getting hurt ourselves. It might work in the movies, but it's not going to work here. This guy might be too dangerous and too strong."

"You're right, Cass," sighed Vickie. She hated to give up the idea of catching the killer themselves. "We should probably just go on with our lives as normally as we can, and leave it up to the police."

They were both disappointed, but somewhat relieved. They had each been showing a certain amount of bravado, which they didn't really feel.

Still, leaving his capture to the police didn't feel right either. This was a problem which required more thought.

They decided to mull it over some more while they had something to eat.

Like Scarlett, they would think about it tomorrow.

Chapter Forty

"I'm going out to get the mail," said Cassie, with a determined look on her face, as they finished their lunch in the sunroom.

"Let me get my cell phone, and I'll come with you," answered Vickie, jumping up from the window seat.

The mailboxes were situated at the end of the road, since all the houses on this stretch of the Parkway, had very long driveways.

"Are we walking, or taking the car?" asked Vickie, returning with a hat in one hand, and her cell phone in the other.

"Let's walk. It looks like such a perfect day, and since we've decided to go on with our lives as normally as possible, we might as well get started."

They chatted amiably as they walked up the road, but both kept a wary eye out for any tall, heavyset men they might encounter.

There wasn't much mail, just a couple of bills and a small brown bubble envelope.

"Wonder what this is?" said Cassie, turning it over. There was no return address, and no name. As they strolled back, Cass said, "It's too nice to stay indoors this afternoon. Let's go down to the falls, maybe we might even stop in at the casino."

"Sounds great to me," replied her friend, always ready for some fun. The suggestion sounded even better because they knew they weren't supposed to be out at all.

When Cassie opened the brown envelope, she found nothing but a cassette tape on which was printed "For Cassie and Vickie."

"Oh, oh," said Vickie. "I've got a bad feeling about this. Where's your tape player?"

"There's a little one up in my room," replied Cassie. "Come on, let's go listen."

Cassie retrieved the old tape player, while Vickie fell onto the bed. The tape was very scratchy, and there was nothing at first except static. Then they heard a man's baritone voice singing. There was no musical accompaniment, just the raw voice crooning "I'll be killing you." That was it, there was nothing else on the tape.

The two friends just gaped at each other. "First the black roses, and now this. What a jokester!" cried Vickie angrily.

"Can you imagine the nerve?" said Cassie, playing it again. It was the tune of the familiar old song "I'll Be Seeing You."

"I can't believe he'd go to all this trouble, just for a little fun. He's toying with us, enjoying himself at our expense. All we did is happen to be in the wrong place at the wrong time. Damn it anyway. Well, we're going to leave it right in the player for Jack and Bud to hear. It's too bad I've put my prints on it, but I was pretty careful. He had likely wiped his prints off anyway."

"He's not giving up, is he?" asked Vickie, shaking her head. "It's true what they say about sociopaths. They do like to taunt and tease."

"You know, Vic, I think we should try out the panic room. We should know just how good it is, or whether it's any good at all. Let's get the cats, and you and the cats go into it. When you're in there, I want you to whisper. I'll stay out here. I want to know whether you can hear anyone whispering or making any noise in there. I also want to know whether the cats can be heard if they meow or make a fuss."

"That's a great idea. We should have tested it a long time ago."

All thoughts of going for a ride, or going to the casino, had been chased from their minds by the arrival of the haunting little tape.

Going back downstairs to find Sugar Plum and Muffy, they checked to make sure that the alarm was on. In spite of their big talk, the cassette had made them nervous.

The two cats were indignant at being roused from their afternoon sleeps, but were quite intrigued with the room, which had not yet been investigated.

"Toodle-oo," said Vickie with a grin, as she closed the door and turned on her flashlight.

First Cassie checked to see whether she could see any light seeping out from the wall. Of course, it was still daylight, so it was pretty difficult to tell. They would have to test it again tonight. "Okay, Vickie, start whispering, and I'm going to put my ear right against the wall."

Vickie loved any foolishness like this, so she was quite happy to oblige. She started whispering obscenities, and then a few insults, just for fun.

"Start talking, Vic," commanded Cassie.

There was nothing but silence. "Vickie, are you talking?" yelled her friend, knocking on the wall.

There were still no sounds from within. Cassie put her ear right to the wall, and listened, but could hear nothing. The walls were thick, and definitely seemed soundproof.

Cassie waited a few minutes for the cats to start meowing, but they were as silent as Vickie seemed to be. Then she heard what she thought was a tiny meow.

Finally, she opened the door. "Were you talking?" she asked.

"Sure I was. Didn't you hear all the bad words I was using?" grinned Vickie. "Sugar started meowing too, but then she quieted down."

Both cats were now settling themselves on the blanket which Cass had put there for them. Vickie picked up Sugar Plum, and began to tickle her. She was a much more vociferous cat than Muffy, who was the calm, laid back one of the two.

"You like it in here, don't you, you little twerp," cooed Vickie. It didn't take Sugar long to tire of the tickling. She voiced her displeasure with one loud meow, as she jumped out of Vickie's arms, and cuddled up against Muffy on the blanket.

Vickie came out, but the two felines were quite happy to stay there. They loved this new dark space. Cass left the door open for them, so that they could come out whenever they chose.

"I guess it's good news and bad," she said, as she and Vickie parked themselves on the bed. "The good news is that it does seem pretty soundproof. If he wasn't listening really hard and concentrating, he wouldn't hear us. The bad news is, if we were hiding in there, maybe we wouldn't be able to hear what was going on out here. We would have no way of knowing whether an intruder had left or not."

"Let's hope we never have to try it out," said Vickie. "It's great to have it though, as long as we have time to round up the two pussums and get ourselves locked in."

"You know, if Dave would only come home and stay for a while, we wouldn't have to feel so nervous. He would be here to protect us, and the killer likely wouldn't try anything. It's just because we're alone that he's being so bold.

It's awful that he seems to like being away so much better than being here these days. Do you think maybe he's having an affair?"

"Oh, Cass. This is Dave, your own Dave. How could you even think such a thing?" Vickie was disgusted with Cass for her evil thoughts. She had great faith in Dave, and thought that her old friend was being paranoid.

"Well, he seems to have changed a lot these past three years. He's more remote, somehow, and certainly much more independent. Maybe I should never have given him that five million to do with as he likes. When I talk about going with him, he almost panics. He always has some reason why it isn't convenient, or why I would be terribly bored, or why it would hamper him in his work. It's all baloney. He just doesn't want me to go over there with him. Now why would that be?"

"I don't know, Cass. I just know that Dave is a really nice guy. He loves you, he loves the kids, and he loves his work. You should be happy that you have such a great husband. If Jack hadn't come back into your life, you would be totally content. Admit it. You're always comparing Dave to Jack these days, and that isn't fair. You should just forget about Jack, and get on with your marriage. That's what I think."

Vickie looked serious, and uncomfortable. There was no way that she would ever admit it to her best friend, but she had also been wondering whether maybe Dave had another woman stashed away somewhere in Europe. His wanderings seemed just too extreme these past three years. She would kill Dave with her bare hands, if she found out that he was cheating on Cassie. Cass deserved better than that, although, the way she was mooning over Jack, maybe it served her right. Who could tell?

Vickie sighed. Life was so darn complicated. She was thinking of her own Brian now. Of course, he had traveled extensively for years. She had never had the least suspicion that he might be playing around.

Brian was too much of a bookworm. He was too interested in dull old history. His idea of an exciting time was to curl up in front of the fire, with a glass of port and a dusty old book about times and people long gone. Putting Brian and some nubile young babe in the same sentence, was a total oxymoron. She had to smile at the very thought.

Chapter Forty-One

It must have been around midnight when Vickie wakened with a start. She had great hearing, and Cassie often teased her that she could hear a butter tart breathing. She was also a light sleeper. Something had wakened her, so she got up quietly and tiptoed to the door. She listened carefully, and to her dismay, she heard noises coming from the first floor. It was a big house, with a lot of rooms, so the sounds were faint, but there definitely were noises.

She padded silently across the hall to Cassie's room. It was always difficult to waken Cassie. She slept like Sleeping Beauty. They had often joked about how she would sleep through a fire, a hurricane, or even a Don Juan climbing into bed with her.

Vickie shook her gently, ready to put her hand over Cassie's mouth if she started to make a sound.

"What is it?" whispered Cassie, fully awake at last.

"There's someone downstairs. He's been moving around for a few minutes. He must be checking out all the rooms down there looking for us."

"How did he get in? I'm sure we set the alarm."

"I think so too, but come to the door and listen. There's definitely someone there."

Cass padded softly on the thick carpeting, and listened intently. "You're right. He's here, and he's looking for us. Where are the cats?"

Sugar Plum was still asleep on Vickie's bed, but Muffy was nowhere in sight.

"Shit. Don't tell me he's downstairs," groaned Cassie. There was no way that she would go into that panic room without her two little feline friends. She always had a fear of someone breaking in and hurting them.

Grabbing a flashlight, she whispered, "Hold onto Sugar, and I'll look for Muff. He sometimes likes to sleep in the little room at the end of the hall. It has that nice comforter he loves."

She hurried down the hall, afraid to use the flashlight in case the intruder might see it. Luckily, there were no impediments along the hallway, and she was able to get right into the small room without turning on the light.

Once inside the room, she flashed the light on the bed, and was thankful to see little Muffin curled up right in the middle, a contented little ball of fur. She snatched him, cuddled him to her chest, and hurried back to her bedroom.

The intruder could be coming up the stairs at any moment. She and Vickie hustled into the panic room, locked the door, and breathed a sigh of relief. They were safe. It was only then that they realized that neither one of them had thought to bring a cell phone.

"Oh shoot. We're stuck in here without a phone," whispered Vickie in a quiet little voice. "Do you think I have time to get yours? It's on your dresser, isn't it, or by your bedside?"

"Yes, but there's no way you're going out there. He's likely upstairs by now, and he'll be searching each room. You can't take the chance. We'll just have to do without it. We're totally safe here." She added that last little bit just to make herself feel better.

Fortunately, the cats were still intrigued with the room, which they had visited only once before. They seemed quite content to sniff around. Cassie gave them some treats, which she kept stored in the panic room, and she put a little catnip on a saucer. She had plenty of resources here for the cats, but nothing for her and Vickie. They had their flashlights, but that was all. The cell phones were of the utmost importance, and they were both lying uselessly in their bedrooms.

"When he comes upstairs, he's going to know that we're hiding someplace. We left the beds unmade, and the lights on. Damn. Did we even close the closet door?" whispered Vickie.

"Yes, I did shut it. At least we did that right. Now let's be really quiet, and see whether we can hear him. We may have to stay in here a long time, because we won't know whether he's still out there or not. Oh, if only we had those damn phones."

They sat quietly for a while, huddled together. Although it seemed like hours, it was likely only a few minutes. Neither one of them had a watch.

"Tomorrow I'm going to buy a clock for this room. It's ridiculous to be in here and have no idea of the time," whispered Cassie. Vickie only nodded in agreement.

They were both thinking of the night they had spent in the woods, huddled in the tiny rock depression. This panic room was infinitely better.

Eventually, they heard the very faint, very distant sound of a phone ringing in the bedroom. It was so faint that they weren't sure whether they were just imagining it.

"That's got to be Jack. I like it that he calls every night to see how we are. I'm surprised he'd call so late, but I told him to call any time he felt lonely or sad," whispered Cassie. "This is good. He's going to be really upset when we don't answer. He'll think for sure that the killer got us."

The phone rang several times, then stopped. Less than a minute later, it began ringing again. It rang several more times, then stopped.

Sugar and Muffy were getting restless. They had eaten the treats, rolled in the catnip, and investigated the litter box, but were now ready to move on to more interesting things. Sugie was scratching at the door, and meowing.

Cass picked her up and tried to sooth her, but Sugar wasn't having any of it. She wanted out, and she wanted out now.

Cassie was clutching her to her chest, trying to muffle the sounds as best she could, when she heard a distant voice calling, "Cass, where the heck are you?"

In the dark, she grabbed Vickie's hand. "Did that sound like a voice calling?"

"I think so, but I could barely hear it."

"It could be Jack. I gave him a key, and the code for the alarm, so that he could get in if he ever suspected that we were hurt."

"Cass, where the devil are you?" That was accompanied with a pounding on the door of the hidden room. "Are you two hiding in there? For Gawd's sake, come out. This is ridiculous. I'm not in the mood for games."

"Dave?" asked Cassie, her face up against the door. "Is that you?"

"Well, who do you think it is, Jack the Ripper? Come on out. There's no one here but little old Chester the Molester."

With huge sighs of relief, they unlocked the door, and stepped out into the bedroom.

"Dave," cried Cassie in delight. "What are you doing here?"

"Well, that's some welcome," he said crossly. "Who did you think it was?"

"We thought it was the killer," said Vickie with a grin. "You shouldn't come sneaking into your own home like that. You nearly killed us with fright."

"Sorry about that. I got a chance to fly home for a couple of days, and I took it. I didn't think there was any need to let you know. I wanted to surprise you," he added, truculently.

"You certainly did that," answered Cassie crossly. "Why didn't you answer the phone when it was ringing?"

"I had gone back out to the car to get my briefcase, and when I raced to answer it, they had hung up. Who would be calling at this hour, anyway? Must have been a crank or a crackpot."

Cassie and Vickie looked at each other guiltily. They were pretty sure that it had been Jack. Of course, it might have been the killer calling to tease and annoy them.

Vickie realized that Dave hadn't hugged Cassie, or given her a kiss the way he usually did. Cassie hadn't tried to hug him either. What was going on here? Things seemed unusually strained.

"Uh, can I make you a cup of tea, or do you want a drink?" asked Cassie, trying to pull herself together. She felt foolish about hiding in the panic room like a couple of kids, and she felt unreasonably cross with Dave for scaring them that way.

"No thanks. I'm really tired. It's been a long flight, and I had to wait nearly an hour at the airport for the shuttle. Think I'll just head off to bed."

As the three of them stood awkwardly in the middle of the bedroom, they heard footsteps pounding up the stairs, and a voice shouting, "Cassie, where are you? Cass, talk to me, dammit. What the hell has happened here?"

Chapter Forty-Two

Cassie had not only given Jack the alarm code, but she had also given him a key to the house. It all made perfect sense. In case the killer did happen to get at them, get into the house and kill them or take them hostage, it would be very beneficial for Jack to have a key and the code.

Unfortunately, tonight was a bad time for him to have both. Dave looked at him in total amazement, as Jack rushed into the bedroom, calling Cassie's name, and looking scared. The usually cool, unruffled, and unflappable Jack Willinger feared that something had happened to Cassie, and he wasn't hiding his feelings. He looked much more concerned than a detective would be. He saw Cassie before he spotted Dave, who was standing over by his dresser, emptying the change from his pockets.

"Cass, are you okay? Why didn't you answer the phone?" He grabbed her hands, and looked right into her eyes, as he asked these questions. Actually, it looked as if he was about to hug her, when he was aware of a voice saying,

"What the hell is going on here? What are you doing here, and how the hell did you get in? Most importantly, who the hell are you, although I think I can guess."

Jack looked surprised to see Dave. "Well, hello. You must be Dave. Finally we meet. I'm Jack Willinger, Cassie's old childhood friend, and Vickie's too. I'm a detective with the Niagara Regional Police Department. I thought you were away in Europe. When did you get home?"

Dave was immediately up in arms. "What do you care when I got home? I asked what you're doing here."

Jack appeared calm, and in control of the situation now. "I guess those are legitimate questions," he laughed, nodding his head slightly. "I've been calling each night to check on the gals. You know, of course, that there's a killer on the loose, and he has targeted them because they, or at least Cassie, saw him throw a woman off a balcony at Edgewater.

They both saw him coming out of an elevator a few minutes later, so he knows that they could testify against him. He made a few attempts against them while they were on their cruise, and now he has followed them here to Niagara, and has been threatening them. I'm sure you know all this, and I'm rather surprised that you weren't here looking after your wife."

Jack said this with a bit of mischief in his soul. He wasn't sure just how much Cassie had told her husband, and he didn't like Dave just on principle. This guy was never around when Cassie most needed him, and he seemed to place much more importance on his business than on his wife.

He continued with his reply. "Since you haven't been around at all to protect them, we're doing the best we can." He couldn't resist that little dig.

"We don't have enough man power to give them good coverage twenty-four hours a day, so my partner and I have been trying to keep a close check on them. When I called tonight, no one answered. That set alarm bells ringing, because they were supposed to be here, safe and sound. Cassie had given me a key, and the alarm code, to use in case they were in any trouble, so, when I got no answer to my phone calls, naturally I rushed over."

Jack didn't seem at all ill at ease with Dave, but Dave was furious.

"Well, I'm so glad to see our tax dollars at work, so to speak," said Dave sarcastically. "I'm really impressed that you would be calling in the middle of the night. That seems a bit above the call of duty. Didn't it occur to you that they might just be sleeping? The entire matter is utterly ridiculous. Cassie and Vickie can take care of themselves. They don't need some cop barging in at one in the morning, and trying to be a hero. I don't care whether you're an old childhood friend or not."

This speech was bad enough, and Jack couldn't help a little grin, as he stood casually, listening to Dave spout off. His nonchalant attitude seemed to rile Dave even further, so that he added more fuel to the fire, much to Cassie's distress.

"We'll take the key back now, thank you, and we'll be changing the code. This house is very safe, and, anyway, I don't believe there's any killer after them. If you knew them as well as I do, you'd know that they both have vivid imaginations, and are always looking for some imagined adventure."

As he said this, he tried to put his arm around Cassie, but she shrugged him off.

Her blue eyes were blazing. She couldn't believe what she was hearing. Dave was being insufferable and rude. This was totally out of character for her usually quiet and laid back husband. What was the matter with him?

"Dave, stop it. Jack is only trying to help, and he's been wonderful. Vickie and I appreciate that he and his partner Bud have been keeping a close eye on us. Certainly you haven't been anywhere within shouting distance, and whether you believe it or not, we are in danger. We've been getting threatening messages, and there's a lot that's been going on. Please don't make a fuss, when you don't have any idea of what's been happening."

She felt sick at her stomach, standing here in her own bedroom looking from Jack to Dave, and seeing that Dave was coming up a poor second.

"Come on, let's all go downstairs and have a drink. We'll catch you up to date." She was trying to diffuse the situation, and help Dave save face. Dave, however, was really wound up.

"I'm not going anywhere except to bed, and I want this cop out of my house." This was said with great disdain, as he stared at Jack.

"Come on, Jack," said Vickie, taking his arm. "Dave's tired. We should let him get his rest. Cass, are you coming?"

"Yes I am," said Cassie crossly, glowering at Dave, before the three of them headed down the stairs.

"Jack, I'm so sorry. I don't know what's happened to Dave. He's usually so easy going and polite. He must be exhausted." She was trying to make excuses for her husband, but she was furious with him. He had acted like a total jackass.

"Well, that went well," laughed Vickie, as they sat in the library. "I've never seen Dave so riled up. He must have had a long and tiring trip." She had always liked and admired Dave, but even she was embarrassed at how rude he had been. You never know about people, she thought to herself, as Cassie poured them three glasses of wine, with a shaking hand. Then Vickie wondered whether maybe Dave suspected, and felt the feelings, which crackled between Cassie and Jack. That was possible, but would be very unfortunate.

"I apologize for my husband," said Cassie, as she handed Jack his glass, "and I'm sure he'll apologize himself tomorrow, once he's had a good sleep. You just really took him by surprise."

She then took a breath, and changed the subject. "Thank goodness it was a false alarm. We wakened, and heard someone moving around down here. Of course we thought that it was the killer, so we dashed into the panic room, and, in our haste and excitement, we forgot our cell phones. We could very faintly hear the phone ringing, but were afraid to open the door and go to answer it. For all we knew, the killer could have been right outside the closet door. We figured it was you on the phone, and were hoping that you would come out to the house to see what was wrong. How in the world could we have known that it was Dave? He should have let me know that he was coming."

"Oh, he likely thought it would be fun to come home and surprise you," said Jack, amiably. "Don't worry about his attitude. It must have been a shock to him to see me rush into the bedroom and make a grab for you." He laughed as he thought of the look on Dave's face. "It wasn't a very auspicious meeting, though, was it? I hope we can get back on more solid ground once he calms down."

As the three old friends sat there, sipping their wine, they had no way of knowing that the unexpected events which were to come, would change their lives irrevocably. This was just Act One in a complicated drama, which was about to be played on the Niagara stage.

Chapter Forty-Three

When Cassie finally went up to bed, Dave was either asleep, or putting up a pretty good pretense. He was lying almost on the edge of the kingsized bed, so Cassie clung to her side, leaving a space the size of a country between them.

The next morning, Vickie took off right after breakfast. She said she was going down to the boutique to have a visit with Steffie and Kitty. She wanted to give Cassie and Dave privacy, as they worked out this little glitz in the relationship.

Cassie didn't want her to go, but Vickie was adamant. She assured Cass that she would be very careful, and would go directly to the boutique. "I'll call you as soon as I get there," she promised.

"Okay, and call me just before you leave to come back. Keep your phone right in your pocket all the time," warned Cassie, as she waved goodbye to her friend. She wasn't happy about being alone with Dave. She was still angry and puzzled by his boorish attitude the previous night. They had been through many quarrels in their marriage, however, and they would get through this one, or so she told herself.

Dave was cold and withdrawn when he finally came down to breakfast. Saying that he had errands to do, he left before Cass could find out how long he intended to be home this time.

She thought it would be good to have a day to herself, and started it by playing one of Muffy's games, while Sugar Plum watched with lazy interest. The game consisted of Cassie throwing a little furry mouse up in the air. Muffy would leap up, catch the mouse in mid-air, rough it up a bit, then bring it halfway back to Cass. He would never bring it all the way back, either through a recalcitrant nature, laziness, or a sense of pride at not being subservient to a human master. Cass liked to think that he was just showing his intelligence and sense of humour.

After the game, she didn't feel like doing any housework, so she made a chocolate cake, (Dave's favourite), put a small pork roast in the oven, and curled up in her comfy reading chair. Muff and Sugar joined her, and the three of them had a pleasantly quiet afternoon.

When Vickie came home around four o'clock, Dave had still not returned. It was almost six o'clock before he came in.

Dinner was stilted and awkward. Vickie and Cassie kept up a steady stream of conversation, while Dave ate churlishly, barely looking up from his plate.

Cass kept thinking of how solicitous and loving he had been when she was in the hospital in Panama City, after the snakebite. He had been right there for her, even postponing his return trip to Europe in order to be with her. What in the world had happened this time? Surely he couldn't be jealous of Jack. He had no idea of her feelings for Jack, or that she and Jack had once been lovers. Why was he acting so childishly? Had something gone wrong in Europe? Was he sick? A dozen scenarios were racing through her mind, but none of them made much sense.

After dinner was finished, and the table was cleared, Cassie said she was going up to shower and wash her hair.

"I'll be down in about an hour, and maybe we can watch a movie," she said brightly, trying to act as if nothing was wrong.

Dave simply said, "Vickie, come and have a drink with me in the library. I'd like to talk with you."

Vickie and Cassie exchanged puzzled glances, as Cass headed up the stairs, and Vickie followed Dave into the library.

"What's up, Dave?" asked Vickie, as she settled into a chair.

Instead of answering her right away, he handed her a glass of wine. Placing his glass on a table, he pulled off the pale blue sweater he had been wearing over his shirt. "Whew, it's hot in here," he muttered, as he sat down.

Actually, Vickie thought it was comfortably cool, but she didn't say anything.

Finally Dave sighed, and put down his glass. "Vic, this is going to come as a shock, but I need your advice. You know Cassie so well. You have to help me figure out how I'm going to tell her."

"Tell her what?" Vickie was suddenly very uneasy. Dave looked sick. He was drawn and pale, and obviously nervous. Was he incurably ill? Was that what he wanted to tell her?

"Okay, here goes. I'm just going to jump right in because there's no easy way. Vic, I'm leaving Cassie."

The words hung in the air like a strange smell. Vickie visualized them hanging there, three ugly little words. Then she could see them breaking apart, and slowly falling to the carpet. She put down her glass slowly, as she stared at Dave, her big brown eyes full of disbelief.

"You can't be serious. Why in the world would you ever leave Cassie? Don't tell me you think you've found someone else? Where in the world could you ever find anyone who would be better for you than Cassie? She's the perfect wife. You hit the jackpot when you got Cassie. What do you mean that you're leaving her?"

Vickie was so incredulous that she was sputtering. It must be some kind of a joke.

"That's just it. She's almost too perfect. She can do anything and everything. She's intelligent, good looking, talented, and full of fun. She's generous and thoughtful. She's got charisma, and dammit, she's rich too. I know it doesn't put me in a very good light, but I resent that she has all that money. Ever since she inherited it, I've hated it. She doesn't need me anymore."

"Are you nuts?" laughed Vickie, shaking her head. "Cassie can't help the fact that she inherited that money. She didn't even want it at first. She gave you five million as a gift right away. You can do anything you want with it. Are you absolutely crazy? Are you telling me that you're leaving her just because she has too much money?"

"No, of course not. I'm leaving her for many reasons. You said it yourself. She's almost too good to be true. Look at that beautiful cattery which she has imagined, designed and built. It's wonderful. She's done a terrific job on it, with your help, of course. People are coming from all over just to see it. I'm sure she's told you that ABC wants to come up and do a segment on it. Imagine, my Cass! She can do anything if she puts her mind to it. The thing is, she doesn't need me,

Vickie, and that's very emasculating. Maybe that makes me a small, petty person, but that's the way it is."

"Well, poor Dave. He has a perfect wife. Oh boo hoo. What a tragedy! Do you know how many men would give just about anything to have Cassie for a wife?" asked Vickie loyally.

"Yes, and I think that Jack Willinger is one of them. I saw how they looked at each other last night. You can't tell me there isn't something going on there. You know, for a very long time I've felt that Cassie was holding back some part of herself. I've always felt that there must have been someone at some point in her life, someone she loved extravagantly. After last night I think I'm right. No, don't interrupt, there's more."

She had started to get up, but she sat back down abruptly.

Dave looked guilty as he said quietly. "You were right earlier on. It's not just the money thing. I really have found someone else."

Vickie simply stared at him. "Well, you duplicitous jerk. I would never have believed it. Who is she? Where is she?"

"Her name is Sophia, and she's in Italy waiting for me."

"Sophia," snorted Vickie. "What is this, an Italian movie? Does she have big boobs and bare feet? How long has this sordid little affair been going on?"

"Come on, Vic. I'm looking for a little sympathy, a little understanding. I need you to help me tell Cassie. It's not a sordid affair. It's, well, I don't really know what it is. I got myself into a mess, and now there's really no honorable way out. I'm not going to go into all the details. Suffice it to say that I met Sophia at the right time. I was pretty depressed. Next thing I knew, she was pregnant, and I was caught in a trap of my own making. That's why I need your help. We've always been friends, you and I."

"Well, you're not getting any help from me, you horse's ass. You have to dump this Sophia right away. Get rid of her. You made a mistake. Now you're going to fix it. Pay her off, so she can go and have the baby some place. Cass will forgive you, and then you two can start all over."

"No, it's more complicated than that." At this point Dave got up and started pacing up and down in front of Vickie.

Vickie stared at him in dismay. "Oh no, she's had the baby already?"

Dave was silent, just looking at her sadly. Then he said, "We have a little seven month old boy. His name is Buckminster Meredith, Bucky for short. There's no middle name. Vickie, he's the sweetest thing on earth. He has black curly hair, and big brown eyes, and he laughs all the time. When he sees me, he just grins. I could show you some pictures, but I suspect that this might not be the right time."

His face had softened, and his eyes crinkled as he spoke about the baby.

Vickie felt a rush of anger. "No, I'm not ready to look at any damn pictures. How could you Dave? How could you get yourself into this muddle?"

"Okay, no excuses. I was lonely, plain and simple. I met Sophia, and she needed me. She has nothing. Cassie has everything. Sophia was fresh and exciting."

"What does that mean, that Cassie is stale and dull?" Vickie was ready to tear Dave limb from limb. She jumped up, and putting her hands over her ears, she exclaimed, "I don't want to hear any more of this garbage." Then, a thought struck her. "You rat," she exclaimed, pointing her finger at him. "Last summer, when you flew home and brought Cassie that gorgeous ruby pendant, that was a guilt thing, wasn't it? That was just you trying to assuage your guilty conscience. What a typical 'man' thing to do. You piece of shit. Your little Italian dolly, Miss Sophia, must have been pregnant then."

She sat down again, and just stared at him in disbelief. "Oh Dave, you've let everyone down, but mostly yourself. Where's the man of decency and integrity we all knew and loved, at least we thought we knew you. You're a jerk with a capital "J"._

"I'm sorry that you feel that way, Vickie. I've always felt that you and I had a special bond. I hoped I could count on you to understand. I'm going to tell Cass tonight, and then I'm flying back to Italy tomorrow.

I know my Cassie, and she can take things in stride. Look how she handled all that mess about her parentage and the inheritance. She's good at rolling with the punches."

"Oh, so you've decided to give her a few extra punches, is that it?" she asked bitterly.

"No, of course not. Give me a break. It's just that I know she's strong, and I have to tell her. I can't let this go on any longer. Sophia and the baby need me now. I wish with all my heart that this hadn't happened, but it has, so I have to do what I think is right. I thought you'd understand."

"Well, you thought wrong about me understanding, and there's absolutely no way you can tell her right now. Think this out, Dave. Cassie has a murderer stalking her at this moment in time. He's determined to kill her. Besides that, have you forgotten that she's just recovering from a serious snakebite? She almost died on us. That's enough on her plate. She doesn't need to hear that you've been cheating on her. She doesn't need to know the sordid little fact that you've got a girlfriend and a baby stashed away in Italy, waiting for you to come back to them."

As Vickie said this, she looked up, and her heart sank. An ashen faced Cassie was standing in the doorway.

Chapter Forty-Four

Cass felt as if someone had poured hot molten lava into her stomach. It burned fiercely for a few moments, then turned to a dull heaviness. It was as if the lava had solidified into a solid mass, and she would never feel lighthearted or happy again.

Vickie ran to her, and put her arms around her. "Oh, Cass, I'm so sorry that you overheard us. You shouldn't have learned about it this way. Look, I'm going to go upstairs and leave you two to sort this out. I'll be awake, though, and I'll leave my door ajar. When you come up, I'll be there for you, just in case you want to talk."

Cassie nodded absently, never taking her eyes off Dave, who was now pacing uncomfortably, looking like a man about to face a firing squad.

Finally, she walked slowly over to the chair, and sat down. Her blue eyes, which Dave had always loved, were full of disbelief. It broke his heart to know how badly he had hurt her.

As he began to talk, Cassie had the strange sensation that her ears were shutting down. She could see his lips moving, and his hands gesticulating, but she couldn't hear him. It was as if she was watching a silent movie. Then, suddenly, his voice cut in again, "and he's so little. I just can't abandon them."

Cassie's life, as she had come to know it, was suddenly and irrevocably changed. Things would never be the same. Well, "they," the elusive and ubiquitous "they," always said that change was good. Where did she go from here? She tried to keep thoughts of Jack out of the equation.

Her heart felt like a fragile crystal plate on which Dave had just stomped. It felt as if it had splintered into a million pieces. It was physically painful, and she wondered vaguely whether she might be having a heart attack. Then, taking a couple of deep breaths, the pain subsided, and she just stared at Dave. Somehow, come to think of it, this wasn't the surprise it should have been. For weeks now she had been feeling that something was seriously wrong. She just hadn't let herself accept it.

Inexplicably, the fact that she was being stalked by a determined and psychotic killer, seemed a non-event at the moment. Right now, she was being killed by her husband, figuratively if not physically. It seemed ironic.

At the moment, she didn't feel anything except that heavy dullness. Later, she would likely go upstairs and stab her pillow to death, or kick the wall till her feet bled, but now she just sat there calmly, trying to make sense of what Dave was saying.

"You can't call me any names that I haven't called myself, Cass. I know I've screwed up royally, but now I have to step up to bat and do the right thing. You have everything, and Sophia has nothing. She loves me, and I love Bucky. That's the picture. I've never stopped loving you, and I'm sure I never will, but for a long time I've felt like an unnecessary adjunct to this marriage. Like the old cliché says, it takes two to tango, and we've both been dancing to different tunes. It happens, and it's sad, but we have to forge ahead."

Cass realized that he was right. Her problem was that she could always see two sides to every story. She was not blameless in this little soap opera. She had been mooning over Jack ever since he came back into her life three years ago. That was when she had inherited all the money too, and had found out the truth about her parentage. All those events had likely changed her considerably more than she had realized. She knew that she had gained confidence, and had more feelings of self-worth now, and she knew that she felt capable of handling any situation if she had to.

They sat and talked for several hours, and it gradually became like a comfortable discussion between two old friends. It hurt fiercely, and she felt like a failure, but she just couldn't be too angry with Dave, regretful, yes, but angry, no. She was just as much the cause of this break-up as he was.

They were both grateful that their son and daughter were adults now. They were away at university, starting their own lives. It wouldn't hurt them too much. It was all very civilized, and Dave looked both bewildered and relieved. It had been much easier than he had expected, but he wished desperately that he could tell her it was all a joke, and just never go back to Italy. Then he remembered little Bucky, and he knew what he had to do.

Dave wanted Cassie to tell their son and daughter. Cassie was adamant that, because Dave was the architect of this fiasco, Dave was the one to tell them, and eventually he agreed. Now there was really nothing more to say.

A very contrite and subdued Dave, said he would sleep in the south wing. It had a lovely sitting room, bedroom and ensuite, and it had not been used as yet. It was meant for guests, and Dave suddenly realized with sadness, that he was now a guest in his own home. Things would never be the same. The thought pierced his heart, and he wondered how he had ever managed to entangle himself like this.

If only he and Cassie could run away and start all over. He still loved her, and he loved her way more than he loved Sophia, but there was little Bucky to consider. He had to do the right thing, and the right thing was to go back to Italy, and take care of the mess he had made. Life was strange, and humans were even more strange.

Cassie spent the rest of the night talking with Vickie. Vickie, having always liked and supported Dave, was torn by this dreadful news. She didn't like Jack, but she had now lost her admiration and liking for Dave. She too could see both sides of the situation, and she felt heartsick for her friends. Cassie, of course, would always come first in her loyalty.

"You know, Vic. I could have offered to give Sophia ten million dollars if she would just take the baby and disappear. She likely would, but Dave seems so besotted with little Bucky, that I didn't have the heart to do it. Also, to tell the truth, I'm not sure that I would give that amount of money just to have Dave stay with me. I'll never feel the same about him now. You know I'm not a very forgiving person.

I just feel so ashamed that I've let my marriage fail. I think maybe I started moving away from Dave the very day that Jack walked back into my life. Remember that day? I danced and boogied all around the kitchen. It was as if the sun had suddenly started shining so brightly that it blinded me.

Adding to that, I think that Dave started moving away from me the day that I inherited all the money. He acted excited and happy, but there was always some kind of an undercurrent of resentment." She sighed at this point, and added, "Do you think it's really been that obvious that I haven't been able to get Jack out of my mind?"

Vickie didn't know how to reply to that one. It was written all over Cassie's face every time she saw Jack, or talked to him, or thought about him. Maybe, however, Dave hadn't noticed. He had likely been too preoccupied with his own troubles. Who knew?

What she did know for sure was that Cassie needed a friend now. Unfortunately the timing was terrible. They couldn't go out and have fun to take their minds off Dave, because they were being stalked by a killer. What a fiasco!

Sugar and Muffin chose that moment to appear at the door of Vickie's bedroom. Muff went right to Cassie, and wound himself round and round her legs, purring wildly. He looked up at her then, and squeezed his eyes shut. Cass had once read that when a cat does that, it is his way of saying "I love you." She picked him up, and rubbed noses with him, then surprised herself by bursting into tears. The usually calm, cool, all pulled together "classy Cassie" was losing it. "At least I know someone who loves me unconditionally," she sobbed, half laughing and half crying.

"You know two someones," said Vickie, putting her arms around Cassie and Muffin. The three of them had a group hug, while Sugar Plum stopped her preening, and gave them a quizzical gaze. Then, assured that things were all right, she went back to washing her tail.

Cassie eventually sat down in the little chair beside the bed. Sugar Plum then did something quite out of keeping with her nature. She would snuggle up beside someone on the couch, but she didn't like laps, and never willingly sat in one. This night, or early morning, she jumped into Cassie's lap, stretched up, and began to lick the tears from her face.

Cass and Vickie couldn't decide whether Sugar was trying to comfort Cassie, or whether she just liked the taste of the salty tears. Whatever the reason, the gesture made Cassie feel better. With Vickie, Sugar and Muff at her side, she could get over this latest crisis.

"Cass, in spite of what we told Jack and Bud, I think that tomorrow or today, since it's almost morning, we should get out of here, and do the tourist thing. It will take your mind off things, at least temporarily, and will do us both good. We'll be careful, but let's ride the Spanish aero car, go on the Maid of the Mist, go up the Skylon, and have dinner out at some neat place. It will distract us, and we'll have some much needed fun."

"Right on, baby. I feel better already. That woman killing monster doesn't scare us. Let him do his worst. We can handle him."

This, of course, was just whistling past the graveyard, and they both knew it. They also knew that they couldn't stay locked in the house today. They needed a diversion.

Cassie continued, "As for Dave, well, what's happened was maybe inevitable, and, in truth, I feel sorry for him. I think he's got the short end of the stick. Imagine being married to someone called Sophia, fathering a baby called Bucky, and having to live in Italy! God help us! That Sophia is going to be a barnacle on his butt for the rest of his life!"

"Yes, and she likely has hairy armpits too," added Vickie.

They dissolved in laughter, as the two cats scurried away to find quieter quarters.

Chapter Forty-Five

The little boutique called "Aunt Aggie's Attic" was so busy, that Steffie and Kitty hadn't had a chance to talk all morning.

Steffie was showing some crystal earrings to a young woman, who was already wearing earrings which dangled to her shoulders. For some reason they looked pretty good on her. On most females they would have been overkill. The new crystal ones, however, were much classier.

Behind all the make-up, Steffie suspected that she was a very pretty girl. Why would any mother let her daughter go out with all that make-up painted on her face? Steff remembered how strict her mom had been with her, and how she had never been allowed to wear anything but a little lipstick. Times have changed so much, she thought, as she handed the girl her receipt. I must be getting old, she thought, with a little grimace.

It was then that she noticed Kitty helping a very large man, who had a very large beard. Whew, that must be hot on a day like this, she thought to herself, as she went to straighten a row of cat trinket boxes. They were all shapes and sizes, in ceramic, glass and wood, and they were favourites in the shop. It was the first spare moment she had had all day.

Kitty seemed to be enjoying her conversation with the large man, who was rather attractive, except for that outrageous beard. She couldn't see his eyes behind the sunglasses, but he was well spoken, and nicely dressed.

"I'm looking for two silver bracelets. They have to be identical, and they have to be rather plain," he said firmly, as he looked into the glass jewellery case.

"We don't have many choices in silver bracelets," murmured Kitty, as she took out a couple to show him.

"Oh, I like this one. Hope it's not too expensive, since I have to buy two of them. Actually, maybe you can give me a discount for buying two." He laughed, and, taking off his sunglasses, he gave Kitty a sort of wink. She wasn't really sure. Maybe he just had something in his eye. Then he casually replaced the sunspecs on his bearded face.

"Please don't tell me that you have two girlfriends, and you're giving them both the same bracelet," she laughed, as she displayed them on a velvet cloth.

"Oh God, no," he answered vehemently. "They're for my twin sisters. I've bought them a pile of gifts already, but just need something else. I like this one," he said, picking up a very plain silver bracelet with a fancy clasp on it. "Tell me it's the cheapest one you have," he laughed again, with a disarming smile.

"As a matter of fact, it is the least expensive one we have at the moment," Kitty assured him, "and we do have two of them. Are you going to have them engraved?"

"Of course. That's the whole point," he laughed, but there seemed no humour in the sound. "Is there a place near here where I can get them engraved right away?"

"Sure. If you go two blocks down to the right, there's a little jewellery shop on this same side of the street. They'll likely do them for you while you wait."

"Great. In that case, I'll take them both, and don't forget the discount."

Kitty thought that he seemed a bit demanding, but it was a good sale, and the customer was always right.

The cash transaction completed, Steffie and Kitty watched the large fellow stride out, clasping his purchases.

"I've never seen him in here before, have you?" asked Steffie.

"No, I don't think so. He's likely a tourist like most of them," shrugged Kitty, heading back to the storage room for more supplies. Just as she reached the door, she said over her shoulder, "Did you see the roll of money he had? It looked as if he had a few thousand bucks in his pocket. Wonder if he's heading to the casino."

She had a nagging feeling that she had seen him before, yet she didn't know anyone with a beard like that. Why did he seem familiar? Likely, if they hadn't been so busy that day, the answer might have come to her.

The next day was Steffie's day off, and she called Cassie to ask whether she could drop around to see her. Steffie had painted a watercolor for Cass, something which Cassie had requested some time ago. It was a painting of the view from the condo at Edgewater Beach Resort. The painting depicted a sunset with all its attendant glory. The purples, reds, oranges and pinks were bold and high spirited. She had captured the magic of the sugary white sand beach, and the eye was drawn to the grace of a single pelican silhouetted against the majestic sky.

Steffie was proud of the painting, and anxious to see Cassie's reaction.

Cassie invited her to come for lunch, so Steffie packed up her painting, and set out along the parkway.

It was a day which couldn't make up its mind just what it wanted to do. One moment the sun was shining in a friendly fashion, the next moment the skies were a dull, sullen gray, foreboding and grim.

Steffie was prone to quite severe mood swings, mostly due to her artistic temperament. Today, she was feeling depressed and anxious, but couldn't figure why. She felt as if there was something she had forgotten, yet couldn't imagine what it could be.

While Steffie was driving along the Niagara River Parkway towards Cassie's new home, Cass was sitting at her computer. She was musing about the strange twists and turns which her life had taken, and was gazing unseeingly at the screen. Thinking of all the money which she had inherited, she couldn't help but feel that she was a very lucky woman. She loved her new home, as well as the freedom which all the money had given her.

On the other hand, there was a crazy killer right on her heels, not to mention her husband of many years, who was dumping her for a hot little Italian number named Sophia. Was she really lucky, or was she incredibly unfortunate? Who knew?

As she printed out some important papers concerning the running of Cassandra's Cattery, the printer indicated that it was out of ink, ---- again!

"Well, phooey, you stupid thing," she exclaimed with annoyance and disbelief. "I just put new ink in you last week. You can't possibly be out of it already."

"What's the problem, lady fair?" asked Vickie, sticking her head in the door. She was cuddling Sugar Plum in her arms like a baby. The cat was on her back, little paws up in the air. Vickie was gently rubbing Sugie's tummy. Sugar appeared hypnotized, and gazed blankly at Vickie, while lying perfectly still. This was unheard of behaviour for Sugar Plum, who was always a bit feisty, and liked to do things her way.

"For a gal who always claims to be a dog lover, you surely do have a way with cats," grinned Cassie. "I'm complaining because this darn printer is guzzling ink like an old wino guzzles rotgut. This stuff is so expensive. It must be about $5,000 per gallon."

Vickie agreed. "Well, why don't you just throw the printer out and buy yourself a new one, oh wealthy one," she laughed.

"That's a good idea," said Cass. "If we ever get the chance to get out and go shopping again, I'll pick up one. I'm still not quite used to the fact that I can afford any darn thing I want, within reason, but I have enough Scottish blood in me that I hate to be wasteful."

She turned off the computer, and they walked up the hall to the living room, to watch for Steffie.

The hypnotic spell broken, Sugar decided it was time to move, and jumping down, she headed for the kitchen. Cass and Vickie stood looking out the front window, blissfully unaware of the excitement which was about to occur.

Chapter Forty-Six

Steffie enjoyed the long driveway, banked on both sides by trees, and clumps of wildflowers. They presented a beautiful approach to Cassie's spectacular new house. Steffie herself presented a beautiful picture, in her red and white crew necked top, white slacks, and red sandals. Her raven black hair was flying freely around her somewhat exotic face.

Cassie and Vickie greeted her like a long lost friend. They had managed to escape the confines of the house the previous day, and had enjoyed a wonderful, fun-filled few hours of playing tourist. Their day had included riding the Spanish Aero Car, taking a trip on the Maid of the Mist, (with Vickie complaining all the way that this would be the day the brave little boat capsized), and lunching at the Queenston Heights restaurant. Now, slightly guilt-ridden, but happy that nothing bad had happened, they were trying to be good, to please Jack and Bud, and to stay locked inside. Almost any diversion was welcome, and they were delighted to see Steffie.

She unpacked the large painting, and waited for the reaction. It was more than she had hoped. Cassie was thrilled with it, and Vickie asked if Steffie would do a similar one for her. She would pay to have it shipped to Vancouver.

"I really love it, Steffie. What a talent you have. I have a perfect spot for it in my bedroom. I'll be able to look at it every night, and remember all the wonderful times we four gals had in Panama City Beach. You've done a fabulous job. I absolutely have to have one," said Vickie impetuously.

Cassie was just as enthusiastic, so they all trotted up to her bedroom to see how it would look. They tried it against one wall, and then another, till they found the perfect spot.

"Cass, I can't believe this house of yours. It's so gorgeous. Don't you get lost in it though? I mean, there's a whole other wing down that hall, isn't there?" asked Steffie in amazement.

"Tell me about it," laughed Cassie sheepishly. "The house was big to start with, and when we bought it, as you know, we added the library and the sunroom, and that entire wing. We just thought that when our kids are married and come back for visits with their children, there would be lots of room for them.

Fortunately Dave is quite willing to let me have the house, without any arguments, simply because I paid for it. I'm wondering now, though, whether I'll find it too big when I'm all alone." There was a slight catch in her voice as she said this. She couldn't picture herself rattling around in this mansion, yet she loved it, and didn't want to live anywhere else. Maybe she would invite some poor homeless person to move in with her. She smiled at the thought. How ironic life could be. Just when they had finally found the house of their dreams, their marriage had gone south. Who ever would have guessed?

They were enjoying a lunch of dainty little sandwiches and tiny home made raspberry tarts with whipped cream, when the doorbell rang.

Cass and Vickie looked at each other without moving. Jack had told them over and over not to answer the door unless it was either Bud or himself. All three of them hurried to peek out a front window. Someone in a Fed Ex uniform was standing there impatiently. He was of average height, and there was no way that he could be the killer. Still, Cass didn't want to take any chances. The small packet he was holding could be dangerous.

"There's something wrong with that guy's face," said Vickie, peering at him through the window. Steffie, the artist, saw it at once.

She laughed quietly as she remarked, "His features are thick, and they look unsymmetrical. Actually, he looks as if his face was left out in the sun too long, and everything has melted and slopped around a bit. Poor guy, I wonder whether he's been in an accident or something."

Cass said, "Keep an eye on him. I'll be right back." She then hurried upstairs to the room which was right over the front door, opened the window and called down. "Would you please just leave the package on that bench over under the tree? I can't come to the door right now, and it will be safe there."

The Fed Ex fellow looked up, and grinned at this good looking babe yelling at him from upstairs. He wished she would open the door. Maybe he could flirt with her a bit, although, someone living in this grand house wouldn't be much interested in him, he told himself glumly. He was sadly aware of what his face looked like, and he knew that there was no woman on earth who was going to find him attractive. He could still dream though. If only he could meet some blind girl, he knew that she would find him witty and gentle. Fat chance of that, he thought, with a sigh.

"Are you sure you don't want to come down and sign for it? Don't want me to get in trouble, do you?"

"If you get in trouble, just have your boss call me. I'll straighten him out," called Cassie. "Oh, before you go, can you tell me whether there's a return address on it?"

The deliveryman looked carefully, then called up again. "Says its from John Doe," he laughed. "Guess someone's playing a little joke on you," he added.

"That's no joke," said Cass. "Is it heavy?"

The fellow shook it, hefted it from hand to hand, and yelled up, "It's very light. It must be something pretty small."

Cassie had flinched as she saw him handling the parcel so carelessly. If it was something explosive, surely it would go off.

"Just leave it there on the bench, please, and get out of the way. It could be a bomb," she warned.

Fed Ex man thought that was hilarious. He liked a babe with a sense of humour.

"All rightyo then," he laughed, as he placed the package on the bench, which was situated several feet from the front door. He then sauntered back to his truck, and took off down the long driveway. This gal was a little off the wall, he decided, but she sure was a looker.

Cass decided that it was such a relatively small package, that even if it was a bomb, it couldn't do too much damage. She was sure, however, that it wasn't anything dangerous. It was likely another stupid cassette tape which was intended to scare them.

"I think I'm going to go out and get it," she said finally. She couldn't stand the suspense of wondering what might be in it. All three of them were standing staring out the window at the innocent looking parcel.

"There's no way it's anything but another tape or some dead flowers," she said, trying to convince herself. "Maybe it's a little dead mouse. He's just trying to taunt us and frazzle our nerves."

"It could be anthrax, though, Cass," suggested Steffie. Her imagination was almost as wild as Vickie's and Cassie's.

"Oh, I never thought of that. What do you think, Vic?"

Vickie shrugged. "I guess anything's possible with that kook. I'm sure it's nothing important, but maybe we'd better wait for Jack and Bud. Do you want me to call them?"

Cassie nodded, and sat with Steffie, while Vickie went to make the call.

While Vickie was on the phone, Cass gave Steffie a bare bones outline of the situation with Dave. Talking about it made it more real, but it also seemed to get easier each time she did try to vocalize this development. She hadn't yet told Jack, and she didn't know when she would. She had to think things out clearly first. She was not prepared to get herself into another situation, much as she would have loved to run right into Jack's arms. She thought she might wait until the killer was caught, and then they would have a long talk.

"I couldn't reach either one of them, but the dispatcher is sending the bomb squad," laughed Vickie, as she reentered the sunroom. "I didn't realize that Niagara Falls even had a bomb squad," she added.

"Well, let's hope they're coming on a wild goose chase," said Steffie, with a worried frown. "We'll feel like three silly paranoid worryworts, but I'm sure they'll be just as happy to find out it's nothing but another tape, or something equally harmless."

There was one good thing about chumming with Cass and Vickie. Things were never dull when those two were around.

Chapter Forty-Seven

It was only fifteen minutes before the bomb squad arrived. There were six of them, all dressed in something similar to hazardous waste gear. The women supposed it was all anti-blast material they were wearing. Still, if there really was a bomb in the package, it likely had the potential of blowing them to pieces.

These were very brave individuals. Imagine having a husband on the bomb squad. At this moment in time, Cassie couldn't imagine having a husband at all. She was feeling a bit bitter and a lot sad. She wondered how long it would take for her to accept the fact that her marriage was in pieces.

The friends talked to the police first, pointed to the package on the bench, and explained why they thought it could be a bomb. When they mentioned Jack Willinger and Bud Lang, they immediately gained more credibility.

"Oh look at that darling little robot," cried Vickie excitedly, as the remote control robot came out of the van.

"Please get inside, ladies, and don't stand near the windows," said one of the policemen. Don't come out till we give you the all clear."

The three friends wanted to see everything that was going on, but they obediently went back into the house, and surreptitiously watched from an upstairs window.

It was interesting to watch all the methods put into play before the package was encased in a bombproof box. Because it was small, it was difficult to think of it as anything life threatening. It seemed silly to have six officers and a robot working on it, when it was likely another harassing tape recording. Still, Cassie and Vickie couldn't take any more chances. The wife killer was definitely dangerous, and he seemed to be very resourceful. They no longer had the luxury of underestimating him.

The men had moved a fair distance away from the house, and were part way down the long driveway.

"They must be pretty sure that it isn't dangerous, or they would have moved it to an open field," said Cassie.

"I'm glad they didn't. This is exciting," answered the incorrigible Vickie.

It was some time before it was determined that the package contained no bomb. Still, it could contain anthrax or some other lethal chemical. By the time it had been opened and examined, and cleared of any dangerous possibilities, most of the afternoon had passed.

By now, Cassie, Vickie and Steffie were bursting with a need to know what in the heck could be in the parcel. When one member of the bomb squad finally brought it to Cassie, she couldn't believe her eyes. In the package had been two small boxes, bearing the name "Aunt Aggie's Attic."

They had been opened by the police, and turned out to be two identical silver bracelets, one engraved with Vickie's initials, and one with Cassie's. On both of them was engraved "I'll Be Killing You," with little musical notes around the writing, to indicate that it was a song.

Steffie gasped when she saw them. "Ohmigawd" she groaned. "He was in our shop. Kitty sold these to him yesterday. I didn't recognize him, but now that I think about it, he was big and brawny, and that was a false beard he was wearing. He had sunglasses too, and I wondered fleetingly at the time why he didn't have them off while he was inside. I just never put it all together. Oh shoot. I'm such a dimwit. You'd think I would have recognized him from all I've heard about him, and from the pictures on the ship. Oh, I'm so darn sorry. We could have caught him yesterday if only Kitty and I had been more alert."

Realizing how badly Steffie felt at having missed such a golden opportunity to catch their stalker/killer, Cass and Vickie hastened to reassure her. They were all on an emotional high, but not a good one. This was just too much. The guy was apparently walking freely amongst them, and they weren't catching on. From now on, any tall man was suspect. They wondered whether they would be fortunate enough to even be given another chance.

It was just at that point that Jack and Bud drove up. They had heard about the call to the bomb squad, and had hurried out to Cassie's home on the parkway.

"So, he's still in town, and he's getting bolder every day," said Bud, shaking his head in disbelief. "If only you had recognized him, this might be all over now."

Steffie felt even worse when Bud said this. He likely didn't mean to be accusatory, but that was how it sounded.

Both Cassie and Vickie jumped to her rescue. "It's not Steffie's fault at all. There was no way that she would be suspicious of that customer. We can't go around being wary of every big man in town. Do you realize how many tall attractive men there are in this city?"

"The fact that he seems to be able to get this close to us any time he wants, shows what a master of disguise he is," said Cassie. She didn't add that the fact he managed to get this close to them, showed how inept the police were, but she couldn't help thinking it. Then she remembered how many cases Jack was handling, and how thinly spread the police were, so she kept silent.

Jack replied, "He's obviously been following you, or else how did he make the connection between you and the boutique. I can't believe our guys weren't able to pick him up. How does he manage to disguise himself so that they wouldn't be suspicious?" He looked embarrassed because of the seemingly helpless police, who were supposed to be following not only the women, but also anyone else who was following them. The truth of the matter was that the killer had the run of the city, and nobody seemed able to spot him.

Cass felt the old urge to put her arms around him and hold him close. Why did the fates love to stir things up?

"I'm so sorry to have caused you all this trouble," said Cassie, as the bomb squad packed up and prepared to leave.

"Oh, don't worry about that. We're just glad that it wasn't a bomb. We don't mind coming out on a call like this. The good thing is that we all get to go home safely," laughed one of the fellows. He was talking to Cassie, but looking at Steffie with admiring glances.

Cass couldn't help grinning. Wherever she went, Steffie drew the eyes of the men.

Finally the squad left, after many thanks for a job well done. Cass asked Steffie to stay for dinner, and called Kitty to join them. It turned out to be a casual, but fun evening, as they rehashed all the events of the day. Jack and Bud stayed for a while, quizzing Steffie and Kitty for any details they might be able to remember about the man who bought the bracelets. Unfortunately, there was no information which the police didn't already have.

"You know, Cass, we just can't let this go on any longer. This guy has been fooling around, teasing you, taunting us, and showing us how inept we are, but now I'm sure he's ready for the kill. He's been proving just how easy it is to get at you. We can't leave you here alone, mainly because we can't trust you to stay safely hidden here. We may have to take you both into protective custody."

"Oh, no," wailed Cassie. "You must be kidding. You'd have to give me some time before we could ride that horse. I'd have to make safe arrangements for Sugar Plum and Muffy. They're my first concern."

"You could take them to your cattery. They would be fine there," suggested Jack reasonably.

"No way." Cass was not happy with the suggestion. "They've been babied and pampered all their lives. They'd die of fright to be put in with all those cats.

All my cats at the cattery are wonderful, but they're little strays, and ones that weren't wanted. They've been abused and teased, and they've learned to fend for themselves, and get along well together in their new environment.

My two, on the other hand, have been raised like family. They're my little kids, and they firmly believe that they are, in fact, little people, not cats at all. I couldn't subject them to that stress. I would have to see whether my old neighbour from Rolling Acres would take them to her place. I think it would be better than having her come here, although, this house really is pretty safe."

"I agree with that. I think this house could be totally safe, provided you would keep the alarm on, and all the doors and windows locked. And," here he looked at them with his detective's glare, while shaking his head. "if you would only do as you're told, and stay inside, he couldn't get at you. With your panic room, this house is like a fortress. I just don't trust you now to stay put. You're a damn horse's ass, Vickie, and you're a pain in the butt, Cass. You both drive me crazy. Why can't you be reasonable and rational? Don't you realize you're putting other people in danger while they're trying to protect you?"

Cass was startled, then she grinned. "I love it when you talk so mean, Jack. Say some more."

He glared at her, then started to laugh. "You two will drive me to drink. I'm an even bigger horse's ass thinking that I can ever tame you, and take care of you. You obviously don't want anyone helping you."

"That's not fair, Jack. We were very sensible this afternoon. We didn't open the door to the Fed Ex guy, and we called the police right away. What more could we have done? Anyway, if we did decide to let you hide us for a while, where would you plan to put us?"

Cass was feeling belligerent, and judging by the look on Vickie's face, she was feeling exactly the same. Neither of them wanted to be pushed around. They felt that they could take care of themselves better than the police could, so Vickie gave Jack her famous "screw you" look.

"Well, you're safe for now. He won't make a move tonight, after that package episode. He likes to spread things out a bit to increase the terror. He's going to let you think about those bracelets for a while. We could move you tomorrow, unless you can convince me that you'll stay locked up tight here."

"You still haven't told us where we would be going," said Vickie in a truculent voice. If they were in protective custody, it would be impossible for her and for Cassie to get out and try to catch this guy by themselves. No, it would definitely be better to stay right here. Jack and Bud couldn't force them out of the house, or could they?

"Don't worry, we'd put you in one of the good hotels down by the falls. You'd be on a high floor, with a couple of guards. The killer wouldn't expect you to be down there. That would buy us a bit of time."

He didn't add that there was no money in the police budget for putting them in an expensive high rise hotel. That would likely be coming straight out of his own pocket, but he'd do anything to keep them safe.

Jack sounded confident, but Cass and Vickie weren't convinced. What fun could they have being locked up in a hotel room? How long could you stare at the nice view? They just looked at each other, and raised their eyebrows. They didn't have to say a thing, but each understood the other. Events were not going the way they wanted. They were definitely not going to be relocated without putting up some resistance.

Steffie just sat quietly, listening to both sides, and wondering when all this intrigue was going to end.

Chapter Forty-Eight

He had really enjoyed watching the delivery of the bracelets, and had almost laughed out loud when he saw the arrival of the bomb squad. He knew he was really getting to the two women, and he could almost feel their anxiety, their nervousness, their loss of confidence.

Those two bitches had really thrown a spanner into the works of his almost perfect life. Just by being in the wrong place at the wrong time, they had seen him throw Gloria off the balcony. It wasn't their fault that they had seen him, or at least, one of them had seen him do the dirty deed, but it certainly had complicated things for him. Still, he had to admit that he was enjoying himself.

It was great fun outwitting the police at every turn. He read the local papers and watched the local television, and knew that there was an unexpected and unusual rash of crime going on in the city. That was pure luck for him. The cops were spread very thin, and didn't have nearly enough manpower to be doing an intensive search for him.

At the moment, he was sitting in a beautiful hotel room overlooking the falls. What a view! He was still holding onto the motel room out on Lundy's Lane, which he felt he would need once his plans were all set in place, but there was no reason that he had to stay in that hole. This high rise hotel, looking right down on the famous cataracts, was much more to his taste, and he felt quite anonymous here. Besides, if you've got the money, honey, why not use it?

He had never been to Niagara Falls, so he hadn't been prepared for just how incredibly awesome those falls were. The entire area was a treat. He had taken a drive out through the country, and had been amazed at the acres and acres of fruit trees, peach, pear, cherry, apple.

There were more varieties than he could count. He knew that this was wine country too, and had seen vineyards galore.

He had even thought about the possibility of living here, but trying to get Canadian citizenship would be too dangerous. It would give the authorities too much freedom to delve into his background. No, once his job was done here, he was heading for Oregon. He had never lived in that state, and thought he'd give it a try.

Today, however, he was having a drink, gazing out at the falls, and wondering how he could get his hands on some of Cassandra Meredith's money. He had been amazed and intrigued upon discovering that she was a multi-millionaire. What a shame and a waste it would be to kill her. If only he could figure a way to marry her first, but that seemed to be "mission impossible."

As far as he could see, she was already securely married. A trip to the reference library had afforded him plenty of information about the very attractive Mrs. Meredith. She had found herself at the center of a highly publicized case involving several murders three years ago. Then just last year she had been somehow involved in the demise of the Black Sheep serial killer. As a result, he had all the info he needed about Cassandra Meredith. She seemed to live a pretty exciting life, and that made her much more interesting.

As he gazed down at the thundering waters below, he pondered the pros and cons of killing Dave Meredith. That would leave the golden Cassandra in the position of a grieving widow, and he was really good with widows. He had had plenty of experience along those lines. Regretfully, however, he decided that there wasn't time to take that route.

As he stared into the angry waters, he realized just how easy it would be to dispose of a body down there. It looked as if there were places along this area where one could dump a body, and have it disappear forever. He must keep that in mind when the time came.

Now, back to Dave Meredith. Unfortunately, killing Dave wasn't a viable solution. For one thing, he didn't seem to be around very much, and, for another, the only reason to kill him would be to make Cassandra a widow. Making her a widow was not feasible, because he just didn't have the time to stick around town and try to win her affections. No, definitely, there was no point in killing Dave.

He wondered, though, about kidnapping Cassie. He had been thinking about it for several days now. He was tossing it around like a dog with a ball. He had never tried a kidnapping, and he knew how dangerous they were. Things didn't usually work out well for the kidnapper or the victim. Still, he wondered whether he could snatch her, and somehow force her to hand over about fifteen million. No point in being greedy. Fifteen million would be a nice healthy sum, but then, what would he do with Cassandra? He liked the sound of that name. It rolled off his tongue as he said it aloud a couple of times.

What would he do with Cassandra, once he had his hands on the money? She was so darn attractive that it would really be a shame to kill her. That friend of hers, Victoria Craig, was not exactly doggy doo-doo either. He had always had a soft spot for red heads, or women with auburn hair like Vickie's. He knew that she lived in Vancouver, and that her husband wrote dull history books. He had done his research well, and knew that she was worth a million dollars. Still, that was nothing compared to what he could get out of Cassandra, if he could just figure out how to play the cards.

The trouble was that he really couldn't kidnap both of them. It would be too difficult to control them. He wasn't actually too worried about Victoria as a dangerous witness. As far as he knew, she had not seen him throw Gloria off the balcony. She had simply seen him getting off the elevator, and that didn't prove much. It was purely circumstantial. Still, he decided, it would be better to have her out of the way completely.

He put down his drink, and got up to stretch. He was in his jockey shorts, and as he passed the full length mirror, he took a good look at himself. He liked what he saw. He was looking at a man with a big, mean torso, concrete-like biceps, and long, strong legs. His hair was growing back nicely, and he had a good, somewhat rugged face, although his eyes were a bit too close together. He stared into those eyes, asking himself why he had such a burning, unquenchable desire for more and more money, more and more conquests and killings. He didn't understand what lay behind these needs, but he knew that they were the most important things in his life.

Finding rich women to marry and then kill, was a game. It was a game to which he made up the rules as he went along. So far, he was the big winner. He couldn't fail now. He wouldn't let himself fail.

Sighing, he poured himself another scotch, and went back to the window. He had pulled the easy chair right over to the glass, so that he could sit and gaze at the incredible view, while he formulated his plan. It would have to be a doozy. It would have to cover all the ifs, ands and buts, leaving no loose ends.

He loved a challenge, and this was a good one. If he could pull this off, he might forget about Oregon, and simply leave the country. He had always had a hankering for Australia, and this might be the time to satisfy that interest. He'd have to check out what the extradition laws were between Australia and the states.

With an extra fifteen million in his pocket, why not get as far away as possible. He chuckled at the picture of himself wearing a Crocodile Dundee hat and carrying a big knife at his waist.

When he got sick of Australia, he could move to Tahiti. He liked the idea of lounging on a beach, sipping a margarita, and being fanned by a nubile young maiden in a grass skirt, silken black hair blowing gently in the breeze. Hell, with his money, he could move from island to island, leaving death and destruction behind him.

On the other hand, he might find a woman who would satisfy all his secret desires, and he could settle down forever. He probably had enough money to do that right now, but the big question was, how much was ever enough? The other question was, where was the woman who could please him forever. By the looks of it, Cassandra might be the one. He was very intrigued with her looks, her feisty spirit, and, of course, her money. How could he win her over though, and get her out of the country?

He sighed as he shook the fanciful pictures from his mind. There was no way that the fancy dancy Mrs. Meredith would ever fall for the likes of him, knowing that he was a wife killer. So - - the matter at hand was how to deal with her and her friend. How could he kidnap one or both of them with the least possible trouble?

Chapter Forty-Nine

The fabric of Cassie's life was now fringed with a mix of anger, anxiety and hope. Her days were like a tangled ball of yarn.

The anger, of course, was turned toward Dave, the quintessential husband who had run off with another woman. What a drab and tired cliché that was! It made her angry and embarrassed just to be caught up in such a hackneyed and banal scenario.

The anxiety came from the knowledge that the killer was determined, and he was getting closer. The black roses, the churlish tape, the woman thrown in front of the bus, the silver bracelets, all showed a purpose and ingenuity which couldn't be denied.

The hope was due to Cassie's lifelong enthusiasm and faith in a good life. She hoped that eventually she would understand and forgive Dave. After all, she had likely been subconsciously pushing him out of her life since the day that Jack had walked back into it. She hoped that she would be able to escape the clutches of the determined killer, and she hoped that someday she and Jack would be together again.

She was pondering all these things, as she and Vickie sat in the sunroom, having their morning tea and bagels.

"You know, we're going to be as fat as piggies, just sitting around this house, having no exercise," complained Vickie, spreading a little more cream cheese on her bagel. "Maybe we should spend half an hour going up and down all the stairs and the long halls."

"Wow, does that ever sound like fun," laughed Cassie. "I think I'd rather mud wrestle."

Vickie grinned at that idea, as she got up to pour more tea. "Well, really, what do you think we should do today? It looks so darn nice out. It's very tempting to just pretend that everything is normal, and go out for a walk or a drive. We could even go down to the casino and gamble for a while." She said this with a hopeful look on her face. Patience was not one of Vickie's virtues.

"I'm with you up to a point," said Cassie slowly. "It's just that, I feel awfully guilty about breaking our promise to Jack. "I want to get out there and catch this guy before he catches us, but I hate to lie to Jack. He's so busy these days, and he's so worried about us. Besides, I have to tell you, my scalp has been tingling like crazy for the past hour. Something's going to happen, but who knows what?"

Vickie used to laugh at Cassie and her tingling scalp, but she had come to learn that it wasn't a joke. Cass really did seem to get some type of warning that something bad was about to occur. When her scalp tingled, they now paid attention.

"Let's put on the radio, listen to some nice music, and read for a while. That will give us a chance to see whether there's something bad coming our way. As soon as your scalp stops tingling, we'll go out for a drive. How's that for a good idea?" Vickie was trying to keep the mood light. She could tell that Cassie was very antsy this morning.

"Okay, I'll find us a good station with background music, while you get some exercise by going up and fetching our books," grinned Cassie, trying to shake off her feeling of foreboding.

Vickie ran up the stairs, gathered the two books from their bedside tables, and was bouncing back down, trying to use up one or two calories, when she heard a loud gasp from the sunroom.

"What is it?" she cried, hurrying towards Cassie, books clutched in her hands.

Cass was very pale, and her eyes looked frightened.

"It's Jack and Bud," she wailed. "They've been hurt in some kind of raid. The radio says that Bud is critical, but they just said that Jack was also hurt. Oh, Vickie, I can't lose Jack. We've got to get to the hospital."

"No, wait a minute. We need to get more info first. If Jack is conscious, he'll be frantic if we show up at the hospital, when we're supposed to be safely locked up here. It could make him have a heart attack or something."

Cassie stared at her in dismay, pondering that awful possibility. Then she began pacing around the room, clenching and unclenching her fists. She looked wild-eyed and on the edge.

"I'm going to call the police department," decided Vickie. "We'll see what we can find out about their conditions. Maybe someone can tell us what happened. Did the radio say whether they had been shot?"

"Bud was stabbed twice in the chest area. They didn't say more than that, except that he's critical. They just said that Jack was also hurt, but they didn't say how. You call the station, Vic. That's a good idea. I've got to calm down a bit first."

Before Vickie could make the call, however, the phone rang. They both looked for the cell phones, then realized that they were still upstairs in their bedrooms. Vickie raced to the kitchen phone, and caught it on the third ring.

"Hello?" she asked, with a question in her voice.

"Hello. Is this Mrs. Meredith?" asked a pleasant male voice.

"No, this is her friend. May I ask who's calling?"

"Please tell her that it's Detective Jim Matheson. I'm a friend of Jack and Bud's, and Jack has asked me to call her."

"Just a sec, she's right here," said Vickie, handing the phone to Cassie.

"Hello," said Cassie, still not knowing who was on the line.

"Hi, Mrs. Meredith. This is Detective Jim Matheson. Jack asked me to call you. He was afraid that you would be worried if you heard anything on the radio. He wanted you to know that he's fine. He got hit across the back with a baseball bat. Fortunately the thug didn't get a good swing at him, so it knocked him down, but it didn't break anything. He's at the hospital though, because he's giving Bud some blood. Luckily they have the same type, and it's pretty rare."

Before he could say any more, Cassie interrupted. "How's Bud? How badly is he hurt? The radio said that he's critical."

"That's what we've heard too. The knife pierced his left lung, and he was also stabbed in the lower part of his heart, as I understand it. He's lost so much blood that it's iffy. They're doing everything they can, though, and Bud's a big strong guy. He'll make it, I'm sure."

"Can you tell me what happened?"

"I can give you the bare outline, but we're not really sure yet. There was a raid on a crackhouse late last night or early this morning. Jack and Bud had been working on the case for a while, so they were in on the raid. Bud insisted on going in first, and Jack was close behind him, watching his back. The house seemed empty, but they were checking it room by room.

A guy jumped out of a closet just as Bud was reaching for the door. It hit him square in the face, and before he could pull his gun, the guy stabbed him twice. Jack got off one shot, but then a second fellow raced out of a bedroom which hadn't yet been checked, and hit Jack in the back and side with a baseball bat. The whole thing was a bad screw-up. It looks as if they might have been tipped off that we were coming."

"Tell me truthfully, are you sure that Jack is alright?"

"Yep, as far as I know. He's going to be really bruised, but the perp missed his kidneys, which is good. He couldn't call you himself, though, because they've got him all hooked up to Bud at the moment, giving him blood. Bud's already had a couple of bags full, but he needed more, and that's a pretty rare type he has, so Jack volunteered. We've always kidded around the station about the fact that those two partners have the same rare blood. That's why they get along so well I guess.

Jack did stress to me that he doesn't want you to even think about coming down to the hospital. You're to stay locked in the house, and don't let anyone in for any reason. He'll likely call you himself once the transfusion is finished."

Cassie did something very out of keeping with her quiet, reserved character. She threw all caution, diplomacy, and good old common sense out the window, and asked Jim Matheson to please tell Jack that she loved him, and that he was to call her as soon as he could. She regretted it as soon as she said it, but the damage had been done. Her little message of love would likely be all over the station in short order. Oh well, nothing she could do about it now.

She did try to explain that she and Jack had been childhood friends, but she knew that wasn't going to work. Now the entire police department would know that she, a married woman, was in love with Jack. Yikes! There went her reputation. What a dumb thing to do.

She asked a few more questions, until she was reassured that Jack was going to be fine. Unfortunately, it seemed that Bud was barely hanging on.

After the phone call, the two women went back to the sunroom to listen to the radio, and try to find out any more details of the disastrous raid.

"Well, that tingling scalp of yours has done it again," said Vickie, shaking her head. "It's so strange that you don't have any other signs of being clairvoyant, but your scalp never seems to let you down. You should go and be tested. Isn't it Duke University where they love to test people with ESP? You might find out that you have other abilities which haven't been tapped."

"I can't think about that now, Vic. All I can think about is poor Bud, and his wife and those three little girls of his. If he dies, Jack will die a little bit with him. They've been buddies for so many years, and they always watch out for each other. Jack will blame himself, even though it wasn't his fault. I'm just so thankful that Jack wasn't badly hurt.

I feel as if the fates are conspiring against me these days. Do you think I've done something to annoy them?"

Vickie knew she was kidding, but she did wonder at why so many things seemed to be going wrong in Cassie's life at the moment. She couldn't help wondering what new disaster might be waiting just around the corner.

Chapter Fifty

It was a very long day for both women. They paced, they talked, they drank gallons of tea, they played with the cats, and then they paced again.

Eventually Jack called, and they talked briefly. "I hear you gave Jim Matheson a very nice little message for me, Cass," he said in his low, sexy voice. Cass could tell that he was likely grinning.

"Oh, you know how silly I get when I'm upset," she joked. She suddenly felt uncomfortable, and a bit shy with him. He still didn't know anything about Dave leaving, and this wasn't the right time to tell him. "How's Bud?" she asked, even before asking about Jack himself.

Jack was immediately serious. "He's bad, Cass. They've given him so much blood, but it took them forever to get the hemorrhaging stopped. He's a fighter though, and he'll make it. He has to," he added grimly. "Amanda's here at the hospital, of course, but she was able to leave the three girls with a neighbour. He looks awful – very white, and so still." He took a breath, then reiterated, "He's going to make it." It was as if he was trying to convince himself.

"Yes, I'm sure that he will. He's in good shape, Jack, and he'll fight with every ounce of strength he has." Nothing could happen to Bud. He was such a nice guy. She refused to think of the fact that nice guys don't always finish first. Instead, she thought of Bud, with his craggy, weather-beaten face, full of decency and honesty. She thought of the crinkly lines around his brown mischievous eyes. She thought of how he loved Muffy, and liked to pick him up and cuddle him.

She remembered Steffie saying that the first time Bud and Jack went into the boutique, she was scared that he would be like the bull in the china shop. She had been happily impressed with how graceful he was, in spite of his large size. Cassie also remembered how kind he was to Vickie the night she was attacked and almost raped. He had stayed and boarded up the back door, and had offered to take them to a hotel for the night, or to post a policewoman with them, in case they felt nervous in the house alone.

She thought about how his whole face lit up when he talked about his three little girls, Gracie, Annie and Maggie, the "midget mafia," as he called them. These memories made her want to weep.

Bud Lang had been there for them in just about every time of crisis, and now there was nothing they could do for him except to pray.

Jack explained that he was staying at the hospital to wait with Amanda, and to be available in case they needed more blood.

Cassie pictured him being totally drained, like the victim of a vampire, by the time they got Bud back on his feet. She wondered how much blood one person could give at a time.

Jack didn't even mention taking Cass and Vickie into protective custody. He didn't mention putting a policeman on guard outside the house. His entire attention was being focused on Bud. He did, however, remind her to stay inside and to set the alarm. Then he was gone.

After dinner, they watched television for a while, but nothing really held their interest.

Her son Mark called just to see how she was coping with his dad's treachery and disloyalty. He was very angry with Dave, and concerned about his mother. Cass assured him that she was doing well, and that he mustn't be so angry towards his dad.

"He's basically a good man, Mark. He's made a bad mistake, which any of us could do, and he's now trying to do the right thing because of the baby. I don't want you to alienate yourself from him. I could beat him with a rolling pin, but it wouldn't accomplish anything. He's suffering too."

"Mom, you're taking this way too calmly. You must be internalizing all your hurt and anger."

"Oo, what is this, Psych 101?" laughed his mother. "I'm calm now, but I've had my moments. The other night I drank an entire bottle of wine myself, yelled at Vickie, and threw out every gift Dave's given me since he met up with Lulu or whatever her name is. I'm debating whether to give that ruby pendant which I never liked or wore, to your sister, or to Vicky. If neither one of them wants it, I think I'll sell it, and give the money to charity. That was bought purely out of a guilty conscience."

Mark laughed, reassured that his mom was going to be fine. Her sense of humour seemed to be intact, and she was a very steady, down to earth person. Fortunately, he had no idea of the other traumas she was handling.

It was after eleven when they decided to go up to bed. Vickie announced that she was going to have a shower, and then try to sleep. "I'm very tired, and my stomach feels a bit queasy. I likely shouldn't have eaten that second piece of pie. It's been a long, tough day, and, as usual, I ate too much. Why do I do that when I get nervous?"

Cass didn't reply. She knew that it was a rhetorical question. She was sympathetic, though, and decided she might as well go to bed too. They wouldn't get any more reports about Bud tonight, and she would pray that he would be much improved by morning.

Vickie went on up ahead, while Cassie put out fresh water and food for the cats. They heard her in the kitchen, and came running for their midnight snack. While they ate, she checked the alarm, turned out the lights, and headed wearily up the stairs.

She was partially undressed when she heard Vickie go into the shower. She was debating having a quick shower herself, when the phone rang.

Thinking it might be Jack calling with an update about Bud, she said, "Hello."

"Mrs. Meredith, this is Tom Nelson from Queenston. Your cattery is on fire. It's blazing out of control."

"Oh no, that's not possible," wailed Cassie, plumping down on the bed as if she had been shot. "Have you called the fire department?"

"Uh, no, but I'm going to now. I just thought you'd want to be here."

Cassie's heart pounded in her chest. Oh please God, don't let it be too bad, was all she could think of, as she said "I'll be right there."

She dropped the phone into its cradle, and quickly struggled back into her jeans.

There was no time to wait for Vickie. She had to get there now. She had to save her beloved family of cats. She hadn't saved all those poor little strays just to have them die in a horrible fire.

Her mind was working frantically as she grabbed her car keys, and raced to yell at Vickie that the cattery was burning, and she was heading there right away.

She couldn't understand how a fire could have started. The veterinarian lived in a small house on the property, and there was always one staff member on in the big house at night. The cats were free to go in and out at their leisure, and on a nice night, many of them chose to sleep outside under a tree or behind a bush. Others loved the big beds and couches inside. She prayed that every single one of them had chosen the great outdoors tonight, but she knew there would be several in the house.

The strange thing was that they had installed a very expensive sprinkler system throughout the old house. Why hadn't it kicked in immediately?

If she had been thinking clearly, she would have questioned who this Tom Nelson was. How had he known that she was the person to call? How could a fire have started? She wasn't sure which staff member was on duty tonight, but had he or she been smoking? There was no smoking allowed in or around the house, so that didn't seem likely. It didn't even occur to her that possibly the killer had set the fire in order to drag her out of her safety zone. A lot of things didn't occur to her, as she ran blindly out the door.

Cass ran into the garage, started her car, and zoomed crazily down the long driveway. The cattery was ten minutes away at the most, but she could make it in five if she flew.

Cassie's thoughts were windmilling in her head. She was picturing the layout of the house. She would have to run right up to the top floor and gather as many cats as she could find. How many cats could she carry at one time? It would be better to throw them into a pillowcase, but there would be no time for that. Would they be okay if she threw them out the window? Could they all land on their feet? She couldn't take that chance.

She wished she had taken the time to wet a couple of big towels. She could have wrapped the cats in the wet towels, and buried her face in them to protect herself from smoke inhalation, as she ran down the stairs with them.

She remembered so well the night that she and Vickie had been locked in the basement of the old burning house. The smoke had been a real killer. Damn. Wet towels would have been a great idea. She berated herself for her stupidity. It would have been better to take the extra few moments and do things right.

Just as she reached the end of her driveway, and was about to make a right turn onto the main road, a car pulled across in front of her. She almost broadsided it. Everything happened very quickly after that. Slamming on the brakes and honking the horn did no good. The car just sat there.

She was half weeping, and half muttering, as she jumped out to demand that the driver move his damn car. Gone were her innate good manners. She would have sworn at him if she had been a swearing person. If Vickie had been with her, Vickie would have done the swearing for both of them. Vickie had worked in the Kingston Penitentiary at one time, and she knew more swear words than a sailor.

There was no time to be lost. Every minute counted. The sooner she got there, the sooner she could save her beloved cats.

She hadn't even taken time to call the fire department, which was a mistake, but it was too late now. Hopefully this Tom Nelson, whoever he was, would call them. She had a car phone, so she would call them as soon as she got this guy out of her way. What was his problem? Why didn't he move? Was he lost? Was he stopping for directions? Maybe she could ask him to follow her and help at the fire.

As she peered in his passenger side window, and shouted at him, he jumped out of the driver's side, ran around the front of the car, and lunged at her. Cass was nearly knocked off her feet. Things were happening so fast that she had no chance to fight him. To an outsider it would have looked like a crazy movie gone wild. She saw the flash of a hypodermic needle, and felt a sharp pain in her neck.

Amazingly, her legs gave way beneath her, and her arms just wouldn't seem to move. Her synapses stopped snapping, or whatever synapses did. They seemed to have melted. Cass herself was having a meltdown. She felt like an ice cube in a pot of boiling water.

It was the strangest sensation. She couldn't even talk. She just stared at her attacker, totally helpless. Her mouth was moving, but no words were coming out. Damn, what had he given her? Nothing on her body was working. Whatever he had in that hypo was magic, black magic. It had cut the legs right out from under her, and it seemed as if she had even forgotten how to breath. The black night got blacker, and from a very long distance, she heard someone saying "We meet again, Cassandra." Then there was nothing.

Chapter Fifty-One

Vickie had been all covered with soap, when Cassie shouted that the cattery was on fire, and that she was leaving. It took her a couple of minutes to get all the soap off, and to dry herself. She jumped into the same clothes she had been wearing, and headed downstairs to look for the keys to whatever car was in the garage. She loved those cats almost as much as Cassie did, and she was sick at the thought of them being caught in a terrible fire.

It took her several minutes to find the other set of keys. Just like Cassie, she didn't give a thought to the fact that she was leaving the safety of the house, and going off into the night all by herself. Jack would have a fit, but, on the other hand, he would understand. He knew how Cassie felt about her cattery, and he knew how Vickie felt about Cassie.

Just as Cass had done, Vickie raced down the long driveway, and nearly ploughed into the back of Cassie's car sitting, still running, with the driver's side door wide open.

"What the hell?" she exclaimed, as she recognized the car.

She jumped out and peered into it. No Cassie. Where in the heck was she? What had happened? Before the ugly thought really had time to crystallize in her head, she knew. The killer had her. It was a total moment of truth. He had thought of the one perfect ploy to get her out of the house. But what would he have done if both of them had been in the car? He would have foreseen that possibility, and would have been prepared. He was a formidable adversary.

Still, how had he managed to grab Cassie? Hadn't she screamed? Hadn't she put up a fight? Cass was no quitter, and it would have been really difficult for him to wrestle her into his vehicle. How had he got her to stop in the first place? Cass was no dummy. She wouldn't fall for something like a body sprawled in the road. Maybe he had blocked her so that she couldn't get past him. Yes, that was likely it. But then, how did he get her out of her car and into his?

Vickie was trying to put the pieces together, but it was all guesswork.

Her mind was running like a cockroach, here and there, and into every dark cranny. She was trying to think like the killer. What would he do with Cass?

He had pushed one woman over a cliff. He had drowned another in a bathtub. One had been thrown off a balcony. He had pushed one in front of a bus. He had tried to throw Cassie overboard. Did he like to do a different method each time? It seemed so. He had never used a gun or a rope or a knife, therefore, what did he have in store for Cass? Her mind was a total blank. Fear had paralyzed her brain. She felt as if she was living in the land of the bewildered. What was happening?

Oh Lord, she really didn't know what to do. She was panting from sheer fright, and her mind was as foggy as a dirty window. She knew one thing though. There was likely no fire at the cattery. She was pretty sure of that. It had been a very clever ruse, and Cassie had fallen for it. Everyone who knew Cass, knew how she felt about her cats. Vickie wondered momentarily how the killer had managed to find out so much about her.

The immediate question, of course, was, where had he taken Cassie? He must have had a place all picked out and prepared, or, was he just going to kill her and dump her? The thought made Vickie's head spin. It was logical that he would kill her as quickly as possible, and then get rid of the body.

Which way would he go? What could she do if she caught up with him? How should she handle this? Should she head down to Queenston, or would he go back towards Niagara Falls? Queenston sounded more logical, because it had lots of bush, and it was close to the river. Still, how would she recognize his vehicle? She had no way of knowing what he was driving. Her heart sank at the complexities of the problem.

Vickie was in a panic. A feeling of terror and terrible anger overcame her. She and Cassie had been through so many tight situations over the years, and they had always come out relatively unscathed. This one, however, seemed the worst. They knew the killer wanted them dead. He had warned them several times with his flowers and tape and jewellery. He had also made several futile attempts to kill them, but this time it looked as if he had won. He had Cassie, and why else would he take her, if not to kill her?

She couldn't afford to waste any time. Closing the door of Cassie's car, after shutting it off and taking the keys, she drove past it, so that she could turn around on the road, and head back down the driveway to the house. She had run out without even locking it. The best thing to do seemed to be to get back there and call for help. Chasing down dark roads, with no idea of where she was going, would be no help to Cass.

She took big breaths as she sped back down the driveway. Why the hell did Cass have such a long driveway anyway? That was ridiculous and pretentious, she thought crossly.

She left the car parked outside, in case she had to leave in a hurry, and raced into the house. She would try Jack first, but was sure that he was still at the hospital. She tried both his home phone and his cell phone, but got no answer. If he was indeed at the hospital, he would have turned his cell phone off. They weren't allowed in the hospital, at least not up in intensive care, which is where he would likely be, watching over his buddy, no pun intended.

Her next choice was 911. She spoke slowly, as she explained that she thought Cassie had been kidnapped, and was going to be killed. The dispatcher was infuriatingly calm, as she asked for Vickie's name, and the address, and why she thought that her friend would be killed. Vickie tried to explain, but it was complicated.

"Look, can you contact Jack Willinger? He's a very close friend of Mrs. Meredith, and he'll know what to do."

"Detective Willinger isn't available right now," said the dispatcher. "Do you feel that you are in any danger?"

"No, I'm safe. It's my friend who's in trouble. Please send someone out here right away. I have to talk to a detective. Jack Willinger knows all about the killer, and everything he's done to try to kill Cassie, please let him know that she's disappeared."

There must have been something in Vickie's voice that persuaded the dispatcher this was serious, and not a prank call. She said that a police car would be there within minutes, and she would do her best to try to contact Detective Willinger.

Vickie thanked her, and hung up. She sat down on a kitchen chair, wondering what to do next. Oh yes, the cattery. Quickly punching in the number, she waited impatiently till the phone was picked up.

"Cassandra's Cattery" said a young male voice.

"Thank you Lord," muttered Vickie under her breath. "Hello. This is Vickie Craig, Cassandra's friend. Is everything okay there tonight?"

"Yes, mam. The cats are bedded down and everything's quiet. Is there a problem?" He sounded worried, as if maybe he had done something wrong.

"You're sure that there's no fire anywhere on the property?"

"Fire? No, there's no fire," said the young chap, concern now in his voice. "Why would you think that?"

"Well, we got a call saying that the cattery was burning. I guess it was someone's idea of a sick joke. Just take a careful look around, will you? If there's anything wrong, call the police."

"Okay, I'll go have a look right now, but I'm sure there's nothing wrong. It's been a quiet night."

Vickie was relieved. It would have been the final blow, if anything had happened to Cassie's beloved haven for cats. She had worked so hard to make her dream a reality, and now the homeless cats of the area were benefiting from her caring heart.

She felt helpless just sitting there, but couldn't think of what she should be doing. Muffy and Sugar soon appeared to see who was making all the noise, so Vickie talked to them. She felt better talking out loud, even though the cats weren't paying much attention.

Within a few minutes the doorbell rang, and she heard the welcome call, "Police, open up."

Taking no chances, she peered out carefully before taking off the alarm, and opening the door to the two men standing outside, holding up their detective badges for her inspection.

It turned out that one of the detectives was the Jim Matheson with whom Cassie had spoken earlier in the day. That seemed a very long time ago.

If only she, Vickie, hadn't been in the shower when the killer called, saying the cattery was on fire. She might have been suspicious, or been able to stop Cassie from going without checking it out first. She didn't know how she would have reacted, but she couldn't help thinking up other scenarios in which Cassie remained safely behind the locked doors, and she wasn't sitting here talking to two strange detectives.

The detective named Jim Matheson did not live up to his nice name. The name Jim Matheson conjured up a tall, slim, good looking man with thick dark hair, bedroom eyes, and a great grin. This guy was average height, with a bulbous nose, and turkey wattle neck. He looked to be late fifties or early sixties, and he was almost bald, with just a little monk's fringe around his head. He kept licking his lips as if there was a residue of barbecue sauce or chocolate icecream on them. He definitely did not impart confidence. The best thing about him was his radio announcer type voice.

Vickie had not caught the other detective's name, but he seemed quite at home. He strolled around rather arrogantly, picking up various objects, and staring at the pictures on the walls, as if he was in an art gallery. His eyes seemed too big for his small face, and it gave him a perpetually frightened appearance. He was also average height, with a head which was too small for his shoulders. Vickie had the insane desire to laugh and call him "pinhead."

She took a couple of deep breaths to calm herself, before telling her story. Actually, she sounded much more calm than she actually felt. It impressed the two policemen, who knew immediately, from what Vickie told them, that Cassie was in serious trouble. They looked at each other without saying a word. They were 90% sure that Cassandra Meredith was already dead.

Chapter Fifty-Two

A groggy Cassie began to waken, shortly before they reached the motel. She thought she might be in the trunk of a car, but at this point, that didn't even register with her as a bad thing. There was tape or something over her mouth, and her hands were tied behind her back. She was very uncomfortable physically, but mentally and emotionally, no fear or anger had set in. There was something wrong with her head, because she just couldn't think clearly. She kept feeling she had to get to the cattery, but couldn't remember why, and didn't really much care.

Gradually the mental fog began to lift, and she felt as if she was coming out of surgery. She remembered looking in a car window, then a tall man lunging at her, and sticking a needle in her neck.

Things were so vague and so jumbled. She seemed to be on her side, and she could stretch her legs out partially, but she couldn't get turned over onto her back or her other side.

It was pitch dark wherever she was, and she was very sleepy. She would just close her eyes again, and things would be better when she wakened.

She did close her eyes, and she did start to doze, but some preternatural knowledge, some innate awareness of danger, began nudging her. Opening her eyes again, she forced herself to concentrate. Where was she, and what was happening?

Behind the tape, her mouth was very dry. She had no saliva, and she was having trouble swallowing. If only she could get some air. Yes, some fresh air would help. Her eyelids felt so heavy that she thought she would just nap for a minute.

When he stopped to get her out of the trunk, and put her in the front seat, she didn't waken. He even removed the ropes on her wrists, but she slept peacefully.

Finally, she became aware that the car had stopped. She still couldn't quite open her eyes. They felt too heavy.

They were at the motel now, and he sat in the car for a moment, carefully studying the parking lot, the windows of the units, and the motel office. Things looked quiet. There was no one around. This was his chance. Lady luck was still riding with him. It had even begun to rain, which was good. There would be fewer people out and about in the rain. He hoped that it would become torrential.

He had already stopped along the way, removing Cass from the trunk, and placing her beside him in the front seat. That had been a bit of a close call, as two cars passed him in quick succession, just as he was about to lift her from the trunk. He had remained calm, however, pushing her back down again, and pretending to search for something. He had kept his head well averted, so that they couldn't see his face. Neither car had slowed down. He had then quickly removed the ropes from her wrists, and loosened the tape a bit. It wasn't time to remove it quite yet. Through all this, Cassandra had slept soundly. He hoped he hadn't given her too much in that injection.

Now they were at the motel, he felt that everything was falling into place, and he hurried around to the passenger side.

Right on cue, Cassie wakened, as the cool fresh air wafted around her face, and raindrops pelted her. She opened her eyes to partial light, and saw a man leaning towards her.

"Hello again, Cassandra," he whispered, as he lifted her from the seat. He stood her up, on her wobbly legs.

"Now, we're going to walk into this nice motel, and you aren't going to say a word. It's very late, and people are sleeping. I'll remove the tape, and you aren't going to say anything. We don't want to disturb people, do we? We will be so quiet. Talking is not allowed. Got that?"

"She nodded blankly, and wondered if there was a bed where she could lie down for a while. She was so sleepy. How nice of this man to help her. He must be a friend. What was his name? She couldn't remember, but she knew that she had seen him before. He had his arm around her waist now, and that felt comfortable.

"Now, this will hurt a bit, but you mustn't cry out. Just clench your teeth and be quiet. Everyone's asleep, and we certainly don't want to waken them, do we," he whispered again, as he ripped the tape from her mouth, and clamped his hand over it loosely.

Tears sprang to her eyes, as she gasped at the pain. He had ripped off her lips. She had no lips now. Would she still be able to talk? That seemed rather funny, and she tried to smile at him, as they headed toward a door.

Her mouth was throbbing and smarting, so there was no question of talking or screaming. She still didn't realize that she was in any danger. Her mind was in a very dark and foggy place. Her mouth hurt so much that she hardly noticed she was staggering. He had a good hold on her. Anyone who was watching, would think that she was drunk, and that her boyfriend was helping her into the room.

Because he had untied her hands along the way, she had free movement. She would look totally normal, just a little drunk, if anyone was watching. He had it all figured out.

She clung to him, as they did the short distance from the car to the motel door. She noticed that it was number 13. What a nice number. She had always thought that it was lucky. She remembered that she had been born on Friday, the 13th of October, but who was she, what was her name? It didn't really matter, her name would come to her soon. Right now, he was lowering her to the bed, and her eyes were closed before she hit the pillow. Cassandra Meredith was slowly drifting back down into the abyss.

He locked the door, and carefully peeked out through the curtains, just to be sure that there was no one around. He stood there for a couple of minutes, his steely eyes searching every part of that parking lot. It wasn't likely that anyone had seen them. His timing had been perfect, and he had given her just the right amount of drug in that hypo. "I should be a pharmacist or an anesthetist," he muttered to himself, as he finally left the window, and stood looking down at the lovely Cassandra. She really was a beautiful woman, and he had her all to himself now.

The blankets in this place were suspect. They were rough and dirty looking. Just touching this one offended his sensibilities. He wished he was back in the fancy hotel room down by the falls. It had sparkling white sheets, soft, clean blankets, and plump, inviting pillows. If all went well, he just might be back in that room tomorrow night. Could he risk taking Cassandra there? No, definitely not. Damn, she should be in a nice clean bed, in a nice clean room with a view. This dump was not for the likes of Mrs. Cassandra Meredith.

Reaching into his pocket, he took out the heavy gold bracelet, which he had found lying by the hot tub, on that infamous night when their paths had first crossed. Gently, he placed it back on Cassie's slender wrist. It looked good there.

Running his fingers through her thick, reddish blond, shoulder length hair, he mused that he had never had a wife this pretty. He had always picked them for their money, not their looks. Well, this one would never be his wife, he knew that for sure. It just wasn't in the cards, but he still wished that he could think of a way to make it happen.

He knew that she would sleep for another hour, and then would waken, a little groggy, but relatively alert. He had time for a drink.

Pouring himself a good three inches of scotch, he pulled the chair up beside the bed, and sat sipping it, staring at Cassie. He liked those long black eyelashes, which covered the blue eyes he had noticed the first time they came face to face, by the elevators at Edgewater.

By the time he had gulped down the scotch, and poured himself a refill, he had come to a decision of sorts. Marriage was out of the question. The best he could do would be to somehow get money out of her, and then kill her. What a shame that would be. In the meantime, however, why not have a little peek?

Carefully, he set down his glass, pulled away the offending blanket, and slowly pulled the shirt out of her jeans. She was wearing a lacy white bra. It was easy to push it up so that her breasts sprang free. Yes, they were just as he had imagined. She had very pale skin, and very rosy nipples. Gently, he rubbed one, and grinned as it responded. This was extremely erotic, and something he had never done with an unconscious, helpless woman.

He was about to undo her jeans, when there were a couple of hard thuds on the wall between his unit and the next one. Next he heard a woman cry out in pain.

Shit! The mood was totally destroyed. Some woman was taking a beating, and was making a lot of noise about it. She likely deserved it. His experience had been that most women deserved a good "dust-up" once in a while.

Unfortunately, however, it brought him back to reality. He realized where he was and what he had to do. Carefully, and with regret, he worked her bra back down over those full breasts. It wasn't his fault that he had to fondle them both as he tried to tuck them back into the bra. Pulling down and straightening her shirt, he tucked it back under her belt, allowing his fingers to reach down as far as possible, just to cop a little feel.

She had a nice flat stomach, but that was as far as his fingers could get, without undoing that damn belt.

She would soon be awake, so he got out the tape and put it over her mouth again. The area around her mouth looked red and sore. Well, that was too bad. He also retied her hands behind her back. He was taking no chances. Cassie looked like a fighter. He didn't want her screaming, or attacking him with her nails.

She began to moan and move a bit, and he watched dispassionately as she regained some semblance of consciousness.

The big question still to be answered was, could he take a chance and let her live, or did she have to die?

Chapter Fifty-Three

Vickie had a solid ball of fear in her stomach, and another one in her throat. She couldn't seem to swallow, and she was having difficulty trying to talk. Cass was one of the most important people in her life. They had been close friends since elementary school days, and, together, they had survived many tight spots.

Her thoughts flashed back to the time they had been trapped in the burning house. Things had looked hopeless that night, but they had escaped. She remembered how, together, they had brought down Willy the Weasel in the woods.

Side by side, they had rescued Kitty from the Black Sheep. They had come within seconds of losing a very dear friend, but, together, they had saved her.

She thought of the night she had been attacked by the would-be rapist, and how caring and gentle Cass had been.

In Key West, Cassie had made them hold the cruise ship while they searched for Vickie. There was no way she was going to leave port without her best friend.

She pictured the two of them surviving the car accident, and running through the dark woods ahead of the killer. That had been a long, frightening night, but they had each other, and they got through it. She thought of how brave Cass had been when she was bitten by the rattler. As always, Vickie had been there to help her.

She thought of the day she had opened the card from Cass, and a million dollar cheque had fallen into her lap. They had shared so many adventures, so much excitement, and always, there had been so much affection.

Regret was nipping at her heels. Why had she taken that shower just then? Why hadn't she insisted that Cass wait for her? Why hadn't she rushed out with Cass, wearing just her housecoat and panties? Why did bad things tend to happen when she was showering? There seemed to be a hundred "whys," but not even one "because."

These two detectives looked as if there was little hope that Cass would be alive. Well, Vickie wasn't accepting that attitude. Surely she would know if Cassie was already dead. There would be such a hole in her heart, that she would know. Right now, it felt as if Cass needed her help desperately. She was still alive. Vickie was sure of it.

She was trying to get into the killer's mind, but so far, that wasn't working. Who could understand or guess the workings of a crazed psychopath, or whatever he was. She wasn't clairvoyant, she had no extrasensory powers, she just had this gut wrenching feeling that Cass was still alive, but maybe not for long. They had to find her.

"Look, fellows, do you know where Jack Willinger is? We have to contact him right away." Vickie had difficulty getting the words out over the lump in her throat, but she managed. She couldn't lose control now. Cass needed her. "Has he gone home yet, or would he still be at the hospital?"

"He's likely still at the hospital with Bud. He's given as much blood as they can safely take from him, so he's a bit weak at the moment. He's likely sleeping, or else sitting in that intensive care waiting room with Bud's wife."

"Well, he would definitely want to know about Cassie. They have a very long history. We have to tell him. Besides, we need his help. He may have enough information about the killer's profile, that he'll have an idea where he would take her." Vickie knew that was a faint hope, but in her desperation she was grasping at the proverbial straws.

These two seemed to feel that Cassie was already dead, and that there was no great hurry. She needed to light a fire under them.

"I'm going to call the hospital. Jack would never forgive me if I didn't tell him what's going on. Excuse me please, I'll be right back."

"No, wait a minute." Detective Matheson said, standing up. "I doubt that the hospital will put you through to him. I'd have a better chance. I'll call him. Do you know the hospital's number?"

"That's a good idea, I'll get the number. If you get through to him, though, I have to talk to him."

It took a few minutes, but finally, Detective Matheson was able to speak directly to Jack.

"How're you feeling, Jack?"

"Hi Jim. I'm feeling okay, thanks. I'm a bit wobbly, but I'll be fine. Bud's holding his own at the moment, so that's really good. That grumpy old bear is going to make it. He's tough." Jack was trying to convince himself that his old pal would pull through, but he knew that Bud was still critical.

"Listen, we've got a situation here. It looks as if your friend Mrs. Meredith has been kidnapped. She's disappeared."

"Oh, God," was Jack's first response. "What's happened?"

"Well, according to her friend, Mrs. Craig, she got a call saying that the cattery was burning. Mrs. Craig was in the shower, so Mrs. Meredith raced out without her. A few minutes later, Mrs. Craig drove down the driveway, and found her friend's car, still running, with the driver's door open. It was parked right at the end of the driveway. Looks as if someone either pulled a vehicle right across to block her, or maybe they used the old body lying on the road trick. Whatever they did to get her to stop her car and get out, it worked. She's gone."

"Let me talk to Vickie. Is she there?"

"Ya, just a minute."

Vickie took the phone from the detective, and began pacing as she talked to Jack. She went over the story again, filling in a few more details.

"She's still alive, Jack. I'm sure of it. We've got to find her." Vickie's voice cracked as she said this.

Jack shifted into his detective mode. "Let me talk to Jim again. Oh, and Vickie, I want you to stay there in case the killer calls. This could be a kidnapping to try to get his hands on some of Cassie's money. Let's hope that's all it is. Get a tape recorder and keep it right by the phone, and tape any call that comes in.

Also, did you check with the cattery to see if she's there? Maybe someone picked her up at the end of the driveway, and they drove down to the cattery together." That was a far fetched hope, but they had to cover all feasible scenarios.

"No, I've called the cattery. There's no fire, and she's not there."

"Okay. Don't worry, Vic. We're going to find her." He tried to sound confident, but Vickie could hear the desperation in his voice. Jack was having one hell of a bad day, first his best friend, and now the love of his life.

"Jack, what about the call telling Cass about the fire. Can you trace it?"

"You bet. I'll get them on it right away. Meantime, you stay safe, and stay there."

They were talking as if they were old friends. Worry about Cassie was bringing them together. Besides, after Vickie and Cassie had saved Jack's life three years ago, the cold war between them had warmed up slightly. Now Vickie felt that if Jack could save Cassie, she would never say another bad word about him.

She didn't want to be left alone in the house. She wanted to be out looking for Cass, but she could see the rationale of staying home and waiting for the killer to call. She just didn't think it was going to happen.

Detective Matheson spoke for a while with Jack, mapping out a plan. "Okay, man, I'll see you in twenty," he said, as he finally hung up.

"We're going to meet Jack at the hospital. He doesn't have his car there. Don't worry, Mrs. Craig, we'll find her. We'll pull out all the stops on this one."

That wasn't very reassuring, but she appreciated his bravado. They had to keep a positive attitude.

She remembered one time at the Kingston Penitentiary, where she used to teach reading to some of the illiterate inmates. She had become friendly with one very quiet prisoner, who seemed truly interested in learning to read.

They had been in the small prison library, working from a Grade One reader, and Vickie had sensed that there was something wrong. Every time she looked up from the book, she caught the prisoner staring at her. Casually looking around for the guard, she realized that he was half hidden behind some shelves, talking to another prisoner. Her heart had started thumping, as she sensed that she was in danger.

It was at that precise moment that her illiterate pupil had lunged across the table at her, ripping her blouse open and kissing her with disgusting wet lips and foul breath. That fear had been real, but it was nothing like what she felt right now, picturing Cassie in the clutches of a psychopath, who killed women as easily as swatting at a pesky fly.

The big house was suddenly too big and too quiet. Once the two detectives had left, Sugar and Muffy came out to see what was happening, sensing that something was wrong. They both sniffed around where the two detectives had been sitting, then came and looked up at Vickie, as if asking for an explanation. Well, maybe they were just asking for food, but she preferred her first idea. She had to smile at those beautiful little furry faces. Cass loved them so much, and now Vickie did too. She wouldn't let herself think of what would become of them, if they didn't find Cassie.

Vickie was trying desperately to close out the awful images which were trying to push their way into her head. She could see Cassie's crumpled body lying in a ditch, or in the woods, or even in the water.

The Niagara River ran right by the house. What if the psycho had killed her immediately, and then thrown her body in the river? That was a scenario she just couldn't handle. That "weasel on a stick" could never get the best of Cassie. Somehow she would get away from him. If Vickie believed it strongly enough, then it would really happen.

Clutching her cell phone tightly, she began pacing from one room to the other, turning on every light she could find. The house would be a welcoming sight for Cassie when she returned. There was no room in Vickie's mind for an alternative scenario in which Cass did not return.

Chapter Fifty-Four

As she gradually wakened from the drug-induced sleep, Cassie became aware of the strong aroma of lime. Actually, the crisp, clean smell seemed to help to clear her head. She lay there, eyes closed, trying to remember exactly what had happened.

Maybe, if she kept her eyes closed long enough, this would all go away. It would turn out to be a silly, scary dream. She had been under a lot of pressure lately, what with Dave's defection, and the killer stalking her. Yes, it could easily be a dream.

Unfortunately, in spite of her wild flights of fancy, Cassie was basically a pragmatist. This time she knew instinctively that she was in serious trouble. This was no silly dream. There would be no knight riding in on a white horse to rescue her. Jack wasn't going to find her in time.

She listened intently for any sounds, and thought she could detect someone breathing. Okay, she wasn't alone. She had better keep her eyes closed until she figured out the situation. She knew that there was tape over her mouth, and she could barely swallow. She needed water desperately. Her mouth and cheeks were burning and throbbing. She wondered whether she was allergic to the tape. Fortunately she had no recollection of the tape being torn off her mouth earlier, and of how much that had hurt.

Actually, at the moment, her mind was so foggy, that there was no recollection of anything that had gone before. The frantic dash to the cattery, the needle in her neck, waking up for a second in the trunk, staggering into the motel, these were all hidden behind a gray, drug induced mist in her mind.

Wiggling her hands a bit, she realized that they were tied behind her back. Yikes! This was not good. There wasn't much she could do with her hands tied behind her, but she certainly would try.

The blanket, which was pulled right up to her chin, was very scratchy, and she needed to get it away from her face.

Suddenly things began to fall into place. The gray mist was lifting. The cattery! Had there really been a fire, or had it just been a clever ploy to bring her out of the house? She convinced herself that it had just been a trick. She couldn't handle thoughts of a real fire. Why had she been so gullible? She knew there was a great sprinkler system in the old house. It would be really difficult for a fire to get started there. Oh why had she been so stupid? She had raced out into danger without one sensible thought in her head.

She knew that it must be the killer who had her, but why hadn't he killed her yet? How long had she been asleep? What would he have done if Vickie had come with her? Had he been prepared for that? Oh how she wished that Vickie was beside her right now. Why had she ever run out of that house without waiting for her friend to get out of the shower?

She needed to figure things out before letting him know that she was awake, but the answers just weren't there.

Since her mouth was taped shut, she had to do all her breathing through her nose, and she was beginning to feel nauseated at the smell of lime. She had always liked that clean, biting scent, but for the rest of her life, if there was going to be a "rest of her life," she would avoid it.

Then she heard it. The bastard was humming, and she knew the tune well. She had always loved that old song, but not anymore. He had spoiled it forever.

He had been watching her closely, and knew that she was awake. Her breathing had changed, and her eyelids were fluttering slightly. She was pretty good, though. Most people would have been taken in by her pretense. He would have to watch her closely. She was smarter than the others, and, strangely, he liked that.

Because he loved to tease and torment, he was humming the very familiar tune to "I'll Be Seeing You." Of course, on the note and tape, and bracelets, which he had sent them, he had changed it to "I'll Be Killing You." He had to smile at his own cleverness. God it was fun to harass and pester the weaker sex. It was like poking a stick at a helpless toad.

What a scumbag, she thought, deciding she might as well open her eyes, and have a good close-up look at him.

"Well, Cassandra, here we are. Welcome to my dream, and, more importantly, your nightmare." He grinned down at her, as she slowly opened her eyes, and stared at him.

"Just relax now. That drug's still in your system, and you'll likely be dizzy if you sit up too fast. Here, let me help you," he added solicitously.

That was another way he liked to tease. He was kind and caring one minute, mean and cruel the next. It kept them totally off guard. They never knew quite how to react, or what to expect.

Putting his arms around her, he raised her to a sitting position. He then pulled the blanket back, and turned her legs, so that they were dangling over the edge of the bed.

"If you promise not to scratch me or try to hurt me, I'll untie your hands." He grinned as he said this, suspecting that she was too groggy to do him any harm.

Cassie indicated with her eyes, that she'd like to take off the tape. She didn't want him ripping it though. She would do it herself, slowly and carefully.

He laughed and shook his head. "Not until you promise that you won't scream. If you do, I'll have to break your neck," he added calmly.

First he untied her hands. Whew! That felt good. They were tingly, and semi-numb, so she rubbed them gently. Next came the tape. It took a while, and brought tears to her eyes, but she finally got it off. Her mouth was stinging, and the surrounding flesh felt raw, but it was wonderful to breathe through her mouth again.

"Could I please have a drink of water," she asked in a polite and quiet voice. She wasn't going to give him any cause to become angry with her, or to put that tape back over her face.

"Sure, we'll go into the bathroom together, and you can have a drink." He knew that there was absolutely nothing in the washroom which she could use as a weapon against him. There was no window, no way to escape. He had made sure of that.

"If you need to use the facilities, I'll let you close the door partway. I won't look, but you can't close it all the way. Don't even think about screaming, because I'll be right outside, and I'll be on you like Attila the Hun before you can get out a squawk."

Cassie didn't need to wizz, and besides, she would never be able to pee with him standing right outside the partially open door. She drank a full glass of water from the tap, something she never did, but it gave her a few moments to think, and she hoped that it would dilute the drug in her system. She needed to have a clear head in order to talk herself out of this.

After drinking another half glass of the awful tap water, she walked slowly and unsteadily back to the bedside. Now came the part where she had to be smarter than he was. Could she do it with her head so fuzzy? Sure she could. She had to. In this case, Cassandra Meredith had no choice.

Giving him an anxious little smile, not too bold, not too pitiful, she asked him what he planned to do with her.

"To tell you the truth, I'm not sure," he laughed. He sat back in the chair, stretched out his legs, and grinned at her.

"I guess I've kidnapped you because I want to get some of your money, a lot of your money, actually. Unfortunately, I'm still not sure of a foolproof way to do it. My alternative, of course, is just to kill you right away, and get the heck out of here. What do you think? What would you do in my place?"

Chapter Fifty-Five

Cass couldn't believe it. He was asking for her opinion. She might be able to talk herself out of this, if she could only convince him that she would give him a lot of money. After all, he had married the other women just to get his hands on their money, hadn't he? Well, she would gladly hand him a small fortune, and worry later about catching him.

"Okay, let's talk about it," she said, with a disarming smile. She knew she didn't look her best, with her face all puffy and red, but she was always good at turning on the charm.

"I do have money, lots of it, and I'll willingly give you a good chunk of it, if only you'll let me go. I'm not the least bit interested in testifying against you, if that's why you want to kill me. Heck, why should I get involved? I don't give a damn what you've done. I just want to get on with my life, and not have to be looking over my shoulder all the time. I've got plenty of troubles of my own. I don't need any more, believe me."

She was trying to act a bit tough, and wondered whether he would buy it. To her ears, it had sounded like a pretty good speech. At least he looked interested, so she continued. She had to make things up as she went along, and she had to make it sound plausible. She tried to remember any good ransom plots she had read, or seen in the movies.

"How about something like this," she said, taking a deep breath. "We could buy two plane tickets to wherever you want. You don't have to tell me where we're going. We'll buy the tickets first, then we'll go straight to the bank, and I'll get five million dollars for you. From there we'll go right to the airport, and catch our flight to whatever destination you've chosen."

She was stumped here for a moment, wondering what to say next. Even to her ears it sounded ridiculous, but at least he was paying attention. There was a slightly sardonic, slightly skeptical look on his face, but she could tell that he was a bit intrigued. Good. She just had to keep talking till a reasonable plan came to her. Dammit, Vickie, where are you when I need you?

"Wherever we go, you could tie me up in a motel, and leave me there. The maid would find me the next day. Meantime, you would have a full day to make your final getaway. You could go wherever you want, probably to some country which has no extradition treaty with America.

I would have no idea where you are. You would have enough money for the rest of your life, and I would get home safely. Of course, you'd have to leave me enough money to catch a flight home." She smiled at him in a conspiratorial way, then added, "It's perfect," with more enthusiasm than the silly plan deserved.

He was silent for a moment, just looking at her. Then, straightening up in the chair, he started shaking his head.

"Am I supposed to believe that in all that time, maybe in the bank, or on the plane, or in the motel, you wouldn't start yelling, and giving me away? Do I look as if I'm stupid? Do I look as if I have it written on my forehead?" He said this, but Cassie sensed that he had liked the plan, at least parts of it.

"Well then, you give me one of your bright ideas," was her quick retort.

Woops, that wasn't too smart. He might just say that his best idea was to kill her right away, forget about the money, and make his escape.

She couldn't take it back though, so she had to stumble onward. "I'm a very reasonable person, and I want to get out of this mess. I'm absolutely willing to hand over five million, and I'm offering you a perfect chance to get away. I'm not going to cause you any trouble. What more can I do? You have to balance that against killing me, and walking away empty handed. How moronic is that?" Oh, damn, she shouldn't call him a moron. She had to watch her words more carefully. Her life was at stake here, and she had no idea what might trigger his anger.

Again he stared at her, then, "You know, maybe it could work," he said slowly. "Let's go over it again. I really like the part about the five million, but I like fifteen million better. What do you think?"

Was he just teasing her? Would he really accept her dumb plan that easily? Had he already made up his mind to kill her? She suspected so, but she had to keep trying. This was life and death, her life and death.

"Fifteen million. Whew, that's a lot. I suppose I could get that much," she replied slowly, frowning as though deep in thought. "It's just that I think going to the bank and asking for fifteen million would really set alarm bells ringing. I could pretty easily persuade them to give me five million for some new project at the cattery, but I don't think they'd go for fifteen without asking a lot of questions."

Cass was remembering the time, almost three years ago, when she had been talking with the bank manager. She had laughingly told him that if she ever came in and asked for more than a million dollars of her own money, he should set off the silent alarms. If she was in trouble, and it was some type of ransom plot, she would give him a secret password.

They had both chuckled, and she had admitted that she had likely read too many mysteries over her lifetime. Still, they had shaken hands on the deal, and he had promised not to forget. As a matter of fact, he had written down the password, and locked it in his desk. Because she had been a new millionaire, she was very nervous about being kidnapped, or having one of her children kidnapped. It had seemed a good idea at the time, and now, it just might save her life. Actually, she realized, it would be better to ask for fifteen million. That would definitely get the bank manager's attention, and remind him of that long ago pact they had made.

John, as he was calling himself these days, had to think about it a little more, before committing himself. He really liked the idea, but at the moment, he liked Cassandra even better. Yes indeedy, at the moment he had more pressing things on his mind.

He had whetted his appetite with his little peek at Cassie's lovely breasts, and he wanted to see more. He was going to get as much out of this adventure as he could. He just might end up having his cake and eating it too. He couldn't help grinning, as he said, "Before we go any further, we're going to have a little party." Then he added something which turned her knees to jelly, and made her forget all the desperate planning.

"You, Mrs. High and Mighty Cassandra Meredith, are going to do a sexy, slow striptease for me. It's obvious that you look damn good in your clothes, but I'll bet you look a helluva lot better without them."

Chapter Fifty-Six

Vickie was pacing the house like a caged animal. She was hyperventilating and sweating, as she strode from room to room, turning on lights, checking the windows, and muttering invectives to herself. She felt so totally helpless. How could she possibly help Cassie?

She needed help, and it suddenly occurred to her that she had to tell Steffie and Kitty. The four friends relied on each other in so many ways. They would never forgive her, if she didn't tell them what was going on. Besides, they might have some brilliant ideas.

She felt better as soon as she had made the calls. Both friends had been asleep, but they had each said that they would be there as soon as they could get dressed. Kitty lived in her home in Rolling Acres, and Steffie was still in her apartment. They decided to drive separately in case they needed both cars.

Vickie had a good hot pot of tea made by the time they arrived. That was for her and for Kitty. For Steffie she had made a big pot of coffee. Steff was a true "coffaholic."

Kitty got there first, and hugged Vickie as soon as she was safely inside the house. Within minutes, Steffie arrived, and they had a group hug. They sat around the kitchen table, sipping tea, gulping coffee, and going over every possible scenario.

"He hasn't killed her yet, that's for sure," stated Steffie firmly. "He would be really stupid to kill her, without getting some of her money first. I'm sure he's holding her someplace till he can get his hands on a few million. The minute he has the money, is when she'll be in real danger. That should give us until tomorrow, though. There's no way he can get the money tonight, is there?"

"I guess not," said Kitty, hopefully.

"I wonder how he managed to get her out of the car so easily. You'd think someone might have heard her scream. Cassie's a fighter. He wouldn't have got her into his car without a real struggle."

"He may have knocked her out with a blow to the head, or he may have pulled a gun on her. That doesn't matter, anyway. The big question is, where has he taken her?"

"With all the hotels and motels in the area, Niagara Falls, Niagara-on-the-Lake, St. Catharines, Welland, etc., it's going to be like looking for one little bird in a great big forest," said Kitty, gloomily.

"It's possible that he's rented some old empty house in the country," suggested Steffie. "There's no way the police can check out every possible hiding place."

"You know, I've just had a brilliant idea," said Vickie. "We should call Cassie's bank manager. He's a friend of hers, and she has some kind of a pact with him. It involves a secret password. She told me about it once, right after she inherited all the money. She was really nervous that someone might kidnap her or one of her family, so she dreamed up this little plot with the bank manager. His name is Brad Harrison, I think. What if we call him at home, and warn him that Cassie might be contacting him to put together several million for her?"

"I'm not sure," said Steffie, frowning. "Do you think we should check with Jack first? He might not like us spreading the word so early. It could screw up some police plan."

Vickie immediately called Jack's cell phone. He answered right away. She told him what she proposed to do, and asked his opinion.

Jack sounded harassed and in a hurry, but he also sounded as if he was definitely in charge. He would do everything humanly possible to save Cass. "Vickie, that's a great idea. Give him a call, and tell him that the police will be in touch with him before morning. Tell him it's imperative that he keep this entirely to himself. If he leaks it to the press or anyone, he's dead meat."

Vickie was temporarily stumped, when there was no listing for a Bradley Harrison in the phone book. "Damn, he's got an unlisted number," she exclaimed, slamming the phone book back onto the little cherrywood table.

"Maybe she's got his number in her address book," suggested Steffie.

"Great idea, gal," said Vickie over her shoulder, as she raced for the stairs. It felt good to keep busy, even though it likely wasn't helping Cassie. At least they knew that they were trying.

The bank manager's number was, indeed, in Cassie's address book. Vickie was a little hesitant about calling him at 2:30 in the morning, but it had to be done. She introduced herself, and he remembered her from the last time she had come into the bank with Cassie. He had a penchant for redheads, and remembered that Vickie had beautiful auburn hair.

He promised that he would be prepared in case Cassie came into the bank, either by herself, (which would be highly unlikely), or with a tall stranger. No matter what crazy story she told him, he would buzz the silent alarm, and the police would be waiting for them outside the bank. It all sounded pretty plausible.

Kitty went to the baby grand piano in Cassie's living room, and started to play. This calmed her, and enabled her to think. The others realized what she was doing, and they gathered around, listening to the background music while they threw ideas back and forth.

Meanwhile, back at the dingy motel on the outskirts of town, Cassie was trying to strip as slowly as she could. She had taken off her shoes first, one at a time, woodenly, and with stiff fingers. The killer didn't like that. He had slapped her on the side of the face, and told her he wanted a sexy dance.

"Look, I don't feel sexy right now. Besides, there's no music. This is ridiculous." She was trying to put on a good show of courage and spirit. She was damned if she was going to let him know he had the upper hand, although that was pretty obvious. Well, at least she wouldn't let him know that he frightened her.

Cass returned his steely-eyed gaze with a firm one of her own. She must not let herself be intimidated by this bully. This was the man who had tried to throw her into the ocean, to turn her into fish food, chicken of the sea, so to speak. Now he's trying to turn me into a stripper, she thought disgustedly.

She was certainly willing to strip, and give him a peek, if it was going to save her life. Doing one humiliating striptease in exchange for her freedom, was a nobrainer. What frightened her was that, if she did a sexy strip, as requested, he might get so worked up that he would rape her.

Somehow, she had to keep him talking. She was definitely smarter than he was, but he had a killer's cunning, which she didn't possess.

Pretending a dizziness which she really didn't feel, she began to undo the belt to her jeans, then staggered, and fell against the bed. "I'm sorry, I still feel a bit dizzy. Just give me a minute, please. Maybe I could have a little more water. That must have been a very strong drug you gave me."

She could now remember the sting on her neck, before everything went black. What had that fool given her? She hoped it wouldn't have lasting effects.

The killer studied her for a moment, then said, "Don't even think of yelling. I'll get you some water, but you'd better be silent, or you'll be dead in one minute flat."

Cass knew he meant it, so she sat quietly on the edge of the bed, closing her eyes, and pretending to be light headed. Her mind was racing, as she tried desperately to think of a scheme to drag this out, and ultimately to save herself.

"Thank you," she said, politely, as she sipped from the water glass.

"Tell me," she said, trying to look really interested. "Do you ever have any doubts about what you do? Are there any self-recriminations, any guilt trips?"

He paused, his drink halfway to his mouth. "Not really," he replied, putting down the drink, and leaning back in the chair. "They were all stupid, far too trusting. Rich women should never trust a guy who comes out of nowhere and starts courting them. That's just Self-Preservation 101," he shrugged. "I have a feeling that you wouldn't be that gullible. With all the money that you've got, you're lucky that you're already married. You'd have to be really suspicious of any guy who wanted to marry you now. Those millions are pretty tempting."

"Well, have you thought any more about the plan to get the fifteen million from me?" she asked. She had deliberately said fifteen rather than five, to tempt him more. As she spoke, she continued to take tiny sips of the lukewarm water. The darn tapwater would likely kill her before he did, she thought morosely.

"Yah, I've thought about it. It could work, but it isn't going to. Your friend Vickie will have called the police by now, and they won't know whether it's a kidnapping or not, but I'm sure they'll have your bank staked out. Nice try, Cassandra, but it's a shitty plan. Unless you can come up with something better, I'm afraid you've run out of options.

Right now you're going to do a striptease for me. We'll see where that leads, and then we're going to take a little trip down to the falls. At this time of night, it should be pretty easy to throw a body over the railing right by the edge. What do they call it, suicide corner? I sure as hell would like to get my hands on some of that money of yours, but I can't see how it would work. I'll just have to be sure that my next wife has a bundle."

He laughed an ugly sort of laugh, and snapped his fingers at her. "Come on, you've stalled long enough."

"Okay, but first I'd like to know. Were you really going to throw me over the railing on the ship, and if so, what would you have done about Vickie? Two people disappearing off the ship would have been pretty suspicious."

She wasn't really interested in his answer, but delaying tactics were all she had going for her at the moment. Maybe Jack was on his way right now. She knew she was clutching at straws, but the thought of Jack bursting through that motel door was keeping hope alive in her heart.

"I must admit, I was in a bit of a panic on the ship. I've always planned my killings very carefully, so that they would look like accidents. I got rid of five wives in five different states, and no one was the wiser. When I realized that you were a witness, I had to do something in a hurry. It was easy to find out what cruise ship you were on, and I flew out there with no real plan in mind. The easiest way, though, seemed to be to throw you overboard. It was more of an impulse born of necessity.

Everything almost worked for me, except for that stupid couple. From where I was standing, they were totally hidden from view, and I had no idea they were there. I must admit that scared me, but I couldn't give up. You and that friend of yours, yummy Vickie, were the only damn flies in the ointment."

Cassie shuddered as she stood up slowly. She could still remember looking down into that rushing water, which looked to be about a mile deep, and full of sharks. Even now it gave her goose bumps. And had he really said that he had got rid of five wives in five different states? Obviously the police didn't have a full dossier on this guy. He was several wives ahead of them.

"What about when you ran us off the road, and chased us into the woods? What were you going to do with us or to us that time?"

"That doesn't matter. You're just trying to delay the inevitable here. Keep stripping, honey. I want to see you dance."

Well, so much for her delaying tactics. She would make the stripping last as long as she could, and the fates would do the rest. Three years ago, another kidnapper had tried to nab her in a parking lot. His plan had also been to throw her over the falls. She had managed to get away from him that time, with the help of two strangers who came to her rescue. Would she be that lucky this time, or was it written in the big book of fate, that Cassandra Meredith was slated to die by going over the falls?

Maybe it was, but Cassie believed that we make our own fate. She wasn't going to give up. She would fight mentally and physically right to the very end.

Chapter Fifty-Seven

She was down to her bra and panties now. He was sitting hunched forward, watching intently, as she took off each item. Unfortunately, it being summer, she hadn't been wearing much.

He was humming that song again, just to taunt her. She didn't want him to see that it was getting to her.

It was a sultry Niagara night, warm and wet. Actually, it had started raining pretty hard at some point, and Cass could hear the rain pelting down outside. The motel room was uncomfortably stale and hot. Obviously the window air conditioner wasn't working properly. It was wheezing like a fat woman climbing the stairs.

She didn't like the look in his eyes. He was getting excited. It seemed inevitable that he would rape her. Maybe she should start screaming now as loud as she could. This was a cheap motel, so the walls were likely very thin. Could anyone reach her in time?

What if she asked to go to the bathroom before taking off her bra and panties? He would leave the door open, and stand right outside it, but could she throw herself against it, and get it locked before he realized what she was doing? She could scream her head off in the locked bathroom. Could he break the door down before someone came to help her?

These thoughts were tumbling in her head like laundry in the dryer. She had to make up her mind quickly. How much longer could she gyrate around before taking off her bra? Then she noticed for the first time, that her gold bracelet was back on her wrist. He must have put it there while she was unconscious. That could give her another few seconds while she pretended to fumble with the clasp. Once the bracelet was off, she would try the bathroom trick, before undoing her bra.

She remembered the night Vickie had come very close to being raped. Afterwards, she had been reluctant to let the police take pictures of all the cuts on her bare chest. She had jokingly said her boobs were national treasures, and weren't for display except on special occasions. Well, that's how Cassie felt about her boobs, and she wasn't going to show them to this pervert unless she had to. One glance at those perfect orbs might send him right off the deep end. She was trying to be witty to herself, just to keep up her spirits. She was in a very dangerous place here, but giving up just wasn't a possibility.

She fumbled with the bracelet, all the while moving gracefully and suggestively in front of her captor. Cassie was an excellent dancer. She had done a few sexy strips for Dave over the years, and she knew all the moves. The trouble was, she didn't want to get this guy any more excited than necessary, but she wanted to make it last as long as possible. It was a fine line she was walking, or dancing.

Finally the bracelet came loose. Cassie twirled it over her head slowly, and then threw it just beyond the kidnapper. Her hope was that he would reach backwards to pick it up off the floor. That distraction would be long enough for her to dash to the bathroom and get it locked.

Unfortunately, he caught it in mid air, and grinned at her. "Now do the same with your bra, but do it slowly. You're pretty good," he said, lasciviously.

Cassie's heart sank. Nothing was working. She should have thrown the bracelet further. Now what? She was running out of ideas. "Please, could I just take a break long enough to have a wizz? I really need to go now. Guess it's all the water I've had."

"Can't you wait?" he glared at her.

"No, I'm afraid I can't. I've really got to go. Then I'll finish up with a great strip. I promise. I know a few more good moves," she added with a disingenuous smile. She was trying to look sexy and titillating to a point, but not enough to inflame his perverted ideas. The longer she could stretch this out, the more chance there was of Jack finding her.

"Okay," he sighed, as he stood up. "No tricks now. I'd hate to have to kill you before you finish your dance."

She noticed that he was still wearing that Rolex watch. It must be one of his favourite possessions. "That's a great watch you have," she remarked casually, still gyrating slowly.

He looked down at it and smiled. My first wife gave me this watch as a wedding gift. It was the nicest gift anyone ever gave me. Susie was a sweetheart, but she turned out to be very stingy with her money. She gave more to her damned interfering mother than she ever gave to me. I've learned that it's much better to marry a woman who doesn't have a mother. They're all interfering busybodies."

Cassie just nodded, and said, "bathroom now please?" She tried to smile at him in a friendly, and possibly enticing way, but her lips felt tight and unresponsive. They simply did not want to smile at this pervert who was a dedicated killer.

Her heart was pounding, as she walked bare footed over the dirty carpet. She hated the thought of touching that grungy bathroom floor with her bare feet, but what choice did she have? Suddenly she realized she did have a choice. "I need to put my shoes back on, please. I don't want to walk on that dirty floor. I promise you'll get a really good dance when I come back."

Every minute she could dawdle, delay and dillydally, was an extra minute to live.

She took her time putting on her shoes, talking to him all the while, so that he wouldn't notice how much time she was taking. Her desperate thoughts were skittering and scattering like barn mice when the resident cat appears. Finally she could delay no longer, so, telling herself that it was now or never, she headed for the washroom. He was right behind her.

Throwing herself against the door, she let out a loud scream. He was too quick for her though. He had obviously anticipated her move. His foot was in the door, and he had his hand over her mouth before she could scream again. This guy was no dummy.

His hand was pressing so hard against her mouth, that she couldn't even try to bite him. She had taken a chance and lost. He was dragging her out of the bathroom, and almost pulling her arm out of its socket in the process. He was furious. All erotic thoughts were gone.

Cassie struggled with every ounce of strength she possessed, but he was much stronger, and she was still a bit light headed from the drug in her system.

He was so angry with her, that she wondered whether he was going to kill her right now. Obviously no one had heard her one pathetic scream. It seemed very quiet outside. Where were all the people? Surely there were others staying at this hot sheet motel. The walls were thin, so why hadn't someone heard her scream? Maybe they had. Maybe the police were on their way right now. Maybe Jack would come bursting through that door any second. Yes, and maybe this pervert would turn into a cockroach, and she could step on him.

"That was a big mistake, Cassandra. I could kill you right now, but I'd rather let you think about it all the way down to the falls. That's going to be a great ending for you."

As he was talking, he was struggling to get some tape over her mouth, but he needed two hands for that. "If you dare make a sound when I take my hand away, I'll snap you in two. Got it?"

She nodded helplessly, but the minute he took his hand away, she shrieked with all her might, and jabbed a finger into his eye.

Roaring in anger, he threw her onto the bed, got his arm right across her mouth, and managed to tear a piece of tape off the roll.

Cassie struggled and flailed with her arms, managing to rake her fingernails down his cheeks, and shaking her head wildly from side to side, so that he couldn't apply the tape. She screamed again, as she drove her finger deeply into his eye. That was when he hit her so hard that she lost consciousness. A short while later, she came to in the trunk of his car, and found that she was trussed up like a chicken.

He had said that he was going to throw her over suicide corner. She tried to picture just what it was like there. The falls were very loud. They roared and pounded as they plunged over the 185 foot drop. It was the place where you could get closest to the one end of the horseshoe shaped Canadian falls. It was the place where it was easiest to pick up a body and pitch it into the thundering abyss below.

She tried to tell herself that it would be very quick, at least she hoped it would. She likely wouldn't even feel the cold water. She would be bashed on the rocks below, before she could actually drown. Hopefully she would be knocked unconscious right away, or would die of fright. There should just be mere seconds of terror before it was all over. She would fight to the very end though. Maybe she would be able to drag him over with her. Unfortunately that was small consolation.

She would pray, and keep her mind on what she was going to see on the other side. Would there be that bright white light which people claimed they saw? Those were people who had died on the operating table, and were then revived. Could their claims be trusted? She had never thought much about it.

Would all the family members who had died before her, be there to greet her? Did she want to see all the family members? She certainly didn't want to see Jenny or Jordan, but it would be wonderful to see her beloved grandmother again, even though that relationship had turned out to be something other than what she had thought. Life had so many twists and turns to it. She had certainly never expected that hers would end this way.

A strange calm settled over her, as with heart stopping clarity, she realized that there was no hope of rescue tonight. Vickie wasn't here to help get her out of this predicament, and Jack might not even know that she had been kidnapped. He was probably still at the hospital with Bud. Poor Bud, what a decent, loveable guy. He was so proud of his wife and the three little girls. He would do anything in the world for them, but now, because of some dirtbag crackhead with a knife, he might be leaving them.

Maybe, if he died tonight, he would be there to meet her, wherever "there" was. Wouldn't that be ironic, if she and Bud were to die on the same day. Jack would never recover from the shock of losing them. Cassie's thoughts were flitting around like flies at a garbage dump. Good thoughts and bad were bumping into each other, as she tried to focus on the problem at hand.

Thank goodness her two kids were adults now. Her death would be a shock, but they had their own lives to lead, and they would inherit all that money. Hopefully, they would use it wisely. She knew that they would keep the cattery going, because they loved cats the way she did.

She would never see her beloved Sugar Plum and Muff again. Maybe Steffie would adopt them. Steff planned to get herself two little cats as soon as she moved into her own condo. Vickie couldn't really take them, because she had dogs at home.

It was sad to think that she and Jack would never get that second chance at a life together. She hadn't even had the opportunity to tell him that she was free now, as free as he was. They had wasted so much time.

Chapter Fifty-Eight

While Cassandra was fighting for her life in motel unit #13, Joseph Warner, the motel owner, was fighting with himself. He had never had much of a conscience, never worried about past actions, but something was really bugging him tonight. He sat in the darkened motel office, peering out the window at his little domain.

He was a thin man, with a pockmarked face, and big ears. His scraggly brown hair was thinning, as well as turning gray, and he looked like the loser he was.

The "no tell motel" as he called it, (although it's real name was the more refined "Vacation Inn"), was laid out in a quasi horseshoe shape, with one arm longer than the other. The motel office was situated on the shorter arm, but it enabled him to see all the units along the curve of the motel. He didn't watch much television at night, but he loved to sit in the dark, and keep an eye on the comings and goings of his customers. He liked to make up stories about who they were, what they did, and what their lives were like.

He hadn't really cared for the tall, brawny fellow who had rented unit #13. He was an arrogant type, condescending and remote. He had paid cash for the room from an obscene wad of money, and had sneererd at Joseph, as he casually stuck the remainder of the fistful back into his pocket.

Joseph had licked his lips at the mere sight of the money, and began visualizing ways he could get some of it. In the long run, however, Joseph, had a "live and let live" philosophy. If they paid, they played. In other words, as long as he got the money for the room, what they did in it was their business. Something about this guy, though, had bothered him.

He had watched the man come and go for a couple of days, but he had done nothing suspicious. Tonight, however, Joseph's watchfulness and nosiness were rewarded. The fellow drove up, and sat in the car for a couple of minutes, lights off. What was he doing? Joseph didn't know.

Suddenly, he had leaped out of the car, raced around to the passenger side, and dragged a woman out of the front seat. He had practically had to carry her. Her legs were wobbly, and she was leaning on him, with her head lolling from side to side. She was either drunk, or very sick. Joseph didn't want any trouble, so he was keeping a close eye on that unit. Something was wrong, but what was it?

Within the past half hour, he had heard a few faint screams, which worried him. Just now, he had heard one loud, desperate one. It seemed to have been cut off in midscream. Should he or should he not, call the police? He was inclined to just let it go, and mind his own business, but his conscience was chewing at him.

He noticed a couple of people stick their heads out of their doors when the screaming occurred, but, likely not wanting to get involved, they had quickly retreated into the safety of their rooms. In this day and age, you could usually count on people minding their own business. The news these days was full of stories of good samaritans getting shot or stabbed for their trouble. Besides, it was raining now, and who wanted to get themselves soaked for nothing?

For some reason tonight, Joseph felt as if his dead wife was urging him to do the right thing, to make up for the very wrong thing he had done before.

The strange thing was that he really missed his wife now. He had never expected that would happen. Even more strange than that, was the fact that ever since the tall man had checked in, Joseph had the uncomfortable feeling that his dead wife was talking to him. Tonight she kept bugging him to "do the right thing." In the small voice, which was nagging him from inside his head, she was telling him "you must atone for what you did to me." It was giving Joseph the creeps.

It was two years since he had killed Maria, so why she would start bugging him now, he didn't understand. She had been a good looking gal when he married her. She was short, but had a very pretty face, and a curvaceous body. Unfortunately, she was lazy and shrewish, and she made his life a living hell. She kept getting fatter and lazier, and more demanding, until one night he had made her really drunk on tequila, taken her out in the woods on the escarpment, and stabbed her to death. He had left her there under some bushes, hurried home, waited a few hours, then called the police to report that she was missing.

His story had been so simple, that it had been easy to believe. She had gone to the movies with a friend, he had explained, tears in his eyes, and fists clenching in a nervous way. No, he wasn't sure which friend it was who had picked her up. He had been in the bathroom when she left, and she had a lot of girlfriends. It could have been any one of them. He had just assumed that they had gone for something to eat or drink after the show, and he hadn't begun to worry until around 1am. It was only after he had called all her friends, and no one had seen her, that he finally called the police.

The police had been suspicious at first. He had no alibi, but they couldn't punch holes in his story. Her body was found four days later, but had been badly chewed by wild animals, likely coyotes. They couldn't even tell for sure how she had died. He had played the distraught husband to perfection, and the case had remained unsolved. That was why he liked to keep a low profile, staying well below the police radar. No point in tempting fate.

The past month or so, however, he had begun feeling guilty about what he had done. He kept remembering how sweet Maria had been when they were first married. She had laughed a lot, and was always ready for a party. He remembered her warm body cuddled up to him at night, and he began feeling real regrets for his terrible deed.

Worse than that, it seemed as if Maria was now trying to communicate with him. When he sat in the dark motel office, his conscience tweaked him, and it was as if Maria was telling him he had to do something good to make up for killing her. He could hear her voice, and it was spooking him. He didn't understand what was happening to him, but tonight he was very antsy.

He couldn't believe his eyes, when the door to unit #13 opened, and he saw the big guy come out, carrying the woman. What really galvanized him into action, was when the guy looked around to see if anyone was watching, then threw her into the trunk!

Joseph didn't stop to think. He simply called 911 before the car was even out of the parking lot. He never took his eyes off it, as the man jumped into the driver's seat, and drove away, not going too fast, not doing anything to attract attention. He noticed that the man turned east down Lundy's Lane, heading in the direction of the falls.

Taking the master key, he hurried to unit #13, and took a very quick look around. He didn't know whether the woman was dead or unconscious, but she certainly had looked limp. He had noticed that her feet were bare, she seemed to be in her underwear, and, he thought maybe he had seen tape over her mouth. Her hands had definitely been tied behind her back.

To his relief, there were no signs of blood in the unit. It didn't look as if the man had knifed her, and there had been no sound of gunshots, so there was no mess. She might have been strangled or suffocated, but at least he wouldn't have to replace the carpet or the bedding. Joseph had a very practical streak.

He was careful not to touch anything, or leave any fingerprints. He didn't want the police to know he had been nosing around. The less he saw of them, the better. Still, he wanted to appear the good citizen, doing his duty and reporting a crime.

As he closed the door behind him, he noticed the woman's shoes. One was on the bed, and one was upside down on the floor. There must have been quite a struggle, he thought, uneasily.

He had just returned to the office, when the first cruiser drove up. It flew into the parking lot, and two policemen jumped out. Behind it came an unmarked police car. He was amazed at the quick response. They must have been right in the area when the dispatcher relayed his call, because it couldn't have been more than three minutes.

He was able to give them the make and license number of the car, tell them which direction it had gone, and describe the condition of the woman, all in about two seconds. The police were back in their cars, and heading down Lundy's Lane before he was even finished talking.

He noticed the tall detective who had come in the second car. He was a handsome guy with a scar on one side of his face. He looked upset, though, and Joseph wondered whether this was a known killer they were pursuing, or whether the woman was someone important.

Chapter Fifty-Nine

With her hands tied, it was difficult for Cassie to move in the trunk. She finally managed to wiggle herself around, however, so that she was on her back, and her feet were free to move. Cass remembered that there was supposed to be some way you could either open the trunk from the inside, or, at least, pull some wires, so that the brake lights would go out. Of course, that only helped if a cop happened to be travelling behind the car, and noticed that the lights weren't working.

Being in her bare feet was now a help. Cass had what her friends called "educated toes." She could pick up a golf ball, or even a tiny object such as a paper clip, with her toes. She had been demonstrating this little talent when all four of them were up at the cottage, and it always made them laugh. Not one of the other three friends could do it. She was now putting her toes to good use. It gave her something to do, to keep her mind off the horrible fate which was awaiting her down at suicide corner.

It was difficult to maneuver in the cramped space, but she was getting the hang of it. Being a rental car, the trunk was totally empty, and very clean. This afforded Cassie a certain amount of room to move her body from side to side. The down side was that there was nothing in the trunk, which could be used as a weapon. Of course, there wasn't much she could do with her hands tied behind her back. She was working at them, rubbing them, twisting them, and trying to loosen the ties, but so far it was futile.

Momentarily giving up on her hands, she used her feet, and methodically felt all along the roof of the trunk, and along the one side. She realized that she would have to get herself turned completely around in order to check the other side. Well, one hurdle at a time. Finally, she managed to catch the edge of the carpet with her toes, and rip it back.

Yes! She could feel some wires, a lot of wires. She had no idea what they were, but she was going to try to yank them all loose. The entire operation offered a very faint hope, but it was better than nothing. What was it they said, "the Lord helps those who help themselves?" Well, she was doing her best to help herself. She had let herself get into this foul situation by being too gullible, and not using her brain. She had run out of the house like an idiot, like the roadrunner being chased by Wile E. Coyote. No, that wasn't quite true. She was more like the stupid roadrunner who ran right into Wile E. Coyote's arms. She shook her head in despair. It was her own fault that she was in this predicament, and she was likely the only one who could extricate herself.

It was raining steadily now, and the wind was coming up. Even the trees seemed restless, as if they knew or understood that something bad was happening. Of course Cassie was unaware of what was going on outside. Her entire world had shrunk to the size of a car trunk. What a demoralizing thought that was!

She tried to figure how far down Lundy's Lane they were. That would tell her how much time she had left before they got to the falls. Twice the car had stopped, and she assumed that they were at red lights. He was obviously being very careful to stay within the speed limit, stop at all red lights, and not attract any attention. That likely meant that there was nobody following them. Her heart sank even lower at that dismal thought.

If only she could remember how many stop lights there were between that moldy old motel and Queen Victoria Park. She tried to think of the cross streets, but her mind just wasn't working. Anyway, what did it matter? They would be at the falls within a few minutes, and it would soon be all over. No, she musn't think like that. She owed it to herself, to her family, to her friends and to her cats. She would fight right to the end.

She was working frantically with her toes, mostly the ones on her right foot. They were more nimble than her left ones. Finally she managed to get what felt like a bundle of wires, caught between her big toe and the next one. Trying to pull them was difficult. There was very little room in which to move her legs. The first couple of times, the wires slipped out from between her toes, and she had to start again.

She was sweating now, even though she was just wearing her bra and panties. He hadn't even had the decency to put some clothes on her, before carrying her from the motel.

How was it that apparently no one had seen him carry her out and put her in the trunk? Was the guy totally invisible? Did he have a lucky charm stuck up his rear end? She could just imagine what Vickie would be saying about now, if she was in this situation. Dear Vickie. She would be devastated to lose her best friend. Hopefully, she wouldn't blame herself for not being with Cassie when the kidnapper struck. Cass knew, however, that she would, indeed, blame herself. Vickie would think it was all her fault for taking her shower at the wrong time.

Good old Vic. What a lot of wonderful times they had shared. Cassie sighed, and got back to the wires. She was tired all over, and felt like quitting, but she had to keep trying.

She wondered whether there was any way that she could position herself, so that she could kick him right in the face, when he leaned in to pick her up. Maybe she could get off one kick, but what good would that do? With her hands tied behind her back, it would be very difficult and time consuming to try to scramble out of the trunk. She couldn't even scream with the tape over her mouth again.

She decided that pulling out all the wires would be her best bet for attracting help, so she went at them with renewed vigour.

While Cassie was taking what seemed to be her last ride, Jack was racing down Lundy's Lane like a mad man, siren screaming all the way. He didn't know for sure where the kidnapper had taken her, but he had a sick feeling that they were heading for the falls. The guy had tried to throw her off the ship. He had thrown his latest wife off a balcony. If he had wanted to kill Cass quickly, he could have strangled her in the motel. For some reason, he liked the idea of throwing her over the railing into that maelstrom. Jack was sure of it.

The only thing in Jack's favour was that he was pretty close on the kidnapper's tail. They had been checking out the motel next door to Vacation Inn when the call came in. What a piece of luck that was. Jack was a firm believer in luck. He figured that the quota of bad luck was all used up for the day, what with Bud getting knifed and Cassie being kidnapped. They were due for some good luck, and being right next door had been the beginning of the lucky streak. He knew it.

If the guy didn't want to attract attention, he would be driving at the speed limit, and obeying all the traffic lights. Jack prayed that the killer would hit every red light all the way down between here and the falls. Luckily, at this time of night, there was very little traffic, so Jack figured he should be catching up to the rental car any moment.

The odd little man at the motel, Joseph something or other, had given them the colour, make, and license number of the rental. That would be a huge help. Jack remembered him from a couple of years ago, when his wife had been murdered. Jack was sure that the little pissant had done it, but there had been no proof, absolutely none. He had that particular murder in the cold case files, and if things ever returned to normal, i.e. if he got Cassie back safely, he was going to reopen that investigation. Well, on the other hand, maybe he wouldn't. Joseph had called them very quickly, and it might just be that call which would result in saving Cassie's life. Maybe he would just leave that case unsolved.

At this time of night, there were very few autos on the road. That was a blessing, and another piece of good luck. He hated those movies in which there was a prolonged car chase through heavy traffic. They were totally bogus and unrealistic. There was no way you could run the car along the sidewalk at outrageous speeds, avoiding baby carriages and pedestrians. You couldn't drive right through little fruit stands, and go around corners on two wheels, without someone being killed in the process. They were ridiculous.

He shuddered to think, though, what he would be willing to do or try, in order to rescue Cass. He would be the first one driving on the sidewalk and turning corners on two wheels. Thank God that wouldn't be happening tonight.

Going through the intersection at Lundy's Lane and Drummond, he was nearly T-boned by an SUV heading north. He was able to take evasive action, and the other driver missed him by a hair. Jack had been speeding through a red light. The poor fellow would likely have to change his underwear when he got home.

Jack was concerned that he still couldn't see the rental car ahead. Of course, it was raining pretty hard now, but that car should be coming into view. Had he been completely wrong about where the killer was taking her? Had he turned off on one of the many sidestreets between the motel and the falls? There were three other cop cars following him now. They all seemed to think he knew what he was doing, but did he?

Damn, he wished that Bud was here beside him. He wondered, fleetingly, how Bud was doing. That big guy just couldn't die. He was the most important person in Jack's life, next to Cassie. Bud and his family were like a second home to Jack. They had really been there for him when his wife Darla had died.

He was in Queen Victoria Park now, speeding along the road, heading right to suicide corner, near Table Rock House. That was the easiest place to throw someone over, or to jump. If, indeed, the abductor had taken her down here, it would be right to that particular spot. You could drive a car illegally through the bus entrance, across the grass, and right up close to the retaining wall. It was the perfect place from which to pitch a body.

Finally he saw it. The black car was parked right where he had expected. The trunk was up, and the guy was struggling with Cassie. She was kicking, and doing everything she could to escape his clutches, but her arms were tied behind her back. Oh God, she was just in her bra and panties. Had this pervert raped her?

Suddenly Jack was out of the car, running, gun in hand, and shouting at the perp.

The next few moments were a total blur.

Chapter Sixty

Cass had done everything she could to help herself, but nothing had really worked. She pulled all the wires that she could feel with her feet, but if they had indeed turned off the brake lights, no cop had noticed. At one point, she thought she could hear a siren, and she prayed to feel the car being pulled over along Lundy's Lane, but that hadn't happened.

As she lay in the trunk, struggling hopelessly, she recalled how scared and angry she had been on the ship, when this monster had his arms around her, and was trying to throw her over the railing. She had pictured herself falling into that black, mysterious and unforgiving water, with no hope of being saved. She had been very lucky that night.

Tonight she was picturing those same strong arms around her, lifting her over the barrier, and dropping her into the churning, foaming, relentless water. She couldn't let him get her that far. There wasn't much hope that she would be lucky twice. She could only depend on herself to somehow outsmart him, before he got her any closer to the falls, but how?

She could feel the car going down Clifton Hill, and her heart sank. If they were going down the hill, then they were very near the falls. Her time was up.

She braced herself, and wiggled around, so that she would be ready when he opened the trunk. Her adrenaline was pumping, and she wondered whether her heart might burst before he ever lifted her out.

The car stopped, and she told herself that this was it. The trunk lid flew up, and he leaned in towards her, a sickening grin on his face.

She made herself wait till he was well bent into the trunk, in order to lift her. Then she pulled her knees back, and jammed her two feet forward, right into his face, as hard as she could.

He let out a yowl, and stumbled backwards. His hand went immediately to his nose, from which blood was pouring. It looked as if his nose was broken. Cass couldn't believe it. That was definitely one for the good guys.

She didn't realize it right away, but the extra minutes that she gained, while her captor took a hanky, and tried to stop the blood flow, gave Jack the extra time he needed to catch up.

Cassie tried to wiggle her way out of the trunk, while the killer was preoccupied with his nose. He was moaning and cursing, and standing with his head back as far as it would go, hanky pressed to his wounded snout. He looked funny, but Cass had no time to enjoy the moment.

Unfortunately, with her hands tied behind her back, it was almost impossible to get herself out of the trunk. Maybe, with enough time, she could have done it, but the killer realized what she was trying to do, and forgetting his bloody nose and aching face, he turned his attention back to her.

He was very rough with her, as he dragged her from the trunk. The pain in his nose was awful, and it wouldn't stop bleeding. Every time he bent his head, his nose gushed more blood. Now it was all over his hands, making them slippery. It was all over Cassie too. He was furious, and wanted to kill her ten different ways, for having ruined his plans and his face.

Cass wriggled and squirmed, and kicked with her feet, making it even more difficult for him to lift her. Even with her hands tied, she managed to cling to the edge of the trunk, so that he had to pry her fingers loose, one by one. This little episode had gained valuable minutes. He eventually managed to lift her out, and was just carrying her to the edge of the falls, when they both heard Jack yell, "Stop right there."

The wife killer stopped, and looked over his shoulder in surprise. He hadn't realized that anyone was on his tail. For some reason he hadn't heard the siren. He had been too concerned with his aching, bloody nose.

"Don't come any closer, or I'll pitch her over," he yelled, more calmly than he felt. This was really bad. In all the years he had been marrying rich women and killing them off at his leisure, he had never been caught in the actual act of killing them. He had always made it look like an accident, and people had believed him. He was a great actor, and he often told himself that he should have been on Broadway. With his penchant for disguises, and his ability to take on different personas, he felt that he could have been a star.

Now, however, he was in serious trouble, the worst trouble he had ever experienced. He stood there, trying to think it through. If he lifted her in order to pitch her over the barrier, into the roiling cauldron below, the cop would shoot him. The mere physical act of lifting her, would expose his own body to a gunshot.

There was no way he could throw her over, and make his getaway. There was no way he could climb over the fence with her in his arms, so that they could take the plunge together. Besides, there was no way he was going into that swirling, thundering water. The bottom line was "no way, José."

Suddenly, he, who always did the string pulling, manipulating people just the way he wanted, found himself with his own strings cut. How had things gone so wrong so quickly? He should never have taken her back to the motel. That was the first big mistake.

No, he didn't have a chance in hell of getting away with this one. The best he could do was throw himself on the mercy of the court, and plead insanity. He would be locked away for a while in some hospital, but after a few years, they would realize that he was sane, and let him go.

They would send him back to the states, and he had enough money to get himself the best lawyer there was. Yep, that was his only possibility.

Wearing a shit-eating grin, he gently stood Cassie on her feet, and put his hands up. Jack was almost sorry that he gave up so willingly. He would have liked to shoot the bastard.

By now, three cars of uniformed police had arrived, sirens shrieking. Strangely, the incessant, blustering clamor of the falls, seemed to subdue the sirens. Looking at all the police who were now surrounding him, he thought wryly that they had really pulled out all the stops tonight. He had never been so frightened in his life, and he wondered vaguely whether this was what his wives had felt during their last moments, when they realized that he was going to kill them.

Jack didn't have to worry about him for a while. The cops weren't going to let him go anywhere. He holstered his gun, and held out his arms to Cass. She ran into them like a rabbit heading for cover. What took you so long, you gorgeous man? Because there was tape over her mouth, she could only think these words.

They stood there, with Jack cuddling her, squeezing her, and kissing her bedraggled face. Cassie's hands were still tied, so she couldn't hug him back, but that didn't matter. Jack was whispering every endearment he knew, and, in spite of the darkness, he could tell by Cassie's big blue eyes, that she felt the same about him.

Eventually, he remembered that she was wearing nothing but her bra and panties. Taking off his jacket, he put it around her shoulders. Then he worked at the rope, which was tying her hands. The tape on her mouth was the worst part of it. Her face was so raw by now, that he knew it would hurt her terribly. He couldn't bring himself to pull it off in one quick motion. Once her hands were free, he let her loosen it herself.

By the time that Cass had her hands free, a jacket covering most of her nakedness, and the tape off her mouth, her abductor was in handcuffs. He was doing his best to be charming with the police, making it clear that he was not the run of the mill felon. He was a cut above the rest, or so he tried to imply.

He was obsequious, overly co-operative, attempting to be funny, anything to convince them that he wasn't bad, just misdirected and misunderstood.

He had been too arrogant. Things had gone his way for a long time, and he had come to think of himself as invincible. Now look at him. From the man who at one time held all the cards, he was now folding like Monday's laundry.

His nose was swelling, and there was blood all down the front of his shirt, not to mention on his face and hands. He felt as if some of his front teeth were loose. His one eye was sore and watery from where Cassie had poked him with her finger. He was a mess. That good looking bitch had really done him in. She was slight, but she was a tiger.

"Cassandra," the "I'll Be Killing You" killer said, trying to get her attention. "My one big regret, is that you didn't get to finish that striptease for me." He leered at her, then turning to the policeman beside him, he added, "You should have seen her, she was terrific, as good as any stripper I've seen. She was enjoying herself too. That was the good part."

It was an evil little attempt to humiliate Cassie in front of these cops, or maybe to ingratiate himself with her, but it didn't work. She realized that he was baiting her, so she just grinned at him and said, "Don't feel badly. I just hope you took notes, because I'm sure it won't be long before you'll be forced into doing a striptease for some of your fellow inmates. You're going to love that!"

The cops guffawed, and John, the stalker, wife-killer, kidnapper, looked horrified. He hadn't thought about what it would be like in prison. Damn! He hadn't thought about a lot of things. He had been too busy teasing, taunting and intimidating Cassie and Vickie. He was done like dinner unless he could pull off an insanity plea. Well, his first step was to get himself the best lawyer money could buy. All that money he had inherited from all those foolish women, was finally going to be put to good use.

Cass didn't have time for him. She was cuddled in Jack's arms again, and that's where she wanted to stay. She still hadn't had the chance to tell him about Dave, so Jack didn't know that she was free, or that she soon would be. He just knew that life wouldn't be worth a nickel if he couldn't have Cassie as his own, just the way it used to be.

Still holding her close, and leering at her, he bent, and, in his best Rhett Butler voice, he whispered, "How would you feel about doing a striptease just for me sometime, Miss Scarlett?"

Cassie laughed, "You better believe it, detective. It would be my pleasure to give you your own personal show any time you say."

Jack grinned, but he wondered at that remark. Where was Dave in this new picture? Something must have happened in their relationship. It was obvious that he and Cass had a lot of catching up to do.

Cass just stood there, surrendering to the comfort and strength of his arms. This was Jack, her Jack, the man she had loved for most of her life. It was all going to work out for them after all.

She was going home. She would see Vickie again. She would be able to cuddle Sugie and Muff. She was going to live to enjoy her beautiful new home. Her kids weren't going to lose their mother just yet. The stalker was out of commission. It was like a whole new lease on life. Everything was possible. She was free! What an exhilarating feeling!

There was so much that she had to tell Jack. It would take a long time to get all this straightened out, but who cared. They had the rest of their lives for catching up. She would willingly be a witness in any trial. She would fly to the states or wherever, just to see the "I'll Be Killing You" killer given a one way ticket to prison. Maybe he would even get the death penalty for all the unfortunate wives he had killed. That would be real justice.

At the moment, however, she just wanted to get far away from those roaring, tumbling waters. Cassie had always been fascinated by the falls. They were so majestic, so overpowering. She had been awed by their strength and beauty. They were one of Mother Nature's greatest achievements. Tonight, however, they had lost their appeal. The interminable noise was frightening, and she couldn't even let herself look at them, without picturing herself being swallowed up in the maelstrom. Somehow, they seemed to be malevolently waiting for her, and she backed away, pulling Jack with her.

Finally, turning her back to them, she put her arms firmly around Jack's neck, and grinned up at him. "Take me home, detective. I just want to go home."

Epilogue

It was three weeks later, and things were gradually getting back to normal.

The "I'll Be Killing You" killer was still being held in the Welland Detention Center, but was about to be extradited back to Florida.

Bud Lang was making a slow but good recovery. He had lost a lot of weight in the hospital, and the day he was discharged, he looked pale but handsome. Somehow, the weight loss made him look much younger. His wife Amanda, and his three little girls were smothering him with love and attention.

This particular evening, Cassie was throwing a big barbecue bash for her very closest friends. Vickie was there, of course. She was sad because she was flying home to Vancouver the next day. Her husband Brian would be back from Ireland, and they were going to head to the Bahamas for a week of fun in the sun.

They so seldom had time to be together, that it would be like a second honeymoon, at least Vickie hoped that was the case. Brian was not the romantic type, but he was loyal and dependable. Vickie had been so fond of Dave, that she had sometimes fantasized that somehow Brian could change, and be more like Dave. Now that Dave had turned out to have feet of clay, she was very grateful for her dear old reliable Brian. She would take him just the way he was.

Kitty and Mitch were sitting on the lawn, and telling everyone about their forthcoming two week trip to England and Scotland. Mitch was going on a book tour, and this time he was taking Kitty with him. Kitty had never been to the British Isles, so she was very excited. Her eyes were sparkling, as she sat there beside Mitch. They made a very handsome couple.

Steffie was going to move into Kitty's home to mind her cats, Petie and little Miss Rosie, while Kitty was in England. Steffie was also excited, because she had an art exhibit coming up in four weeks, in one of the big art galleries in Toronto. She had never done an exhibit before, and was anticipating a wonderful adventure. An art connoisseur and patron had been in the boutique the previous winter, and had bought several pieces of Steffie's work. Since then, he had come over from Toronto a couple of times to talk with her, see other pieces of her work, and persuade her to do a showing.

All Steffie's Niagara Falls friends would be there, as would Brad and Jill. Brad had promised to bring everyone he knew as well. Vickie didn't want to be left out, so she had promised to fly to Toronto for the occasion. Kitty and Mitch would be back from England by then, so it promised to be a huge affair. It was all rather electrifying.

Jack and Cassie had done a lot of talking, and a lot of planning. They were biding their time until her divorce was final, but they were looking forward to a wonderful life together. The pair of them couldn't get the silly grins off their faces.

Neither liked to think about how close Cassie had come to dying. At first she had had nightmares about being pitched over the falls, and she wasn't sure that she ever wanted to see them again. Sometimes, on a perfectly clear, still night, she could hear the distant roar of the cataracts, and in her imaginative mind, it was almost as if they were waiting for her, calling out to her, just biding their time. She tried not to dwell on that dismal thought, and was concentrating on what it would be like to eventually become Mrs. Jack Willinger.

Jack had decided to mend fences with Vickie. They had disliked and distrusted each other for so long, and it was time to call a cease fire. They both loved Cassie, there was no doubt of that. Actually, that was the trouble. Each had always been jealous of the time Cass spent with the other one. It was ridiculous, and had to stop.

With that in mind, Jack had invited Vickie out to lunch. Cass was not included, but she was delighted to see them go off together. All her life she had wanted them to be friends.

It had apparently been a successful meeting of the minds. Vickie came back after lunch, full of praise for Jack, and admiring how much he had matured over the years. Jack spoke of Vickie in glowing terms, stating that he had never really seen or appreciated her witty side.

Cass withheld her judgement. She suspected that there would be plenty of squabbles along the way, but it was a good start.

Vickie was just biting into her second hamburger, when Cassie walked over to her. "You know, Cass," she muttered, between bites, "you'll have to give me plenty of notice before you and Jack get married. I'll need time to take off about fifteen pounds, so that I'll look svelte and beautiful as your matron of honour. I'm assuming that you are going to ask me to be your matron of honour. You wouldn't dare have anyone else, would you?"

"Of course not, you goof," laughed Cassie. "It's not going to be for a while, and then I think it will be a fairly small affair. Just imagine the fun you and I are going to have, picking out dresses and planning the whole thing, when we get nearer the time. You'll have to come well in advance, and stay till you get me safely married off.

As a matter of fact, we've been talking about flying the wedding party and all the guests down to the Bahamas or Florida for the wedding. Wouldn't that be fun?"

"What a great idea. Gawd, I'll have to take off twenty-five pounds, so that I'll look good in a bikini or a sarong. You know, of course, that we'll have to try to stay away from any mysteries," laughed Vickie. "We won't have time for them until we get you safely hitched."

"That's right, but just think. Once I'm married, you and I will be able to help Jack with some of his cases." Cass was kidding, but she had said it loud enough for everyone to hear. Jack just groaned, and muttered, "Lord help us all." Bud grinned broadly, as he looked at his old pal. Jack was going to have his hands full with this one, and Bud was grateful that he'd be around to see the fun.

It was a wonderful party. They ate every bit of the potato salad, baked beans and hamburgers. There was nothing left of the strawberry shortcake. The wine had been plentiful, and the coffee was strong.

Mitch was a great raconteur, and he kept them laughing at his many stories. Kitty beamed proudly. She really loved this guy, and grinned at the memories of when they had first met. They had started off on the wrong foot, and seemed to dislike each other intensely. Those feelings had all been washed away, though, the night they had nearly drowned.

By the time they were all finished eating and clearing away the dishes, the mosquitoes were coming out, so they went inside to finish the evening in the large sunroom.

Sugar Plum and Muffin were delighted to have them back inside. They hadn't left Cassie alone since the night Jack had brought her back safely. They seemed to have sensed that something was seriously wrong. Tonight they had sat at the screened window, watching all the festivities, and mewing loudly to get Cassie's or Vickie's attention.

Now that everyone was back inside, the two cats were in their glory. They wandered around, sniffing feet, jumping on laps, then jumping down again. They spent a lot of time with Kitty, obviously smelling signs of Petie and Rosie around her ankles. Muff usually slept on Bud's lap anytime Bud came to the house, but tonight he was concentrating on Cassie. Finally they had come to rest, Muffy in Cassie's lap, and Sugar on the back of her chair, looking over her shoulder. They were taking good care of her.

As Cassie sat looking around at her friends, she felt a great sense of contentment. It had been a wild summer. So many things had happened, but it had turned out well for everyone. Cass had spoken with Dave a few times, and he seemed to be adjusting to his new life with Sophia and Bucky. She wished him well, because if he hadn't become involved with Sophia, she would never have been free to start a new life with Jack. It was funny how things worked out.

She was toying with an idea which had been in the back of her mind for some time now. She felt that she would like to try writing a book, maybe several books. Of course they would be mysteries, and of course, Vickie would want to be in on them with her. They would co-author a series of murder mysteries. The more she thought about it, the more she liked the idea. She would mention it to Vickie tonight, and see what she thought. Knowing Vic, however, Cass was sure that she would be ready and eager to jump into a new venture, and she would love the idea of writing books. They certainly had plenty of experiences from which they could draw.

Looking around at the roomful of close friends, Cassie felt very grateful. She had come close to losing all this, her friends, Jack, the cats, the house of her dreams. She had been a bit cocky, a bit too sure of herself, and a bit too cavalier in her dealings with the "I'll Be Killing You" killer. After everything that had happened, she promised herself that she wouldn't take anything for granted ever again.

Things seemed to be going so well for all of them at the moment. It was very serendipitous. Life was such a precious gift, and Cass had learned that it was important to make the most of every day. She knew all too well, that you can never be sure about what lurks just around the corner. Hopefully, there were a lot of good things in store for all of them. There had been enough bad news this summer to last quite a while. The good thing was that they would all be together, friends and family, to face whatever surprises the future had in store.

The End

Printed in the United States
133008LV00002B/136-183/P